For
dear Iris ++
from Greta +
christmas 15

Under Charred Skies

Under Charred Skies

GRETA SYKES

authorHOUSE®

AuthorHouse™ UK
1663 Liberty Drive
Bloomington, IN 47403 USA
www.authorhouse.co.uk
Phone: 0800.197.4150

Published by AuthorHouse 10/06/2015

ISBN: 978-1-5049-9018-9 (sc)
ISBN: 978-1-5049-9017-2 (hc)
ISBN: 978-1-5049-9019-6 (e)

Print information available on the last page.

Any people depicted in stock imagery provided by Thinkstock are models, and such images are being used for illustrative purposes only. Certain stock imagery © Thinkstock.

This book is printed on acid-free paper.

UNDER CHARRED SKIES

Lene has died peacefully after a long life, and her daughter Vera must travel to Hamburg for the funeral. During the train journey from London her thoughts about the past reawaken. During the seventies her mother used to visit her in London and surprised Vera with revelations about a past that she had never before spoken about: Her love stories, the cultural richness and idealism of the Weimar republic, her hopes for a socialist future, her work with the resistance and the fate of the exiled poets. Nazi tyranny had turned her life more upside down than Vera had ever imagined. Vera made notes about the stories of her mother who had sworn her to secrecy until the day she died. Now the time had come to tell her stories.

For Oliver and Stefan

I would like to thank the following persons for their generous help and support:

Karl-Heinz Rabas from the Stadtteilarchiv Rotthausen, Andreas Jordan from the Gelsenzentrum and my sister Ute Woltereck for research assistance. My thanks also go the Jean-Michel Palmier and his book 'Weimar in Exile' (Verso, 2006).

The actions, places and persons in the book focus on historical facts, yet have been written with due regard to creative freedom.

PROLOGUE

I was almost ready. The 10.29 left St. Pancras station for Brussels. From there the Thomas Tallis leaves at 13.15 for Cologne. The 17.48 would take me from there to Hamburg. There was nothing else to be done. I had to rush, if I was going to make it to the funeral in time. I'd promised myself I wasn't going to fly. I needed time on the train to sit and think. So much had happened, but now so much more was about to happen. My brain was fluttering with thoughts like so many seagulls on the beach. Mother had died peacefully after a long life. I would meet with the others at the funeral, and a story would have to be told.

The pink hand luggage case was ready and locked. I checked my face in the mirror. Was I beginning to look like mother? I saw the tears she shed when I left the country. Wrinkles! Crying leaves wrinkles. I gave her wrinkles and made her sad. I sighed while putting on the mascara and eyebrow lines. I used to show her how to colour her eyebrows, and she always managed to get it a bit wrong, but she enjoyed the tuition. She liked learning things. All her life she was prepared to learn something new. Maybe that had helped her to live such a long life. That and her secrets.

When I decided to leave the country our relationship was at a low ebb. My late nights, studies of philosophy (what job can you do with that?) and various boyfriends were a cause for constant arguments. I didn't want to have readymade answers from her. I fled. I left Germany. In London I felt safe. I could begin to work out what sort of life I wanted to live. The old buildings helped. A city that had not been burnt down! A city with history. I spent months walking through the streets of London. The old yellow and red brickwork of the Georgian and Victorian terraces was comforting to me. The narrow, ancient streets in the city. Pudding Lane. Borough market. Then one day the visits started. I had two small children by that time and was writing my first book. She was to make this journey many times. I lived behind Regents Park near Baker Street station. Every day we walked through the cast iron gate into the park by the lake and over to the rose garden. It was always summer when she came. She fell in love with the rose garden. Its wide avenue from the tall gate in the inner circle contrasted mysteriously with the small paths behind grasses and summer flowers. One of them led up a small hill and down past the waterfall to the roses. The many colours and shapes of bushes. The climbing roses. All had names and she admired each name, colour or scent. We sat down on a bench. At the time I harboured many angry feelings towards her, which I hoped she wouldn't notice. But thinking of her now several decades later I can understand a lot more about what went on inside her. She had done her hard work. The father of her children had volunteered to join the army and afterwards he was in prison. Then he died not much more than ten years later. After his death she might have experienced a kind of rebirth, when the memories of her tumultuous past came back to her. She needed me for her to relive her past. She had to tell it all to me. Now I was glad and relieved that I didn't give up and allowed my frustrations to burst forth. I listened to her whole story. I looked back in the mirror. Wasn't I now about the age she was when she wanted to talk? At the time I forced myself to make diary entries for all her visits, recounting our meetings and her tales, although I was often not in the mood to do so. Now I was pleased and content. Her story was important and now it needed to be told. I was determined not to let all that had happened fall prey to forgetfulness and oblivion. After all, memories are a powerful weapon against men's exploitation by men. The first time she visited was unforgettable. Here is my diary entry for it.

Diary notes, 7ᵗʰ July 1969

We sat down on a bench. Gabriel had fallen asleep and my little Daniel played with a car.

"You left to become a poet and now you have children instead! I'm happy about that, but it is also strange."

I was stunned. What was she talking about? It is true that I had been a wild child, a radical bohemian. Now I was a mother of twenty-five with two small children.

"Why is it strange?"

"It happened to me too."

That's how it all began. She looked at the blossoms tenderly. The wind blew the scent into our nostrils. London and time ceased to exist. I was puzzled and intrigued and looked at her focusing the distant blue sky with its small cumulus clouds.

"What do you mean?"

"I once wanted to become a poet or a painter too. I had many friends who were poets, painters and socialists."

I looked at her, thinking that's women for you! But my mother? Surely not! Such a devoted housewife! I didn't understand. Her eyes were still on the distance; her hands lay in her lap. She was as still as if she had been painted there next to me. I was almost startled to hear her speak.

"I want someone to know what really happened. I've decided that you need to be that someone. My peace baby!"

When I was small she sang to me 'Guten Abend, Gute Nacht' and 'Weisst du wieviel Sterne stehen' at bedtime. She sometimes whispered to me 'my peace baby' before she got up and left the room. Never in front of anyone else. And not for many years. I never thought of asking her what she meant. It was like a secret pact between us, a mystery that gave us a momentary sense of supreme intimacy. I loved her at those moments.

"What whole story are you talking about, mother? I don't understand."

"Before I had all my children I had a life as a young woman. I had friends and relationships. I was politically active, just like you. I studied and worked. Like you. But I never spoke to anyone about this life. It took place before the Nazis came to power. I was very happy in those days. You can't imagine how high our hopes were. We thought we were going to have

socialism in Germany. My father, your grandfather, was an outspoken socialist. I learnt a lot from him. You would have liked him. All my life I was loyal to him. But later, after I married my husband, your father, everything changed."

She stopped for a moment and turned her head to look at me, maybe to see the effects of her words on me or to see if I was still there. I sat there motionless and breathless. Gabriel cried, I had taken him on to my lap. Mother held Daniel on her lap. He looked sleepy and closed his eyes. The softness of her voice was like a song in the wind. The last thing I had expected was that my mother, the disciplinarian of my life, would come out with a story that resembled my own chaotic strivings for meaning that I am engaged in. I was not sure whether I would like what she was going to tell me, and I began to feel uneasy. My stomach rumbled, and I longed for a cup of tea. We got up and walked to the cafe.

"You mean everything changed when you married our father?"

I felt almost sick. My little boy started crying.

"Shall we go to the cafe and have a cup of tea?"

"That would be very nice."

She looked taller when she got up, as if she had grown or had become more upright after her words. I felt smaller and very vulnerable. My muscles ached. The weight of what she might expose felt heavy. We walked slowly into the afternoon sun. She sat down outside in the garden with the children, while I bought our drinks.

"There is a lot I have to tell you, but I have to ask you one favour, though, before I say any more."

"What favour is that?"

"You must keep my story a complete secret until the day I die. I want to be able to entrust you with it. Can you promise me that?"

My mother's dark eyes shone, as she looked directly at me. With some of the hot tea inside me I felt reassured and strengthened.

"I promise you that. You know me. I can keep a secret well."

She looked pleased and smiled. She was not one who gave hugs freely, but this time she leant over and we embraced each other.

"Your father was a Nazi, but he never told me so. He was so in love with me that he decided to spare me this particular truth. I only found out *when I already had children. And later on, after the war, well…you know that we were still together… but I have to tell it all in order."*

We wandered back. Daniel chased the ducks and Gabriel watched from my arms.

"You're lucky to live so near to this beautiful park."

We crossed back over the curved bridge towards the exit. We spoke no more about her story. A ceremonious spirituality was between us, as if an imaginary altar had been erected. We were going to observe the shape of her story unfold there over time. She came back many summers. I felt quite brave suddenly. Whatever she would impart I would need to brush aside my own doubts and my misgivings about the German past.

End of diary notes.

Money, tickets, passport. A bottle of water. I took my raincoat off the hanger and hung it over my arm. I might not need it, but judging by the weather I probably would. This summer was extraordinarily wet. The taxi was waiting outside, and it wasn't long before I sat comfortably installed in the Eurostar train with my cup of coffee in front of me, the Guardian front page glaring at me. 'Germany isolated', 'Angela Merkel stubborn', 'Greeks burn German flag'. I put the paper away and took Sartre out of my bag. Reading about the past was easier to bear than the comments now unleashed by the press. In 'The Reprieve' Sartre's characters are unable to act in the face of the betrayal that led to war. Is Angela Merkel unable to act? Is Europe again at the beginning of self-destruction, some arguing, with Germany leading the way? Swastikas had started to appear on posters in southern Europe. The financial crisis. That was really what was at the heart of it. And wasn't it the same country as in my mother's story, the US, that determined which way the wind should blow? I closed Sartre, keeping my finger on the open page and shut my eyes. I felt uneasy and nervous. The past seemed to creep back like a weed, or was that just an appearance? Had I not left Germany many years ago to escape from a past that seemed to be locked into a politics of oblivion? Don't mention the war! What did your father do in the war? Our parents kept stony silent faces. The walls of our small kitchen enclosed us in the silence. I tried to breathe deeply, but could feel that I was hyperventilating. My breath raced in and out of my lungs and made me feel dizzy.

It was during the first year of my philosophy studies. I decided to leave the country. The past was like a cement wall on my chest. I felt buried under it. My life was like blotting paper that had absorbed the ink of Germany's recent history. I had involuntarily inherited a past, and I decided to run away from it. But could I really do this, or was I damned from the beginning? I left for England. I was going to be free, free from the past. I lived a life of a stranger. You speak good English! The foreign town welcomed me. We were so many strangers here. The foreign language didn't contain all those familiar words. Schuld. Eine Schuldenlast. Konzentrationslager. Truemmerhaufen. Verbrannte Stadt. I obtained a British passport. Now I was British. Or not? Or was I a German with a British passport? Blonde and blue-eyed. They could all see I was German. The pupils in school asked:

"Miss, are you Hitler's girlfriend?"

"Miss, how was it when you used the showers in the camps?"

Two World Wars and one World Cup. The snide looks. The derision! My British passport hadn't prevented me from being a foreigner. I was condemned from the start. The original sin. I closed my eyes and tried to breathe more slowly down to my feet to calm myself.

We were in the tunnel, darkness hummed around the compartment. I could hear music from somewhere, or was it in my head? I was thinking of Free Will and was searching for it in my life. As my breathing slowed down I felt sleepy and dozed off. After a while I woke and saw with relief that we were travelling through France. The green meadows shone in the sun. I began to be able to shed my ruminations. I thought of the clothes I was going to wear at the funeral. I had an elegant black suit. And I had her secret. I was looking forward to seeing my sisters and brother, but I also knew that it wasn't going to be an easy step to disclose my mother's story. Perhaps no one wanted to know about it anymore.

We arrived in Brussels Midi. I took my pink suitcase, my handbag and coat and looked for the Thomas Tallis. I love train journeys. I found my seat and relaxed. I tried to imagine how it was going to be to recount my mother's story. I took pleasure in watching the north German plain fly by at great speed, and began to doze. It was evening when I arrived. I took a taxi straight to the hotel where we all had booked our rooms. I paid a brief visit to the bar after checking in, found none of my siblings there and so went up to bed.

The next morning noisy embraces and greetings drowned details of individuals in a blur of small talk, smiles and laughter. Not everyone had been able to come. My oldest sister had problems at home with a sick husband, so she wasn't there. Instead a couple of cousins had joined us. The drive to Ohlsdorf, more akin to a forest than a graveyard with many chapels in a large wood. We had to go to chapel seven. Those of us who wanted to were able to view my mother before the coffin was closed. Only two of us went. We stood silently looking at her dear face, a tiny smile at the edge of her closed lips in her wrinkled face. She had died at a ripe old age and seeing her made me feel a peaceful sadness. I wanted to ask her how it had been in those years with Klaus. Was I Klaus's child? Can you be genetically the child of one man and in your heart that of another? She smiled softly at the edge of her closed mouth and I was inclined to feel that she agreed with me.

A small crowd collected in the chapel, and the pastor told us of the milestones in her life, two world wars, five children, her charitableness and kindness, her humour and love of her family. Tears were shed. Bach hymns were sung. The angel at the side of the altar lit up briefly from a beam of sunlight. I thought of her story that was hidden from those present and that now had to be brought to life. Some of the colourful scenes she had related to me passed in front of my mind's eye, her friend Olga's kiss with Hubert at the Emscher, the night walks with Resistance fliers in their pockets with her friend Inge, her secret meeting with Klaus, her lover, in Mainz. The two small children who stood lonely in the rain, deserted in a burnt out town. I thought of our conversation, when she asked me to make sure the story was told and published in the end.

Diary notes, 15ᵗʰ July 1969

Mother is leaving in a couple of days. All in all, it went well, I think. We didn't get on each others' nerves too much, at least I hope not. She seemed at ease anyway, but then she was never someone who was open about how she felt. Apart from now in relation to what she wants to reveal. We were walking back from the park with the children when she came back to the subject of secrecy.

"You know I asked you to keep my story a secret until I die."

"Yes, and I said that I would keep it a secret."

"But I do want you to tell my story. Don't just keep it to yourself, even if I carry on living for a few more years, it has got to be told."

"Sure, I will, I won't neglect it, you don't need to worry." I was beginning to feel that she was making too much of a fuss and getting me to sign and seal a contract with her on this.

"I don't worry, but such important things happened then. They are all still relevant and will be for many years to come. Like what happened to my friend Olga, whose daughter was turned against her own mother by the Nazis. Or how my friend Inge and I sorted information about the exiled poets and writers and how they were hunted in the Netherlands and in other countries although they were antifascists. Well," she mused and looked at me, "has anyone heard of these writers and poets recently here in London or in Germany? I haven't. It's as if they've been swallowed up in a black hole."

I looked at her. Was she going to start telling me more details now, when we were on our way back and everyone was hungry? I felt impatient and tried to hide it, but she was right. Much of the existence of these artists and writers was as good as forgotten.

"Of course, but you must tell it all to me one thing at a time. I can't take it in now."

"What I'm saying is that there is a lot to it, the politics of the international support for the Nazis and the bravery of people. You have to think about what might be a good way to present it, when the time comes."

"What do you mean?"

"What form you are going to put all of it into..."

"Yes, sure, I shall have to think about that. Well, I could turn it into a novel, would you like that?"

"That might be a good idea, it's got to be attractive to people, so they want to read it, but you need to choose the format. You're going to be the one who'll have to write it all down."

We had reached the gate and left the park behind. The noise from the cars drowned out any further talk about this.

End of diary notes.

As the pastor spoke and my eyes were on the angel who was now in darkness I thought of that conversation. She liked the idea of a novel. It would make sense. I would be able to shape the many fragments I was expecting to hear into something that formed a coherent narrative. Something that people might be keen to read. The older sisters might be taken aback. My brother would not believe me. But the story was more than a family story, so their hesitations should not stop it getting to the people. Our fellow human beings, their children and the children of their children needed the memory of this time. It was their defence against the exploiters of their time. Now it would also become my defence against exploitation. I looked around me at the mourners. They were perhaps thinking that a past was now going to be buried. Our mother was now part of the past. She was going to be buried. But her secrets were alive. They would live on and breed new actions that would eventually produce socialism, the socialism she had defended. The socialism which Alfred Zingler and his wife Margarethe had defended. Socialism was not just to do with bread and money alone, but included culture. The whole human being. I cherished these thoughts about her secrets. Hadn't they also given me strength in my own convictions? In them rested my ability to act. I had guarded them carefully for many years. Forty years of silence. Forty years during which she grew old, very old, while her eyes remained shiny coal black until the end.

The pastor had finished. We followed the coffin to the grave, saw her lowered into the ground next to her husband. We threw flowers and a spadeful of earth. I thought of Klaus, her lover. Where was he now? Who knows, perhaps they were together somewhere now. The evening meal at the hotel with a good glass of wine soothed us all and somehow bridged the distances between us for a short evening. The next morning we would all disappear into different cities and I would start to dig. Dig deep for memories for a better future. I would dig and write and unearth the names she had mentioned and bring them to life. Walter Hasenclever, the poet; Carl von Ossietzky, the writer; Karl Schwesig, the artist. Liesel, who introduced my mother to the social democrats in Berlin. Klaus, who she fell in love with.

Diary notes, 20th June 1970

This year she came early, in June. It didn't suit me at all. I had appointments booked with a publisher. The children needed a lot of patience. But everything had to wait, because she wanted to rid herself of her past. I had little time to contemplate her concerns. We rushed into the park. It was in full bloom. The colourful flower beds were a feast for the eyes. We had brought bread for the ducks. Daniel fed them. Gabriel was asleep in his pushchair.

"I don't know where to start. I want to make it as short as possible. On the other hand I can't just leave out important events, do you understand? It's not easy."

"Just start wherever you like..." I mumbled impatiently.

"You must understand I was only seventeen. That's when I became aware of politics. Inflation. Murder. Suicides. Soldiers in town. The occupation. You can't imagine it now."

I remained silent and wished she would start at last. With the essentials. I dearly hoped she wouldn't stir up everything I had tried to forget or things I was comfortably unaware of.

"I don't know anything about some occupation. Just start somewhere."

"Yes, it must have been the year 1923, when a friend of my parents took his own life."

Then she started. We sat on a bench behind the tall trellis circle. It was early and we had the rose garden almost to ourselves. It was a beautiful day and my impatience had given way to a pleasant mixture of pride and curiosity. About her entrusting me with her secrets. She spoke and I listened. I had never heard her talk so much before. It kind of shot out of her, as if someone had opened a valve. Sometimes she was almost hectic, she stood up and walked a few paces, grew red in the face or pale. She used her hands to shape thoughts and feelings in front of our eyes. Tonight we were especially tired and went to bed early. Her tales reached right into my dreams. I think all beginnings are hard.

End of diary notes.

At some point her visits and stories became an integral part of my summers. I decided that I just had to give her this time. There was a lot I didn't know about politics or the economy. The role of the American banks when Hitler usurped power, for example. The betrayal of the citizens. It wasn't very surprising. We're still living under the threat of the same elites so many decades later. Then, at some point, I grew very intrigued and involved and stopped feeling bored and frustrated. I checked when that was. It had to do with two facts, which were also recorded in my diary entries (14th July 1972). I was better able to deal with my own life, and our relationship with each other became warmer and more close. I began to see her as a woman who had fought for her love and for justice, and not just as my mother. She had a remarkable capacity to love, as others may have such an ability to hate. I wanted to learn that capacity from her and was grateful to her. Her last visit to talk about her secrets was in 1975. It was a remarkable year. Not only was the summer good and almost tropical for a London climate, but there were also so many things that happened which we valued. The Vietnam War was lost by the Americans in spite of all their superior weapons and chemicals. The Helsinki Accord was signed. We were optimistic and confident about the future of Socialism, which already included half of Germany.

Now I sat again in the train back to England and had time to reflect on my thoughts after the excitement of seeing everyone again. A feeling of warmth rose inside me. I felt fond of my siblings, as different as they seemed to me. I looked out of the window. Some say that the year 1975 had been one of the best for mankind. More people were then better off than any time before or after. Before is not surprising, but after must make us think. The old elites were pulling strings again: Profits were privatised and debts were socialised. Socialism for the few. Had they stolen our utopia, the hope for a better future, I was wondering. Instead we now had the total surveillance by the American security services. We were living in a world reduced to the present tense of a life of shopping, questions of ethics or conscience discarded. The dictatorship of the presence without past or future. What does that mean for our children?

The restaurant service of the train pulled me out of these miserable ponderings. Yes, a coffee, please, and a croissant. The sun lay green on the fields and cows with full udders stood still like sculptures. The coffee made my thoughts more positive. Hope lay in my mother's stories which I would now retell. They would reconnect us with the past and give us a new optimism. I was glad that I had the diary entries, as they spoke to us so directly from the bygone time. I imagined that she intended her story to be more than just a family story, more like a piece of history.

CHAPTER 1

THE FUNERAL

"I love these green tiles with the fish and seahorses on them, don't you?"

"Yes, I do, so atmospheric! As if you were by the sea. I hope you'll sing for us, well, after dinner anyway..."

"I might, if I'm not too shy in front of ..."

She looked round to see if Hubert was near. He was following the two friends into the low ceilinged cavern with fish lamps, ceramic tiles around the walls and fish nets spanning across the ceiling. It was so cosy! They were led to a plain wooden table. The waiter lit a candle and brought the menu.

It was Olga's eighteenth birthday. Hubert, her boyfriend, had offered to pay and Lene was invited. They had fresh plaice and white wine and toasted each other frequently in an exuberant mood. Going out to a restaurant wasn't exactly a usual experience. Outside the heavy snow muffled passers'-by footsteps, along with the sirens from the mine towers, the screeching of the trams. Fresh snow was still drifting through the air and sparkling in the light of the gas lamps. Olga smiled with glazed eyes and glowing cheeks, when she stood up and sung for them a burlesque tune from Carmina Burana. Her voice sounded lovely. Hubert took her in his arms and kissed her, while Lene applauded.

"What a great voice you have! I bet you'll be an opera singer one day; I can just imagine you on stage! Hubert and I will get free tickets to hear you and we will applaud you extra loud."

"I'd love to be on stage, singing and wearing those amazing costumes that you get to wear, silk, lace, with décolleté, long gloves, fabulous shoes..."

"The stage! You know what is going on behind the stage, it's a decadent world!" said Hubert, and his big eyes rolled with pretend danger. They doubled over with laughter about Hubert's funny face.

"Hard work, that's what it is. Eight hours singing a day, that's not very decadent."

They had often talked about their creative careers, Lene as a writer and Olga as an opera singer, when they used to come home from school. You could easily imagine Olga on stage with her operatic figure with a full bosom and broad hips and there was her remarkable voice. Next to her Lene was a skinny rake with buttons for breasts, although she was taller than Olga with broad shoulders.

"All right, I'll just be singing in a nightclub, then."

"No, don't say that, I didn't mean to put you off, you should keep your aspirations. I try to hold on to mine, but I can see that I shall end up as a bakery manager, like my mother," Lene sighed.

"Now you're wrong and giving up your ideals. If I'm going to be a singer, you will become a writer. Let's shake hands on that."

As they shook hands a small bright flame of hope lit in her heart. In that moment she loved Olga deeply.

After the party Lene trotted home carefully, watching her steps on the snow covered paths. With her eyes fixed on the icy pavement she almost ran into her uncle Jakob.

"Out so late, Lene? Shouldn't you be at home?"

"Oh, Uncle, you gave me such a fright, I never saw you coming towards me."

"Well, no you couldn't have, you were talking to yourself and staring at the street as if you'd seen a ghost down there. Are you all right?"

"Thanks, Uncle, I'm fine. I've just been out with my friend Olga to celebrate her birthday. So glad to see you anyway, the streets seem so empty tonight".

"Well, there's been quite a bit of trouble. Not sure if you've heard, but French Troops have started arriving this evening. They are occupying Gelsenkirchen. Also, we've had some bad news about a family friend. Your parents will tell you about it, I don't want to worry you now, it's late, get yourself some sleep, dear."

"Now you're worrying me more, who was it, Uncle Jakob?"

"You remember Herr Müller? He was found dead in his cellar, he hanged himself, and they believe it was to do with his debts. His wife found him and called the police. I've just been to see her. She's in a terrible state."

"Dear Lord, that's awful, I didn't even know he had debts, what did mother and father think?"

"Have a word with them tomorrow, Lene, best get some sleep now. I'm pretty tired myself, but see you soon, OK?"

They had reached Lene's house. She waved goodbye, shut the door and gingerly climbed up the stairs to her bedroom. She looked out of the window across to Dahlbusch mine silhouetted black against the sky, with coal trolleys rumbling through the air. She listened hard and was certain she heard the sound of men in boots crunching over the snow. It sounded only a few streets away, or was she imagining things?

She dozed off into a restless sleep with vivid dreams. She saw soldiers walking, rifles in hand. Tight groups of uniformed men in darkened streets. Erich, her brother, turned up, a beggar in rags, his eyes wide with terror. She woke early and could hear her father going downstairs to the kitchen for his breakfast. Rosa was usually the first and made coffee and toast for the bakery staff and Hermann Deppermann. Lene had no more taste for sleep. She washed in the enamelled wash bowl and jug in her room, taking an absent-minded look in the mirror and wiping her hair into some order. She looked again. Her hair reminded her of the other death. It was Grandpa's, a year ago, when she locked herself up in the bathroom to cut off her plaits. *I didn't want plaits any more. First the left plait was gone, then the right one. Cut them off at my neck level! That strange grinding noise of the metal blades on a thick bunch of hair! It was so loud and took ages. I felt nothing when the noise happened and the plaits fell down. I just thought good, they're gone. Then the door rattled.*

"*Lene, what are you doing? Come down.*"

I heard nothing.

"*Lene, come out. Don't lock the door, child.*"

I was in some sort of trance and heard nothing. I kept looking in the mirror and seeing this strange person I did not know. A girl of seventeen. Tall, thin, blonde. No plaits. Eyes dark brown, almost black like coal. I know her; she thought, maybe I don't want to know her, she is sad.

"*Lene, do you hear me?*"

That was my mother. I came out of my stupor and picked up the plaits. I pressed them into my pocket like stolen goods.

Lene took her eyes off the mirror, as if it had caused the memory flash. The smell of coffee wafted up and she ran down the stairs. In the kitchen the fire was already glowing in the hearth.

"You're up early, Lene, are you going to college today?" her father asked.

"No, I'm not," Lene replied. "How are you?" she asked her father. "Not too bad, but we've got troubles, Lene. I can't tell you now. I've got to get to the bakery. Your mother will tell you. Have some coffee and toast anyway."

Her father left the kitchen through the open door to the courtyard of the bakery. She followed him with her eyes and noticed his bent back. The smell of yeast and dough wafted into her nose, warm, luscious, sweet. It gave her a sense of belonging and safety. But it was getting in her way now. She felt nervous and itched to know more about what was going on. She looked around the room and her eyes fell on the notice board. She saw the note with Frau Müller's telephone number and 'urgent' written over the top. It was probably going to be one of those bad days where everything goes wrong from first thing in the morning. She wandered over to clear some of the dishes and tidy up the table for the rest of the family, when Hilde, her older sister, entered the kitchen looking at her with one of her cold blue-eyed looks. She felt wary and puzzled about Hilde. She always poked her nose into things. This morning was no exception. She started muttering about her being out late and bringing the family into disrepute. "Girls your age shouldn't be out in the street at night."

Lene tried to ignore her, but Hilde's watery eyes followed her. Hilde could be so annoying! She'll marry a priest one day, as father says, Lene thought scornfully. There's no one else left, except the soldiers. The war had buried them in early graves, in Normandy, in Verdun, in Russia. The rest of the day drifted by in a blur of routines and mishaps, after her mother and father had gone out to see Frau Müller and help her make arrangements for the funeral. They were expected back late. A tray of loaves burned and sent waves of acrid smoke through the yard into the hall and kitchen. Marianne, the shop assistant, was seething, her chest rising and falling like a yo-yo.

"The shoppers are going to lynch us. First there is the price they have to cope with. 500 marks a loaf! And now they have to wait for the next tray of loaves."

The shoppers gave vent to their irritation.

"What's next, we won't be able to afford a loaf with the price going up the way it is."

"What sort of peace is this! Prices going up like that. We can't feed our families."

"They spent our money on weapons and uniforms, now we have to bear the cost of their adventures."

Empty shelves in the shop made the shoppers nervous, awakening the fear of an empty stomach. Lene, Hilde and Marianne scurried from the shop into the bakery and back to find out when the next set of loaves was ready. The house and shop were like a rabbit warren with many doors, rooms and entrances to different parts of the premises. The once red brick building had grown soot coloured from the coal dust, just like the other terraced houses in the street. From the shop you had to walk through the kitchen and into the hall where a door led into the yard outside the bakery and round the corner to the large gates for automobile deliveries. Years ago two houses had been turned into one, when the Deppermann family grew to six children, with live-in staff like Rosa the portly maid, and apprentices who at times were accommodated in the bakery itself. Around the turn of the century number 59 was inhabited by two widows called Strack and Schuetz. Then there were Buiting and Doornlarge who were workers. An electrician called Franz Fuhrmann and the nurse Anna Hessbruegge had also once lived there. One after another the lodgers were given notice. Hermann and Mathilde Deppermann eventually asked the last lodgers to move out and had the place renovated to have enough room for the children. The bakery remained at the corner of the street at number 61. The blue enamelled sign above the entrance read: 'Dampfbäckerei Deppermann', which meant Steam Bakery Deppermann. A pretzel was hanging on a decorated iron holder outside and you could hear it clink, if the weather was stormy. Of course it was no longer steam but coal that was now used in the bakery.

Lunch-time was sacred. The shop was closed, all the staff and family ate in the kitchen together and banter did not stop, even if Hilde kept frowning.

"Sometimes I want to throw a cream cake right into Frau Schweinsdorfer's face. She complains too much," said Ruth, the youngest of the shop assistants, who was only sixteen.

"Do it," encouraged cheeky Josef, the bakery apprentice, a good looking lad with curly blonde hair that popped out from under his baker's hat at the back.

"Shut up, Josef, don't be giving the girl ideas. Stop running down our customers." Hilde looked frosty-eyed around the table.

"But they all want white bread! Imagine that! White bread, as if we could have a magic wand and make white flour happen. I keep having to tell them, only at weekends."

Hans and Josef were messing about with their food and attracting angry glances from Hilde, which made them giggle. Josef excused himself and left for the bakery. Erna sneezed and left the kitchen complaining of 'something in the air' that she was allergic to. The others laughed behind her back, because it was time to clear up. They finished their potato soup and ate a good piece of rye bread, followed by a cup of peppermint tea. Rosa, Mathilde's 'angel', and Lene made sure little Hermann and Hans, Lene's younger brothers, helped to put everything away. It was always Hermann who diligently looked to help and Hans who suddenly disappeared and had to be called back, like his older brother Erich. Erich was another story altogether, because he had come back from the war a changed person. No one ever said much about it, but he puzzled them and they felt a mixture of wariness and irritation about him. He was grumpy and sullen at home, his hair unkempt and constant stubble growing on his face. He had taken up his law studies again and seemed to be enjoying the company of his fellow students. He was out of the house a lot. Rumour had it that he was sometimes found drunk and dishevelled in the bars of the town and then stumbled home through the street arguing loudly with anyone who cared to listen to him. Perhaps he was practising his legal debating powers. His mother never gave up on him, though.

"He's seen a lot of death, just remember that. He's been in the killing fields of the war. It's made him callous, he's just unhappy."

The afternoon of that same day saw the bread price increase further to 650 marks a loaf. Scuffles broke out in the shop, when customers rushed to get their loaf. Marianne asked people to be patient and wait their turn or come back later, when they started to argue.

"You're trying to get my place in the queue, you rascals, let me go."

Hilde was good in those situations. She marched majestically from behind the counter into the crowd bringing a loaf with her. She gave it to the lady who had felt she was being squeezed out, saying:

"Frau Kahnemann, pay me next time and take this loaf now. We are all in a rush today and people are tired of queuing. That's why they are getting bad tempered. Don't take it to heart."

After a hectic and tiring day the shop was finally closed for the night, and the women sighed with relief when they could lock the door. In the evening the bakery staff and shop assistants left for their lodgings, and the family ate on their own, Rosa being the only extra person who stayed. She was like a family member. Her quiet and friendly round face was much loved. She had a quick way about her and could pick up no end of washing, loaves or plates with her plump, strong arms and hands. Rosa had a room in the attic of the house. She had her own key and went about her ways as she wished, although Mathilde liked to see everyone back home by ten o'clock.

Mathilde and Hermann returned from their visit to the bereaved Frau Müller looking exhausted and resigned. The table was laid with bread, salami and potatoes. A pot of tea was ready under the tea-cosy. A fire crackled in the hearth. The washed pots and kitchen utensils hung sparkling in the shifting light. It felt homely and calm. As in most evenings tiredness was almost as overwhelming as hunger. After a short prayer the food was eaten silently. By the time the dishes were cleared, enough liveliness had returned for them to sit in the lounge and share the day's stories.

Lene collapsed into the patched armchair watching the lights from the coal wagons flicker through the room and hearing her mother's knitting needles click. Hermann sat on the sofa with his newspapers next to him, and Hilde had pulled the thick velvet curtains, shutting away the outside world for a short peaceful time. Lene curled up safely in the lap of the family like a cat, while she listened to her parents.

"Poor Lisbeth Müller was in a bad way. She's in a state of shock and couldn't stop crying. She doesn't know how she'll cope with the debts her husband left. Apparently, he did some dealings with shares that failed. Neighbours brought some stew. We all made sure she ate something. She looked very upset, eyes swollen with tears. On the way back we met Uncle Jakob. He's been a great help. The funeral is going to be in a week's time. She's lost her son to the war and her husband to the inflation. Now she's only got her daughter."

Hilde suggested Erna could go over and assist Lisbeth Müller.

"Erna, you're good at nursing, aren't you? You could go and keep Lisbeth company."

"You always think of something for me to do, you know I'm waiting for my training place," Erna said agitatedly. She knitted her brows and looked accusingly at Hilde. This look always amused Lene, because she could put it on for the smallest reasons. She smiled, whereupon Hilde frowned with a look that said 'you keep out of this'. Erna had started to pull the skin on her fingernails, something she always got into when she started to get stressed.

Hermann had 'der Volkswille', the social democrat newspaper in front of him.

"Listen to this. The town council have refused to hand over 100 million marks to the French. Our workers are suffering badly. The French say they don't want a war, but just to have what belongs to them. But what we've got now is worse than war; it's a slow creeping death. The workers are expected to work for international capitalism."

"You will have to be careful, father," Hilde warned. "This shop could easily become the target of the French, if you refuse to sell them bread, or the nationalists, if you do sell the French bread. It's complete madness! I can see a huge problem coming our way."

Lene had admiration for Hilde's confident way of explaining a situation. She had a grasp of politics, although she and her father constantly battled over their views. Lene usually sided with her father. Mathilde pointed out that everyone was exhausted and suggested they all go to bed and get some rest. When Lene got to her bedroom, the essay papers she was working on were still strewn about. She sighed. She had had no time to do any college work all day. She peeped out of the curtains. A tight and pale moon was stuck lop-sided above the shafts of the mines. Their sharp outline cut a dark hole into the sky.

Then came the day of Herr Müller's funeral. His untimely death had brought home to them how much life had changed for the worse. The war now seemed easy in comparison. During the war you had soldiers doing their duty at the front and citizens doing their duty at home. But now it was not clear what these duties were and who was to do what. Foreign troops were in town as if it was war. Some people made lots of money, others became poor suddenly and lost everything. Some wanted the Kaiser back and ran crazed through the streets beating people up. Others wanted the republic or demanded a path to socialism. Money kept losing its value and thereby confused the worth of labour and goods. What was it that people these days could depend on? So spoke the pastor, when he held his sermon. Herr Müller's trust had been betrayed. He was led to believe his savings were in safe hands with the bank, but was disappointed. He was mortified and did not dare to tell his wife. She was left to pick up her life's pieces with a dead husband and a funeral to be paid for. The pastor had shown forgiveness and allowed the burial to take place on the cemetery. Suicides had become almost commonplace.

The muddy path on the graveyard filled early with mourners, whose polished shoes sank into the rain soaked soil. Many friends turned up from the neighbourhood and stood quietly under the sulphuric clouds hanging low in the sky. The black soggy snow fell caked in soot on their coats. They stood uneasily, shuffling on their feet and looking about themselves, as if to watch their backs. Each one of them had seen violence erupt within moments and die down in unexplained ways. Now it rose again like a bird of prey, while the funeral was taking its sad and ceremonious course. More mourners arrived in dark coats; some women wore hats with veils. Older ones bent slowly on walking sticks, as they followed the carriage with the coffin. Another carriage carried Frau Müller and her daughter with uncle Jakob, his wife Sophie, Hermann and Mathilde with the Deppermann children and bakery staff in the next one. The procession was about to cross the railway line, when the mourners were alerted by a noise. A throng of men was shouting and yelling, arguing loudly. There seemed to be a dispute as to the direction a large number of railway wagons should take. They were being shunted hither and thither from one track to another. Red and navy uniforms of French soldiers could be seen amidst a throng of railway workers. The payment in coal! The reparations! The conflict that had been all over the newspapers. In front of the passing carriages the noise suddenly grew, when a gang of men in German uniform suddenly ran into the arguing crowd. A cacophony of shouting followed wielded truncheons, batons and various other tools. You could make out the

German soldiers beating the crowd regardless of whether they were railway workers or French soldiers. Sticks and clubs flew through the air, and as sudden as they had turned up the uniformed Germans disappeared. Then all went quiet. The carriages had moved on, the men had vanished. The mourners, frightened eyes, pale and silent, squeezed into their seats, as if to disappear. Lene's heart galloped, she felt dizzy and dirty, the skin dry in her face. The silence was broken, when someone asked. 'The Freikorps, isn't' it? No policemen were in sight. No one appeared to have seen the attack apart from the mourners, some hidden away in carriages, others protected from view by the vehicles. That was probably lucky. Witnesses could often suffer the same fate as those who were attacked.

While the pastor softly intoned about the suffering the Müllers had to go through Lene started day dreaming about her own family and how odd they all were. Her mother, a delicate yet assertive woman who could have a quick temper, when her hand could suddenly fly and leave a stinging sensation on one's cheek. Apparently, though this only happened once, when a sales girl had thrown bread away. Bread was sacred, it could not be thrown away. Hilde was so funny with her watery pale blue eyes, her uprightness as if she had swallowed a ruler and her hankering after the monarchy, but Erna! No one could make her out. She was the opposite of Hilde, dreamy and withdrawn into herself and yet she had sweetness about her and an easy smile that flitted over her thin lips. Hilde was quick with work, while Lene had seen Erna only work in the kitchen that one time, when a water pipe had burst and everyone had to help. It's strange how you see people do certain things, but never certain other things, she thought. It was as if each person in her family came to do certain tasks, but never other ones, like actors on a stage. Playing roles! She always saw her mother giving orders, sorting out trouble, organising the staff and sewing or knitting upstairs in the lounge. She saw her father going off to the bakery in his white hat and baker's trousers and jacket, carrying trays of loaves or cakes, a cloud of flour coming off him like spring pollen. She saw him with his back bent, heavy bags of flour bearing down on him as if to break him in half, his face red with the effort of it. She saw him with his small blue eyes focused on the velvet curtains or the lounge ceiling, when he made one of his proud points about the social democrats or the communists. Or with an exasperated line between his eyes, when Hilde gave forth about the wrongs of the Weimar Government. Hilde had a quick mouth putting people in their place; she was like another parent, and dare anyone not do the right thing, she hounded them relentlessly and pointed out their wrongs in public. Older siblings! Lene sighed and looked at the painting with angels playing musical instruments and Maria in the middle holding baby Jesus, while the pastor voice hung over the hushed little community of mourners.

That same evening, when they were already settled down in their places in the lounge the door bell rang and loud noise could be heard from the street. Mathilde beckoned Hilde to go and have a look to see who is there, and she went downstairs. They saw soldiers. French soldiers. They asked for something in their language. Hilde made signs to say 'not here'. Lene peeped down from the stairs and saw blue and red uniforms, helmets cutting shapes into the entrance towering above Hilde. "Not here, this is a bakery," said Hilde again and again and pointed to the enamelled Brezel sign. Finally they left.

CHAPTER 2

THE INFLATION

"Citizens! The enemy has marched into our country. They disregard our human rights. They threaten one of our most successful industrial regions and ruin our ability to abide by the Treaty of Versailles. We accuse the enemy before the European population and the whole world of an act of aggression. We raise our voices loudly to declare that the holy right of our German people to its own land and soil is being violated. We will do everything to stop your suffering as early as we can and ease your pain..."

It was the Reich's President, Friedrich Ebert's speech. Hermann read it from the 'Volkswille'. He put the paper down and took a sip from his cup of peppermint tea and looked to check the impression his words had caused. It was one of those evenings, when all the work was done, when the whole family sat together in the lounge with a cup of peppermint tea.

"What's the use of big words and speeches like that, the man is a loser." Hilde was unforgiving with her comments.

"Give him a chance! The situation is not of his making, and the French have made a bad problem worse for him and all of us. He's trying to appeal to the leaders of other countries. Not a bad idea, they should listen! I think his speech is powerful."

Hermann sat back on the sofa stretching out his tired legs and glancing at the ceiling stucco. The bakery work meant standing all day. Mathilde's knitting needles clicked.

"What's the use of such proud declarations? He ought to come and listen to the people in the shop and their complaints. The money has lost so much of its value. It has lost its relationship with work, creating debts everywhere."

"Another problem is the farmers who keep their produce from us," Mathilde interjected. "Just as well we've got bread which we can trade for goods."

"I looked in at the greengrocer to see what he had to sell. No carrots, no cauliflower, no potatoes, just turnips." Erna made an offended face, as if she had been personally insulted.

"Forget meat, unless you try and buy it on the black market," Hilde pointed out sharply.

Hermann always tried hard to explain the actions of the government, even when it became complicated.

"Here it is in the 'Volkswille' of the 21st February 1923: The German are not the only ones – the working classes in France and Belgium are suffering too. The Brussels paper 'Le Peuple' ran an editorial on this under the title: A loaf of bread at 1 franc 15 centimes: "Today Monday the price of a loaf of bread per kilo rose for the second time. This means that Belgians are spending 300,000 francs more for their bread."

"I wonder who wrote that," Hilde mused. "Why do their soldiers bother us, when they have their own problems?"

"At least it has nothing to do with us," Lene announced, "we are neither policemen nor soldiers."

"You should keep well out of their way, anyway," was Hilde's tight-lipped general warning. Her watery blue eyes blinked dangerously.

Erna was stuffing the body of one of her dolls. The wooden carved head lay by her side. She tried it on now and again.

The weather turned rainy with heavy clouds hanging low over the coal mines and steeples. Lene was on her way to see Olga. She had not seen her friend since the birthday party, but she still felt a special warm feeling in her heart from the moment when they had shaken hands on their future careers.

As she walked down Karl Mayer Strasse she could feel the cold wind on her face in spite of the spring sun. She wrapped her scarf tighter around herself and doubts crept into her mind. What if Olga was really serious about Hubert and didn't stick to her word? Why had she not been in touch, she often popped into the bakery on her way to the shops? Lene felt puzzled. The world stood still in the afternoon sun. A few crumpled up handbills were rustling in the slight breeze. Out of curiosity Lene picked up one of the bills, unfolded it and read it. It was a call to attend a public meeting at the local mine to discuss Passive Resistance towards the French soldiers in town. Lene pushed the paper into her pocket.

The way to Olga's led past the Dahlbusch coalmine. She was in awe of its monstrous shape. Its towering structures cut a dramatic silhouette into the cold sky. Clouds raced past it. It sat there like a giant sleeping animal, humming with inner noise, heat and human and machine labour. Like a regular breath thousands of workers poured in and out of the tall gates, as if a force of nature. Shifts changed day and night.

Scalding fires illuminated the sky from the towers and their big wheels. Coal dust blew like swarms of tiny insects settling on hair, nose and lungs. Coal carts travelled on thick *wires* through the air from the mine shafts to railway terminals for the coal to be transported east, west, north and south.

At the road 'Am Dahlbusch', she crossed over a bridge passing the coalmine works and then turned right into Bromberger Strasse. Something made her walk faster. Olga lived near the crossroads with 'Am Graftweg'. Olga opened the door and beckoned Lene to follow her into her bedroom. She crept back under the covers.

"I don't know what is wrong with me, Lene, but I don't feel well. I've lost my voice and I have a bad throat. Hubert said he'd come round, but my dad won't let him come in. He says it's not right he should see me in bed. He's so old-fashioned, he makes me laugh."

"If you think that's old-fashioned, you should get to know mine," Lene laughed and added, "would you like some tea or water?"

"No, don't worry, just sit and chat with me. Mother's going to bring a tray of goodies in a minute. She knows you're here. You know how fond she and my dad are of you. They think you're a good influence on me... especially now that I'm going out with Hubert." Then she whispered:

"Funny how differently they behave when Hubert visits. They're on edge and keep asking him questions. I don't know why. He's good-looking and very successful in his work."

Olga looked dreamily at Lene and smiled when she talked about Hubert. She did not notice Lene's hesitation. It was difficult for her to find words for her uneasy feelings, and she felt awkward. When she spoke her words came out in spite of her feelings:

"It was great the other night on your birthday. Hubert is a real gentleman and he looks very much in love with you. And he has a good income. What's his job, have you asked him?" Olga ignored Lene's question.

"Did I tell you that he spoke of marriage, when he brought me home that night?" Olga smiled broadly and brushed her hair out of her face. She took a small mirror and looked at herself. Lene saw a chance to vent her feelings.

"Oh, that's nice! But there's no need to rush into anything, Olga. You've got plenty of time, you're only eighteen. Don't you want to do your music studies first? I'm dying to see you as an opera diva!"

"Why should I study, when he has all the money we need? He says he's going to buy us a big house by the river. A big river like the Rhine."

Lene imagined that Olga was already seeing herself strolling over the lawn of a lovely mansion and arranging the garden furniture for a party, the Rhine willows gently rustling in the breeze.

She hesitated, feeling uncomfortable about Olga's words. What about her independence? Somehow growing up in the bakery, where so many women worked, made her suspicious of dependence. You could see the pride in her mother's posture about being able to run the business. All the women in the shop worked for a living and could support themselves. If her father, God forbid, ever died, her mother would know what to do. She thought of Hilde who had such commanding abilities. She could probably order an army about, if she had to. Ruth and Marianne, one of them only sixteen, but they worked. When they received their pay at the end of the week, she had often seen them look proud and excited and whispering to each other about the little things they might want to buy for themselves or their family. It might be a new spangle for their hair, or special buttons for a dress.

"Don't be thinking of getting married, what about me? We've got to do interesting things first. Just imagine what it would be like, being a singer, maybe perform in the theatre, Olga. You'd be bored just staying at home. You like a bit of adventure, don't you?"

"What's adventurous about working?" Olga muttered, digging herself deeper into her featherbed. Lene struggled to comprehend what Olga said. Maybe it was just that she wasn't feeling well. She tried again.

"All you need to do is do the studies you planned to do, and then look for a job in the music halls or the theatre as a singer or a performer. Even if you don't then work immediately, at least you would have those skills and could get a glamorous job in an opera house or a music hall. We would all come to hear you and applaud you. That is adventurous! Hubert would also be very proud of you."

It was impossible to enthuse Olga today. "Sounds like a lot of work to me. Anyway, my mother and father don't want me to study singing. They say there are an awful lot of bad things going on. The singers get seduced by the actors and directors and then you start to look old and no man will marry you. I want to marry and have children."

Lene looked out of the window. Drops of rain hit the window leaving stains of soot on the outside. She felt sad and anxious. How was one supposed to lead one's life as a woman? Surely, the only way was to learn something and be to able to earn one's own living. Even if you married, you would have the choice of working or staying at home, rather than always having to ask your husband for money to go shopping.

"Your mum and dad have their point of view, and you can have another point of view, in the end you have to decide on your life, not your parents. I think you've got a great voice, you should get training for it." Lene looked at her watch.

"Look at the time, I can't wait till the goodies arrive, I just wanted to see how you are. You've got to get better first and then see how you feel. Just don't worry about all of this now." Olga looked at Lene gratefully and their friendship felt deep and solid for them. She stretched her white arms out and Lene bent down for a hug.

"Get yourself well quickly, there's all this stuff going on in town now. French soldiers have occupied the whole place."

She was on her way to the shops. A gusty wind was blowing rain into her face. Needle-like drops struck her on her cheeks. She was pulling Hilde's worn woollen coat closer around her burying her hands deep inside its big pockets. She squeezed her eyes nearly shut to stop the pointed raindrops lashing her pupils, but couldn't help noticing several fliers stuck on a wall. Each had a photograph of the face of a young woman, French soldiers in uniform in the background. The girl's name was written in thick letters at the bottom. The caption read: 'This woman is fraternising with a French soldier bringing shame to the German people.' Someone out there would feel encouraged to spot one of the women and attack her. It was an invitation to violence. This could be me! she thought. I've got to help protect these women. She looked about herself to see if others felt like she did. But they all hurried to do their shopping.

She had reached the throng around Ahlsdorf, the town's illustrious department store with the imposing glass windows displaying luxury goods. There were obviously still people who could buy them! She walked in after having gazed at the exhibits of underwear when, suddenly, French soldiers appeared as if from nowhere shouting at people to leave the shop immediately. Everyone was shunted and pushed about as if they were a herd of animals. Word had it that the soldiers had wanted to buy some writing equipment. When the staff of Ahlsdorf refused to sell it to them under the order of 'passive resistance' they gave the employees ten minutes to change their minds. When they refused to do so, the soldiers proceeded to close the whole establishment down. Shoppers were told to leave using the back door. The surrounding shop workers immediately decided to close down too according to a solidarity agreement. Lene stood and watched the shops shut in amazement. Children cried; women shouted; men bustled; there was mayhem. Frustrated groups of shoppers stood in the street and protested loudly, but they were unable to take action. Within moments the police appeared and dispersed the discontented crowd. They had to go home empty-handed.

Lene managed to buy a newspaper and some matches at a street stall. On the front page of the 'Ruhr Echo' she read that the French soldiers had left the telegraph office which they had occupied previously. The paper reported that it took the army a long time to move out, because they had so many stolen goods accumulated from many different buildings, including all the tools owned by the telegraph workers. All the stuff had to be loaded on to lorries. Mattresses, clothes, bicycles, electrical equipment, food and telephones. Files with paper documents were taken out into the yard and burned. Public records would be lost for good.

Walking back she mulled over Olga and her own decision to start college. She was enjoying it very much. It removed her from dreary bakery duties for parts of the week. There had been a family discussion about this and the usefulness for a woman to have further education. Her mother had supported her, while Hilde had demanded she stick with her duty in the household. They offered a range of topics that she was keen on.

She had witnessed thousands of workers from the mines demonstrate in the streets of Gelsenkirchen, calling for the right to vote for all men and women. They wanted a republic and declared that the Kaiser was responsible for plunging the country into war and poverty. They did bring about the fall of the Kaiser. The Weimar Republic had been declared with a constitution and citizens' rights. Women were given the vote! Change had been brought about by the power of men and women! Had the Russian people not won a revolution and were now in charge, the Tsar gone? Things had happened, change had taken place. Yet, when she looked at the streets of Gelsenkirchen, its aged, blackened brick terraces, the dirty paving stones, the soup kitchen smells, women in aprons looking worn out, she wondered if change had really taken place. It seemed invisible. How had the Kaiser been made to resign? How had the sailors in the Baltic Sea agreed to stop the ships leaving the harbour? How was such change brought about? In someone's mind as an idea? Was it like a caterpillar metamorphosis? Or did it happen like the eruption of a volcano, out of anyone's control? Perhaps such matters were not knowable. How did Olga's desires to marry appear? Due to chemicals, pheromones, pathways in the brain?

The house was quiet, when she reached home. She ate a piece of rye bread with cream cheese and walked upstairs. Her parents were sitting with Erna and Hilde in the lounge. Erich was out and Herman and Hans sat at a small side table and played chess while Hilde was doing some stitching. The table light drew a warm circular light on the little group. Her father was in his armchair as usual, the newspapers by his side, and her mother on her sofa. They seemed to be in the middle of an argument.

"Passive resistance, they call it, but I say they are just forcing the problem on to the people."

Hermann spoke with a quiet frustration in his voice. You could hear it tremble. Tiny stubble showed on his chin, his beard always grew very fast. His face shone, and his cheeks glowed red from scrubbing them after the day in the bakery.

"They are telling us to stop producing to help them against the French! How can we? Just not serve them?"

"It's true, you can't single them out in the shop. They also bring good food with them to pay for a loaf, sausages, wine, apples…" Even Hilde agreed on this point.

"It's not the French I mind, they are poor soldiers who have been ordered into this. Many of our local customers are able to give us food or coal or they ask for credit. The money is just not worth much at the end of the day. It's fortunate that we have been able to keep going. Some of the other bakeries have shut down. No flour, valueless money that won't buy you something to fill your stomach."

Mathilde joined the discussion.

"Your father is right, we are bakers and bakers bake bread. Politicians make politics and soldiers go to war. We've got to bake, the local people need our bread. What would become of them? Or of us, if we did not bake?"

"You forget people feel incensed. There's a pride to resist the French, can't you see? There's a lot of them that really want to show the French their anger. Occupying the Ruhr, what gives them the right to do so? Our government is weak. They should stop the French now. I say the Kaiser would not have allowed them to put their troops into our town. They won't last." Hilde carried on doing stitching. Her metallic voice jarred.

"The Kaiser, the Kaiser! Look at what he's done, taken us to war and lost it."

"Wait till you hear what I saw." Lene couldn't wait to tell her story and see what they were going to make of her experience. "When I was at Ahlsdorf earlier the French soldiers turned up, and the shop assistants refused to serve them. They made everyone leave through the back door and then shut the shop. All the shops in the streets shut down as well."

Hilde beamed. "I told you so! They are all supporting the resistance. We've got to resist too," she insisted.

"I'm not sure. It's certainly not a good idea for us. They are only following orders. They want to do something. They are frustrated. This resistance thing is mainly hurting our local shops and businesses and what is it gaining? It just means we have even fewer goods to sell, because no goods are produced. The French are here. They want their reparation money. It was agreed after all. The resistance will ruin our economy and our currency even more."

"Do you know who's behind these calls to resist, Hilde?" Hermann looked exasperatedly at her.

"The 'Freikorps', the unemployed officers. They are fanning the flames of conflict with the French. We've just had a war, do you want another one?" Hermann was shouting at this point. He turned the colour of beetroot.

"It's the nationalists! They are going on a rampage about the French, they are using them as an excuse to harass ordinary people. You know what I mean, the fliers about local women. They have a war mentality, a hate mentality. They think it's glorious to fight and they feel powerful in their uniforms. Also, what do you think we bakers should do? Stop producing bread? Who would be helped by that?"

"Come, come,' Mathilde soothed over, 'no need to get worked up, Hermann, we're just having a chat."

"I know, I know, but where, I wonder, does our Hilde get her views from? The church you go to? Does Erich talk like that? We're a social democratic household. I don't like to hear nationalist views spouted. You seem a little angry, Hilde. That won't help, if you want to find a man. They don't like an angry woman..."

"That's it, you always have to tell me I won't find a man.' Hilde jumped up and started marching to the door. "C'mon, Erna," she beckoned to her sister, "our father thinks we are going to end up a pair of spinsters."

Hilde always used Erna or Lene, when she was annoyed; but Erna did not move.

"Don't get upset, Hilde, I like you debating with father," Lene said soothingly. And Mathilde added: "Now you all calm it down, we're just trying to have a quiet relaxed evening. You're spoiling it, the two of you. Erna isn't taking it to heart, are you?"

Erna sat pale and freckled, her eyes on the limp body of the doll. The material needed to be sewn now. She stopped with the needle and was now rubbing her hand. They knew this meant she had some pains in her wrists. She looked up, with the expression of a surprised sheep in the field, startled, yet unaware.

"I've got the eczema again, mother, I think I'll go upstairs. I've got to put some of that tincture on my hands," she muttered. She got up and both of them left the room. You never knew with Erna what was going on inside her.

"I can see Hilde siding with these warmongers. I hope she hasn't got a boyfriend amongst them. It would be better she stayed single than bring a nationalist into the family." Hermann spoke quietly to Mathilde.

"Shish, Hermann," Mathilde put her finger on her mouth and nodded in the direction of the boys with their chess. "Leave it! She's a good girl and won't do anything daft. We ought to invite Lisbeth Mueller to have a meal with us one of these days."

The room fell silent for a while, while everyone followed their own thoughts. You could hear the Dahlbusch work siren and the clattering of the trams in the distance. Flickering lights now and again travelled around the room from one of the many thousand fires in Gelsenkirchen.

She always watched the display before going to bed. Tonight it looked more like a huge fire in the blackened sky. In her dreams the handbills about the women turned into nasty stories. One of the girls on the nationalist poster was beaten up in a narrow street near Ahlsdorf on her way to work. She could see her twisted arm and blood and a man running away. An ambulance carried her away. In another dream she saw the Dahlbusch machine workshop rooms, where hammers and tongs for tightening bolts hung. The workers held their mass meetings. A single bulb hung from the ceiling and lit up the dusty faces tattooed with soot. The smell of smoke, iron cogs, coal and sweat was pungent. Instead of her family she heard the workers argue fiercely about the passive resistance and whether to support it or not. Once when she was still at school the whole class had visited the local mine and admired the enormous machinery that filled the dark, coal dusted building on all the floors, the huge tools, spanners and anvils in the workshop. They could only imagine the workers in the flickering light, the oversized shadows of their restless and shifting bodies, worn bleak eyes, exasperated features simmering with frustration and tiredness.

"If we don't work for the French, they'll get rid of us and others will do it. At Westerhold they've already agreed to work for them. They'll have jobs and earn money. This gives us little choice. If we don't do the same, we might just as well give up, because they can easily find other workers to replace us at Hibernia and here at Dahlbusch. It's going to end in mass redundancies."

"I won't work for the French and that's it. Why, we produce coal and then they steal it off us and take it to France. We've got to defend our coal, let's stop them."

"Passive resistance, easier said than done. It's always us workers who have to carry the can when there's trouble. They call for war, we have to fight and die. They call for passive resistance, we have to starve and lose our jobs."

"C'mon, you can't just give in to them, the workers are resisting. Ahlsdorf and all the shops in the centre were shut, because the workers refused to serve the French. How brave was that? We've got to support them."

"Foolhardy, I say, all you're doing is playing into the hands of the 'Freikorps' and those uniformed posers. They're stirring it up against the French. You should know those chaps are all too eager to kill socialists like you. They've done it in Hamburg, Saxony, Thuringia. You should be siding with the French. They are poor workers like you."

"C'mon, comrades, we've got to decide, we can't just stand here and practice philosophy. Let's stop the French stealing our coal. Let's go."

Lene tossed and turned, half waking from the dream then sinking back into it, exhausted and fascinated in equal parts. Dawn crept leaden through the curtains. She felt stiff as if she had been sitting in a meeting all night. She peeped out of the window and felt as if she was still in her dream with actions carrying on relentlessly. French and Belgian troops were already crowding the street at this early hour. Soldiers were marching; the column of red and blue uniforms was disappearing along Karl Mayer Strasse. She opened the window for some fresh air. Downstairs the household was moving through its routines like a carousel. It was dizzying how everything seemed normal and people were carrying on as if they had no control.

"The soldiers are in the street outside," she said abruptly.

"I know, can you bring the rolls into the shops."

"I know, I know, I know, that's all everyone is saying and then they act as if nothing can affect them." She noticed the 'Volkswille' lying on the table.

'The soldiers have taken over the airfield near the woods. They took over the local public houses, town halls and sports grounds. Office equipment was thrown out. It was replaced by their own machines and equipment. Records of pensions, employment and other official documents were shoved into dustbins.' She couldn't stop reading. 'Miners' strikes took place against the occupation. Court-martial sentences for disobedience. The death penalty was imposed on anyone sabotaging the transport lines, because the French were going to extract the coal in payment for the reparations they had not received. Fights broke out in many places and French soldiers were pelted with sticks, stones, lumps of coal, bolts of metal. Citizens were arrested. The town of Gelsenkirchen was asked to pay 100 million marks in damages for an incident in which police sergeant Hutmacher was shot and killed by a French soldier. In the thick foggy evening other policemen who arrived as the scene were beaten with rifle butts and kicked until they collapsed streaming with blood.'

"What's the matter with you? Everyone's busy, work has to be done and you're sitting here pondering the meaning of life. Where are the rolls, we need them urgently."

"Have you read the papers?"

"Read the papers! I haven't got time for that. We've got to sell bread. Your father isn't joining the resistance, so we've got to bake and bake. There's huge demand, other bakers aren't open. C'mon, Lene. Nothing we can do. As your mother says, we are bakers, we bake."

Hilde looked at her younger sister with a mixture of annoyance and pity. She could waste so much time bothering with things that had nothing to do with her. The government had to solve these problems, not a young woman who had work to do; yet she could see that Lene was upset. She patted her on the shoulder and nudged an apron into her hand. There was something salutary about everyday duties. They could both feel it and by setting an example Lene followed Hilde like a duckling. Write the bread prices up! Fetch the rolls! Make sure enough paper bags were hanging ready to stuff them with loaves or rolls! The boxes for cakes! The small price labels for pieces of tarts in the glass cabinet! Wipe the crumbs! Brush the floor! Clean the cloth, clean the bread knife. Adjust the scales. After writing the new prices on the blackboard she carried it past the customers to the shop entrance next to the mirror, where the women took brief stolen glances before they left the shop. Women queued with large bags and rucksacks stuffed with paper money. A loaf cost a trifling 1250 marks today.

CHAPTER 3

THE FIFTY THOUSAND MARK LOAF

Inge knew Lene was going to be on time, she always was. She brushed her short brown hair back, took a brief look in the mirror, picked up her satchel and nodded a goodbye to her mother in the crowded kitchen that smelled of boiled turnips. Her younger brothers were hungrily shovelling their porridge into their mouths. Her older brother and father had left for the early shift down the Hibernia mine. Every time she watched them as she left an uneasy guilty feeling slipped through her mind about going off to college.

"You must go and learn more, my child," her mother and father had insisted, "it's no good depending on our men these days. They send them to war, and if they come back they are crippled. Or they are down the mine with too much hard work... Learn something, girl!"

They were a proud working class family with a high regard for education, women's rights and the future of the republic.

"The republic needs women like you, my girl, you have to take a lead role, when you've finished studying. Don't worry about us, we'll manage somehow. One of the family needs to become educated, we've already got your brother going down the mine, the young ones will surely follow him..."

They believed firmly in a socialist future for Germany. Talk like that had persuaded Inge to take up the challenge of learning; in turn she had talked Lene into joining her, which was easy enough. Her school friend Lene had been top girl in her class and eager to learn whatever was put in front of her. Her father's passionate belief in the social democrats was shared by his daughter. Every Monday morning they started the week together. Lene rang the door bell punctually, and the two of them left for the station to catch the Dortmund train. Waiting in the hubbub of the colourful throng in the station felt like a naughty escape from their busy households and all the bad news. It was a relief to be able to study. By some mysterious powers the collapsing world stayed outside the hallowed walls of the respected Helene Lange college. Lectures were held, as if no French soldiers were holding citizens to ransom. Lunch was served in the canteen, regardless of food shortages. Teachers turned up to teach in spite of the wage freeze and the cuts in public services.

Inge always had stories about the mine to tell. She had a laconic way of delivery even when reporting on a death in the mine or the viciousness of the employers towards political activists.

"They buried Joachim last week, he was one of Emil's mates. The older chap he always used to tell us about."

"What happened to him?"

"He got squashed when a support collapsed. Of course the mine owners won't replace him, they just make the others work harder. Damn them!"

Her brother Emil was one of the political activists; a tall and broad shouldered man with wiry reddish hair popping out from under his miner's cap and a prominent nose, giving him a bird of prey-like appearance. Inge enjoyed Lene's enthusiasm for her stories, even when they were sad.

"My family are just small shopkeepers," Lene sometimes grumbled, when she was annoyed.

"No, they aren't. They are crafts people. Bakers belong to guilds who have their own powerful work and learning solidarity," Inge rebutted.

"But they work in isolation. Each master baker has his own business, unlike the miners who need each other." Lene was right, but Inge never rubbed it in. They talked about the handbills showing women's faces.

"Emil is organising a miners' defence of women group, they already talked about how to take action."

They could both see that such solidarity action was possible for the miners, but perhaps impossible for a baker to take. Lene looked at Inge as if an angel had appeared. "Emil, he's great, your brother, tell him I want to join the group," she stuttered. Inge's big warm eyes shone.

One Sunday in May the Deppermanns invited Lisbeth Müller, Uncle Jakob and Aunt Sophie for coffee and cake. The sun shone through the windows of the dining room, making the soot, dust and skin particles visible in its beams. Karin looked pale. She was younger than Erna and Thilde and of smaller build with short red hair and a ready smile in her freckled face. She worked as a shop assistant at Ahlsdorf, which was considered a lucky position to achieve. She wore elegant clothes which she could get at a workers' concession rate available to employees. After her father's death both her mother and Karin relied on her income. They soon all chatted about the funeral back in February. How death had come to him unexpectedly and how they missed him! How the first daffodils had peeped out of the grass in a surprise show of nature's will to survive, when the coffin was lowered into the grave. How they had covered it with earth and flowers. How the tea and sandwiches had felt soothing in the old church hall near the graveyard. Frau Mueller wiped away a tear. Had it been an act of fate? God was still holding his loving hand over them all, if they could believe it.

"He was a victim of the bank and their advice," Lisbeth stated. 'I can't forgive them for exploiting a poor hard working man like that.

All he's done in his life is work. They don't treat you as a person; they just use you and rob you."

Her voice trembled with the sense of loss and rage she felt. Her face was flushed and her lips quivered.

"Don't upset yourself, dear!" Mathilde tried to soothe her friend's feelings, "You have suffered and there is injustice, but you have Karin and what can we do but carry on and make the best of things."

"Have another piece of cake. It's our English apprentice's party piece," Hermann added.

"Mm, it's tasty, have some more, mother," Karin added encouragingly to distract her mother from her sadness and frustration.

Aunt Sophie started to fidget with her handkerchief between her hands. She could not tolerate expressions of much emotion. She behaved as if she was about to sneeze. Uncle Jakob knew his wife's habits and patted her calmingly on the arm.

"Only the rich can dream up such ways of making money. The Junkers, big land owners that they are, are laughing all the way to the bank, because their debts have vanished. Say they have to pay 25,000 marks for a mortgage. Well, they can pay it easily now, because 25,000 marks is about the price of a piece of meat," commented Uncle Jakob.

"And the farmers! You wonder what they think we're supposed to eat. Shoe leather, I suppose. They just don't sell their goods. The shelves are empty," Hilde insisted.

"Don't we know it, what with the bakery. We have daily struggles to lay our hands on the flour we need for bread," Mathilde explained.

"Not so for my hairdresser Lucia! You know what she's like, a bit of a trend setter," burst out Aunt Sophie. "She's having better trade than ever. All the French soldiers are having their hair cut at her salon. She says the French have a lot more style than the Germans and they pay with fancy goods."

They all looked down at their plates and started to put a piece of cake in their mouths in an attempt to hide their embarrassment. Aunt Sophie could be so tactless. Her long thin face had cheerful little eyes, as if she had just made a joke. She had bright lipstick that she painted over the edge of her lips. Above a high forehead she wore her hair in a bun on top. She turned innocently towards Lisbeth, unaware of the ruffled feelings she had caused. Lisbeth and Karin looked at Mathilde for help, but it was Thilde who had a quick reply.

"She'll need to worry about the passive resistance that has been put in place. You're not supposed to work with or for the French," Thilde said, her watery blue eyes blinking sharply in Auntie's direction.

"She's an excellent hairdresser, though. She's having her salon renovated with the money, she says. It's going to be very flash..."

"Better get home now anyway," Uncle Jakob, ever the tactful gentleman, was mindful to stop a political row emerging. The visitors left. Perfume from Aunt Sophie lingered in the dining room and on the stairs long after she had left and tinged the air with hairdressers' ambience.

Hermann's newspapers had more information on the situation in town. French troops had stopped food deliveries from the USA for children. There was no transport to move it. Rotthausen station was occupied. The 'Ruhr Echo' and communist 'Workers Press' were forbidden by the French. Gelsenkirchen was now said to be experiencing real scarcity of food. Potatoes, milk and meat were not arriving due to train stoppages. The town council had organised some deliveries on lorries. Citizens were advised to queue at the post offices for food rations.

Lene felt restless and got up in the night to have a drink of water. She found her father in the kitchen with the 'Rheinisch-Westfaelische' newspaper. He had been unable to sleep.

"Hold on to your purse, Lene dear, when you go to college and into town, make sure your handbag is safe and closed, you've got to be so watchful! All this stuff is going on out there. Hear what they say in the paper: 'Demonstrators with clubs, sticks, rubber tubes and other weapons were threatening the shopkeepers to open up or have their shops robbed. The day before many shops were already broken into, window glass lay on the pavement. Seventy were injured last night, five deaths. Burnt documents are lying in the streets.' Here! See what they did to Ahlsdorf. All the windows are smashed, the goods strewn about, the counters turned upside down. Thieves everywhere."

He seemed to have shrunk into the chair as if the news had crumpled his bones. She looked at his dear tired face and saw the deep creases in his cheeks and between his brows. She stroked her father's head lightly in an urge to comfort him. She was so fond of him. Was he not someone who took an interest in the world out there, not just in his own little life? There was something grand and magnanimous about him, something big and free like a bird in the sky. She stroked his head again with these thoughts. She urged him to get some rest, saying: "Ahlsdorf! That is awful, such a beautiful shop. Why destroy it? How's that going to help anyone? We've just got to take it from day to day, father. Don't worry about me, I'm very careful."

It was another Monday morning, when Inge met Lene in the station on platform six for the 7.20 am train from Gelsenkirchen to Dortmund. Often trains were cancelled. Strikes, equipment stolen, workers locked up; one thing after another could stop the trains. This June and July seemed particularly bad. All the same, the hustle and bustle of the station was entertaining: the running passengers in their hats and jackets over their arms; the women with shopping baskets, bags and umbrellas; some in fancy stockings and high-heeled shoes; the speedy fly posting boys. Yelling newspaper boys; ragged beggars and colourful gipsy women with babies on their arms. The thousands of workers in their various work clothes, caps on heads, newspapers or thermos flasks in their hands. The station was noisy with whistling conductors running up and down the platform, looking at their watches, rushing travellers to get on or off the trains. Huge steam locomotives arrived and departed like giant prehistoric animals snorting clouds of condensed water into the station hall. For moments they were wrapped up in fog without seeing anyone in the crowded space. When a train left it puffed noisily, releasing steam to set the engine in motion. The mixture of sounds was like a piece of music one has become familiar with and enjoys because one knows it so well. This morning they were lucky, because the train was ready to leave. It was only a thirty minute journey, and the theatricality of the station continued on the train. Some people appeared to get on any train that moved. They were often traders or gipsies who wanted to deal in goods and tended to have heavy bags, which they carried on their backs or dragged along. Some had rucksacks tied carefully at the top. Inge and Lene made a game of guessing what was inside the different holders. Often they became oblivious to the other passengers, as they chatted, and watched the houses and trees fly by on the outside. A few brown and green fields, some black and white cows, horses and sheep raced past the window and then came Dortmund with the Hansa coking plant and smoky chimneys of the Hoesch-Westfalen mine. They walked the fifteen minutes to college near the old Bodelschwingh castle. Helene Lange was a celebrated feminist who had fought for women's rights, and the college played a proud role as a leading educational establishment setting standards for equal rights and educational achievements for women. Broad stone steps led up to thick oak double doors of the solid brick building, where they entered a shadowy hall with a shiny terrazzo floor. Sturdy oak benches looked more like exhibits than inviting visitors to seat themselves. Women suffragettes proudly gazed out of portraits lining the wood panelled walls. Helene Lange held pride of place, and nearby was one of her pupils, Gertrud Bäumer. A poster of Gertrud Bäumer was pinned to the wall near her portrait. It announced her forthcoming visit to the college. Inge and Lene waved goodbye to each other, as they had different classes to attend.

Lene had an art class today with her favourite teacher, Fräulein Bäcker, who often peered over Lene's drawings with her large warm brown eyes. She gave her extra advice and praised her work. Today Fräulein Bäcker gave a seminar. 'Have you heard of Paula Modersohn and Heinrich Vogeler, girls?' she asked the class. None of them had heard of either of them. She announced that they were going to study these two in detail. She called their style 'Jugendstil' and said that it was very influential amongst German painters. The college usually offered a trip to the artists' colony in Worpswede. They were encouraged to explore the concepts of symbolic colour, patterns and themes in the paintings. Paula Modersohn's 'Old woman by the poorhouse duck pond' and Vogeler's 'Spring' were shown to them. The two artists' place in the wider art community was discussed. Fräulein Bäcker explained that one of Germany's most celebrated poets, Rainer Maria Rilke had lived amongst the community in Worpswede and wrote about them. 'We have to become children, if we want to achieve the best': she quoted his thoughts about Worpswede. 'Artists love enigmas, and art is love that has been poured over enigmas.' Fräulein Bäcker had a way of celebrating the artists she talked about and their work. She also didn't mince her words when it came to describing some of the traumatic events that occurred in their lives. She told them that one of the Worpswede friends was found to have shot himself in an act of emotional desperation over whether he could become a close member of the group. When Heinrich Vogeler found out that his idealised wife had started to live with another member of the artist community he suffered terribly, Fräulein Bäcker explained. She told them that the peasants' lives, often pictured romantically in their paintings, were in reality brutal, dark and poor. They cut peat in a melancholy landscape of heather, birches and low skies over glistening rivers.

After such lessons Lene was full of fantasies about her future life as an artist or poet, and Inge had an inimitable way of bringing her back down to earth again.

"And then you woke up and found you had to run the shop and sell bread."

By the time they arrived back in Gelsenkirchen reality had returned. Inge was off to her miners' home and Lene to the bakery. Inge probably did not ponder about her existence any further, but she realised Lene would.

"You're such a romantic! Mining and baking are essentials. We need to stick with them, otherwise we starve or die of cold. The rest is fancy stuff we can't afford."

"You're a pragmatist, Inge. Food and politics, that's all. But we have to wonder about the meaning of it all, where we come from, our soul, why we do what we do. We're not ants, after all." She looked at the sky and shivered, sensing the size of the cosmos above, while Inge called out, "Bye then, got to go and cook," and disappeared behind her front door.

At home in the lounge the talk was about the Müllers again. A new problem had hit the family. Karin had lost her job at Ahlsdorf. After the luxury store had been ransacked it was closed and staff members were told that their service was not required until the warehouse had been renovated. The family would probably have to live off the soup kitchen until Karin got her job back.

"We have to help those two, isn't it terrible?" Mathilde mused.

"The Müllers are not the only ones."

Hermann was reading in the 'Volkswille' again. "In the last two months we've had twenty suicides. And that only here by the Ruhr. And then there are all these paper factories turning out bank notes. It's bizarre! A hundred and fifty printing presses producing notes that become valueless the same day."

"Why doesn't the Government sort out the inflation?" Lene wondered.

"They don't really want to. The inflation helps them reduce the cost of payments to France. Now they have to pay with goods without getting anything in return. People who have saved money can now only get less for their money. But if you're a baker or a carpenter you can sell your wares and receive goods in return. The rich, though, are especially fortunate. Their debts have melted away like snow."

Hermann had talked himself into a bit of a rage, his face reddening. His voice became louder as he spoke. He had slipped to the front of his chair and was waving his arms in the air to explain.

"Thanks, father, I didn't mean to get you worked up."

"It's not you, Lene, it's the situation! When I think about it it makes me mad. At least we have the Rapallo Treaty from last year. That helps us not to have problems with the Soviets as well."

"Rapallo, Rapallo, that's probably why the French are in the Ruhr," Thilde hissed sharply. "They probably think we have common plans with the Soviets."

"What nonsense have you picked up! That Rathenau was one of our best politicians. That's why the reactionaries killed him. In broad daylight. In Berlin-Grunewald. Shocking thing."

Hilde clicked loudly with her knitting needles, as if she wanted to command her father to be quiet with them. Lene admired him. He knew so much. Here in the lounge she felt safe, but when she thought of the outside it seemed full of theft and dread.

The curfews did not stop robberies. In the back streets that reeked from urine, fear and hate, thieves were ubiquitous, often wearing a suit or a uniform. Everything was stolen and sold for cash or goods; water meters, furniture, ladders, sinks, telephones, filing cabinets. Cuff-links were sold for peas, lentils and flour, porcelain for meat, milk and bread. The black market flowered. Between exhausted sleep, the shop work, the train station and college Lene walked in her darned dress with long strides clutching her satchel, her thoughts full of hope one minute and dread another. The Berliner Illustrierte cost a mind-chilling 500 marks. The loaf of bread in the family's shop was by now 3,450 marks.

The rich were hidden away, but sometimes you could see them parading their wealth on the streets, a silk jacket here, a glimpse of diamonds, a silk-stockinged high-heeled foot stepping into a limousine there. The new wealthy businessmen needed opportunities to spend their money, and pretty young women were an ideal way of showing off. Overnight colourful, seductive looking nightclubs grew like mushrooms and appeared, lights blazing, and beckoning their opulent clients. When the police raided them, the astonished guests fled through cellar windows that were covered with heavy carpets. The tricked officers only found wine menus. They showed the cheapest wine at the price of 3000 marks.

During the heat of the summer the Freikorps men organised further provocations which led to Bloody Saturday. A policeman was murdered in a knife attack. A large rabble gathered outside the police station with a lot of officers locked into the building. The reactionaries had cut the telephone wires, so that they could not ask for assistance. The same troublemakers turned up to fight the following weekend. Police rushed into the mayhem and made liberal use of their truncheons. In spite of much effort to protect it the miners' café 'Glueckauf' was robbed, and the coats and possessions of the comrades were stolen. Windows were smashed.

In late August bread prices rose to an unimaginable 50,000 marks. A litre of milk was 20,000, a litre of beer 30,000. A cup of coffee came at 15,000. Customers arrived at the bakery carrying their paper money in huge bags and linen baskets. Often it was still wet from the printing presses. But it was colourful. Lene had to write the unbelievable figure of the bread price on the blackboards outside and inside the shop, and the chalk shook between her tense fingers. Her blood pumped in her temples, as if she had invented that outrageous price. She eyed the street for any loitering reactionaries looking for trouble. The street was bathed in glistening sunlight, as if the heavens above were mocking the troubled community. A deserted street! The strange concert of town noise was the only thing going on: work sirens screeching; tram bells clanging; blackbirds twittering; horse drawn coaches clattering. That's all. When the women arrived for their bread she felt for them, as they studied the bread price of 50,000 marks on the blackboard outside the shop. Some did rub their eyes. Was it tears or was it disbelief, or dismay? The women's voices were full of exasperation. They had each a story to tell! How hard it was to feed the family. Why did no one have pity on them?

"A quarter pound of bread please!"

"Two hundred grams of bread for me!"

"Is it made with turnip flour? And what sort of price is that!" one asked, and crinkled her nose at the thought of turnip flour.

"Well, it is turnip flour mixed in with ordinary flour, otherwise you wouldn't get a loaf at all!" Lene was annoyed. As if the price was the bakery's fault! It was just too easy to blame others, when they didn't understand what was happening. Others were calm and patient and had prepared themselves. They handed over wrapped up vegetables; someone even gave meat. Another one a bag of coal. There were the inevitable wads of paper money and grateful looks for their loaf. Grateful that another meal was safe, but dreading the next day and the one after, with hollows in their cheeks and shadows under their eyes, as they thought of their children.

CHAPTER 4

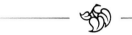

SOUP KITCHENS AND RAFFKES

"They've raised the price of coal to buy new equipment and now we're out of a job."

"Doesn't make sense, does it? Now they have to pay for our soup!" The worker grinned grimly.

"They don't give two hoots for us. We might as well starve," said another pulling his cap into his face. The soup kitchen queue was filling the street with men with good hands that could work hard but were not wanted now.

"It's those pneumatic drills! They've robbed us of our jobs!"

"They can bore away at the coal easily. You could never do it with a pickaxe at that speed."

"And when we strike, they get rid of us. We can't win!"

Such were the angry talks Emil reported from his comrades. Inge spoke with bitterness when she reported the conversation and added,

"Do you know the price of coal now? It went from 468 marks in March to 1208 marks in July. A nice little earner for those busy on the stockmarket!"

"Yes, they're laughing all the way to their millions."

"The newspapers call money the most perishable ware, worse than fish."

"The ones with money put it into goods, the Raffkes! They hurry and swop it for a watch, ties, hats, conserves, cigarettes, you name it."

"You bet! Nothing is safe from their greedy hands: door handles, gully lids, drain pipes and even urns from graveyards vanish."

"They even grabbed our plant pots from the window sill."

The way Inge spoke the word 'Raffkes' with such disgust, rolling the 'r' made Lene smile. They shared the small pleasure of Schadenfreude about these hated people, as they walked back from the station.

"Not the tiniest bit of solidarity in them! They'd steal their own mother's dinner!"

"Fancy robbing our own council! It already hasn't got enough money to pay for the unemployed. Believe it or not, the street lanterns in Karl Mayer Strasse went missing, they removed them. The street was plunged into darkness."

After saying goodbye to Inge Lene peered at the sky. It had a glassy moon looking fragile as if about to fall down and break. The lights of the Dahlbusch mine flickered through the thick air. She thought of the previous Sunday, when the Deppermanns had been on a family walk by popular request, especially from Lene. She wanted to visit Grandfather Winterwerb's restaurant on the Emscher river. The sun was out, it was a cool but bright day. How it had all changed! The previously pristine river embankment looked bleak with rubbish deposited among the tall grasses and wild flowers. The water was an inky colour. A cloud drifted over the sun throwing shadows over the family.

"I don't know how fish can live in this, I certainly can't see any," Lene said. Hilde complained: "Why do people leave their rubbish piled up here? It's such a nuisance, you can't enjoy nature when there are broken bottles, waste paper and food waste lying about."

Nearby, Grandmother's flower garden still displayed some of its past beauty of hardy mauve asters and zinnias. Lene peered into the restaurant, but found it was closed with the shutters clean but locked. A faint scent of earth and flowers brought back images from her childhood.

"And you thought you could have tea and a cake here like during Grandmother's days. I told you it would all be shut down." Hilde had a way of being triumphant that irked her.

"Well, it's still nice to see the old place, someone must own it, because it's well secured," commented Mathilde.

As they turned to leave the Emscher behind Hilde pulled Lene sharply by her sleeve and pointed behind her. She whispered: "It's your friend Olga." Both had drifted a little behind the rest of the family, while chatting about the old times. Lene's heart stopped. On the lonely path by the river Olga and Hubert were kissing in a close embrace. Olga's jacket lay on the ground. Hilde stood huge in front of Lene, piercing her with small pale watery eyes and spoke in an accusatory tone, lips pursed tight. She went into a tirade.

"Young women like her these days, no shame, she's not even married, no wonder they get into trouble. She'll be pregnant in no time. I don't know what you're doing with friends like her. You don't want to follow in her footsteps."

For a moment Lene was transfixed. A small breeze had come up, and Olga's skirt fluttered slightly, Hubert held her head with one hand with his arm wrapped around her.

Lene said nothing but was moved. There was such endearing passion in those two. You could feel the heat even from the distance. She knew Olga loved Hubert. Why shouldn't they kiss? It was only natural. She didn't see anything wrong with Olga's behaviour, but something bothered her. Was Hubert a 'Raffke'? That would be bad, but it didn't give Hilde the right to speak in this moralising tone about Olga. She didn't say anything. It would only lead to one of those arguments.

When Hilde announced what she had seen Olga do on one of the following evenings, Lene was furious with her. What was the point of worrying their parents about this minor detail? What drove her to have it in for Olga?

41

"I told you, Olga is no good as a friend for Lene, I think you need to stop her seeing that girl," she started.

Hermann was looking at a newspaper and Mathilde was engaged with her sewing. Both looked up. They looked tired and uninterested. They did not need more trouble to worry about.

"I've got proof now. I saw her kissing that man, when we walked on the river last Sunday. Lene saw her as well. She can't deny it."

"Is that so, Lene?"

"Yes, she was kissing her boyfriend. What's wrong with that?"

"She isn't married. She'll be pregnant before long."

"You don't become pregnant from kissing."

"Don't be daft, I know that, but other things follow once you kiss in public."

Hilde's watery eyes sparkled with self-righteousness. She looked agitated and twitched her head like a chicken scratching for seeds. She gesticulated with her hands while she spoke. Luckily the doorbell rang, and Friedrich came up for a visit. Hilde went to make some fresh peppermint tea. She looked sullen. Her campaign to enlist their parents against Olga had failed.

"I just popped round for a quick chat, hope you don't mind."

Hermann and Mathilde beckoned for Friedrich to sit down.

"I just wanted to tell you what Wanda, my girlfriend, saw in Berlin, when she visited her aunt. Lene, you'll be interested in this, I know you're keen on Berlin. She was waiting to catch the train back to Gelsenkirchen. She bought herself a cup of tea standing up and paid at the counter in the waiting room. She said she watched a woman order a coffee at a table. It cost 6000 marks. But when she went to pay the price had gone up to double that amount. The woman tried to run away quickly, but they caught her and marched her off. You can become a criminal just by having a cup of coffee and sitting down with it."

"Now that is a story!" Mathilde looked up from her knitting in disbelief, so did Erna.

"The poor woman, what happened in the end?"

"Well she was in trouble! When she started she probably had enough money to be able to afford to sit down for a cup of coffee in Berlin, but the next minute she didn't. Wanda told me she was wearing a fancy fur collar on her jacket, so she wasn't poor."

"Do they charge you for the chair and table?"

"Oh yes! You can have your coffee standing up or be waiter served, that costs more, also you pay when you leave. Meanwhile, the cost shoots up, crazy! She also told me that you see the war invalids standing with their one leg and crutches everywhere, begging. Can you imagine begging, after they already gave an arm or a leg for the Kaiser. It's criminal."

"I'm really fascinated with Berlin, Friedrich, what else did Wanda tell you?"

"She said they don't even use the trams any more. The tram tickets cost too much. So they walk or cycle, but Berlin is a big town, not like small Gelsenkirchen. You have to walk for hours to get from one part of town to the other. They have wide, long avenues in Berlin, like the one called 'Unter den Linden'. They are theatre mad in that town, she said. There's crowds of them waiting patiently to buy tickets. The lucky ones trade in foreign currency, like dollars or pounds and make a big profit. The rich walk about in patent leather boots, decorated with diamonds and furs. It's another world."

In the summer the warmth stretched like a tent full of fumes from the town. Gelsenkircheners went out in summer dresses and colourful hats determined to enjoy themselves despite everything. The theatre at the Stadtgartenhalle was particularly popular. This summer the play was Wilhelm Tell. Lene went with Inge. Inge's brother Emil had got a lot of tickets through the mineworkers' union. Lene was excited when Inge picked her up. They laughed and joked as they checked out each other's dresses with the new raised hemline. They pointed at each others' legs, whether they were shaved or not.

"You've got legs like a giraffe!"

Inge was a stout young woman with thick calves and broad hips.

"And you're like an elephant!" laughed Lene, tall and willowy.

"Will the men be keen on giraffes or on elephants?" they giggled.

When they arrived at their seats the mine workers were already in their places around Emil. Burning glances from the eyes of a couple of dozen young men followed the two young women into their seats. Emil had to explain again and again who they were and how it came about that he knew such lovely young princesses. After the performance Inge and Lene had trouble in escaping the attention of Emil's comrades who invited the two women to stay out and go dancing. Eventually they agreed to be accompanied home by Emil and his mate Rudolf. Lene walked arm in arm with Emil, Inge with Rudolf. The miners' Christmas ball was mentioned.

That autumn was impossible ever to forget. The Rhineland declared itself an independent republic and Berlin was haunted by riots. The whole country was reeling like a ship in the sea about to break apart. The government coalition was fragile. Over three million citizens went on strike demanding work, food and a stable currency. In Munich a little known lance corporal called Adolf Hitler shot at the ceiling of a Bierkeller where a gathering of conservatives took place and shouted that the end of the republic was nigh and he was going to march on Berlin, like his hero Mussolini had done in Rome. Proclamations, refutations, claims and counterclaims echoed from the calls of the newsboys. The chaos was a fertile ground for doom mongers who appeared knowledgeable about the future and lavished forecasts of the end of the world on the unwitting bystanders.

"Pray for your soul, brother, our government is at the end."

"It's a town of thieves, I suggest you pack your bags and go if you want to be safe."

"There's going to be a revolution, make sure you have your gun ready."

"We're all sinners and God is punishing us."

"The final Judgement is upon us."

Others spoke of the past rationally and tried to rekindle a sense of order. Lene attended a social democrat gathering with Inge. The speaker tried to evoke a belief in the republic by talking about the achievements since the war. First he recalled in passionate language the catastrophic blows that befell the young Republic.

"Comrades, let's not forget how much has been achieved! In 1918 we still had a monarchy. Now we have a republic. It's true that we have inflation and the French Occupation to deal with. And the Freikorps and Monarchists are after a bloodthirsty revenge for Versailles. But we need to remind ourselves of how much has been achieved." The speaker stopped and glanced about at his audience, then continued.

"We have a constitution now. Social democrats fought for such a constitution for fifty years! I need to remind you how we have languished in opposition, imprisoned at times and banned under Bismarck. Now we have a mass party. We have the right to vote for women! We have free elections involving every citizen. The German people, united in their many tribes, have given themselves this new constitution. We desire to serve the inner as well as outer peace. We aim to work towards social progress with the help of this constitution."

The speaker watched the effects of his words and concluded: "It's worth remembering that this constitution is a huge achievement in our war torn country. Our chancellor Ebert called it 'the birthday of German democracy'. It deserves to be treated with utmost care and appreciation by all citizens. That means working with the constitution, not against it."

On their way home the two women talked about the speech.

"A lot of the time it feels more like a big burden, this constitution, don't you think?" Inge mused. "We're carrying the can for all the mistakes they are making."

Inge's family, being communists, tended to be more critical of the activities of the government than her social democratic friend.

"All the same, there's no way back, maybe people don't know how to make use of democracy."

"The ruling class wouldn't allow it to take shape anyway..."

Lene didn't reply. At home Hermann brought the big news to the table:

"The government is terminating 'Passive Resistance' from tomorrow onwards, the 26th of September. And they've got the agreement that the French troops will leave by July 1924." He turned to Hilde, adding: "You see, it's not all bad. You've got to give them that! They are making an effort, even with Ebert and them all having little political experience."

He was referring to Ebert's working class background, which was the cause of many evil wishers' arguments against the president.

On the 15th November that year the Ebert government introduced a new mark worth one trillion old marks. It was pegged at the 1914 level. The US banker Dawes set up a commission aimed at pouring money into the German economy. When Lene came home from college the following week the young apprentices were invited for supper. They sometimes had little money and nowhere to stay. It was a custom amongst bakers to let out the baking room for apprentices as sleeping accommodation. It was warm there. It brought in a little money, and allowed the apprentice to be ready for work early in the morning. Johnny had arrived from London. He had stories to tell that made them gawp.

"You can't imagine the dirt. No one has time to sweep out. Cockroaches run over your face while you sleep. Once one of them was baked into a loaf. I saw the customer pull it out by its legs."

"Don't go on, how filthy is that."

"There is a terrible heat underground, that is the other unbearable thing."

"Underground, what do you mean?" Lene asked.

"Yes," he replied. "The bakery room is often underground in a cellar to save on space and heating. The heat, though, is almost unbearable. Then there were rats and mice."

They stared at his face in awe of what he must have suffered. He looked chubby, though, with a pink complexion, dimples in his cheeks and flat blonde hair.

"What's the pay like?" Hilde asked.

"Payment is so mean, you can just about buy food from it, that's why you live in the bakery room, because you couldn't afford a room in a house. And you can't save any money, it's not enough."

"We discussed the right to vote at college today." Lene was keen to relate her latest experience at college. "Gertrud Bäumer spoke at our school. She's a member of the National Assembly!"

Hilde watched Lene's eyes sparkle and her face light up. She felt cheated and was envious of her little sister's experience. They give these young things ideas above their station, she thought, and quickly found a way to cut down the excitement.

"Could you first put your coat outside on the hanger where it belongs, Lene," Hilde reprimanded her, but she couldn't stop Lene.

"You should have heard her speak! You really missed something. She said the Republic and our constitution are at the heart of women's new hopes. Women should have access to higher education, be able to go to work and earn a living and not depend on a man, she said. Imagine, she helped to organise for women to get the vote in our constitution."

Silence followed while they were all chewing some bread, although both her parents looked at Lene with encouraging smiles. Astonishingly, it was Erna who spoke first. Her face opened up and blushed.

"Well, Lene, that's so wonderful! I would like to meet her too. Is she also coming to Gelsenkirchen?"

Before she could reply Hilde had to give another rebuke:

"You should finish eating before you speak, Lene. I thought they were teaching you manners at that school, but they obviously aren't. Anyway, I've never heard of that Gertrud what's-she-called."

"Gertrud Bäumer! She's a member of our National Assembly. Don't you believe girls have a right to higher education and work?" Lene spoke the word 'our' with special emphasis. She looked provocatively at Hilde.

"Hilde, Lene, why do you two always argue? Calm yourself, Lene, you must be hungry and tired after your long day at college and travelling." That was Mathilde's reaction. Lene noticed that Hilde

47

diminished the college by calling it 'school', whereas her mother did not. Turning towards Hilde Mathilde added:

"You leave the girl in peace! She is learning something and why shouldn't she get a bit passionate about her new knowledge? I am glad they're teaching some sort of citizenship to our young women."

Lene threw a grateful glance at her mother and saw out of the corner of her eye that Hilde bit her lip and tightened her mouth around a mouthful of food she had just put in, her eyes down on her plate. Hermann had read today's paper which now lay on his lap. When the girls quarrelled he used to dissipate the arguments by focusing on the events in the world outside the lounge.

"You might want to know what the 'Volkswille' had to say today, girls and boys", he started. "We've just had news that the Government of Stresemann, our Reichskanzler, has resigned. That's the second time that the government under Stresemann has resigned. This brings us to the sad result that since 1920 seven governments have resigned. What does this mean for the people of Germany who have voted in good faith for their government to create stability and safety? Instead, we've had to witness uprisings and shootings that don't seem to abate. The death of Rathenau this year in June and the deaths of Gareis and Erzberger during the last couple of years are only the most prominent examples of the dire state of it all. We were unable to reach a member of the National Assembly to discuss these matters with us."

"Yes, because that Gertrud what's-it was holding forth at your school."

Hilde was ignored for that remark, instead Erna wanted to know more about Lene's news.

"I thought that was so interesting what you told us, Lene. I wish you could tell us more of what you're learning at college. I wonder if she could help me?"

They found an excuse to go up to Erna's room where all her craftwork materials were piled in boxes and baskets covering all the surfaces. It did not bother Erna. The chaos added to the conspiracy the sisters felt. The question Erna wanted to ask was could Gertrud

Bäumer be invited to Gelsenkirchen. Lene said she would find out if it could be done. They hugged each other, and Lene had to inspect Erna's eczema to see if it was healing. Later in her sleep Lene dreamed of Erna and other women standing for election to the assembly dressed in smart suits and deciding on new laws for democracy in the country.

When she came back from college on another evening Lene heard strange voices in the kitchen. She stopped and her eyes fell on the girl with the milk jug that was just visible in the dingy hall. The kitchen door was ajar and she could hear her father walk to and fro on the stone slabs by the fire place. His footsteps sounded tense. A man's voice could be heard with a soapy dissonant voice:

"God has been kind to me. He provided for my education, because my poor parents died when I was only a child. I was lucky that a distant uncle took pity on me. I knew then that God was going to take care of me."

Silence followed. You could hear the fire in the stove. Cooked parsnip soup smells lingered. Lene held her breath. She could hear her father pace the length of the kitchen floor.

"Have you spoken to Hilde?" His voice sounded tired and aggravated. She knew he didn't hold the church in high esteem and cared little for solemn vows directed at God. "Wars, wars wars", he sometimes exclaimed in the family circle, 'how could a God allow people to have so little understanding that they continue to kill each other?"

"No, Herr Deppermann, I have not. I wanted to come and see you to talk this over with you. You know your Hilde often looks in on the services I conduct. I have talked with her on a number of occasions and gained the impression that she's a faithful member of our community."

"But, Pastor Meier, you have not even spoken to her. Does she know of your intentions? She's a young woman with a mind of her own. You can't assume that I'm going to persuade her to marry you, when perhaps she has very different thoughts on her mind."

Lene gasped pressing her scarf into her face to stifle her breath. She knew Hilde was going to marry a pastor and now here he stood in her father's kitchen.

"Excuse me, Herr Deppermann, I do appreciate what you are saying, of course she must make up her own mind. But God's will has opened up my heart to her. I'm only asking you for your support, because you are her father and she'll listen to you."

Lene squeezed the shawl over her mouth, fearing her breath becoming too loud. How dare he ask for Hilde's hand behind her back?

"Pastor Meier, I'm afraid I can't help you with your endeavour. If you would like to get to know my daughter Hilde, you'll need to find an opportunity to speak to her yourself. I'm sorry I can't say any more about this matter, it's not really up to me."

She could now hear her mother intervening in the conversation that was about to turn quite sour.

"Pastor Meier, don't misunderstand my husband, he doesn't mean to be sharp with you. You have to understand where he comes from. He believes strongly in the rights of his daughters to decide their own fates. He sees it as separate from one's belief in God. We are pleased that you came round to see us and make your intentions clear. You'll need to find the courage to speak to Hilde yourself. She can stand up for herself."

"Thank you so much, Frau Deppermann, thank you. God willing, I shall soon be back with some good news. I'd better be on my way now. Thank you again for listening to me and God bless."

Lene quickly scrambled up the stairs with her coat and bag to get out of the way, when she heard that the conversation was ending. From upstairs she could hear her parents lead the pastor through the hall. The front door was opened and shut behind him.

"I can't stand his manner, a pastor in my family," she heard her father say, as the two of them walked back into the kitchen. That night Lene had a dream. The pastor in a flowing black gown crouched on the floor with a thin black cloth spread like ink around him. He was pleading with Hilde, begging for forgiveness for his emotions for her, while Hilde stood tall and cool in her shop apron, her high collared dress and stockings and looked down on him. Lene could see the pastor's flushed face, his red blotched nose and bulging, slightly blue lips. Say no, Hilde, she moaned. She woke feeling a cramp in her stomach. The flickering lights from the coal mine circled around her bedroom walls, as the trolleys with coal shuffled through the air. As they did every night and day after day. The familiar illumination had a calming effect on her. Like a fairground, she thought and fell back into sleep.

One foggy evening as Lene hurried from the station to see Olga, she accidentally spotted Hubert on the tram. The carriage was packed with workers and employees on their way home. The smell of damp woollen coats, sweat, bad breath and alcohol was pungent. She wound her way towards him and greeted him cheerily. The grey eyes in his long finely cut face seemed to find it difficult to focus on her; they remained distant, as if he didn't recognise her.

"How are you, Hubert, you look distracted and worried." Lene did have a way of being disarmingly honest.

"Oh, Lene, its you, I was miles away in my thoughts," he made out. She knew that this was not so, he had seen her, but had tried not to be seen, she felt.

"You look a bit ill, are you coming down with a cold? Are you coming to see Olga, because that's where I'm heading."

He looked at her intently. "Are you going to Olga's?" he repeated, as if surprised and taken aback. Lene nodded.

"Olga is pregnant", he stammered, and she could see his eyes becoming moist.

Hubert seemed unprepared for the situation and looked to her like a boy whose toy had gone wrong. What a mess, she thought, but said:

"Oh, that's nice. Are you going to marry her?"

Hubert's face was pale and he gasped: "Of course I will, if there is nothing else we can do."

They stood in silence while the tram shook and squealed. Poor Olga, Lene thought he's come to try to persuade her to have an abortion. Hubert suddenly looked pleadingly at her:

"You go and speak to her, Lene, she loves you and trusts you, you tell her to go and have an abortion, it's the best for both of us, she's too young, and so am I. I'm not sure how the money situation is going, you never know these days and jobs are hard to find. We'd have trouble in supporting ourselves and a child."

They had got off the tram with a crowd of others, all dispersing in different directions. Soon the street corner near the Dahlbusch mine and the bridge was empty. In the early darkness the street lights shone as if from another planet, not breaking through the deep blackness around them. The wind tossed odd soot flakes into their faces. She knew Hubert was feeling wretched and it made her feel similarly forlorn and hopeless.

"No, Hubert, it's you who needs to go to her, you are responsible, both of you. I am sure you'll sort it out between you. Remember you love each other. It's not for me to interfere or take on your duty. Believe in yourself and speak openly to her." After a moment's consideration she added:

"You must promise me, though, that you will ask her what she wants to do, you must ask her," she repeated. "She's got a right to speak for her own body, she has to carry the baby or abort it. That's her decision, not yours."

While she spoke Hubert's face had first sunk between his shoulders and his chin hung inside his scarf, his eyes averted, as if he didn't want to take in what she said. His eyes opened with a shine, when she mentioned their love for each other, and she was glad to see it, because it meant there was love in their togetherness. She even saw a brief smile on his lips, when she asked him to believe in himself. When she spoke about asking Olga for her opinion he first made a noise as if to object, then stood quietly and let Lene finish.

"You're right, Lene, I am glad I bumped into you, my God, really I am! First I didn't even want to see you, because I felt so bad and confused. I feel more certain, and I'll go and see her now and I promise I'll ask her."

"Good luck, Hubert, see you soon," Lene called and turned to go home. Fog had welled up from the river while they stood by the bridge, and before she knew it she had started to cry. The tears were rolling out of her eyes unstoppably, and she stood still and was now leaning on the bridge, looking at the huge mine towers with their trolley cars travelling through the dark sky.

'Why am I crying?' she wondered and immediately realised that she was sad about whichever way Olga was going to make up her mind. She saw her friend drifting into a far distance into which she could not follow, into a different life from hers altogether, almost a different universe. She was either going to have an abortion or get married. Either way she would be emotionally troubled and experience life from a new perspective, one that was a long way from Lene's. 'We're so far apart,' she whispered to herself. What would her parents say? She was anxious about Olga and her friendship; but she was also relieved. She had made the right decision and not given in to Hubert's pleas. She stood for another while looking at the endlessly travelling wagons full of coal, the fire from the chimneys of Gelsenkirchen and then went home.

CHAPTER 5

THE WANDERVÖGEL

In January the news of Lenin's death was in all the papers. Hermann's 'Volkswille' offered readers a review of his life and work. How the Germans had helped the revolution by allowing Lenin to travel through Germany in a sealed train. The nationalist press screeched 'End the Bolshevist experiment now'. Hermann employed another apprentice in the bakery, because trade was beginning to get back to normal since the new money had stabilised people's finances. He was another Johnny from England, where the other one had returned to. They called him Johnny Two. He had to share the bakery quarters with another apprentice. Early in the morning they rolled up their bedding. Lene told him how Johnny One had filled them with curiosity. Since then Johnny Two had endeavoured to outdo Johnny One with vile stories from London.

"You can't guess what happened! The apprentice's finger was baked into a roll after he had accidentally chopped off the top of his forefinger. They had to search inside all of a hundred rolls to find it again. Even though it couldn't be sewn back on, he insisted on having it back. He had fainted after the accident and someone had swept it up with flour and added it to the dough."

"Disgusting," Lene and Hilde commented. Rosa stared at him in disbelief. Erna left the kitchen, she said she was feeling sick.

One day a strange contraption stood in the middle of the table. Friedrich and Hermann were bent over it and fiddled with it excitedly. It had a lid and the bottom part contained a lot of different small metal cylindrical components.

"Ah, Lene, have you seen what Friedrich has made for me?" Hermann called out with a smile. "It's a radio, you can hear news on it. He's such a skilled man to make something like this after work."

Friedrich beamed all over his face. He smiled proudly and studiously bent over the box brushing a small wire over the another wire inside the box.

"Put on the earphones, Hermann," Friedrich commanded, "tell me when you hear something." They watched Hermann place the black earmuff-like bakelite pieces with their arm over his head and looked intently at the tiny cylinders in the wooden box.

"Yes, there it is, I can hear a voice," he shouted, "no, it's a bit of music, let me see, it's the Blue Danube, Friedrich, just out of thin air." Hermann was beside himself and his voice rang like a child's. "Do you want to have a go, Lene?"

"You have to tickle this wire. It's called a 'cat's whisker.'"

Friedrich sounded proud.

"I made it, they tell you in the papers how to do it. It's a present for all the nice cups of tea I'm having in your house."

Lene heard hissing and then a bright voice.

"...Then it was observed that the light of stars was deflected, as it passed near the sun during the eclipse of 1919. This proved that Herr Einstein's theory of relativity was correct." The voice faded and a hissing ensured. Lene pulled the earphones off her head and gasped:

"Did you hear that, about stars in the sky, I never heard anything like that before, but now it's hissing."

Mathilde came into the kitchen and looked at the three bent over the machine.

"This is where you are, we need to sort out the details of the engagement. Lene, dear, your sister has some wonderful news for you. Go on, Hilde, tell the girl," she added when Hilde appeared behind her.

"I'm getting engaged to be married, Lene," Hilde announced proudly, lifting her chin and looking down from up high.

"Congratulations," Lene said simply and stared back at the wooden box.

"I'm going to see off Friedrich, Mathilde, he has a long day of work tomorrow, so will need to leave shortly. I think it's a bit late for a discussion about the engagement, shall we do that tomorrow?" Hermann looked tired suddenly, and the matter was postponed to another day.

Lene lay in bed later and saw the stars that had their light bent by the sun in the eclipse. In her dream she was swirling through the blue air of the atmosphere flying higher and higher and then climbing on top of a bright curve that reached down into the sea. She jumped and dived deep into the ocean, swimming with fishes.

A week went by before Hilde's engagement was properly talked about in the family circle, and even then it was hard for Mathilde to get a word in, because Hermann had read in the 'Volkswille' about the release of a group of 'Reading Circle' members who were known national socialists.

"It doesn't surprise me that mayor Wedelstaedt has released these fascists from prison. He was always on the side of the Freikorps and has never spoken out against rampaging gangs of rightwingers. You know that he actually made out the so-called 'Reading Circles' were just ordinary people in a book reading group? He's always on about the danger from the left and calls our mine workers a mob. What a disgrace! Not a word of the Wehrwolf."

"Who are the 'Wehrwolf'?" Lene asked.

"They are some of the new formations into which the Freikorps and other nationalists organise themselves. They also join these so-called 'Reading Circles'. That's a joke, because no reading goes on there, just agitation against workers and communists, Jewish people, gypsies and the French."

"Hermann, Hermann, stop, Lene! Don't ask him more questions, you know he can't stop, it's his favourite subject. He'll go on about it till the cows come home. Listen, we must talk the engagement through. Who is to be invited, what food are we offering? Hilde, girl, speak up, its your event," Mathilde was getting exasperated and feared she was going to be left with all the planning by herself.

"Just a minute, Mathilde, we will sort out Hilde's engagement, but our children do need to know about the dangers that are building up all around us. Don't forget what happened in Munich. That lance corporal Hitler attempted to overthrow our government, staging a march on Berlin from one of those Bierkellers – copying Mussolini who is now installed in Rome. In Rome they handed power to him, just like that!"

"The dressmaker, I don't know what the woman is thinking about, she put frills all along the bust and the waist of my wedding dress. I had a row with her..." Hilde's mouth spat the words out.

"There's no point having a row with someone when you want them to do you a favour, dear. You don't want any frills, just tell her to take them off," her mother said soothingly but with an undertone of frustration. Lene looked at her mother and sister wondering how they could discuss such minutiae, when some unknown soldier was threatening the country's government. She tried to hide in her seat. Erna ignored the goings-on. She was painting eyes on to the face of her wooden doll.

Olga stood in front of the mirror looking at her face and then turned sideways to see the small bulge of her belly. 'I'm pregnant. I am going to have a baby! Even my parents are excited now, especially since Hubert came round and talked to us. He actually asked me what I wanted to do. I thought that was very good of him. Yesterday he came and brought me flowers and said he would marry me!' She smiled at herself and looked at her reflection while smiling. 'He loves me.' Then she recollected the stern looks in her parents' eyes and the words they used, words like 'duty' and 'embarrassment' and doubt flickered, but only for a moment. She took the hair brush and combed through her long brown hair. 'The doctor says I must do some exercise every day and I need to eat good food.' She tied her hair into a bun and looked out of the window. Snowflakes and more snowflakes. The world outside had disappeared in the whiteness. The baby will be a summer baby, she thought. Her parents had gone out. She would write her invitations to the wedding. 'Lene would make eyes, when she finds out. I don't think she really trusted Hubert, as if he would run away and leave me.' She felt warm and happy inside herself. A small human being was growing inside her womb, and the father of the child was going to marry her.

Hermann brought a couple of newspaper articles that reviewed the Kapp Putch of four years ago. At the time they had so many other worries, they didn't even realise how much the young Republic had been thrown into grave danger by the Kapp adventure.

"When the extra papers reported the violence in Berlin there was soon a growing sense of disquiet. By four o'clock large groups of people moved towards the old market from all areas of the town. So the crowd soon grew to over a thousand. From the balcony of the offices of the public gasworks speakers from the Social democrats, Communists and Christian trade unions addressed the demonstrators. The secretary of the German metalworkers union spoke and argued that it was time for all the workers to act together now and defend the Republic against the Kapp traitors. Otherwise, he argued, we will lose our eight hour day and other achievements of the revolution. Other speakers also asked for a united front of the Left against the Right. There was emotional applause from the audience."

Hermann paused and looked up. Only Lene, Mathilde and Erna were in the sitting room, each with their work, but indicating they wanted to know more. Hermann explained,

"The workers all over Germany abided by the call and that is how Kapp was stopped. The Ruhr workers formed the 'Red Ruhr army'. Those good people helped to defeat the nationalist gangs. The fighting went on until the middle of March and led to many deaths and wounded which were mourned in all of Gelsenkirchen. You can say what you like, but the point to be made is that Herr Kapp was responsible for all these deaths and injuries so soon after the war in order to create a dictatorship of the nationalists. The defence of our town cost the council over 720,000 marks. Guess who's paying that bill? The working people!"

In March a rush of tiny green leaves seemed to have grown overnight. The wedding was planned for June. On a bright morning with spring sunshine, Lene found a hand-delivered letter in the letter box addressed to her. She opened it to find a wedding invitation. It wasn't Hilde's wedding, it was Olga's. She stared at it in surprise and then relief mixed with regret. 'He's done the right thing, I'm so glad.' Then she had second thoughts. Maybe it wasn't that straightforward, perhaps pressure had been put on him; it was possible that it wasn't all happy and sunny now. Well, as long as Olga was happy and could keep her baby it was surely all right. Then it occurred to her that she had to tell her family about the event. She opened the folded card again to look at the details. Heilige Kreuz church in the Bochumer Strasse on the second of April. That was really soon. It had to be, considering that she was now a good two months pregnant. The reception was to take place in Walter's restaurant where they had celebrated Olga's birthday. Hilde was probably going to make the usual snide comment. Lene braced herself for it. That evening in the lounge with the velvet curtains drawn and the lights flickering from the smelting and mines she told them. Hermann was reading the 'Volkswille', and Mathilde was sewing a dress. Hilde stitched a veil to a small hat. Erna was sewing a body for one of her dolls. Young Hermann and Hans were playing chess.

"I've had an invitation to a wedding."

Everyone looked up, wondering how it could be that Lene already had an invitation to Hilde's wedding, when they hadn't even been printed.

"Its Olga's wedding to Hubert. She's getting married here in the Heilige Kreuz church. She's really looking forward to it, and so is all her family."

Everyone looked again for verification into Lene's face to see if this was true. Her mother was always able to find the appropriate words.

"Well, congratulations to her! You must tell her parents and Olga we are very pleased for them. When is the wedding?"

"On the second of April."

"She's had to get married, hasn't she. I told you, Lene, that girl's no idea what she's doing, she's obviously pregnant." Hilde's sharp tongue spat out the words. Erna's face had lit up with a gentle smile that was also sad. Lene thought she must be thinking that everyone around got married, apart from her.

"It is rather quick, with no engagement and all, I suppose, times are changing, and the young people are in a rush to marry for their own reasons we may not understand."

"We do understand them." Hilde could not stop herself. "If you're pregnant you have to get married. What choice have you got? Be a single mother?"

Hermann changed the subject of the conversation after adding his good wishes. He didn't like moralising about other people. He knew how much pain people suffered, and that sometimes difficult decisions had to be taken. Lene was glad to get the matter out of the way and felt grateful to her father for moving on to another subject. She had to go and see Olga as soon as possible, maybe tomorrow. That night she dreamt of Olga. Slate grey and pale pink doves were fluttering overhead, and her white wedding dress was trailing a long way behind her and looked frayed, as she stepped up towards the church entrance. She kept turning around to look for someone, while she held tightly on to her father's arm. Lene wondered who she was looking for. She had to take care walking behind without stepping on the beautiful trail of white cloth. Suddenly it dawned on her who was missing. It was Hubert.

During the spring all the papers analysed the Dawes Plan. Germany was to take part in a conference in London that summer, at which the details of the negotiations were going to be decided. Hermann was bent over the wooden radio box. He tickled the cat's whisker, and found a voice that was discussing the Dawes plan:

"We have our specialist in foreign affairs, Herr Leuter, who will explain to us what the Americans are planning to achieve with the Dawes plan. Herr Leuter, why are the Americans suddenly taking such an interest in helping Germany?"

"Our industrial production has shrunk by 50%, unemployment is rising, land is not being tilled, the people are exhausted. The Americans don't like what they see. They think if Germany stays economically weak, there will be another revolution. They want to prevent that from happening. They need a strong Germany. They want Germany as a bulwark to the expansion of Bolshevism and..."

The voice trailed off. Hermann looked up. Lene had entered the kitchen. She had heard the last words.

"We are becoming the plaything of very large world powers," Hermann pondered aloud. "The Soviets want us to have a revolution and become like them, the French want to wipe us out, the English don't really care at the moment, they're busy with their empire, and the Americans want a bulwark to Bolshevism. The Americans are watching what is going on in Russia. Too many rich people are forced to give up their money. The industrialists are being expropriated. They are afraid this might happen here, if we stay poor. They are going to bribe us with their money."

"Can I ask you a favour, father?" Lene had other things on her mind.

"Go ahead, Lene."

"You know about Olga's wedding. It's only a couple of weeks from now, and I have to have a suitable dress and also need to buy her a present. I thought it was best to ask you now. You know what Hilde is like, she might get ideas that money meant for her is going to Olga. You know she doesn't like Olga."

Hermann looked at his daughter and nodded absentmindedly in agreement, as he withdrew some cash from his pocket. For a moment they had the same thought: thank God, the money was actually worth something now. You could rely on it to have the same value today and tomorrow. She left immediately for Ahlsdorf, where the colours and exotic scents soon enveloped her in a suggestive world of luxury. The aisles were laden with red, pink and yellow scarves, lace and leather gloves and hats dangled from hooks and shelves. She wondered what would please Olga most. She might like a piece of dress material, as she had time on her hands. There were printed silks, gleaming taffeta, Scottish wool, printed cotton and linens. Her hands slid over the texture of a lovely flowered design in batiste and imagined Olga wearing it as a pretty summer blouse. She decided to buy a piece of the flowered batiste. For herself she soon decided on one of the new style lose pinafores with a jacket.

The second of April was a windy and dry Saturday. The washing fluttered in the yard. The loaves on the trolleys were cooling. Mathilde's yellow daffodils glinted. The sun travelled in and out of clouds. Lene and her parents represented the Deppermann family at the wedding. The church bells rang out. They all fell silent and turned round. Olga and Hubert, accompanied by their parents, were slowly walking towards the altar. Olga's dress did not have a long trail, as in Lene's dream. A short sky blue mohair jacket with raised shoulder pads gently wrapped around her womanly figure and only exposed the white embroidered dress from her waist down. The pleated skirt rustled with every step she took. Hubert in a black suit, tails and a top hat held on to her closely. Their eyes were raised above the community as if looking at a horizon. Olga's eyes glistened, and she had a serene smile on her face. Her brown hair was curled and hung in soft waves down beyond her shoulders, and she had flowers tied to a small veil over her head. Hubert looked very young and almost frightened. Bach's 'Ein feste Burg ist unser Gott' (A Firm Castle Is Our God) was sung. There were prayers. Hallelujah, Amen. Each murmured their prayer with their own fears and wishes in their minds, but all of them heard the collective voice of the families wishing for good to happen and for an end to the strife and fear. The pastor's speech alluded to Olga's and Hubert's youth, their lack of knowledge of the ways of the world, but also his belief that they would help to construct a better society through their love for each other. The angel above the pulpit was lit up and glistened in a beam of sun that was broken up into rainbow colours coming through the altar window. It was all very moving.

'Closed to the public due to wedding' the sign read outside Walter's. The fishes on the ceramic tiles shone in the light of a multitude of lit candles making them seem three dimensional and as if swimming in the sea. Flower garlands decorated the ceiling. Wine and champagne flowed. Blue and red bulbs were lit and created more darkness than light. Three Russian musicians turned up with two balalaikas and an accordion and soon the dancers swirled and spun, as if they never wanted to stop. After a start with Viennese waltzes, 'The Blue Danube', 'Vienna woods' and 'Wine, women and song' the musicians moved on to Russian classics 'Kalinka' and Volga dances. They evoked in their sounds the distant, wide steppes covered in ice and snow, the sleighs with bells and the Ural Mountains. Lene danced with Alfred, the youngest, skinny brother of Hubert. He had lovely amber eyes. The music made Lene feel pleasurably dizzy, and Olga whispered in her ear,

"This is wonderful, isn't it? I can see you're enjoying dancing with Alfred. Maybe you'll marry him! He's sweet, isn't he?"

"I'm so happy for you, dear Olga, this is such a lovely wedding party." Lene embraced Olga warmly and they smiled with glazed eyes at each other.

Diary notes, 16th July 1971

On the third day of her visit to London I lost my temper with my mother.

"You go on and on about this woman Olga. What has that got to do with me and with your secrets? All your family knew Olga, it really isn't a secret..."

A slight rain had started and we opened the umbrellas and walked towards the cafe. She was silent, which made me feel worse than if she had defended herself. I was tense and irritated. Here was my mother glorying in her friend's wedding a good forty years ago. What did it have to do with me? I had no interest in weddings. I was a feminist and believed strongly what Engels had written about 'Private property, the family and the state' and was on my guard not to have the wool pulled over my eyes.

"What was so important about Olga marrying that you need to tell me that now?" I asked impatiently. Was this storytelling an attempt to subtly tell me what to do, as she had done back in Germany? She didn't blink and looked absorbed inside her own world.

"It remained so strong in my memory, and so linked with what followed that I don't seem to be able to move on unless I mention it. You see, for instance, I hardly remember Hilde's wedding, apart from the wonderful cakes. But Olga! Her fate was so closely tied up with mine. You'll see in a minute what happened to her. Forgive me, it might seem selfish to you now, but I just need to talk about her. It's like a script inside me."

I grudgingly submitted to her wishes, but felt inside a rebellion growing. We sat down in the cafe and had a coffee. It helped and gave me the energy I needed to let her carry on. Strange, she was so much in her own world, almost as if she was hypnotised by her own account. Then she talked about Inge, her other trusted friend.

(end of notes)

"I'll do that, mother, get yourself a rest," Inge was gently edging her mother away from the sink and on to the kitchen chair. She felt little resistance from the large woman with the mournful face and tight grey bun. Inge pushed up her sleeves exposing her strong white arms and took some of the many dishes to wash in the soap filled water, chatting to her mother as she did so. She had noticed how tired her mother looked recently. It made her feel more guilty about her attendance at college.

"Let me give up college, it's not that important, mother, you can't manage all the work on your own, what with Grandmother here. Anyway, what are we learning at college, I'm never going to be able to use all that knowledge."

Her mother shook her head. "No, don't give it up. We'll manage." She sipped her tea.

How many times had Inge made this offer? Around the supper table in the narrow dark kitchen where they all sat closely together, both parents kept insisting that she mustn't give it up. It was as if her attendance at college held a spiritual value for them. If it was rescinded a vital part of their world would collapse. The smell of dinners with baked, boiled or shredded turnips hung in the air.

Outside balmy yellow summer weather brought neighbours out to chat. Women with bare arms and rollers in their hair hung their washing on the line and used carpet sticks to beat the old dust out of the furnishings. There was a cathartic feeling in these activities, a form of renewal was in the air. Yet inside her parent's house Olga lay with the curtains drawn and the window closed.

"Open the curtains, dear, let the fresh air in, it'll do you good," urged her mother. When her mother saw Olga roll under the duvet she sighed and picked up the baby from the cot and walked with her. Olga didn't move.

"Poor little thing," Frau Reichardt whispered, "what will become of you in these times? Your mother is suffering from depression and the rich are robbing the people." She dared not ask when Hubert was going to come again in case Olga didn't know. His visits had become less frequent, but he always brought presents with him. Marta, nicknamed Matti, was now three weeks old and luckily Olga was breastfeeding her. She complained bitterly about the pain she was suffering after giving birth. She soon expected her mother to help, saying she was in pain or tired. That is how it continued. Now the doctor suggested she was suffering from depression.

"Depression! When you have a wee little baby to take care of." Frau Reichardt said nothing to Olga, but it upset her a great deal. She dared not speak to her husband about it, in case he had no understanding of this depression thing. She walked into the small yard with Matti and lay her on a blanket in the grass. The blackbirds were singing and the creaking coal trolleys could be heard in the distance.

Erich turned up one evening in the Deppermann lounge. He recounted stories of legal battles that he had to deal with in his office. He was always in a grey suit, white shirt and tie. They eyed him cautiously and wondered about his clothes that had been said to look dishevelled, un-ironed and with stains, as if he had slept rough somewhere. He never spoke about his private affairs. His work stories were of robbery, assault and victimisation of employees. He had very regular habits. After telling his tale, he checked they were all right, had his cup of tea and then suddenly walked out. There were still rumours about spending time in the bars of town. Hermann and Mathilde's attitude to such tales were to ignore them and not to speak of such matters. Once Erich had left Lene's mother told a proud story from her visit to her daughter's new home in Gladbeck. Erna looked down at her craft work and did not utter a word. Lene felt for Erna while her mother told a tale of married bliss. There was no husband in sight for her.

"The lovely spacious house they have and a vegetable garden and conservatory! They can grow their own food. Thilde has her hands full of work. She did the flower arrangements in the church."

The tea cups clinked as they sat in the lounge exhausted from the day's work. Hermann looked pale and worn; his legs kept twitching. They knew he had restless legs from all the standing in the bakery. He didn't like it when they wanted to talk about it and always changed the subject to politics and readings from his newspaper the 'Volkswille'.

"The 'Stahlhelm' and the 'Wehrwolf' organisations are both active in Gelsenkirchen. Here it is in black and white. Lene, listen to this," Hermann started.

"'Stahlhelm' is for young men without military training and the 'Wehrwolf' is mainly made up of previous soldiers, officers and Freikorps men. They are fanatical German nationalists, and specifically anti-Jewish. Then there is the National Socialist Deutsche Arbeiter Party (NSDAP). They are from Munich and speak about being socialist, but actually attack workers regularly. They're a very dangerous group! Not many members, but brutal and full of hatred towards Jewish people, communists and social democrats."

Hermann looked around his family to see if they were paying attention, but only Lene gazed at him. Nevertheless, he continued.

"They have many rich benefactors. The 'Volkswille' wrote the other day the big industrialists have a combined wealth of millions of marks. They can apply this wealth to force the hand of our government. The IG Farben boss Duisberg openly announced that he wants to join the government to be able to influence their decisions. Then there is the Dawes plan with the American money..."

"Surely, with all that money these people have more rights than someone who has no money. It's not democratic to be able to use it to influence government decisions..."

Lene mused, when the doorbell rang. Friedrich was passing by and wanted to see how they all were. Hermann greeted him warmly with a hearty handshake and urged him into a comfortable chair. Lene fetched another cup.

"We were just talking about the 'Volkswille' article about the 'Wehrwolf' and 'Stahlhelm' groups. As soon as you think life might be getting easier, new problems come up."

"My friend Inge saw one of those Stahlhelm groups attack a man on the tram the other day," Lene said, putting a cup of hot peppermint tea in front of Friedrich.

"She said they called him a 'Jewboy' and kicked him unconscious, then just ran off."

"Yes, that's the sort of thing they do to stir up fear. They use violence and generally create an atmosphere of alarm among the citizens," Friedrich joined in.

"They want people to get used to extreme violence. Sometimes they make up stories just to frighten folks. The stories they should write about are the accidents in the mines. They are real and often preventable, if only they cared enough. But the wealth all goes into the wrong hands."

"Yes, the safety regulations are just bypassed to save the bosses money. They don't prop up the galleries well enough, so that rock collapses on the men. Four of the lads had accidents in the last three weeks. One was Ernst Rabe. He was hit by falling coal. It squashed his arm. Then there was Walter Nischke. When he was hit by coal wagons they fractured his leg. Rudolf, another lad from my gang, a drawer, was run over by a wagon and had his foot broken. And there was Jens Meier. He was struck by falling timber. It's being kept quiet by the bosses, but the workers are furious and want safety increased."

"The poor lads, where are they now?"

Everyone had looked up and stared at Friedrich. Even when you knew that mine workers had accidents, being told about the details these poor men had experienced made them feel upset and full of pity. Friedrich told them that the injured miners were improving now in the local hospital. They looked at Friedrich's face and saw that the emotion about the men in the mine had made his face look ashen and tired and his skin sag. Lene was thinking about Emil and his comrades. Friedrich added into the silence:

"It's a good thing that none of your boys are going down the mine." Hermann added:

"I know about the mine. It was my family's tradition to work there. We lost an uncle in one of those accidents before the war. A whole seam collapsed, the wooden supports broke and buried ten men. They took two days to dig them out. By that time all of them were dead."

Friedrich nodded his head and saw in his mind the rumbling cages, pulleys and cables flying by in the beastly darkness of the pit. Mathilde, visibly moved, urged the men not to upset themselves. Erna blushed and smiled, while she addressed Friedrich.

"If you ever need someone to help with looking after one of your comrades let me know. I am attending nursing training so I might be able to help."

"Well, Erna, what a very kind thought, I will bear it in mind, there is always someone who needs a little looking after. Still, I'd better be on my way now. Thanks for the tea, Lene, dear."

Lene looked at Erna. She had changed so much since Thilde had moved out. She looked more at ease and confident and to everyone's surprise actually participated in the conversations. She was sewing the straw-stuffed body of one of her new dolls to the wooden head and neck. She looked at Lene with her warm doe-eyes.

"Lene, dear, I just thought of the woman from the general assembly again, what was she called, Gertrud Bäumer I think. If she comes to Gelsenkirchen, let me know because I also want to hear her speak."

"I'm glad you mention her, because we're having a picnic for the year one students. The college is organising for Gertrud Bäumer. We are going to be in the Gruga park in Essen, just outdoors, so I think you can also join in." Erna beamed all over her face.

Hermann had dozed off with the newspaper on his face.

The day of the picnic was a Saturday. Hats or no hats, sandals or more elegant shoes and jackets. All evening the sisters ran in their underwear between their two bedrooms across the hallway and up and down a short flight of stairs. Lene climbed down to Erna's room, her button breasts in small bra cups, her knickers fluttering. They told each other they had nothing to wear and then dug out skirts, dresses and blouses from drawers and spread them over the floor. Erna's heavy breasts heaved.

"If I could give you half of mine we could both have perfectly sized breasts," she joked. She was shy about her large bosom. They laughed and teased each other. Erna brought her eczema cream.

The women gathered on the open space by the Margarethenhöhe. The sky was bright and the grass was tall and yellow. Glasses of home-made sweet wine were handed round and the mood became carefree and very jolly. The fresh air gave them an appetite and the food tasted like never before. The students tugged one another along the grass by the leg and a game of chase followed that few could resist. They ran and tumbled. They jumped over each other and fell into the soft summer grass with giggles and laughter. They were in stitches and held their bellies. They pulled at each other's dresses and jackets, teasing each other about their clothes, pointing with fingers and then swopping blouses because they had taken a fancy to each other's clothes. Erna sat quietly, her face in a rosy shimmer and lit up by a smile. She chatted with some of the young women and listened to their stories of dreams of their future and falling in love. It made her feel less lonely. She was not alone with her longing for love. The director of the college stood up and the women quickly settled to listen to her. She introduced Gertrud Bäumer.

Gertrud was a strong looking woman with a bright and intelligent face. She looked confident and cheerful at the student gathering and spoke to them about the modern times they were living in; the inventions; electricity; the telephone; the radio; the eight hour day; social welfare. She mentioned the Weimar Constitution and the proud achievement of the women's right to vote. It was a new hope and a new beginning for the country! She also warned that life was not necessarily going to be easier for women.

"Men will fight to maintain their rights over us women, mark my words. I have with me a good friend of mine who will talk to you in a short while about the type of discrimination that we will have to fight wherever it appears. My friend is called Marianne Brandt and she works with the Bauhaus, the avantgardist architectural school in Dessau. But before I let you listen to her let me mention another woman who is also a heroine of mine. Men have their heroes who they worship, and we women need our heroines. One of mine is Bertha von Suttner. On the 18th of April 1906 Bertha was the first woman in the world who received the Nobel prize for peace! She wrote a book against war. It was called 'Down with the weapons'. It became a huge success and was translated into several other languages. You can find her book in our library, and I suggest you read it. Now let me ask Marianne to speak to you. She is a young woman like all of you who was given a place of study at the famous Bauhaus. The Bauhaus has a constitution that guarantees women the same rights as men. Give Marianne some welcome applause."

There was excited applause when Marianne stepped forward. She was a slight woman with a clear ringing voice.

"Fellow students, women, comrades! I am thrilled to have been asked to address you on this wonderful summer day in Essen. I have travelled from Dessau where it was raining. I am indebted to Gertrud, because as a member of the National Assembly she has done so much to support the women at the Bauhaus. In case you don't know what the Bauhaus is...."

Inge was whispering something in Lene's ear, that made them both giggle and lose concentration.

"... the unity of art, architecture and craft. We believe in creating a whole new vision of life and art in harmony..."

"Look at those people, they are all in a sort of uniform, walking uniform, big boots..."

Inge pinched Lene's side and made her squeak.

"Stop, you're making me laugh..."

"We're proud to learn side by side with the men, but then we found out that we weren't allowed into some of the workshops, for instance the metal, cabinet making and painting workshops. They started a workshop just for women, and we resisted. We weren't going to be treated as second class citizens. You can see that in the most modern and progressive situations men will still..."

There was huge applause. The women beamed, laughed and clapped. They got up to meet Marianne and Gertrud to shake their hands and be close to them. They were inspired and felt a better world was possible with justice and equality for women and peace for everyone. Inge helped Erna up and pointed to the group of women and men with their walking boots. The evening sunlight threw beams of light past trees creating shadows.

"You're wearing good boots. Did you walk far?"

"What a great day we've had!"

"I'm proud to be a woman after meeting Marianne."

"Where did you walk?"

"Yes, it's lovely today, lucky for us, because we had a long walk to get here and we're famished now."

They were all asking questions at the same time and found out that the walkers were from the Wandervögel organisation, a new craze of being in close touch with nature by walking and wandering everywhere, often for miles.

"It's an elixir to a happy life, you ought to try it."

"Why don't you join us one day?" another suggested, a muscular looking blonde with a bob. Lene took out a scrap of paper and wrote down her name and address. Her name was Susi. Susi, Gertrud, Berta, Marianne! They felt serene with the images of these wonderful women in their minds, heroines, as Gertrud said, 'we all need them'.

They chattered away and Erna watched them with a smile. They were on the train back home.

"Bertha von Suttner, she was well ahead of us. If we could ever achieve such things," Inge mused, "how can we contribute from our tiny life in a miners' family home, dark and with few books? She must have had a lot of books at home."

"When I'm at the library, 'I'll look up the Wandervögel. Father asked me to get a book for him anyway. These Wandervögel might change our lives. I have the same trouble you have with all the work in the bakery. What time have I got to spend on big ideas?"

"Yes, they are big ideas. We women always think of love, but we also need to get going with the big ideas," Erna mused. They watched the fields speed by.

At home Mathilde and Hermann were keen to hear their stories. Bertha von Suttner! A great woman! The Wandervögel and their vision of a renewal of society in touch with nature!

"We live in this dirty city with all the coal mines. So much dirt everywhere! You can't hang the washing out. It gets covered in soot. It was different when my parents had the restaurant by the Emscher! How easy life was then!"

The stories had brought up memories for Mathilde. Lene looked out of the window and saw the full moon. It stood above the mine shafts. The coal trolleys each picked up a small piece of its light. The big wheel rolled, cutting the sky into cake slices.

CHAPTER 6

OLGA

Olga's mother picked up little Matti and rocked her in her arms. What's Lene going to make of her, when she sees Olga like this. She looked at Olga, who lay under the cover.

"She doesn't even wake up when the baby cries. If I wasn't here to help, how could she manage?" Frau Reichardt muttered to herself.

Finally Olga opened her eyes and stretched herself. Frau Reichardt put the baby in her arms. As if she was an automaton Olga, removed her nightdress from her breast and pressed the baby to her nipple. She hardly glanced at her mother, who looked down at her daughter in disbelief. What had become of her lovely girl? She felt anger at Hubert, but that didn't help because he wasn't there, and was it not Olga herself who had to take responsibility for her condition? Why? Other people had much harder lives and coped, why not her? Still, they just had to get on with it, and she had news to tell.

"Olga, my dear, Lene is coming round shortly, she's really looking forward to seeing you, she says."

Olga looked up briefly as if she remembered something from the past, then sunk back into her pillows.

"Come on! Let's make a real effort. You want to present Matti to her with pride. Let's get you dressed when you've fed her."

Olga's huge body lay motionless, her eyes were half closed. It was as if she was letting Matti feed without herself having to be involved. The doorbell rang.

"That must be Lene," she called and left Olga's room, carefully closing the door behind her. She shot out and hugged Lene as if she was her own missing daughter. The strong broad shouldered woman was holding back her tears. The deep shadows under her eyes belied the smile on her face.

"I'm so glad you've come! You must talk to Olga, she's in a terrible state. We don't know what to do and how to help her. Come in the kitchen with me, and I'll make a cup of tea."

Frau Reichardt soon joined Lene, and they both had steaming cups of tea in front of them. It was peppermint tea, just like at home. Lene waited to hear what Frau Reichardt had on her mind.

"Lene, the truth is that Hubert isn't really ready to be a father. He's always busy. When he comes, he's perfectly nice and loving to us all and cuddles the baby. After a couple of hours, though, you can see that he has other things on his mind. He speaks of work in Duesseldorf and Frankfurt. That's quite a long way away. He says his career depends on him working so hard that he has no time. He says he loves Olga, but I think she's stopped believing him and now can't face the future. She still loves him, but every day she's becoming more withdrawn and won't even talk to us about him. We can't speak about the future or Hubert. She yells at us, telling us off, telling us it's our fault and so on. It's become unbearable to have a conversation with her. I think Hubert is well meaning, but the baby has come too early for him. He didn't want to be so tied down early in his life. But he can't face up to it either, so he pretends everything is normal and all right, but it makes it worse for her and us. We live in a sort of limbo, not knowing what to do and what to expect. Is this a marriage? Are they a couple? No one knows. He hasn't spent a night with her since the arrival of the baby. It's days since Olga has got out of bed. That's how bad things have become."

The words poured out of Frau Reichardt. Tears had started to well out of her eyes.

"I'm so sorry that you're upset," Lene said, "but Olga is a good, strong woman. This is surely just a temporary thing. It's all been very speedy. She might not have had time to adjust. She is young. She will recover. We just have to take good care of her and the baby. Also, she might still be exhausted from the birth."

Frau Reichardt looked up. Lene made a lot of sense to her. She might be very tired. Perhaps it had much less to do with Hubert than with her tiredness. This thought cheered her up. She dried her eyes, and her shoulders moved away from her ears, allowing her to take a deep breath.

"I knew it would be good to talk to you, Lene. You are such a treasure! Let me take you to see her. I'm sure that you can cheer her up too."

Lene just saw a pile of blankets when she went into Olga's room. Olga was completely smothered under pillows and a duvet. The baby's cradle stood by the window. Lene went to look. Little Matti was fast asleep. Her snub nose rosy next to a tiny fist, a golden glow of hair around her face. She looked gorgeous and peaceful. It made Lene feel more certain that things were going to be all right. Lene sat down by Olga's bed and called her softly. After a bit the pillows moved and Olga's head emerged. She looked pale with deep rings under her eyes. She had cut off her hair, so that a short shock of brown surrounded her puffed face. She looked at Lene for a while without responding, as if she didn't recognise her.

"How lovely Matti is, so cute, her little face! You are lucky to have such a nice healthy baby. How are you feeling, did you have a good sleep?"

"I'm not really sure how I feel, Lene, I have been in bed continuously for the past weeks, as far as I know. I've got no energy. I seem to have changed personality. I am fat and slow and tired all the time. I don't really want anyone to see me, but with you it's OK. I do want to see you. Chat to me! My mother is getting on my nerves. She keeps looking at me as if I've lost it and have gone mad. She keeps asking me about Hubert. I don't know what Hubert is up to! To be honest I've stopped caring. He's busy, but he's my husband and should help to look after the baby, or at least be with me at night. It's all very weird. I've stopped understanding what is going on."

"Olga, you're doing fine. Just think how tiring it is to give birth. I think you're exhausted. Just stop worrying. You have a lovely baby, and you need time to recover. Hubert, well, who knows. It's not like you're in financial trouble. You've got a roof over your head and a caring mother and father."

While Lene was speaking she observed Olga carefully. Wrinkles around her eyes and on her forehead gave an indication of how the labour of the birth had engraved itself into her face. Her eyes had become more focused as she spoke, and she could see that Olga's face had somewhat brightened.

"I've got an idea! Why don't I do your hair and put some make-up on your face, some lipstick? We could also dress you up in bed. You don't have to get up," she reassured Olga, who'd started to look perturbed.

"That sounds like a good idea. I feel so ugly and fat."

Lene went into the bathroom and brought a brush, a comb, sponge, towel and Olga's make-up gear. She got Olga to sit up in bed, brushed her hair, sponged her face and dried it. She took care with a face cream, a foundation crème and then carefully used her make-up equipment, mascara for her lashes, eyebrow pencil, eye shadow and finally a red lipstick. She took her time and chatted with Olga about things going on at college, the outing with the Wandervögel. When she'd finished she gave Olga the mirror to admire herself. Olga smiled.

"Funny, you know, I hadn't even thought of make-up and lipstick. My thoughts just keep going round in circles as if in a prison. Most of the time I don't even know what I'm thinking. I suppose you can't call it thinking. Its just a mush in the head, a labyrinth, if you can imagine what I mean."

"I can quite imagine it. It comes from being exhausted. You had to work hard to give birth. You need time to recover and not to worry about anything. Do you want me to find you something pretty to put on, without getting out of bed? You can just wear it in bed."

Olga nodded and Lene went to look inside her wardrobe. She pulled out a couple of tops and showed them to Olga. Olga fancied a pink blouse with ruching and small buttons. But they found it was too small now. Her breasts had become enormous and popped out of the buttons. Lene found a wide red top that was designed to hang loose. Olga put it on, and looked at herself in the mirror. What about a nice scarf? This one here, wrap it round your neck! That looks great now! Have a look! Olga checked herself again in the mirror and Lene saw that her facial muscles moved towards a smile. She was glad. She needed gentle encouragement and no reprimands until she gained strength.

"I remember when I wore this last, I think it was that time we celebrated my birthday last year. We had fun then..."

"Never mind that! We're going to have fun again." Lene cut her thoughts off quickly to stop her from dwelling on the past.

"We've got to get a good routine going for you and the baby, when you're ready. Just let your mother spoil you for now. You shouldn't get upset about her. She loves you a lot and just wants the best for you and the baby."

She gave Olga a big hug and promised her that she'd come back every other day or so. Olga still had a vague and distant look on her face, but there was a hint of a smile around her eyes.

Lene rushed to the library to find out about the Wandervögel. She found a book on display that was obviously new. It was by someone called Gumbel, on the left and the law. That'll be interesting for my father, she thought, and took it with her. She found an article in a paper about the Wandervögel movement. It started as a youth movement in Berlin in 1896 and aimed for the renewal of life, it said. Long hikes to celebrate nature, nude bathing, early morning dew walking, eating natural, ideally vegetarian food and wearing natural cloth were the hallmarks. The poet Friedrich Nietzsche was mentioned, who spoke of life as if it was a powerful drug all by itself. Lene read: 'You have to have chaos inside yourself to give birth to a dancing star.' And: 'Life is the unity of body and soul, dynamism and creativity. We must break out of materialism and return to nature. We must venture out to new horizons and find our true selves again.' 'Give birth to a dancing star,' she thought, 'what lovely poetry. Do I have chaos in my mind? Probably! But no birth to dancing stars yet.'

The words stuck in her mind. She wanted to feel closeness and renewal. Had Olga not given birth to something new, someone new? Was this the same as being creative, writing a poem? She had a letter in her pocket from Susi about a walk, and she had to drop in on Inge before she went home. Karl-Mayer Strasse, Steeler Strasse, Rotthauser Strasse. The blackened sooty house fronts made her feel like holding her nose, thinking of the coal dusted tenements they all lived in. She began to have Wandervögel thoughts in her mind. She reached Inge's house. She led her in. The walls in her house were decorated with pictures of mines, wheels and men with charcoal faces. Miners stood in the lounge. The kitchen was full of people, so they went into the lounge.

"I've just come by to ask you if you fancy a walk with the Wandervögel. Susi wrote to me, it's in two weeks."

"I said I'd help with tea and coffee at the next action meeting the miners are holding, I think it's that same Saturday. Let me ask Emil."

Inge went across to the kitchen and brought Emil back. Emil listened to them and then announced with a cheeky smile in his face:

"OK, I'll make a deal with you. Go to your Wandervögel do that Saturday, and then the next Saturday you can both help at our fund-raising meeting. We also need a team to go out and take down those posters with local women on them."

"That's a deal, I definitely want to help with that," Lene quickly told them.

It was a sunlit Saturday morning when they met with six other young people at the railway station. The train to Köln did not take long and soon they began their ramble along the river Rhine. Everyone had brought something to eat, so that they could have a picnic when they got hungry. Blonde Susi made them laugh all the time, as she exchanged jokes with Ute whose bottom wobbled at every step.

"I'm losing weight this minute," she told them, "that's the only reason why I'm punishing myself with these walks."

"You'd hate to miss our walks, you would."

"Would I! You can bet I wouldn't!"

Sturdy Erwin with builder's shoulders, lanky Jan, petite black-haired Rita and Ulrike were ahead of them. They learnt that Ulricke was a trained runner.

"Do you remember that time we were washed out by rain?"

"That was a lark, we were soaked to the skin. It was quite an experience."

"Yes, and then we were turned away at the inn. No wet clothes inside here. Charming people! What were we supposed to do?"

"And we were hungry!"

The sand of the river embankment was soft and white. Willows in bent and ragged shapes hung their dangling branches into the water ripples. There was a tinkling sound. The group had a speedy and well practised stride. Lene and Inge had to get used to it. It was startling at first, but after a while the strength and energy felt good.

"Think of our lungs," Inge said to Lene, "they're probably full of soot." Her eyes sparkled. It was a blue day. The sky looked like a field of forget-me-nots dotted with Marguerite clouds. The picnic was unwrapped and they sat down on the sand. Sandwiches with tomato and cucumber were shared out. Home-made pastry, carrot salad, crumble cake. Jan brought out a bottle of white wine, which was handed around.

"Have some wine! It's amazing how good food tastes out in nature, isn't it?"

"It's like you've never eaten properly before!"

"You're exaggerating now, what about turnip soup?" Everyone laughed. They were all fed up with turnip soup. Wine in their blood, they lay back and watched the sky and felt close to nature. Inge thought of her dark miners' home and her weary mother. Lene was thinking of the dirty chimneys they had to live with, when Inge nudged her. She looked up and saw Rita and Jan begin to take off their clothes.

"Are you coming for a dip?"

"I didn't bring a costume."

"You don't need a costume here, Wandervögel love nudity! Come on, don't be shy!"

"Ouch, I stepped on a nettle."

"Stop it, you're tickling me!"

"Lene, Inge, are you coming? Don't be shy, we're all nature's creatures!" They were now giggling, as bras, suspenders, stockings, knickers and any other clothes they were wearing ended up in neat piles on the sand. The men stepped into the waves, tiny fluffs of hair on their chests and pectorals perched unconsciously. Inge and Lene joined in. Wandervoegel was for them, warts and all. Soon they were all squeaking and giggling in the cool water.

"Watch out, there are dangerous currents!"

Inge with her womanly body ambled towards the Rhine followed by Lene, androgynous and muscly. They swam, and the currents tugged on them. They had to swim harder. 'We're Rhine maidens now, we're guarding the gold!' Lene thought. The sun threw sparkly ciphers amongst the swimmers. At the end of the day they parted with kisses and promises to join in the next outing. Worn out from their unusual experience Lene and Inge sat on the train like two sphinxes, unable to move or talk, pondering the enigma of the day.

"How was your day out?" Mathilde asked Lene.

"It was a long walking day full of nature, mother, very enjoyable."

"Nature, what a good idea!" her mother replied. "We don't even have any nature around us any more. Look at that dirty Gelsenkirchen! It never used to be like that. Soot and coal dust everywhere. If I think of the restaurant by the Emscher, where I lived with my good parents. God bless them…"

Hermann had other things on his mind. He was reading the book Lene had borrowed from the library.

"Lene, you're a treasure! It's all in this clever book you brought from the library."

"There are over three hundred murders of leftwing politicians by rightwing radicals that have never been punished. Rathenau was the exception. One of his murderers was shot dead during his arrest, the other one committed suicide. This Emil Gumbel has done all the research and has concluded his devastating findings. It doesn't surprise me, but its shocking! The way the law is practised in the Republic carries on as if we were still a monarchy. There are hardly any lawyers from a social democratic background who are cognisant of our democratic constitution."

Lene beamed. She was too tired to talk, but felt proud that she had been able to please her father.

The squeaking of the coal trolleys could be heard while they silently sipped their tea.

Lene visited Olga every other day. Tonight the miners poured out of Dahlbusch from the evening shift. A smell of sweat, work and flames soaked into Lene's nose and reminded her that she had promised to help on the miners' action day, the following Saturday. She pictured them working underground. They have to hang a token of their identity around their necks so each can be identified in an accident. The safety lamp. The trawling in tubs to the seams. Water stands in the seams. She shuddered. The works sirens yelled as she joined the stream of men, when someone pulled on her sleeve. It was Emil.

"Hi Lene, you're still coming, aren't you? The miners' action day, it's next Saturday."

"How funny you should be here this minute and tell me that! You know, I just remembered about it when I smelt all the heat and dust from the mine. My God, look at you!" she exclaimed. "The state you're in! I wouldn't have recognised you. Your face is black and glossy like a piece of coal."

"That's exactly what I feel like after a whole day of digging. In the end you just become a part of the charcoal face of the earth. Must have been trees, all of this a long time ago, maybe we'll become trees again, if we stay down long enough."

He laughed, but it was a sour laugh full of fatigue.

"Oh, you must be tired from your work, Emil, and I'm on my way to a friend who's had a baby. I have to give her a helping hand to cope with her new life. About Saturday - you can count on me."

Frau Reichardt opened the door.

"She's better, you know, Lene. I think she's improving. I'm so grateful to you for coming to help us. Have a look at Matti, she's so lovely. I think Olga is now beginning to enjoy her as well. Go and see for yourself."

Olga was still in bed, but sitting more upright and she held Matti in her arms and let her play with her hair and touch her nose and mouth.

"How are you doing, Olga? Look at you and Matti playing together! She's lovely."

Olga smiled. She cuddled and kissed Matti and got her to clap her little hands, which made Matti laugh. They laughed too. When Matti fell asleep Lene chatted with Olga and made her laugh by telling her stories. Olga could not get enough of the episode about the Wandervoegel's naked bathing in the river Rhine.

"Were there no police?"

"Not a soul."

"Did nobody stop them or complain?" She couldn't believe it.

"Did the men get undressed too, and show their private parts?" This made Olga laugh out loud. It was the first big laugh she'd had. Lene was overjoyed.

"You can't imagine what it's like. Once you stop worrying about all that. It's just so natural. Out in nature, on the sandy beach by the willows, the river rippling and murmuring. Everyone in the nude. You get a sort of sense of freedom that overwhelms you, and you know the others feel it too, so it brings you close to them. I can't explain it."

Lene was looking for words to describe what she had experienced. No one mentioned Hubert. They had decided it was best to forget about him, as he hardly ever turned up. They couldn't make him come, and talking and worrying about him seemed to make Olga sad and listless. Instead they talked a lot about the baby, spring, how the baby was going to enjoy the flowers in her mother's garden and what fun it would be to dress her in a pretty dress when she was bigger. Lene could see that Olga was improving. She continued to fuss over Olga's looks, putting make-up on her, mascara and lipstick and brushing her hair and then showing her the result in the mirror. They kissed before Lene left.

On Saturday the miners' fund-raising day took off. There were coloured balloons and flags outside the entrance to the community centre advertising the event. Families with their children ambled into a large hall full of stalls. On the stall of cheap goods you could buy toys, household goods and tools. Another stall offered socks, jumpers, scarves and gloves. The Deppermann bakery had donated bread, rolls and cakes which another stall offered. Smells of cabbage, potatoes and coffee drifted across together with the merry chatter of the families, the screeches of their children. It mixed with the scent of soap on freshly washed bodies. Inge spotted Lene at a book stall, and they soon pointed out favourites to each other.

"Have you read this: 'The Suffering of Young Werther', by Goethe?"

"You bet, we did that at school. Look, here's Heine, I'd like to read Tolstoy and Chekhov."

"Have you got the time for Anna Karenina? It's a long story."

"Here's our good old Karl Marx, and August Bebel. My father reckons he's read some of their stuff."

"Poems by Bertolt Brecht, they look interesting!"

"Inge, Lene, you need your steward's badges, come along, the political speeches are starting in a minute." That was Emil with his mates who handed them their badges.

"Are these the Rhine maidens, guarding our gold? Wish they guarded my gold!"

"Don't be rude!"

"What's rude about that? We should have a nudist party at the end of our fund- raising."

"If we make over 5000 marks, I'll join the nudists today."

"That's if her indoors lets you."

"Oh, come, how will she know? It's only natural, I'll tell her."

"Leave the girls alone, boys." That was Emil. Then he said to the girls:

"Sorry, I did tell them about your outing. It was too good a story. Don't worry about them! They don't mean any harm."

"He's right, we don't, we just like a good laugh."

Lene and Inge took the banter with equanimity, while fixing the badges to their jackets. People were gathering in the hall, which was now nearly full.

"Just stay here and keep watch. You can come inside and listen, but make sure you guard the door. You know there are people who might want to disrupt proceedings."

Emil looked at them to see if they understood. The noise grew with the excitement as more men and women crowded into the hall until no chairs were left and people had to stand up at the back. Alfred Zingler, the editor of the 'Volkswille' went up to the platform and sat down with the miners' leader.

"Comrades, fighters for peace and work! We have today the pleasure of the company of one of our foremost supporters of our proud social democratic tradition, Alfred Zingler. Alfred is the editor of our newspaper 'der Volkswille' in the department of Gelsenkirchen for communal politics, art and science. There will be time for questions at the end."

There was enthusiastic applause. Lene and Inge stood at the back watching the doors as more people turned up. The crowd fell silent as Alfred began to address them.

"Comrades, colleagues, women of the Republic! I am thrilled to speak to you today. Our social democratic tradition and our aims for the working people are very close to my heart and also that of my wife, Margarethe. Margarethe, show yourself," he called.

She stood up in the front row and turned round, waving to the throng with her small round hand. Alfred told the assembled company about all the roles Margarethe had in the local community, from running a sewing club for workers' wives to assisting the theatre in planning and organisation. Alfred spoke about his own extensive experiences in journalism; his work in the local youth organisation, theatre, the folk choir and the local Wandervoegel. Lene dug her elbow into Inge's side when he mentioned that. They both giggled. He spoke of the need to be organised and for socialists to fight side by side with the communists, explaining that they both had the common aim of winning rights for working people and defeating nationalists and warmongers.

"It would be wrong not to speak the truth here, the truth as we all know it, even if we wish not to look that way. You know that women have been attacked and hunted down like animals. You know that socialists and communists have been attacked in broad daylight. You also know that Jewish people have had to suffer insults and violence. I feel it's my duty to warn you to be aware, to keep your eyes open! Record and report these abominable incidents when they occur! Don't look the other way! If you do, this can happen to you or your family. These people are a danger to the Republic. The groups have names like Wehrwolf, Stahlhelm and National Socialists. We must never underestimate our enemies."

As he spoke a commotion grew louder behind the double doors. Lene and some of the men got up to see what the noise was about, when a couple of men stormed in shouting at the top of their voices "Bolshevist pigs!", followed by others making their way towards the stage.

Several men immediately shot up and confronted the men, asking them to vacate the hall. Alfred was moved out of the hall for his own safety. They carried on shouting and shoving. A fist landed in one of the miners' faces. This brought about a roar of fury from the assembled crowd with more men jumping up. A couple more ringleaders tried to muscle up against the miners, but were soon overwhelmed and thrown out of the hall. Their followers swiftly escaped. The incident, like so many of that sort, was quickly quashed, but left a bitter and tense feeling in the hall. Alfred returned. He was confident and calm, saying,

"Speak of the devil... I told you they are after all of us. Comrades, let's finish with a song and our promise 'United we win, divided we fall'."

They sang the 'International'. As if to prove the interruption to have been a complete failure the men's and women's voices rang out powerfully and confidently accompanied by a couple of musicians who were sitting in the front row.

After Alfred's speech the families returned to the stalls. Inge and Lene were at a stall of home-made make-up powders and potions, lipstick and nail varnish. They teased each other while trying out lipstick and blush powder.

"You look like a film star!"

"Look at you pouting with that colour, no, that mauve is better, oh let's go to the cinema, they've got a new film at the Phoenix."

"No, first let's have a look at these clothes, maybe we'll find a new frock." They were engrossed in experimenting with make-up when Emil turned up with a small man with long ash-blonde hair and deep set eyes. He was wearing a striking necktie in red and black.

"Girls, I want you to meet Karl Schwesig. He's a local artist. He has an exhibition upstairs which you ought to see. Karl, this is my sister Inge and her friend Lene. Do show them your work. The two of them are quite artistic themselves."

Inge looked at her brother, then at Lene.

"C'mon Lene, let's have a look. Karl, will you show us your work?"

They went upstairs and were soon engrossed in looking at Karl's lithographies, depicting miners, townscapes and portraits of individuals. Each piece of work showed an aspect of the mines: the shafts; coal trolleys; giant hammers and anvils, and workers at work. Karl was a softly spoken man. He seemed a little shy at first, but soon told them how he'd become an artist. They had reached an old settee with a wobbly coffee table beside it. The women dropped into the sofa with a sigh and beckoned Karl to sit with them. Karl didn't seem quite so small when seated, and they noticed that his backbone was rounded from what must have been rickets. As he quietly chatted he turned his head now and again to see if his audience was paying attention. Inge was leaning back into her seat, and he only caught Lene's eyes. She saw a quiet deep flame in his pupils. It was an odd feeling for Lene suddenly to sit close together on the sofa with this strange man who started telling them about seaside holidays he'd had. She could feel the sea, almost hear it, when he spoke in a low singing voice that could have been that of a musician.

"My aunt lived by the sea in St. Peter Ording. She always took me for walks on the mud flats when the sea was out for miles, and we looked for shells. She brought the shells home and we painted them with her nail varnish. I loved the colours on them, they brought out the wonderful forms even more. In my work I approach the men I draw as an aspect of nature, of the sea, stones, pebbles."

As he spoke Lene could see the sea, as grey green as his eyes. She looked straight ahead at the charcoal drawings of coal trolleys and big wheels and saw the sea rolling in turquoise waves towards the mud flats. She turned to look at Inge and saw that she had dropped off. A tiny whistling sound came from her mouth.

"I drew for my brother who'd gone to fight in the war. We used to write to each other, and he'd say how much he liked my work. He died in 1917 in France. I found his death hard to bear."

"I'm sorry about your brother, Karl. You must have been very fond of him."

"I was. He gave me so much encouragement. It's because of him that I insisted on studying art. I went to Düsseldorf art school, but I also learnt a lot at the Folkwang Museum in Essen."

"What's the Folkwang like?"

"Well, it's one of the best in Germany, sort of world famous. The 'Bruecke' artist, the 'Blaue Reiter' ones from Munich, they all exhibited their work there. It's all because of the founder, Karl Ernst

Osthaus. He was a pioneer of the arts. He had strong beliefs in the unity of nature and the arts."

As Karl spoke his hands flew up in the air and drew shapes, to sculpt the thoughts in his mind, but for Lene they became alive, as if they were birds. She shook her head, feeling silly, as if she wanted to shake herself into reality, thinking she must be tired.

"I must be going home soon, Karl. I'm feeling quite tired."

"I'd like to do a drawing of you, Lene. You could come to my studio, but you'll have to be quite patient. I like to take my time..."

Lene burst into a nervous giggle, clasping her hand over her mouth as if to suppress a yell.

"Don't get me wrong. I'd like to do a portrait of you. You have very special eyes and lovely eyebrows. Your nose is feminine, but you've got a cheeky glint in your eyes," he announced, but he said it in such a dreamy way, as if he wasn't quite present and was speaking from another room or sphere. Lene marvelled at his intuition, and his ability to see things that she'd never heard anyone else talk about. Inge woke up.

"Goodness me, I forgot all about time and things. I just fell asleep, I was so tired."

"You missed Karl's childhood story. Shall we go down now?"

They found the main hall cleared of stalls and people gathered in groups chatting. Lene could see her parents with Friedrich and the Zinglers. Both Friedrich and her father were avid readers of the 'Volkswille'. They chatted animatedly, and Lene joined them, waving goodbye to Inge and Karl.

"My daughter Lene, she was a steward here today, Herr and Frau Zingler," Hermann announced with a proud smile.

"I heard you talk about the Wandervögel. I've been on one of their walks," she said.

"That's a wonderful initiative," Margarethe enthused. "I try to walk with them as often as I can, and Alfred as well, but you know we have so many other duties. They're such a positive bunch, socialists, you know. How did you find out about them?"

"We accidentally bumped into them on a college outing in Essen."
She didn't mention the nude swim.

"Oh well, there you are! I was going to say you must join, but
you're well ahead of your time, young lady, or should I say comrade,"
she said laughing in an encouraging way. Lene looked at her. She
had smiling, warm brown eyes that twinkled with humour. She
wore her dark brown hair parted in the middle and held loosely at
the nape of her neck. Some curly strands had freed themselves and
rested on her shoulder, giving her an easy-going expression. She was
a slight woman, as was Alfred, her husband. Lene found she was
taller by a couple of inches. She beamed into Margarethe's bright
face.

"Of course, comrade, I'd like to come and see you in your sewing
class sometime. Not that I'm any good at sewing, but just for a chat
and to see how you do things. You seem to do lots of work with the
mining families here."

"Definitely, do come along sometime! There's a lot of work to be
done, and an extra hand is most welcome."

At this point of the conversation the men turned round to
Lene and Margarethe and suggested they all go for a meal at the
canteen of the newspaper. A small round woman joined them and
was introduced by Friedrich as his fiancée Wanda. She looked rosy
cheeked with curly brown hair surrounding her face. Her large bosom
was most noticeable. It seemed to protrude ahead of her. Lene stared
with undisguised perplexity for a moment, until she realised what she
was doing and quickly turned to look at her father instead.

"If you're off for a meal, you must excuse me." Wanda spoke with
a baritone voice that could have been a man's. "I've run our stall all
day. Friedrich, you go if you want, but I've had it for the day."

Friedrich put his arm around Wanda, who looked even smaller
now because he was so tall next to her, his arm seeming almost to
push her to the ground.

"Well, let's be off then, I'm not that sparkly myself."

Lene was intrigued to meet Wanda. She was the person who
had been to Berlin, and she was her father's best friend's fiancée

with the voice of a man and an enormous bosom. They bid Friedrich and Wanda goodbye and left amidst further greetings to those who were still lingering in the hall. It was a bright evening outside with a red glow from the sunset covering the town's buildings. Thick green bushes glowed in the light. The air seemed to be mingled with a fresh breeze coming from a long way away, as if from the sea. Lene saw the mud flats in St. Peter Ording and Karl's grey green eyes.

CHAPTER 7

KARL SCHWESIG

Diary notes, 4th July 1972

It's now the fourth year of her visits to London. This time I was on the verge of cancelling it. I was furious with her. What are her real aims with her stories, does she have any secrets to tell, or are they just subtle ways of trying to influence me or reprimand me? I was confused, and wished she hadn't come. This business with Olga's baby and her post-natal depression. Is she trying to imply that I'd had post- natal depression? It's that feeling of vulnerability in the presence of an experienced mother, who keeps giving advice when you've just given birth to a child. I'm not in that situation any more. I have my own experience. I am the mother of two healthy and lively children. I feel I need to hide my own life from her, in case she makes sly allegations and drops subtle hints. I'm now in a lesbian relationship, but have asked my girlfriend to stay away while my mother is here. It's so awkward and upsetting for my lover and me. I told her my husband was on a business trip. I didn't dare to cancel her visit in the end. She is my mother after all, but I can't stop my anger flaring up, especially when she starts telling me about the artist she fancies.

"When I still lived at home you frowned about all my boyfriends. None of them were good enough, my nights out were a moral disaster and here you are telling me about an affair..."

"It's true, I couldn't deal with it. When you were still at home I blanked out all my own adventures…"

"And now I have to listen to you talking about them, after you made me suffer with your reprimands."

She was silent and looked at the sky. She looked sad, and my empathy got the better of me.

(end of diary notes)

The bombshell news came on the 28th of February 1925. Friedrich Ebert, the president was dead.

"Ebert dead! We're going to be in even more trouble now."

"I'm not going to miss him. He was responsible for the death of Rosa Luxemburg and Karl Liebknecht."

"You bet, the ones who killed them are still alive and well. Ebert just couldn't stop them, they're a law unto themselves."

"I fear the worst for our republic, it's got too many enemies."

"God help us, I think we shall need it." Everyone talked in the streets.

Had he not signed Germany's first democratic constitution? He was like a parent to the republic and had given it stability. Now he was dead. The news of his death rolled like a tidal wave of mourning through the nation. Forgotten were the hate tirades that had been conducted by newspapers and politicians of all colours. Forgotten were the enmity and the endless legal battles that he had been subjected to, the whole mass of dirty tricks to ruin him. The defamations from the left, the right and the middle classes who despised the 'Saddlemaker'. His health gave way. He died of blood poisoning following acute appendicitis.

The Deppermann household rang with his praise. Hermann and Mathilde, despite reservations they'd had about some of Ebert's political decisions, remained loyal to him in their attitude. Was he not a man of the people like they were? They understood that just because a democratic republic had been declared it didn't mean that the people would automatically turn into democracy loving citizens.

Quite the contrary! The outspoken democratic aspirations of the many had driven the traditionalists and monarchists into a frenzy of reaction. Friedrich dropped by on the night of Ebert's death.

"Poor man! He was hunted down like an animal. But he could have built a better alliance with the left wing if only he'd kept people like Kapp in prison, or those gendarmes who killed Rosa and Karl! He let them out of prison after very short sentences."

"He was hunted down like a fox. I reckon he tried to build alliances, but it was a difficult job, because the communists always wanted to go too far. The Germans were not ready for a Russian Revolution, but they thought they were." Hermann had a different angle on the topic.

"The social democrats themselves didn't always agree with Ebert. He betrayed the workers with that Noske. That man should never have had the job of defence minister. He refused point blank to stop Kapp and intervene with the armed forces."

"I remember. It was a terrible day. Ebert had to quickly leave the government offices at 5 o'clock in the morning, otherwise that gang of mercenaries would have locked him up. Unthinkable!"

"The workers saved the republic! They stopped everything from moving, and four days later Kapp had to give in."

"He had too many enemies, and they are still with us. That's the most important thing for us to remember." Hermann spoke and slapped the upholstery of the armrest for emphasis.

Small and large black, red and gold flags were soon available at all news-stands in the country. They were the colours of the republic, initiated by Ebert. The nationalists carried on with the colours of the monarchy in black, white and red. The Deppermann household was quickly decked out in black, red and gold flags.

"These flags alone should make people think," Hermann said in defence of Ebert.

Now that he was gone the citizens became aware how much Ebert's battles had also been theirs. Hundreds of thousands came out into the streets to say their farewells at Potsdam Station in Berlin, where his corpse was put on a train to be taken to Heidelberg for the funeral. Thousands lined the streets in Heidelberg. Black, red and gold flags flooded the streets. People were crying in the street. Lene and her family were poised over their radio to listen to the impassioned speech of Paul Loebe, the new president: 'Darkness lies over Germany and its people. Only from afar can one see the dawn of a new morning. Fate has denied you the fruits of your toil, the experience of calmness in the country. When the flag of real peace one day flutters over Germany and Europe and justly distributed wealth reigns, then the German nation will bow their heads over your grave.'

Olga rocked Matti in her arms, as she stood by the window looking at the mine towers. Fog made them look soft. Ebert was dead. It all seemed quite distant to her, as if life outside was taking place on another planet. What difference would it make? Frau Reichardt came in and stood next to her.

"Ebert is being buried today! There are thousands out there mourning for him, but did they lift a finger to help that poor man? It's disgusting. Hypocrites, that's what they are! It makes you wonder what will become of the constitution now, they are treating it like a football."

"I can't follow all this political stuff, it's going right over my head. I'm just glad to be able to cope with my little one." Olga sat down. Matti had fallen asleep in her arms.

Inge was washing the dishes, while her parents discussed the situation around the kitchen table. Turnip soup steamed on their plates.

"He wasn't a bad man, but he did make some big mistakes. He should have cleared out the whole legal system, the judges, the lawyers and all. Prussians the lot of them! You heard that Gumbel wrote a book about it. Hardly a single rightwinger has been brought to justice. It's a disgrace!"

"There's also the army. He didn't have a chance to get on top of those old structures, the army officers and the Junkers with their estates. It makes you wonder what lies ahead of us."

Lene looked out on to the coal trolleys. They rolled on and on as if into infinity. Their dispassionate unstoppable motion felt offensive to her on this emotional night of the burial. The big wheel silhouetted against the sky like an emblem of impassiveness. It was foolish, of course. How could the coal wagons or the big wheel react, they were not beings with a heart and soul. The relentless rhythmical travelling of the coal from the depth of the earth through the night sky started to make her feel anxious. Where was all the coal going? Why were all the fires burning day and night, filling the clouds with toxic air; the heat and dirt underground? What was it all good for?

There was college the next day, and they were too busy to spend any more time on Ebert, the funeral and dark fears. In the art class Fräulein Bäcker continued her tale of the Worpswede artist community. They were going to visit it with a solid understanding of what they were going to encounter. Fräulein Bäcker had a seductive manner when she talked to the class. Her warm brown eyes shone. Her voice was soft and almost inaudible, so you had to strain to hear her, but the story she told was tantalising. Every one of the young women sat up and bent their ears so as not to miss a single word. How did she manage to look so deeply into my eyes, Lene wondered. It made her feel unable to move or even breathe, she was so attentive.

"Picture a dark, lonely landscape of moors, peat bogs, heather and birch trees. The socialist Heinrich Vogeler who lived in the village with Otto Modersohn and Paula Modersohn-Becker. You remember I told you he suffered very much, when his first wife left him for a younger man. But he transcended his suffering into new ideas and a positive direction for his life. He used his house to create the 'Arbeitsschule', a new type of education in which children learn by doing. The children study geometry by measuring their vegetable patches and by creating maps of the surrounding area. The one day he met the beautiful brown-eyed Sonja Marchlewska, the daughter of a Polish communist who had worked with Vladimir Lenin, the leader of the Russian Revolution. Sonja had come to study Vogeler's artistic and paedagogical ideas. The two fell in love with each other. They set up a sort of Red Cross called the German Red Assistance.

It was meant to look after the children of political prisoners. By June 1923 the first children arrived. Heinrich was overjoyed. Not only had he fallen in love with a gentle and soft-eyed woman. By late June he and Sonja became members of the 'Society for the Friendship of New Russia'. Other famous members included Albert Einstein, Heinrich Mann, Ernst Rowohlt, Max Pechstein and Ernst Toller."

Fräulein Bäcker finished, but the students looked at her. They all liked a good love story. Outside dusk had arrived in the park around Helene Lange college. On their way home Lene and Inge noticed the evening star Venus sparkle.

On the day Lene met Karl, the painter, and he'd asked her to pose for him she had blushed because she'd thought that he meant that she should take her clothes off. She was reassured that he just wanted to do a portrait. That night she touched her arms and shoulders in front of the mirror. She unbuttoned her blouse and looked at her breasts as if they belonged to someone else. She held them in her hands, they just fitted into the cups of her palms. She touched her nipples. A tingling ran hot and cold down her spine followed by a sensuous feeling in her body. She knew she was going to meet with him. A real artist! She had a letter from him inviting her to his studio. She visited one Saturday in July. Summer heat made the soot particles stick in the air as if glued. You had to breathe them in. It was soot and cigar smoke that made her throat scratch, especially when she stood in a queue waiting for a tram or walked past a cafe. It reminded her instantly of Fritz, her sister Hilde's husband. She saw him sitting as usual with a broad self-satisfied grin on his face, the cigar in his mouth, his legs hanging wide apart from his leather arm chair, a round belly protruding just below his grin. Disgusting, she thought. How can Hilde bear it with him. Her mother never even mentioned him when she praised Hilde.

It was a sweltering Saturday when Lene visited Karl. His studio was on the top floor of a large block of flats in the centre of town. From there you had a view of the usual mine shafts, the public baths and in the distance the station. He was waiting for her on the landing in his painter clothes, trousers covered in charcoal dust and dried colours, a loose blue shirt open at the neck and a neck-tie in turquoise and green. She noticed again how grey-green his eyes were.

"Well, how nice to see you! Do come in! Fancy a cup of coffee? It's not the real thing, I haven't managed to get that yet from my favourite corner shop".

He beamed and strolled off energetically ahead of her towards the kitchen through a chaotic huge lounge with roof lights that were open, and large side windows. Chimneys, the ubiquitous coal trolleys, church steeples and not far away the railway station roof.

"Yes please! Can I have a look around?" Lene called out, when she saw the wilderness of paintings, easels, canvasses, brushes, pencils, books, newspapers and the shelves full of ornaments of various descriptions. They included miners lamps, small copies of miners' tools, stones, pieces of coal, a mini coal trolley and other collectors' items. The ceiling was high and included the roof space, so that you could see the beams that had been exposed to create more space. She heard Karl put the kettle on, and saw a low bed close to the floor occupying much of the space. Lene noticed that clothes were freely strewn over the unmade bed, something that in her mother's household was severely frowned upon. A musty smell of turpentine, oil paint, soot and summer heat pervaded the room. A burnt fragrance akin to ground coffee appeared.

"I hope you like this. It's my favourite way of having coffee, when the real thing is unavailable. This one is made of burnt acorns and dried and burnt potato peel, called Muckefuck. It's a sort of taste you get into a habit with. There's still no real coffee, you just add lots of milk if you can get it."

"I know Muckefuck, we usually have it with carrot, barley and beechnut, or whatever can be got hold of in the bakery that can be turned into coffee. You know that we have a bakery in the Karl Mayer Strasse. Here, I brought you a cinnamon whirl."

"Lets share it, I'll get us a plate."

They sat down by a coffee table with a sofa and a canvas chair. "It's a great flat, isn't it. I really like the view you have of the town below, it feels good to be so far above it."

"I agree, that's what keeps me here. It's not that good as a studio, because I'm having to jumble everything together, my bedroom, living space and studio. So it makes for quite a bit of mess. But look," he got up at this point," I just love the cityscape from here. These are the places I love to draw over and over again. Our work spaces, the mining towers, big wheels, trolleys. The workers, the fire, the elementalness of it all. We are creating a new society here. Think of all the inventions that have come out of all the materials that are found in the earth, the radio, telephone, telegraph."

"Tell me more about you becoming an artist."

"I've always been fascinated with the shapes of things, buildings, the colour and texture. So painting was an obvious choice. I fell in love with the architecture of the industrial towns. I went to study at art school in Düsseldorf. We had some fantastic teachers, also visiting artists like George Grosz and John Heartfield, who came from Berlin. Berlin is really the centre of all the new art movements. You know Dada?" Lene shook her head. "It's a sort of anti-establishment art movement that makes fun of everything that people take seriously, like the army, the Prussian uniforms."

"I haven't been to Berlin, but we learnt all about Worpswede in college. I have a fantastic art teacher at college. She told us all about the artist community there and Heinrich Vogeler. I think it's quite a bleak and dark landscape, with all the moors, but kind of romantic and mysterious. He was a romantic, wasn't he?"

"Actually, I met Vogeler, because the art school had links to Worpswede. Its not that far from here, certainly closer than Berlin. He struck me as a very kind and good hearted man. I am a bit, what shall I say, maybe traditionalist. I want to stick to one theme, and that is to celebrate the workers and their environment."

Karl saw that Lene was watching him dreamily, and changed the subject.

"But we are chatting and chatting, it's really nice to talk to you, Lene. I could go on for hours, but I want to get started on the portrait. As you know, I'm a slow worker, so I won't finish it today."

Lene felt hot and took her jacket off in a moment of shyness. She felt aware of her strong arms and shoulders and could feel her breasts pushing into the white summer blouse that she had opened at the neck.

"Is this your portrait chair, or should I say torture chair? Surely, it must be terrible to sit still for very long, I'm not sure if I can do it."

They both laughed.

"We'll try. Don't worry! If you get tired, we'll stop and have a break. And we won't finish today anyway, you just come back for another sitting."

She made herself see her sitting for the artist as a task that her mother had given her, like all the other work she did. That made it quite easy. She relaxed and sat on the chair looking out of the window. She could see a group of large birds flying by in formation. They could be geese or ducks, she thought, and so her thoughts wandered to the outside world. She only vaguely noticed Karl's intense gaze, his grey-green eyes and the softness of his blonde hair, his long fingers holding the charcoal, the rapid movements of his hands on the paper that seemed to swing his whole body into action like a dance. There was only the scratching of charcoal on paper, until Karl spoke.

"Time for a break," he called, and almost woke Lene out of a trance.

"You're a brilliant model! Lene, you keep really still. I thought you said you couldn't."

"Oh, I was just joking. Funny, I think of myself as not being able to sit still, but actually I love it and start to feel sort of dreamy." She jumped up and walked to the window where they stood next to each other. Karl pointed out his favourite sights below and told Lene of his visits to the mineworkers to draw them in action. Lene told Karl about her friend Inge and her brother Emil and his political actions.

"That's what I mean. This place is bubbling with action, nearly everybody is aware that we are living in extraordinary times. I want to record some of these actions. Mind you," he added, "not all of it is something that I want to draw."

They both stood both gazing out of the window as they chatted. She noticed that he lay his arm round her shoulders and gave her a squeeze. His arm felt good and for a moment the warmth of his body so close to hers sent an electric pulse through her. Luckily, he took his arm away casually, as if nothing had happened, saying:

"You have fine shoulders, Lene, almost like a man," and laughed into her face a cheeky laugh. "They're like your face, strong and upright, with your feminine nose and the soft shape of your lips that contradicts your rebellious charcoal eyes. It'll be tricky to get these expressions right on my paper," he added, almost speaking to himself.

"Well, you're the first artist I've ever sat for, and I suppose you would say things like that. You have to look at people and study their faces in detail," Lene argued, studiously avoiding the sensuous undertones in Karl's remark. He responded to her shyness by asking her to continue her sitting, and once he had his pencils and charcoals in his hands he seemed quite absorbed. She had time to calm her inner self and return her gaze out of the window to regain her hypnotic state until it was time to go. At the door he pressed a small kiss on her cheek and asked her to come back the following week and maybe they could also take a walk by the river. She agreed and quickly left to be on her own with her emotions. Outside rain had arrived and gushed from the sky in long, grey sheets. She only had a thin jacket. It didn't matter. On her way back she called at Inge's and couldn't wait to tell her what had happened. She suggested they go to the nearby churchyard. Inge looked at the sky and at Lene, rolling her eyes as if she wanted to say you're crazy, then shrugged her shoulders, grabbed her raincoat and they walked off. Inge was like that. She was a great friend who would find time to follow a sudden inclination.

"I have to talk to you, I saw that artist guy from the miner's fundraising day today."

The words rushed out of her mouth, as they pulled their jackets close and ducked their heads. The grassy path squidged soft water into their shoes. In the graveyard the colours had washed out of the flowers left by mourners. The gravestones glistened darkly.

"Did you let him kiss you?" was Inge's first question. Inge's eyes had widened to a huge question mark, her mouth stood open. She was in work clothes from helping her mother at home with sleeves rolled up and buttons open on her blouse, her curly neck hair touching her shoulder.

"I feel so excited about it. No, we didn't kiss, not on the mouth, but he kissed my cheek, as I left. I do like him, he is so interesting to talk to. I know he's quite a lot older than I am, but I had a fantastic day with him. He started to draw me, and I just went into a sort of calm state. He told me I was a very good model."

"You know what that means, Lene, he wants you in the nude!" Inge laughed.

"That's what I first thought as well, when he asked me that day of the miners fund-raising. But he told me then that he mainly does portraits."

"Well, he would say that so as to be polite and make it easy for you to feel OK about visiting him. Lene, you have to be careful. You know what people are like. They talk and gossip and watch behind their curtains."

"He lives up in the block of flats near the station, not anywhere near us, so people don't know me there. Also I saw no one going up in the lift. Inge, what shall I do? I won't be able to sleep tonight!"

"I know what's the matter with you. You've become infatuated! Make sure you do plenty of other things to get your mind off him. There's another miners' event next Tuesday. Why don't you come to that and meet the boys? That'll be distracting. Also our next Wandervögel..."

"I'm not sure I want to be distracted. It feels so strange and marvellous to be excited. I feel really light. As if I had filled up with air like a balloon and was floating in space."

"You've fallen in love, Lene. Treat it like a virus infection. You need to recover from it. C'mon, do other things..."

"You're cruel, Inge. Haven't you ever felt like this? It's awful and wonderful at the same time." Inge shook her head. She laughed with her shoulders and suddenly gave Lene a hug.

"You are a one," she said, "don't get me wrong. I have no sort of moral sentiments about your feelings. No, I think it's rather great, or sort of thrilling. I don't know how I'd feel. We're so matter of fact in our household. We just think of work, food and sleep. Mm...that's not quite true, because we're all into the politics and get excited about socialist ideas. But love and all that... I'm not sure."

They had walked and were standing under the arch of the church portal, but they were both already drenched in rain and were shaking the water out of their hair.

"You did get excited when we met the Wandervögel people and you love walking with them."

"Well. Yes. True. But I do like my peace and when I go home I kind of shut things out. I get excited about having a good sleep." She laughed. "Really! There's nothing to worry about. Why don't you just enjoy it and see what happens, but don't let things happen too quickly. Must go back, they're waiting for me, supper to sort."

They hugged each other. Lene felt relieved. She looked gratefully at Inge, thanked her and waved goodbye. Lene's heart fluttered as if she had a swallow in her chest, a bit calmer now, but still circling the skies.

CHAPTER 8

THE ZINGLERS

Inge's words rang in Lene's ears. Was it love that she felt, or just the excitement of something very new, something she had never experienced before. Her heart beat a little faster, and everything seemed more colourful. He had a crooked back. It didn't matter to her, indeed his vulnerability endeared him to her. She breathed in the familiar smells, the sour-sweet odour lingering from the bakery; her mother's sandalwood scents drifting down the stairs; a faint smell of soap. The rapping of the grandfather clock in the kitchen and voices murmuring upstairs clicked into place for her. A door was being closed. Someone had gone to the toilet. Kitchen smells of potato and leek soup and fresh bread.

"Is that you, Lene?" her mother called down. "Make sure you have your supper, dear, you must be hungry."

Lene smiled and realised she was ravenous. She had soup, lovely bread and butter, peppermint tea and a roll with jam. The food tasted extra good. She popped her head into the lounge, greeted her parents and told them she would just get herself sorted and come back for a chat. In her bedroom, she took her clothes off, looked dreamily in the mirror and went into the bathroom to wash. Her reflection in the misted mirror gave her a new sense of selfhood. She put on her pyjamas and dressing gown. She had no problem thinking of a story of her whereabouts in case her mother asked. Her own newly found shrewdness surprised her. It was like discovering a previously undetected mole.

When she went into the lounge she saw that her father's friend Friedrich and a mate of his who she didn't know were present. Newspapers lay on the floor. Friedrich must have arrived and surprised her father while he was reading them. Lene was pleased because no one was going to ask her now about her own outing. They were engaged in one of those political discussions that she enjoyed.

"Do you know how old Hindenburg is? Our new president? Seventy-eight years old! Can't you see what they've done, giving us this ancient chap as the representative of our young republic? The right-wing parties have ganged together to present us with a war legend from a long gone victory. It's a shambles."

"I have my own theory about this," said Friedrich's friend Paul. "There's a lot more treacherous hidden stuff going on than we are told or most people know. The big shots in industry. Like Duisberg and what's his name, the IG Farben one. They're constantly muddying the waters and throwing in money to bring about developments they want. What can we do in the face of all that money? We, the working class, haven't got money to throw at situations. Money does change things, Karl Marx already said that. Money can turn one thing into its opposite, and so democracy goes out of the window."

"I told you Paul would put it all in Marxist terms, he's read the books. Actually, Duisberg is the IG Farben man, he dictates the events," Friedrich put in.

"This stuff is all coming from America. They have watched the Americans with their economics and now they're copying them. They gang together and then start to exert control, by joining in government committees."

"Our biggest problem is going to be Article 48 and the power Hindenburg basically has, being elected not by parliament, but by plebiscite. This article reduces the power of our parliament. That's why they're calling it the Dictatorship article. The president can annul parliament, if he feels it's necessary for internal security. Additionally there is article 24, which says the president can dissolve the Reichstag. You can see what that means! Whenever they think the time is right for it the president can choose to go back to a monarchy."

"C'mon, you're exaggerating now! Surely, we're a long way from that. I think the social democrats will prevent such developments. They're still the biggest single electoral party."

"But look at them! They're not what they used to be when they were in opposition. I wonder if having power has gone to their heads. There's that chap Max Weber, the sociologist, elevated to rubbish Karl Marx, he invented the plebiscite idea."

There was a moment of silence while they all digested the dramatic knowledge that Paul brought to the conversation. He must be doing a lot of reading, Lene thought, and looked at him intensely. His face was flat like a pancake with a small nose and wide cheekbones, a round chin and ears that stuck out. But in that round face his eyes sparkled in a brownish green light, as if from a deep cave. They seemed to be looking from somewhere far away. He sat very upright, his arms resting on his crossed legs, and his hands gesticulated as he spoke, making shapes, as if he wanted to place his arguments somewhere in this room like pieces of furniture.

"What it illustrates for us is that most of the middle-class parties that allowed this article to be part of the constitution aren't keen on a properly functioning democratic system."

"Quite so! Their slogan for everything is 'We're fighting Bolshevism'!"

"The universities are full of chaps that propagate the idea of rule by decree. They joke in their lectures about our constitution and ridicule it in front of their students."

"That's outrageous!" Lene was incensed. "The republic has been voted in using political power. Maybe the parties ought to have more control over what goes on at university?"

"They ought to, but how can they exchange all the lecturers in a couple of years?

"Do you remember November 1922? That's when they started to choke our constitution and democracy. You wouldn't believe it happened, unless you'd lived through it! Chancellor Wirth stepped down and Cuno, the general director of a shipping company was put into his position. He wasn't even in any party. It was pure power politics, nothing else."

"Wirth uttered the words 'The enemy stands on the right' that cost him his job."

"Have some more mint tea, Paul. What about you, Friedrich and Hermann?" Erna got up and poured everyone another cup of tea. She looked at Lene and seemed to sense something was going on for her. Her doe eyes shone with a shy but roguish glimmer that perturbed Lene. How could she know anything - or did she look different?

"I wouldn't be surprised if the Americans actually paid some of these lecturers. Imagine you're sitting on a huge amount of profit from the war, while the rest of us Europeans are bankrupt. So all they need to do is bankroll some rightwingers to come out with reactionary views."

"That's what the Dawes Plan is all about, to strengthen Germany to stop the Soviets making inroads. Money is their tool."

"Where did this Dawes come from?"

"The man's a banker. He's a leading light in the J.P. Morgan bank. His theory is brief: 'Business, not politics'. The communists call it enslavement by American capital. Not far wrong." Paul was shouting now. They could see he was furious, his hands fighting battles in the air.

"Lene, can you fetch me the sewing basket?" Mathilde asked. "Actually I think it's in Erna's room, isn't it, Erna? I might just as well start on the buttons before I finish tonight. You might also put the kettle on again. I think this is going to be a late night the way the men are talking."

Erna looked up and nodded towards Lene, her cheeky smile still lingering. "It's by the window on the small table."

Lene hurried, because she didn't want to miss the conversation. Paul seemed to know a lot, and the discussion was fascinating. She turned the kettle on in the kitchen and made another pot of peppermint tea. When she returned the conversation had turned to everyday matters. The price of flour, sugar and butter; the miners' wage cuts. Where one could get a good piece of meat. She yawned and suddenly felt tired. She bid them all goodnight and went to her room. Before drawing the curtains she gazed out at the sky. The stars seemed to speed across the sky, everything seemed in motion. The universe is all moving and we are moving with it, she thought vaguely. She was trying to feel the movement of the earth in space while she watched the coal trolleys float through the air as they did every day. She stared at the tall towers' black silhouettes against the sky. It was a fairground feeling, after you've been on a helter skelter. You can't stop spinning.

Olga brushed her hair and put on some lipstick. Her mother was playing with Matti in the garden. She felt at ease, although looking at her huge belly and breasts she sighed, thinking 'How will I ever get rid of the weight?' Size 18! But she was in a jolly mood. Lene was coming to celebrate Matti's first birthday with her, and Olga was going to show her that she had recovered. In fact, she was proud. Her little girl had started to take her first steps.

"She's walking!" Olga exclaimed, as soon as Lene arrived. "Come and look at her, she's with mother in the garden." They drank tea and ate cake. They laughed about Matti's funny little faces and yelled with pleasure when she took some more steps. They were so close, but also so distant. Olga with her child cocooned in her mother's house and Lene adrift in a secret love affair that she couldn't talk about. Lene made an excuse and didn't stay long.

"I've got so much to do. I'm helping Frau Zingler now. She's the wife of the 'Volkswille' journalist. Didn't I tell you about her?"

Lene had indeed arranged to meet Margarethe Zingler at her sewing class. This took place in the August Bebel house, which had recently been built and was financed by the social democratic party, the workers' welfare organisation and the socialist youth organisation. Margarethe ran the sewing club of the workers' welfare as well as an advice centre.

"There's lots to do, Lene. You can see the women here have work to finish, but I sometimes can't manage to get round to everyone,"

Margarethe said, when she saw Lene arrive. There were about nine women who sat around tables with sewing baskets by their feet and all manner of equipment and materials spread in a creative disorder over four tables. Scissors, tape measures, thread, cotton, pins and needles, chalk, patterns, pieces of cotton, wool and chiffon were everywhere. The women hardly looked up to see who had come in. They were deeply engrossed in what they were doing, apart from when they needed something. The atmosphere was busy and contented, with casual banter and requests for scissors.

"Where are the scissors?"

"Can I have the pins?"

"The tape measure's disappeared. Oh, it's always you, Barbara!"

"Stop it, girl, don't give me any lip!"

"What do you mean lip, it's going to be my fist in a minute!"

"Don't make me laugh, your wee little fist wouldn't knock out an ant."

Such banter caused uproarious laughter. No one took it seriously. It added to the comfortable feeling the women had for each other. They were talking while working and laughing about the jokes, all of it with great good humour.

"You're a great lass, Margarethe. Since this class has started I've got all my men in new clothes and there's even a dress for me nearly done. It's saved me a lot of money."

"I wouldn't know what to do without the class, Margarethe," said another. Lene dutifully walked around as Margarethe had asked. She watched here, helped to make a decision there. It was nearly five o'clock, and tidying up took place briskly. The implements were locked away together with the half finished clothes.

"They're a great bunch of women. I really enjoy this work," Margarethe told Lene after they had all left.

"They work all the time. They're prepared to do everything for their families, such loyalty you only get in these working class families. Well, my dear, have you got any more time? Because if you have, we'll have a coffee down in the canteen and a nice little chat."

"I'd love to. There's so much I want to ask and find out about your work and how I can contribute."

They had reached the canteen. Margarethe fetched a pot of coffee that was standing by the sink, got two cups and some milk and they sat down.

"I'd love to hear how you became who you are. You and Alfred your husband. What were things like for you, and where did you come from?"

Margarethe began her story, as they sipped the hot milky coffee.

"We were both born in 1885 in Silesia. His town was Szprotawa, mine Jawor. Our parents were both protestants. Alfred was really going to become an actor, he had a lot of cultural education at school. Are you sure you want to hear all this, because I get quite involved when I start telling our story."

"No, no, I mean yes, I do, I'm very interested. Do tell me." Margarethe needed little encouragement. Her cheeks had become rosy and her eyes glistened. She had rolled up her shirt sleeves, because her own story was giving her extra heat.

"Alfred began to study acting and gave classes in languages, as he was very talented linguistically. He took a job as a journalist at the Breslauer Morgenzeitung (Wroclaw Morning News). Then he started to write about the arts and the theatre. That's how his interest in acting remained with him."

"In my family," she continued, "languages were also encouraged. I learnt English and French. I worked for the co-op in Breslau. We met and fell in love when we attended a theatre performance of 'The Robbers' by Schiller. He was making notes for a review, when I passed him and asked him how he found the play. We started chatting, and he asked me out there and then. We married in that same year, on the 26ᵗʰ of September 1914. The war had already started. We were lucky, because Alfred had a problem with his hip and didn't have to serve in the war. You know, Lene, what 'soul mates' means? Well, Alfred and I have always been like that, very close and with deeply shared feelings. We both became politically interested in the war years. Just reading about the victories and hearing the stories of what really went on behind the scenes. The brutal slaughter of so many men! It just showed us that our Government was misleading us and that you had to organise yourself politically. Maybe I'm wrong, but I think, when people are politically on the left, which is what we were, they have a stronger bond with each other. They share a hope for the future and an idealism, when everyone else tends to become cynical and self-centred. Are you with me, Lene?"

"I am, I mean, I know what you mean, because I feel so close to my father. He's the political one in my family. And he has a strong friendship with his close friend Friedrich. Both of them are socialists."

"I knew you'd know what I'm talking about. There's a sort of deep loyalty feeling," Margarethe replied, and smiled warmly at Lene. She continued.

"We moved to Tilsit (Sowjetsk) in East Prussia. We both worked for the 'Tilsiter Zeitung' and decided to join the Social Democratic party."

She looked at Lene, who was watching her attentively.

"We didn't want to stay in Prussia. So we first went to Regensburg, which was further south, and from there we went to Hagen and onwards to Gelsenkirchen. We've been here now three years and have become real locals. Alfred became a member of the workers' welfare and 'Freidenker organisation' and we're both committee members of the theatre 'Die Volksbuehne'. You already know that we're with the Wandervögel and friends of nature."

"So for you culture and politics are very important," Lene summed up.

Margarethe looked at her thoughtfully. Lene was surprised by the confidence and enthusiasm that beamed from Margarethe's face. She sat holding her hands on her lap, but energy seemed to fill every fibre of her body.

"You know, Lene, that's a good question. For us socialism and culture belong together. Whoever separates them ruins either one or the other. That's why we need to invest our work in both."

"That makes a lot of sense to me, Margarethe. Funny, I've never heard it expressed like that, but I felt it must be so. I hope you'll stay put, so that we can work together." Lene could feel inside herself a glowing of the same passion that she'd noticed in Margarethe's face.

"Definitely, we will! You might particularly like to help in the theatre, I think you'd find that interesting. We need dramatists and many others. Neither of us intends to move away from here. I like the people. Such a colourful mixture from all over. It's a strong place for social democrats. Why don't you come sometime to the Volksbühne theatre with us and join the town's cultural committee? You can't believe how excited people get when something that is planned actually gets done. A lot of them just want to sit and criticise and then drown their worries in a drink. The state we're in here in Germany is not good."

"How do you mean it's not good?"

"The Reichstag isn't strong enough. And the industry bosses pull strings on behalf of big money. You see how they manoeuvred Hindenburg into power this year? An old man who did a bit of fighting in the war? We've got to work to strengthen democratic thinking in all areas of our life. That's what Alfred and I are after."

Lene told Margarethe that she often heard her father talk about just these dangers. While Margarethe talked they had got up and were walking through the kitchen to the back and into the garden. It was a green wilderness, overgrown with grass up to their knees. There were some evening primroses shining their yellow faces in the dull light. Snapdragons bloomed in bright yellow and orange. Lene said it did need a bit of gardening work. Margarethe took it as an offer, and enrolled Lene to help clear the jungle. Lene left in case Margarethe had further ideas of work for her.

She jumped on tram number one and then to number three and got out at Inge's house. First she was going to walk home from there to give herself time to think, but then in a quick change of mind she found herself suddenly ringing the doorbell. Inge opened and begged her to come in quickly in a whisper. She was pale and dishevelled and seemed not to have dressed properly, although it was close to supper time.

She pulled Lene through the hall up the stairs and into her bedroom and shut the door. She sat down and her head slumped into her lap, her hands in front of her face and sobbed. Lene was aghast. She sat down beside her friend and put her arm round her. Inge was shaking with quiet sobbing. She could not bring out a word.

"Inge, my dearest, what's the matter, is someone ill? Has there been an accident in the mine? Tell me, I can't bear seeing you like that and not knowing what's upsetting you!"

Inge was still shaking silently, and Lene squeezed her gently close to her and stroked her back. Inge started mumbling, yes, there had been an accident, but no one had died.

"But my mother always gets such a shock when such news reaches home. This time she ended up falling ill with the dread of it. Fearing my father or brother had died. We had to take her to the hospital with suspected tuberculosis. She's under sedation. We're not allowed to speak to her." She cried bitterly. Lene was shocked and dismayed.

"At least no one's died," Lene muttered finding her words again, "and your mother's in good hands, they'll look after her well. Of course you want to speak to her, but it's better for her if she isn't spoken to and is left to be very quiet. You can recover from TB."

Inge lifted her tear stained face and put her head on Lene's shoulder. Lene stroked her hair out of her face.

"You're a pal, Lene! Yes, I mustn't despair. There's always something, and this time it really hit me, because of mother. She's usually so strong, and without her the household will fall apart. I can't do all the work she does. I'd have to give up college and still not manage. But now we have to make do without her for a while."

The two young women sat on the edge of the bed for a long time holding each other and contemplating the vicissitudes of life. Just when you think things are all right, then something else smacks you down. They tried to make plans, talk of college, think of the Wandervögel, but nothing cheered them up.

"You'll have to go on your own to the walks."

"No I won't, I can't go without you."

Inge couldn't shake off her worries, they kept creeping back.

"I'm so worried about mother. I never thought of death as so close before. Yes, death in the mines, injured men, you hear that all the time, but my own mother, that's different. She is the heart of our family, without her nothing would be the same."

"Don't think about it like that," Lene said. "She's not going to die. That's what you have to think now. That will also be the best for your mother, thinking positively like that. You've got to make yourself have hopeful thoughts, not sad thoughts."

"I'm sorry, Lene, I'm just miserable now and not very good company. Come and see me soon, I must get myself sorted and visit my mother now."

CHAPTER 9

TIME OF HOPE

Lene, Olga and her mother were crossing the busy Bahnhofstrasse to get to the shops. Olga's mother was holding little Matti's hand tightly. The sloppy snow splashed up on their legs and the little girl looked like a furry ball in her thick woollen coat, scarf and hat. They were going to buy food for supper, and it was market day. The display of vegetables and fruit was a feast for the eyes these days. Cabbages, potatoes, carrots, leeks. There were many kinds of apples and pears. Flour was offered in big open bags; milk was poured from big cans; eggs could be selected into small baskets. The meat stall had an impressive variety of sausages, salamis and smoked meats. At the cake stall she marvelled at Streuselkuchen, Butterkuchen and Schwarzwälderkirsch. They were all going to have a piece of cake with their coffee. Happily Olga's depression was now in the past. Olga had even asked her mother if she could attend college and study to become a nursery nurse. It all happened very quickly soon after Olga filed for a divorce. Hubert generously offered to make a financial arrangement that would secure money for little Matti. They were discussing the new plans now.

"Attending college is a great idea, Olga." Lene was really pleased for her friend.

"If you can look after Matti, I can do it, mother. I've thought about it all. I want to be able to go to work. That's my biggest wish now."

"But don't you want to be with your child?"

"I can be there for her after college every night, can't I? I want to become a nursery nurse. They will always need people like that, so I can find work and look after myself and my daughter."

"My poor girl, you're only twenty and already a divorced mother."

"Don't look at it like that, I've got a lovely, healthy daughter and I'll be able to earn my own living. Women these days can be independent, can't they, Lene? You've always said that to me. I'll learn something and go out to work."

"At least you're over that depression."

"Don't think about it any more. It's in the past now."

"Yes, let it just be the past now." Olga and Lene spoke in chorus. Lene added,

"As long as we think we can't change the world, it won't change."

Lene didn't remind Olga of their big dreams of artistic careers. What could she say? Her own dreams lay dormant. At least Olga had some practical, alternative plans. She had a place at college with clear job prospects. She had Matti, and she had a loving family home and knew how she saw her future. Lene had a loving family home, but her work in the bakery was far from satisfactory. Young Hermann would take over the bakery after her father. He was ageing quickly with a bad leg that ached on many evenings after the long days standing and rolling dough. Lene dared not think of her time after college. Life looked dangerous one minute and dreary the next. If she thought of the bakery it was dreary. If she thought of Karl it looked exciting but impossible.

Her father's leg had become very painful at times, where he had injured himself many years ago. An inflammation flared up now and again, and immobilised him. Bakers spend a lot of time on their feet from early morning. Hermann's leg had started to swell up and turn blotchy and red. First he had tried to ignore the pain that came with the swelling, but when he showed it to his wife one evening, she was startled.

"You can't walk about with this leg, it's badly swollen. You need to rest it until it gets better."

It was better the next morning, but by evening it had swollen up again. Lene noticed that her mother's face was starting to have a small frown instead of her usually cheerful expression. She looked worried and tired and had begun to urge young Hermann to speed up his learning of bakery tasks. His apprenticeship was not finished yet. The radio was now in the lounge, and they often listened to it.

"...We need to use the American techniques, that have been shown to be so successful there. Politics needs to be made by the men from industry. For that reason I welcome the decision to form the steel industry with Herr Thyssen in the lead. It is to the credit of our American friends Charles Dawes and Owen Young from JP Morgan bank that we can aim to create an industry worthy of the German people..."

"Do we have to listen to this on the radio, Hermann, it upsets you anyway?" Mathilde said anxiously.

"I've got to know what's happening. These huge companies can monopolise wages and hours of work. You watch, it'll lead to rising unemployment and political extremism in the streets."

"It is already, look at the number of unemployed here. It stands at two million. They have American money to buy machinery, that gets rid of people's work. That means the company earns more money, people lose their wages, and the state has to pay out extra in welfare."

Hermann's friend Friedrich had joined them with his fiancée, Wanda. Her red curls bobbed, as she nodded her head animatedly in agreement with his arguments and then turned to Erna. Friedrich's pale blue eyes shone with a bright rage. His usually pale complexion looked ruddy. He seemed to have put on weight. Wanda was now leaning towards Erna, speaking fast and quietly in her baritone voice. Lene couldn't hear what she was saying. Erna's face showed shock and disgust. She was scratching her wrist with her fingers, and you could see the eczema flush under the impact of the irritation. Lene noticed Wanda's narrow back. She looked so slim from behind, making her voluminous bosom and belly surprising, when you saw her side and front.

Hermann had his leg on a stool. The swelling was quite apparent. They had spent some time looking at it and discussed whether it was receding or not. Mathilde had wrapped cooling bandages soaked in camomile extract around his leg. Hermann looked comfortable now. The conversation was as ever heated. He hadn't lost any of his political fervour.

"It's the power hammers. I'm not saying it would be better if the miners had to continue using pick axes, but what's the point of introducing new tools and taking the jobs away from the men? Its impoverishing the state. They have to pay benefits for the out of work, and the extra profit goes into the hands of the industrialists."

"And those same industrialists are financing political groups on the right. Guess who is financing the NSDAP? It's our good old Thyssen, head of the steel industry. I read in the 'Volkswille' that he paid them the tidy sum of 100,000 gold marks back in 1923. Another one of their apologists is Dietrich Eckart. He wrote an article called 'Bolshevism from Moses to Lenin'. You can see the shape of their hate campaign: they're linking anticommunism with anti-semitism. All of them are sworn enemies of our republic."

"What do you expect when the president of our republic, Hindenburg, is himself a member of the 'Stahlhelm' groups who keep marching under the monarchist red, black and white flag? They're directly challenging the constitution of the Weimar republic."

"Thank God for the 'Reichsbanner' organisation! They're the best we have at the moment."

Wanda had joined the men's discussion.

"Who are the Reichsbanner, Wanda?" Lene wanted to know.

"They're called 'soldiers of peace'. They were formed as an organisation of republican war veterans in March 1925 to oppose the warmongering 'Stahlhelm' and other groups like 'Wehrwolf'. The Reichsbanner's aims are to support the Weimar constitution.

Membership has grown massively to over three million members in just a year."

"You should come sometime, Lene, there's great comradeship in the events they organise, a real people's movement. We need strong young people like you and your brothers."

She looked at Lene and eyed her expectantly. A comb had loosened some of her curls that now fell into her face, giving her a wild look. Her bosom was wobbling above her belly. Lene saw a warm fire in her eyes.

"I think the Reichsbanner is really important, because many people who have become disillusioned with politics and might drift to the reactionary parties are joining up. The other choice is between the social democrats and the communists."

"And the communists don't even support the republic," Friedrich added.

"Not really, let's not go into this now, Friedrich, my dear, its a long argument that we both know well, but it would take all night to explain. Shall we go home, Hermann must be tired."

"It might be best to call it a day now," Mathilde joined in, "we do have tiring days here in the bakery. Our young Hermann is to take over from father, and it can't happen soon enough. Look at his leg!"

Lene put on new red shoes. In fact, she had left Karl Mayer Strasse with old worn street pumps. In her hand bag were her new shoes. Putting these on stirred excitement in her heart. They were so beautiful! She felt seduced by the shoes. It was strange that she didn't want Karl to notice her lovely shoes. She was afraid to stir up strong emotions in him. Or was she even more afraid of her own emotions? She wasn't sure. She didn't show them to her mother, but one evening she went to Erna's room wearing them and asked her what she thought. Erna was in her dressing gown writing a diary. She always wrote a diary. She looked up with her doe eyes.

"The shoes? Oh let's see, yes well they are lovely, Lene, where did you get them?"

"I saw them at Ahlsdorf in the window. Funny, I just had to get them. Do you ever feel like that Erna, like something grabs you and you really have to get it? I don't understand it, we were never like that before."

"I do, Lene, I feel like that, when I go into town. They do have such wonderful things in the shop windows now. I think to myself, shall I try this dress on or buy some lipstick? But, my dear, what's the point for me? No man has ever turned round to look at me. I'm too shy, I'd blush if they did. So, then I get disappointed and think to myself it's not worth it. Then I go to the craft department and buy a wood carving knife or colours for my dolls, maybe a piece of material for their clothes."

"You shouldn't think like that, Erna. You're a beautiful woman with such gorgeous auburn hair and kind eyes. Any man would be lucky to have you as his wife."

Erna looked at Lene and blushed with pleasure for a moment. The words had sparked nice feelings in her, but she quickly dropped her head and, looking at her diary, seemed to think of what she had written there.

"No, Lene, it's no use. The years have gone by. I'm twenty-eight now. The war is long over. The men have come back, but the one that was meant for me probably died on the battlefield."

She looked sad and resigned. The skin on her face lost colour and looked drooping. For a moment she almost looked like an old woman. It frightened Lene, but she held her feelings inside her.

"You surely don't believe that there is one specific man that was supposed to be your husband and that no other one could be the one for you? That's silly. That cannot be. I know of women who've had a man and left him, and then gone with another man. So that would mean they were entitled to two men – and you only to one?"

Erna's face lifted. She got up from her chair and walked over to the window.

"Well, my child, I must say I hadn't looked at things like that before. I know there are women, shall we say loose women, who go with several men and even get paid to be with them, like prostitutes. I'm not completely ignorant. But we're different. Surely we're looking to find the man God has chosen for us. We've got to be patient for him to turn up, but in my case, it might be getting too late, I'm too old. It's different for you. You're young."

"What makes you think we're completely different from the women you call loose women? Some of them may be exactly like us. They may have fallen on hard times, their man has left them. They need money. They need to earn a living. They may have a child or an old parent to look after."

Lene was of course thinking of Olga. No way would she be a woman with just one man. She was lively and attractive. She would meet someone else and have another relationship. Lene also thought of the women in Berlin and Susi. If only Erna knew! She looked at Erna as she stood by the window. She had put on weight and looked a bit stodgy in her frumpy and heavy olive green dressing gown. Not a good colour, Lene thought. She looks as if she's given up.

"You need to believe that there is a relationship out there for you, it will make you look and feel happier."

"Don't be silly, Lene! Now you're talking nonsense. How can my thoughts be visible? They're very private. I don't tell them to anyone. My diary has all my thoughts in it. It's a kind friend to me, but you are too," she hastened to add.

While Lene wondered if she had said something that might upset Erna her sister had walked over to her and gave her a hug.

"You're my dear little sister, Lene. I'm always astonished at how clever you have turned out, much cleverer than the rest of us. But I'm tired now, that was such an interesting conversation I have to sleep on it."

Lene was thinking of her conversation with Erna when she put on her shoes while leaning against a tree. She rang Karl's doorbell.

"Come in, Lene, I've missed you. Are you all right? You sound out of breath."

"Oh, it's nothing, maybe me running up the stairs." She knew very well that it wasn't just the stairs that had made her out of breath. She had to get a grip on herself. She chatted, and the words spurted out of her mouth.

"It's all these things going on, Karl. I'm worried about my father. He has a bad leg and doesn't seem to be coping too well with the bakery work any more. Also we had Friedrich, my father's friend and his girlfriend Wanda come round and talk about the Reichsbanner. I wasn't sure about her at first, but I like her now. She has very warm eyes, and she knows a lot about the Reichsbanner. And then my sister Erna! I'm worried about her. She thinks she'll never get married, and she's sad about it."

Lene went on talking about her week, her studies at college, Olga and the baby, Inge and her family. When she stopped Karl suggested they go and have a look at his recent work. Lene saw the drawings he'd done of her and felt flattered. She didn't comment. Some pastels hung on the wall that were miniature explorations of townscapes. She pointed them out and expressed her admiration for them. They were by the window looking out. The blue hour emerged over the chimneys. Karl put his arm around Lene's waist and gave her a gentle hug. It felt so good in the blue light.

"Let's have something to eat and drink, shall we. You must be hungry."

He went into the kitchen and brought a glass of wine for them each. She was startled but tried not to show it. Wine! What would that do to her! Karl carried on bringing bits and pieces into the studio with him. A plate with cheese. Some biscuits. His slow movements made her feel calm, as if time and events didn't matter.

"To you and me, Lene! We've known each other nearly a year now!" Karl said and gave her a glass of red wine, lifting his to clink with hers.

"Yes, to you and me. I had no idea, it just shows you how fast the time is going. Is it really a year ago?"

"Yes, do you remember the miners' do? You came up to see my exhibition. You asked lots of interesting questions about the arts, politics, going on walks - you're quite an amazing person, Lene, and very special to me."

Lene swallowed hard to hide her rising nervousness again.

"I really like coming to see you, Karl. For some reason I love being surrounded by all that art and the art materials you have here. The smell of paper and inks, oils and pastels is a sort of magic. Are you going to do some drawing today?"

"Let me show you what I've been working on."

They walked along the length of the studio past the drawings he'd done of her. She felt flattered seeing herself there captured in a moment of her life, young and slender and full of vibrancy. Karl had recently worked on miniature townscapes, each a square of board neatly hung behind glass portraying the streets of Gelsenkirchen with its people. They were back by the window.

"The blue hour," Lene murmured, and Karl gently wrapped an arm around her waist and held her tight, which caused a searing warmth to run down her spine and belly.

"Look, the stars are coming out." He pointed at the sky and bent his head to kiss her neck. His long hair tickled her. He turned her towards him and his eyes seemed to sink into her face as he pressed his lips gently on hers. Against all her will to keep abreast of what was happening she felt swept away by a wave of longing. She responded to his kiss and felt his tongue seek out the shape of her mouth. They stumbled to the sofa. As if it was the most natural thing in the world they sank into each other's arms without ending the kiss. Everything went dark in Lene's head. Oblivion filled her brain. Time stood still. She felt Karl's hand cupping her breast through her silky blouse. She felt his lips on her neck. Her back arched in a surge of passion. She felt delirious and hardly noticed how he loosened the small straps on her red shoes and strip them off her feet. She felt his long artist's fingers caress her feet. She sighed with pleasure. How gentle he was! Something stirred her into thoughts and she wrestled from his embrace. They had some wine and cheese and chatted, both struggling with the inner vibrations that were shaking them.

"...my favourite colour? I don't know, I just love bright colours," she said, answering his question helplessly.

"The Bauhaus ones actually defined colours in terms of shapes, believe it or not. They asked students to put a shape to three key colours."

"What, and then they added up their views and came to a decision?"

"Funny, isn't it, you'd think a colour could be any shape, but it was part of their philosophy to define things."

His grey-green eyes smiled, and she noticed his lips were full and inviting. In the growing shadows of the evening the wine started to roll through her veins and fill her brain with a pleasant vagueness. In the middle of talking about shapes and colours Karl again turned to her and took her face in his hands and kissed her. Her lips burnt. A tram screeched and a dog barked. The outside world came back to her, and she smelt the soot in the air and heard a neighbour's door banging. She looked down at Karl. His head lay on her breast, his hair tussled and tickling her neck, his arms wrapped around her waist and bottom, and his legs twisted in and out with hers.

"What's the time, Karl? I've lost all sense of the outside world," she muttered. He turned his head and kissed her again, shutting the words in her mouth. "Just stay, can't you just stay here?" he murmured into her neck.

"I can't, really. I've got so much to do."

He embraced her as if to hold her tight and whispered words she didn't understand into her ear. She pulled herself away from him and stood up. "Give birth to a dancing star, that's what Nietzsche said. I feel like that now." She bent down and kissed him and went into the bathroom. She didn't take long. She had to catch the tram home. The family would be in bed asleep. Life outside the studio drifted back into her mind, as she tidied her hair. They kissed again and as she left they whispered to each other 'See you Saturday'.

The next week was packed so Lene had no time to think of Karl. College work had to be handed in. Hers was an essay on Hermann Vogeler. She had the bread deliveries to do, Erna to worry about, who kept wanting Lene to come and chat with her in her room. Susi had written to her about the next walk. Berlin flickered on and off in her mind, and she thought not now. She had a political meeting to attend, which she had agreed to do with Alfred and Margarethe Zingler. This was a discussion and planning meeting with the social democrats. The meeting had been called to analyse recent political events and plan how to take things forward in the light of rising unemployment. Within a year the unemployment figures had increased from zero to two million.

The meeting took place in the small hall of the 'August Bebel Haus'. The hall was packed. All the wooden chairs were occupied, many people were standing at the back. The entrance doors were all carefully watched. You had to. The sudden appearance of louts from the Wehrwolf or Stahlhelm or that party called NSDAP needed to be planned into every meeting these days. Lene sat with Margarethe. Alfred spoke.

"Comrades, it's important that we see the success we have had this year in the light of wider political and economic developments. One of the key events for us on the left has been the people's referendum on the expropriation of the Junkers in June this year. If our government had acted as they did in Austria, we could have finished with all these exploiters soon after our revolution. The Austrians took over all the landed property. Their National assembly voted in April 1919 almost unanimously for this, leaving only personal wealth in the hands of the aristocrats. We missed such an opportunity. The courts are staffed with people trained in the law of the monarchy. Many of them have never accepted the constitution of the Republic. They act as if nothing had changed. This is why for instance our valiant Herr Gumbel has found that most political murders of the post-war years were committed against the left, with few people ever having been tried and imprisoned for their deeds. We have conservative sociologists preaching at the universities. Unbelievably, they take their own views as gospel and complete truth."

There was a roar of laughter from the floor about Alfred's comment. Alfred stopped and then continued, when the noise had abated.

"One of these so-called sociologists is a man called Karl Mannheim. I wonder what his take home pay is for having such views. Of course, take home pay isn't part of his context!"

Another roar of laughter greeted Alfred's comment.

"But back to our lords and ladies! Hundreds of marks have been paid out over these last years to these exploiters. Every year the Hohenzollern receive 600,000 as compensation, the duke of Mecklenburg 400,000. And what do the working people get? Pennies, as you well know!"

Screams of anger and applause.

"You might remember that in May it was discovered that the lords of industry were plotting a right-wing takeover with their political friends. Back in 1923 that hero of the monopolising industry, Herr Thyssen gave the NSDAP 100,000 marks. Since then they haven't just been sitting on their backsides. One thing you can say for those chaps, they're busy! They're rearming Germany in secret. You mark my words! And it's contrary to the Versailles Treaty. They've formed secret companies to hide their activities. One of these companies is a clothing firm! They profess to sew folk costumes. Instead they are producing uniforms. Others produce weapons. These are the same people who campaign against our republican flag. The black, red and gold one from the revolution in 1848. They smuggle in the use of the monarchist flag. The black, red and white. Behind the flag, though, much bigger manoeuvres are going on."

Alfred stopped and had a drink of water before he continued. Expectant and serious faces sat waiting for him to speak. You could have heard a pin drop.

"You'll remember the Dawes Plan, but that has now been added to by the Locarno Plan, fixing the border with France, but not with the East. And that's the important thing. They want to keep their options open with no certainty about the eastern border. There's no doubt that both plans are intended to turn Germany into an economic bulwark against the Soviet Union. The money that America is pouring into our country beggars belief. The communists call it the Enslavement of Germany under American capital. Hundreds and thousands of dollars are flooded into Germany's private industry to fatten it up. Reparation payments are made to France and England, who in turn have to pay their debts back to the US. You can see the purpose of it all. The US is creating a bulwark against Bolshevism."

"This, comrades, is the environment in which our expropriation referendum took place. It was a massive success for socialists and communists. The revelations about the rearmament, secret deals in industry and rising unemployment stirred the people into action. You remember that 14.5 million people voted for the expropriation of the Junkers in June 1926."

Loud applause greeted Alfred's announcements. He continued:

"Take election results as a comparison. There have been no election results for any party that have reached such tremendous results so far. I'd like to suggest that this result is powerful and an indication of the democratic inclinations of our citizens. This should give us hope, comrades. I would like to conclude by saying that we need to build on the optimism and confidence that can be seen at the heart of this powerful vote for democracy. That in the end the vote was not turned into a reality, well we can thank the machinations that are currently going on in our ruling circles. As you know, they manufactured a tiny rule change, which then demanded that you had to have an absolute majority of 20 million to bring about the asked-for change."

A man stood up and asked to speak.

"Comrades, I do welcome our comrade Alfred's positive interpretation of the expropriation referendum, but let's not forget that there are people who try to turn vengeance into a virtue. I have here some newspaper extracts from the speeches and would like to read you this. A man called Pohl, by trade an apothecary addressed the crowds on 'Deutschlandtag' in August last year with these words: 'German women, German men, you, German Youth, dear Bismarck citizens! We have lived through the most powerful day in the history of Gelsenkirchen. On this unforgettable day, after the unbearable suffering of the two and half years of occupation and unspeakable suffering of our people, the French have finally left the holy ground of Westfalia.' I'll save your ears from the rest. But don't forget that the right-wing press keep harping on about the terrible deeds of the French."

Another man got up to speak.

"Comrades, our colleague here is right, I saw the march on the 'Deutschlandtag', and I heard the speeches. They went on and on about the French and stirred racist feelings. Only thirty odd houses had the black, red and white flag hanging out of their windows. Just thirty! And the crowd that had turned up for their special day was a miserable thousand. Now how many turned up for our Reichsbanner constitution day? Over 12,000!"

The man sat down to raving applause. There were noisy thanks for Alfred's informed speech, and the meeting was brought to a close with the singing of the Internationale.

CHAPTER 10

KINDERSPEISUNG NOT PANZERKREUZER

On the 20th May 1928 the people celebrated a huge victory. Crowds flocked to the Stadtpark, where stalls with sausages, potato salad, rolls and cakes attracted large queues. Tea, coffee and beer were on offer. The social democrats had achieved their best results yet, the NSDAP their worst. In order to find money for a huge rearmament programme to build an armoured cruiser the right-wing coalition had simply and cold-bloodedly cut the annual five million-mark food programme for malnourished school children. This news followed the failure to expropriate the Junkers in spite of a majority vote for it. These dismal events made excellent headlines and lent extra venom to the voices of the newspaper sellers.

"'Kinderspeisung statt Panzerkreuzer' (food for children instead of armoured cruiser)" shouted the newspaper boys. The comrades jostled each other, embraced and chatted happily in the lush spring green of the Stadtpark after the election results had been announced. Musicians were quick to pick up jolly tunes and cash in on the good mood.

"We've taught them a lesson, those warmongers, what would you be producing an armoured cruiser for unless you intended to go to war?" was Emil's comment. Hat pushed back on his head, his thick hair sticking out, his eyes had a laughing and happy appearance today.

"A great result, but don't think the military will just accept it..."

"Oh c'mon, let's celebrate today, we've got the majority, and that's excellent news. They have to listen to the left now. You've got to believe in the democracy we have now, otherwise you play into the hands of the cynics and reactionaries."

Rudi, Emil's mate Rudolf, always had a positive view on things, and he was right in a way. You could get too pessimistic and harbour conspiracy theories in your head, until you felt paranoid about every footstep behind you. Still, you shouldn't underestimate the powers pitted against working people.

The miners from the Dahlbusch mine were conferring with each other, when Friedrich and his girlfriend Wanda turned up with Paul. Sausages with mustard in a roll in one hand and a glass of beer in the other. They pricked their ears, always keen on political debate.

"The only problem is that the democracy we have now has as many holes as a Swiss cheese. We can believe in the constitution as much as we want. The army, the Junkers from the Elbe, the industrialists, they have the rich backers. We don't," Emil retorted.

They exchanged greetings and for a moment the talk went over to more mundane issues about the quality of the beer, the sodden grass they stood on and the best place to get a good piece of meat. But Paul couldn't leave it there. His pancake- shaped face shone with the pleasure of the success.

"Comrades, we've got a success story! The social democrats at 29.8% and us communists at over 10%. That's a fantastic result! But think of our enemies for a moment! We're still in deep trouble. A different set of parties in our government every year since 1919. There are over twenty parties. They make the government fall over minute disagreements – and the social democrats are not without blame in this direction. And then we got the new floating voters of office clerks."

Friedrich wiped the beer foam from his mouth and added:

"Add to that the unemployed at about 18%. Don't think for one minute that unemployed families vote for revolutionary change. They want stability, food in their mouths and jobs, and they'll listen to anyone who promises to give them that."

"Look at the success of the communists! It shows that people are beginning to understand that the social democrats can't deliver on their promises or haven't got the guts to stand up for their convictions."

"But it's only 10%, Paul! You can't change society with 10%, especially when you've got enemies the size of the Thyssen's steel bosses to face up to."

"Guys, let's have a bit of fun before we all get morose again. Look, here come the Zinglers and Lene." Wanda turned and pointed in the direction of the park entrance.

"What an excellent day, we're going to have a social democrat as chancellor for the first time in eight years," said Alfred. He was always the man to look confidently and positively into the future.

"Yes, as long as the nationalists don't pull the rug from under his feet. I bet you they'll try their hardest," insisted Wanda.

"Well, not just the nationalists. It'll be the army and industry who will intervene to rescue their programmes. Remember, they've lived it up on American money which is paying secretly for rearmament programmes amongst other things."

They strolled over to the beer tent. With a glass of beer in each hand they wandered along the tables with fancy goods or food and ended up by a book stall. Wanda picked up a small magazine called 'Der Uhu' and showed it to Lene.

"Look, you'll find this interesting, Lene, if you haven't seen it before. See, it has Kurt Tucholsky, he's a good one to read. Such a funny but politically sharp poet. Here, look at this! He said in 1922: 'The German political murders of the past four years are tightly organised - with incentives from anonymous backers - they always kill from behind - sloppy investigations - lenient punishments - suspension of sentences. That is not bad justice. That is not poor justice. That is no justice at all."

"Do you want the Uhu? I'll get it for you. How much is the Uhu?" Wanda asked and paid for it.

She handed Lene the journal. Within moments Wanda had found another journal that she seemed to know well. She looked at Lene warmly and smiled.

"Friedrich, come and have a look! Here's that John Heartfield on the front of the 'Arbeiter Illustrierte Zeitung'. He produces some great photo montages."

Friedrich and Alfred turned round to look at the AIZ, as it was called. "Willi Münzenberg's creation. Yes, let's get one of those, he's one of ours." "I'm having one as well. He's a remarkable man, an example to us all, such energy. I don't know how he does it. He's everywhere, running a business that actually makes money, working for the Comintern, running magazines, he's a communist hero of mine," was Alfred's comment. Not that Alfred was much different, thought Friedrich.

"You're pretty much like him, Alfred," he said. "You organise events, direct plays and write them, hold public meetings and generally carry our cultural life on your shoulders."

"Well, I'm trying to do my bit, but Willi is something else, he's a powerhouse for socialism." Under their weathered workers' caps, one tall, the other slight, they had broad but conspiratorial grins on their faces. The sense of having a shared vision shone in their confident eyes. Thinking of Willi and the radical left literature warmed their hearts. Laughing and chatting they wandered between the tables with beer glasses and the laden book stall. The sun shone in the clear blue sky. Children ran and played with balloons and hoops.

Lene rang Inge's doorbell. Inge hugged Lene on the doorstep.

"My mother's on the mend, isn't that wonderful?"

Lene looked at Inge's tired, pale face and the shadows under her eyes, but saw that she was smiling.

"I'm so glad, Inge, what a relief."

They went to sit down in the kitchen, and Inge brewed some tea.

"She's on the mend, but needs to stay in bed resting for at least another two weeks, the doctor says. So I have to do all the work, get the boys ready for school, do all the cleaning and tidy up after Emil's political meetings.

"Are you still infatuated?"

"Don't ask, Inge! I am, and I'm enjoying it, but you're the only one I talk to about it and that isn't easy."

"You're telling me! Who do you think I've got to talk to about the worry and tedium of minding a sick mother and a household with three men?"

"I'm sorry, I must seem so egotistical to you with my love affair."

"No, no don't apologise, Lene, it's life. You happened to come across a love affair, while I came across my mother falling ill. It's not your fault, it's nobody's fault. She's doing better though, so at least my efforts are rewarded."

"In fact, it's not all rosy at home either. My father is getting quite weak and needs to rest his leg every night. It swells up badly. But the other thing that's happening is the visit to Worpswede. That's really what I wanted to ask you, whether you'd be able to come. Oh do, Inge, it would be a good break for you and such fun to go together."

"I can't, Lene. Really, it's impossible. If I took even just a morning off, the household would fall apart and my mother, well I need to take her drinks all day, Wash her, make her get up for a bit, help her dress, do her hair..."

"I understand, of course, she still needs you badly. She's lucky she's got you, Inge, you're a good daughter to her."

These words were like balm to Inge's heart. No one had said anything like that to her, and she had worried so much that she wasn't doing a good enough job. She looked gratefully at Lene.

"Thanks, Lene, I needed those words, funny how no one thinks of saying something supportive. You're the only one."

They hugged and Lene left with her heart full of sadness for her friend. Back at home Lene noticed the intensity of her mother's sandalwood smell which put her on her guard. Worry and stress always made her mother use an extra dose of her perfume. She found her mother and father in the lounge. Hermann had a thick white bandage around his leg.

"Your father has had a blood clot, Lene, he's just back from hospital."

Somehow Mathilde always managed to look serene, even at this moment. She was calm and a small tired smile flickered over her silky skin that seemed to express something like 'Lene, this is life, and we have to bear it with grace.' The other event that caused Mathilde much stress was Hilde's pregnancy, which did at last happen. When her mother found out that Hilde was pregnant, she showed agitation for the first time in her life. The sandalwood smell hung about the lounge and her mother's bedroom like a cloud. That was when Lene was sure her mother used the smell to reduce feelings of stress and anxiety. A grandchild was going to be born! Would it go well? Was Hilde doing too much hard work? Did her husband care enough for her? Would there be problems during the pregnancy? Her mother's worries were quite out of character, Lene thought. Mathilde took to visiting her oldest daughter almost daily to help. She seemed not to trust Fritz all that much. There were even arguments in the evening about this, and Hermann urged his wife to calm herself and stop worrying. Yet finally a little girl was born. Mathilde was overjoyed. Every evening some knitting of a little jacket, a hat or tiny shoes occupied her. The smell of sandalwood subsided. For a while the talk in the lounge almost only focused on nappy rash, diarrhoea, a first smile, a runny nose and the mother's tiredness.

This summer, with Alfred's encouragement the Volksbühne theatre decided to put on a show of Bertolt Brecht's new play 'Threepenny opera'. Alfred never tired of telling people that socialism wasn't just about better wages and shorter working hours, but also needed to include cultural and creative activities during leisure time. Lene hurried to the theatre in the afternoons, and often stood with Margarethe on the stage discussing the stage design and the costumes with the performers. When she arrived that afternoon she could hear the noise of arguments, shouting and urgent footsteps rushing hither and thither. The actress Katharina was to be Polly Peachum and she was furious. She didn't like her dress. She looked sullen and was smoking one cigarette after another.

"You can forget about me being in this show if you don't get this dress sorted out. It's frumpy and baggy, it's hanging around my waist like a bag. How can I look wild and sexy with that?"

The other actors looked fed up and bored. Maybe this was just one tantrum too many.

"My sister Erna is good at sewing, I'm sure she'd do the trick with the dress. Shall I take it with me tonight?"

"That'll be great, Lene," Margarethe called out with relief. "Lene, sweetie, can you ask your sister for us? The show must go on."

They decided that it was best if Lene took the dress home with her immediately. When she told Erna that the theatre director was begging her to make the dress more interesting and lively for the production, she was beside herself with pride and joy. Both sisters dug through the materials in Erna's chest of drawer to find suitable lace and silk with which Erna could add a bit of magic to the dress. She didn't scratch her wrists once during the work.

It was July when the performances were due to commence. The Volksbuehne was flooded with demands for tickets. Crowds queued and jostled outside the box office. Olga and Lene walked arm in arm.

"My first day out to enjoy myself! I can't believe it, Lene, that we're here together and going to the theatre. To be honest, I never thought I'd recover from that depression, but here I am!"

Lene pressed Olga's arm with joy in her heart.

"It's fantastic, I'm so thrilled. It's good of your mother to let you come to the theatre. She really is a very generous and kind woman."

Olga was almost back to her old shape and the popular fashion of loose dresses helped to hide the extra weight she still had. They sat in the stalls. The lights faded and the first songs caused shivers down their backs. The performance was stunning. Polly Peachum wore her gipsy dress. How outrageous was that Macky Messer! All those women after him, unbelievable! And he was in with the police. That was London for you! So many beggars! Corruption, criminals hand in glove with the police. Was Berlin perhaps the same?

The chatted and chatted all the way home and couldn't get enough of talking about everything. As they walked home together, Lene told Olga about Karl. Olga was stunned.

"You have a secret affair, and you didn't tell anyone?"

"Well, yes, but only one close friend."

"I couldn't," Olga said, "I just have to blabber about things. Maybe that's my mistake. Then I always drag people into my affairs. You're so clever, Lene. How do you get away with it? What will happen? Are you going to marry him?"

"I always think I've got to be careful, otherwise someone is going to mess up my plans. It's not really about marrying. He's older, anyway. Also I still want to do so much, before I get married." She didn't know how to describe the confused mixture of feelings she had.

"You are a one! You're not going to make my mistake, are you? Getting married as soon as you fancy someone! If I hadn't been so stupid to fall for that Hubert...but who knows. I might still get somewhere." Lene watched Olga with hope in her heart. She wished so much for Olga to be ambitious and that the old dream of them both being creative would come true. Olga continued.

"Yes, you were always that way, Lene. You're a very strong person. You're one of those women's rights people. Like Rosa Luxemburg. She was a revolutionary and see what happened to her. She got murdered. Lene, be careful! You also do politics. I don't want to lose you. They pick people up and they just disappear." Lene was so touched by Olga's words. She knew Olga cared about her, even if her words came out in a bit of a muddle. Olga did have similar desires to hers, she knew that, and she was very fond of her.

"Thanks for worrying about me, Olga. I've got to act, it's sort of in my blood, I just have to get involved."

They hugged and said goodbye outside Olga's house. Lene had walked her home and then went back to her own house. Everyone was asleep when she got in. Upstairs Lene drew the curtains after looking at the coal trolleys. She sighed. She wished she knew how her life was going to be. The coal trolleys travelled silently. She opened the window and breathed the air. An owl hooted. Didn't Olga have something wonderful, a child who she had to take care of? A child can make you forget the difficult times you live in, because you're busy taking care of someone who is helpless. I have to choose to be busy and work hard...so I suppose I have that freedom...her thoughts trailed off as she watched the bright moon. It was low in the sky, sinking into one of those chimneys in front of her.

Interior Minister Severing finally concluded a deal with the employers, giving in to their demands. The industrialists sensed success was theirs. The Zentrum party slipped to the right with Ludwig Kaas as the new leader, mirroring events in Austria. There a Catholic called Ignaz Seipel had formed an 'anti-Marxist' unity list. With loud proclamations the 'Vienna tax Bolshevism' was condemned. It consisted of a proposal to build social housing and offer welfare support for workers and their families. The holy order based on God's will rather than the will of the people was being rebuilt.

Alfred agreed to speak on the subject of a United Front for socialists. A heavy patrol of young men stood guard outside the offices. It was a cold November, and frozen snow filled the sides of the pavements. Stresemann's Young Plan was occupying all the headlines. It clarified the reparations payments. The nationalists had a field day! Open quarrels broke out between communists and social democrats over this issue. Was the Young Plan a good thing or not? Lene joined her comrades at the August Bebel House.

"The enemy is powerful! We must not underestimate them. We all know that the Nazis only gained two and a half percent in last year's election, but don't forget who is paying for them: the electric company boss Albert Pietzsch, Fritz Thyssen, Ernst von Borsig, just to name a few. Our poet Bertolt Brecht said about them: 'Everyone knows that the crimes of the rich are hidden and protected more by their perceived improbability than anything else. The politicians can only get away with it because one imagines their corruption to be more refined and delicate than it is."

Alfred wanted to continue, but heckles from the floor interrupted him. Several lads stood up and argued noisily.

"Fine business, working together, but we don't share your point of view, comrade. Look at the Young Plan Stresemann has just agreed. The working class is supposed to pay for the war for another fifty-nine years! How can you support such measures?"

"It's all very well quoting our poets, but we need action to stop the Young Plan now."

Another called out 'What unity, if we don't agree?' but was told to be quiet.

There were a number of others who seemed unsettled. Alfred must have thought it best in the situation to address the issues raised straight away to calm the mood down.

"The Young Plan, comrades, is not a social democratic piece of work, as you know. The way I see it it's not our biggest problem. It is reducing our present payments on reparations. That's important for the working classes in the here and now. Also, think about it. You don't want to get into a campaign about it, otherwise you'll be siding with the National Socialists."

There were boos and shouts from the floor.

"As I said, it's not our biggest problem. A good aspect about it is that we'll pay less than now, something like two million instead of two and a half million per year and we'll have control of the Reichsbahn again. That business about fifty-nine years, well, which of you believes that that's of immediate importance to us now?"

More objections came from the floor, especially when Alfred pointed out:

"Comrades, let's not confuse the working class! If socialists join the Nazis in their condemnation of the plan we will confuse them. Our demands must be different from those of the NSDAP. Why do you think they named themselves so similar to us? They want a mix up. All their policies are a confused bunch of slogans aimed at muddling things up. They aim to confuse people."

Alfred's wise words fell on deaf ears this time. Several people shouted at each other. The meeting did not calm down until a speaker from the communist party went to the podium and urged comrades to be prepared to receive their fellow socialists with politeness and interest. However, many people didn't feel like listening any more and began to walk out.

"A bit of a mess, isn't it," Lene said to Margarethe. Margarethe thought it was quite serious that there was so little patience from comrades.

At home Lene joined the others in the lounge. She was feeling anxious about her father.

"How are you, father?" Her father was resting his leg on a stool and was reading 'der Volkswille'. He looked up and instead of answering asked Lene about the meeting.

"It was a bit of a mess, father. You know Alfred spoke about the Young Plan and how we needed to be united with the communists to make a united front. Of course they're against it, so are the Nazis, and he said that is confusing for people. I thought he made a good point, but people didn't hear him out. They kept interrupting him and shouting. Many people left early, so did I. Not a good meeting at all. It makes you wonder how we can work together across the..."

"That's not good news, Lene, it's exactly what we don't need, people splitting over minor issues. We've got such huge problems coming our way. I always thought that the defence of the constitution was one key issue and joining forces with the communists another one, as you know, Lene." He sighed.

Lene looked at him. How old he looked suddenly, or was it the light? She felt a stab in the stomach. Her father had sunk into his chair, as if his bones had shrivelled. His skin looked sallow, his hair was quite thin now. She could see his scalp. She noticed that he must have lost weight. He looked a worn-out old man, but his spirits were still lively. She wanted to say something, but couldn't. The words got stuck in her throat and behind her eyes and blocked her tears. Maybe it's just me, she thought, as no one else seemed to take any particular notice. There was more chatter. Mathilde talked about Hilde's baby and what a good job she was doing. Young Hermann and Hans debated bakery problems and whether the apprentice Johnny should be sent back to London. Erna was painting a face on a new wooden doll. It was reassuring that some things never changed.

Political events seemed to speed up. Stresemann died on the 3rd October. A mob of intriguers threatened the social-democrat-led Mueller government from all sides. The air was thick with conspiracies real and invented. They were like drugs that the people consumed, as the news was screamed out from street corners. What was right, what was wrong, who to turn to, when the governing parties had so little control? Late in October the American property bubble burst and the flow of easy short-term credits suddenly ceased. The government coffers emptied and payments for the growing number of unemployed were stalled. Newspaper boys shouted themselves hoarse. The streets were ringing with shock announcements.

"Wall Street Crash, read all about it!"

"The banks are losing millions! Banker jumped to his death over Crash!"

Citizens gaped at headline displays. The newspaper boys yelled. Dogs urinated on lamp-posts. Soapy rain, sour soot and sodden leaves mingled on the pavements and made them slippery. Local folk rushed dabbing greetings into the cold air like brush strokes of paint. They had to go on. They had to believe in each other. The bonds of solidarity were the one thing they could rely on. But betrayal was lurking and could be smelt like a rotting cadaver.

The final days of October were filled with pain and sadness in the Deppermann household. Hermann's ailments were increasingly weakening him, until one day he didn't get out of bed any more. He complained of aches and being unable to stand up on his legs. He didn't want to eat. His wife, Lene and Erna kept a constant vigil at his bedside. The hospital was suggested, but he refused. He accepted pain killers. He insisted he was going to stay at home. Mathilde gently urged him to accept treatment, but it was useless. As they kept watch they felt that he was preparing to die. He wanted to be in the circle of his family. They read to him. They made him tea, They played him his favourite possession, the radio. His friend Friedrich came and spoke about the dangers in the political developments.

Hermann quietly accepted all the offerings with a small smile on his thin lips. His round eyes developed a dark fire in them. He watched them and held Mathilde's hand. On the 16th November Hermann passed away in his sleep.

The household became silent and filled with tears. When they saw each other they held handkerchiefs in front of their faces, sniffing and sobbing. Around the kitchen table, in the lounge, in the bakery, his huge and caring presence was now felt like never before. Without him it was a different house, a different family, a different life. The misery of his death overwhelmed Lene. She had so loved her father, always looked up to him. He had been her guide in her politics, her actions, her beliefs. She felt a huge hole inside her and thought it could never be filled. Nothing else was important, all her work, her meetings, her friendships paled away against this loss. How could the coal trolleys carry on moving through the night, when death had come to her family? She was surprised how calm her mother stayed. Only the pungent sandalwood smell told her what she must be going through.

CHAPTER 11

THE CHARITE

After another public meeting Lene, Inge and Margarethe went for a cup of coffee in a nearby cafe. Inge and Margarethe knew about Lene's state of mind. She looked drawn and pale. They knew that she had thrown herself into more work since her father's death and she looked exhausted. Margarethe came straight to the point.

"Lene, you look under the weather, why don't you try a change of scene?"

Inge watched Lene and asked her about the bakery and her mother.

"Do you still have to work in the bakery? Surely you have your brother. He must be in charge now, and he has your mother. She's still strong, isn't she?"

"Yes, young Hermann is running the bakery, and my mother continues to do all the administration. It's going reasonably well..." She hesitated and tugged on her hair at the back of her head, then added, "I've got to be honest, I resent the bakery right now and I wish I could get out of it."

"Look, you're being used, Lene. I want to be quite honest. They use you as cheap labour. You need to learn a profession. It would get you out of the bakery, out of the place where your father died. You need to move on, I think. Don't you agree, Inge?"

Their cups of coffee arrived, and the three women busied themselves with pouring it and adding milk and sugar. The little spoons clinked in the cups.

"I agree," Inge added. "In a way it doesn't matter what you study as long as it's useful, so that you can get work with it..."

"Get out of this town for a while. How about Berlin. You did say you'd like to go there, didn't you?"

Lene looked up. She felt bewildered. How well her friends knew her. For a moment she felt spied upon.

"Yes, I would like to go to Berlin. I always did, I told my father that as well."

"So, we'll try and get you to Berlin," Margarethe said firmly, relief lighting up her face. "I've got an idea. I have a friend whose daughter studied with a professor called Sauerbruch at the Charite, the big hospital in Berlin. I could ask her to give me some details."

Inge and Margarethe looked at Lene's face to see if she might like that idea. They saw that she looked less miserable.

"Just let me have details of what you've learnt already and I'll send it on to them."

"Lene is a fantastic student. We studied together at college in Darmstadt and in school," Inge added.

After Margarethe had gone Inge and Lene carried on chatting.

"I would like to live somewhere else as well, but I know I have to stay with my mother. Also I'm going out with Uwe now. You know him, he's a friend of Emil's. We might get married and maybe have children. He's sorted of hinted at it." Inge laughed.

Lene's eyes glazed over. Another friend who's going to have a child! Pain rippled through her stomach. Inge saw Lene's absent-minded look, but put it down to the confused state she was in. They chatted for a while about the dire state of politics and how difficult it was to create Alfred's dream of a United Front and then left.

Within a week or so Lene had heard from Margarethe. Lene had an offer of attending a course in physiotherapy. She accepted it immediately. There were some arguments in the Deppermann household. Sandalwood smells emerged.

"How did you get the idea to go to Berlin? It's such a big city and so far away from us," her mother asked.

"That's true, but they need physiotherapists in Berlin. And I'll be able to earn my own living. Here you have two baker sons and one of them is able to run the bakery very well, aren't you, Hermann?"

"Lene, you must do as you wish. We can't stop you. I'll miss you, but you don't need to worry about the bakery, that's for sure," was young Hermann's reply. He looked self-assured and she hadn't expected him to say anything else. He was always kind and caring and had respect for other people's points of view.

"Physiotherapy!" sneered Hans in a different tone. "What's that, then? I've never heard of it. Why don't you study medicine, isn't that more useful?"

"Actually Physio is a part of medicine and can be used to help people through exercise who have been injured and get them fit again. It's quite practical," Lene explained, ignoring his teasing tone.

When Lene looked at Erna she saw that her older sister had tears streaming down her face without her making a sound. Lene rushed over and hugged Erna who was now sniffing audibly and scratching her wrists. Lene took Erna's hand and held it in hers and pressed her cheek to her sister's.

"Don't cry, dear Erna, you'll make us all upset. I won't disappear, it's just a couple of years of study, then I'll be back."

"I shall miss you so much, my baby, you're my favourite. What shall I do without you here?" Erna was inconsolable.

Lene beckoned her to come and go to her room together. They left the lounge and went to Erna's room. Mathilde nodded to Lene to indicate she agreed they should go upstairs to Erna's room. Erna flooded into tears now. They sat down on her bed, and Lene spoke quietly to reassure her.

The departure date was only a few days away. Lene went to say goodbye to Karl. She felt sad but calm and happy and Karl even found opportunities to make light of her departure and give her cuddles. She could feel he was sad too, but he didn't complain. He held her in his arms for a long time. They stood at the large window overlooking the town.

It was a Wednesday when she had to catch the train. Lene was surrounded by her family in the station. Inge came and stood with them. She had already said goodbye to Olga. She was surprised that even Thilde turned up briefly.

"Lene, be careful! There's a lot of trouble in Berlin. You've got to expect it and make sure you are safe. Don't go walking in the streets on your own!"

Margarethe and Wanda also turned up and waved to Lene from the stairs leading down to the platform. The women hugged, laughed with joy and promised to write. "I'll miss you, have a fabulous time in Berlin, you lucky thing!" were Wanda's words. Hermann and Hans stood arm in arm with their mother. The locomotive pulled into the station with a roar and a whistle. The steam flooded the hall momentarily and all held handkerchiefs over their mouths. The engine came to a halt. There was much rushing, shouting and running up and down the platform.

"Here's your seat, give me the bags!"

"Let me help you up."

"This is the compartment. I wonder who's travelling with you."

"Do take care, won't you."

Everyone was helpful, nervous and excited. One last hug and a kiss for her mother. Then they all stood on the platform with their handkerchiefs ready for waving. The last she saw of them were their handkerchiefs fluttering in the steam, as if they were seagulls caught in a storm.

Steam puffs rose into the sky as the train ploughed through the countryside with stops at places with evocative names: Hannover, Braunschweig and Magdeburg, where it crossed the river Elbe. It grew dark and the distant street lights flickered. At 21.45 the train pulled into Berlin Hauptbahnhof filling the voluminous hall with billows of steam. Lene made her way to the student accommodation. Luckily the directions to get there were very clear. She was handed a key, and after a short while she sank worn out on to a narrow metal bedstead, breathing a deep sigh when she smelt the fresh linen.

At eight o'clock in the morning she found herself in the lobby of the student hostel with three young women and a young man who were all eyeing each other furtively. Lene introduced herself to a young woman standing next to her who looked shy and anxious. She found out that she was called Annegret and came from the Rheinland. They had hardly any time to begin a conversation, when a woman dressed in a smart suit showed up and exchanged a jovial greeting with the orange-haired concierge who appeared to be called Mamsell Napoleon. The suited lady was Fräulein Ute Meier, Professor Sauerbruch's personal assistant. She addressed the waiting group.

"Welcome and good morning, ladies and gentlemen! I'm glad you've all managed to get here on time. Let me introduce myself. I am Fräulein Ute Meier. I'm responsible for recruitment and administration for our students. I'm going to take you over to our seminar room and library now, where we will all introduce ourselves, and then I shall inform you about the study routines here at the Charite."

Fräulein Meier pulled her red and blue silk scarf straight and tucked it back into her jacket, turned and left after waving a greeting to Mamsell. Her auburn hair was short and curly. She led them through an impressive entrance portal and a grand lobby along a narrow corridor to a small auditorium with raked seating so that everyone could see the speaker easily.

"Do take a seat. After our introductions I shall give you a brief history of the Charite. That will be followed by tea and coffee and a visit to the library."

The students introduced themselves in turn. Annegret came from a small town by the Rhine and a large lady was called Hannelore. She came from Lübeck and had already worked as a nurse without finishing her training. She wanted to complete it now. The swarthy not so young man with short cropped dark blonde hair and a moustache had come from Munich. He was called Wolfgang. He treated everyone to a long speech about his experience in the war and how Germany needed to get itself sorted out, there was just too much politics and he wanted to do something practical now. Lene wasn't sure what he was talking about. The taller of the young women was called Heidi. She looked sporty with noticeable calf muscles. She was from Berlin and had short blonde hair. The last of the three other women was a slightly older looking auburn lady with her hair loosely held in a knot, a bit like Erna. She had a deep voice, so that they looked with surprise at her expecting her to look like a man. She said she was called Lieselotte. She was also from Berlin. Fräulein Meier listened attentively to each of their stories and then moved on to tell the history of the Charite.

"The Charite was established in 1710 by King Frederick I of Prussia just north of the city walls. At that time bubonic plague was devastating towns and villages in the nearby countryside, and he feared it was going to reach Berlin. However, thankfully, it did not, so the new building was made available to the poor, unmarried mothers, prostitutes, alcoholics and the like. In 1810 the Humboldt University was built, and the Charite was integrated with the university. Since then we've been extending our study courses into many directions and are proud to say that the Charite is one of the most distinguished university hospitals in Germany and maybe in Europe. We are proud to be able to offer the best training for students who are diligent and willing to put in hard work and study. At the end of your first week a reception is held for all our newcomers. You mustn't miss it, because you'll have a chance to meet all our professors, colleagues and other new students."

Tea and coffee was on offer a while later in a student canteen on the top floor. With a coffee in her hands, the like of which she'd never had before, Lene marvelled at the view of Berlin. This was really her first glimpse, as it had been dark when she'd arrived during the night. Fräulein Meier took them on a tour of the library, study rooms, lecture halls and the different departments. The students were handed their timetables. The nurses' course had a number of overlapping sessions with those for physiotherapy. Fräulein Meier, tugging on her blue and red scarf, explained the canteen rules to them.

"You need a pass to get anywhere," she said. "You won't get a single potato in the canteen without your pass, or be able to take out a book in the library. If I were you I'd keep the pass on you all the time, because some of the teachers are fussy and might not let you in the lecture hall if you can't identify yourself. That's the Prussians for you," she added with a smirk. She pulled up her eyebrows as she said so and looked sharply around the group in front of her.

Lene saw Annegret later at the student hostel, and they spontaneously decided to take a stroll around the famous Alexanderplatz. Lene recalled Susie's stories and wished she'd had time to get in touch with her and find out where her friend lived. The big city with its potential adventures had a soothing effect on her recent woes about her father's death. They both looked in awe. The grey and rough shabbiness of it all took their breath away. The buildings stood like forlorn, neglected stone monuments in the midst of a shifting and swaying throng of people, forever on the move. A dishevelled man with a limp and a torn coat approached them and asked for money. Another younger man with a hat covering his hair bumped into the limping one and started cursing loudly. The two women walked on stiffly and fearfully without saying a word.

"Hold on tight to your bag, Annegret, there are probably a lot of thieves here. Let's walk quickly," Lene whispered, as they tried to move past a group that had collected outside a pawnbroker's. The smells, screeching of brakes, horns clanging and yelling of newspaper boys were intoxicating. Automobiles, coaches, cyclists, pedestrians, fine ladies and rough looking ones, gentlemen with bowler hats and umbrellas filled the plaza. Drunken men barely able to stand on their feet lolled by a newspaper stall, arguing loudly about the rights and wrongs of government decrees. Ownerless dogs sniffed urine on lamp-posts and trees and left their own messages. People with carts called out whatever goods they happened to offer:

"Buttons! Buy your perfumed sweets here! Ladies, we sell panties and suspender belts in pretty colours!"

The sausage stand looked appealing. The smell from the onions was pungent, but the sizzling brown 'Bratwursts' were too tempting to their empty stomachs. Their hunger was suddenly overwhelming. They stood with a piece of hot sausage with a wodge of mustard in their mouths.

"Delicious! Eating in the street is what my mother always said you never ought to do as a well brought up girl, but here we can enjoy it," she said to Annegret.

"Me too, I've never eaten food out of my hand into my mouth. It's coarse, my mother told me."

Not only had they eaten their first hand to mouth sausage in the street, they then entered a small bar in a side street of Alex and ordered two glasses of beer. "Never had beer in my life, wine yes, but not beer."

"We had neither wine nor beer in the Deppermann household to my knowledge. Peppermint tea was the staple." Lene did not mention the secret wine she had with Karl.

It was such a strange feeling to cross these boundaries of their protected childhood and youth that they looked about themselves to see if anyone might point their finger and accuse them of misbehaving. But no one bothered to even notice. The people there were mainly as young as they were, and preoccupied with themselves. They clinked glasses.

"Here's to our Berlin studies, Lene, do call me Anni. That's what my family call me."

"Yes, here's to our studies, Anni. It's great to have a pal straightaway. It makes it less lonely, being far away from my family."

After their first night in Berlin the weeks raced by once they got into their routines. Statuesque Mamsell Napoleon at the student hostel kept order. She had a sharp eye for bad behaviour and could tell people off as if they were school children. But they also found out that she had a heart of gold and would help by making hot tea, if one of her 'children' as she called them was cold, hungry or tired.

Lene spent a lot of the time with a physiotherapist called Gustave. Her huge hips and behind wobbled sideways and her strong bulky arms made her look like a boxer. Will I get arms like her, Lene wondered. Gustave was a jolly fortyish woman who joked about her asthmatic husband who was a smoker. She told Lene how she often just about rescued him from drowning in his own phlegm, and wondered if she should maybe let him be. Lene was shocked by such cold-hearted comments. The students followed her wobbly bottom into the hospital rooms, both female and male ones and examined the ones who needed physiotherapy for broken legs, arms, pelvis, or who were recovering from diseases of the lung.

Gustave had an easy and witty manner with the patients, which Lene thought sometimes bordered on coldness. It made her cringe at times. There was an old man who could hardly breathe because his chest rattled like dried peas in a box. Gustave walked up to his bed, and called out:

"August, wake up, time to stop rattling, I'm going to use the sucking machine. Oh, you do look a bit under the weather today, didn't your favourite nurse bring you some breakfast?"

With those words, she told Lene to pull the curtain around his bed saying "You don't mind another pretty young thing assisting me, do you? Always happy for another female to pay attention to you, aren't you?"

Lene smiled a greeting, pulled the curtain shut, tried to ignore the awful rattling and held the instruments ready for Gustave to use them. It was hard not to feel sick. She had to swallow several times and control her thoughts. Think of nothing, she kept saying to herself, trying to ignore the painful procedure of relieving the sick man of his congestion. A lot of her work consisted of holding instruments ready for Gustave, but at other times she observed her making a diagnosis by talking to patients and watching her while she felt collarbones, vertebrae, knee joints, ankles and wrists. The human body became a skeleton for her with muscles attached that pulled and pushed bones. She became aware of postures, slumped creatures, humped ones, one-legged, one-armed, ones in wheelchairs. How much there was that could go wrong! It was surprising so many people managed to stay upright and mobile, especially when you saw the drinking and smoking that was going on. At every street corner groups of smokers discussed the evil ways of the world and spat on the pavement to make their point.

Gustave had to be dealt with carefully, Lene decided. In the third week she suddenly turned on Lene who stood behind her and shouted:

"Are you with me or in a dream world of your own? I told you to go to the medicine cupboard and get some elastic bandages. I can't afford to have people's attention drifting in this work, dear."

"Sorry, Gustave, I was looking at the woman coming towards us on crutches."

"No excuses, I can see you're a bit of a dreamer. Now don't take it to heart, I've got to train you. You hear me. Otherwise I'll lose my job and I've got children to feed."

Lene was impressed with her matter-of-fact way of looking at her job. She didn't hold big idealistic visions in her mind like Lene. Instead, she saw work as a necessity of life. Lene found out more at coffee break. Gustave was her jolly self again and chatted about her husband.

"He's a useless work-shy scumbag. And my three children? Well, I bring them up pretty much by myself. The courtyard where we live and they play, when I'm out at work, it's full of dogs, drunks and beggars. It's not a pretty life you've come to see here, I'm telling you. We're at the end in Berlin! You watch, there'll be more trouble soon, because it can't go on as it is. There's too many of them have become unemployed and that gives them bad ideas. Too much time to waste. Fights and street brawls almost every night somewhere and people end up in hospital and need to be patched up by a surgeon. They've got more than enough to do. What on earth made you want to come to Berlin?"

"I needed to get away from my mother's bakery and get myself a profession. I want to be able to earn my own living. Also I wanted to come and be in Berlin. Get to know it. I have a friend who told me lots about it."

"Very honourable of you, too many of them hang around and just look for a guy to hang on to and marry. And then there are babies to look after and the guy leaves them. It's a shambles! Those poor sods, not enough to eat, their mother goes out to snare woodcock, because the bugger left her."

It was a busy schedule for them. During the day practical work and some lectures, and most evenings Lene had to study, which she didn't mind. There was comfort in others being in the same position, and they all shared the kitchen. Mamsell Napoleon, her hair from time to time more orange than a carrot, had to rebuke them. She liked perfect order and cleanliness in the kitchen and would threaten them with fines, but it never came to that. Lene often cleared up just to make sure Mamsell didn't get annoyed with the students. Anni also shared that sense of responsibility, but a lot of the others did not. They also often seemed to have friends round in their rooms, which was not permitted after ten o'clock. You could hear music and laughter. You could hear other noises too. The beds were squeaky. In the mornings grey tussled figures in dressing gowns made their way to the toilet or bathroom. Sometimes you could hear weeping.

Lene and Anni both worked hard, but from time to time they enjoyed the offerings of Berlin that Lene had been so keen so find out about. They went to the Schiffsbauer Damm theatre, where the writer Bertolt Brecht had his plays and looked with curiosity at the advertisements and photos. On the advertising hoardings were colourful posters with words they had never seen, like surrealism and expressionism. Anni was a dear girl, and Lene became very fond of her. She was clever and quiet, but she could ask sudden unexpected questions, like 'Did your mother and father sleep with each other after they'd produced all their children?' How did Lene know, she'd never asked them. Certainly her mother was not too old to have more babies, so did they stop having sex? Anni also made jokes that they then both laughed about. Maybe it was just the way she said things with her nose crinkled up and her eyes smiling cheekily that tickled Lene's sense of fun.

The two women went to see Fritz Lang's film 'The Nibelungen' which showed a gigantic dead dragon by a pool of blood into which Siegfried dived to protect himself. Anni pulled a face as if she was the dead dragon many times after they had seen the film to make Lene laugh. They laughed all the way back from the UFA-palace where the film was shown, mimicking actors and pretending obstacles in the street were stage sets.

Walking past the zoo they noticed panic in the street. People were running and screaming. A lion had managed to escape and was roaming the streets. Cars, trams, buses and fire engines filled up with pedestrians who were seeking the safety of a vehicle. Lene and Anni themselves quickly jumped on a bus, not caring where it went, and spent half the night travelling to get home. They heard on the radio in their kitchen the lion had to be shot in the early hours of the morning.

One day they had lunch in the canteen with Lieselotte who was on Anni's nursing course. Soon they were talking about the nurse in charge of teaching, who was called Engelbrecht.

"She's called Engelbrecht, but we call her angelbreaker and have a good laugh about her. She's a tough old Berliner who's seen better days, a bit of a cynic. She knows her stuff, you can learn from her, but you've got to be on your guard with her otherwise she'll have you for breakfast."

"Can I be quite frank with you, Lieselotte?"

"Sure, go ahead. Also just call me Liesel, that's what everyone calls me." Both Liesel and Lene looked at Anni to see what she was going to say. Anni looked angry and embarrassed at the same time, her face had reddened.

"That woman has got it in for me, I am sure. Have you noticed how she always has a go at me?"

Liesel looked surprised and then thoughtful. Her bass voice rang out and made people turn and look. Anni looked at her beseechingly and she spoke more quietly.

"She's a rough and ready bitch, Anni! That's all! I don't think she has it in for you. I think she can hardly tell us all apart. It's her normal manner, the way she talks. Very Berlinish! They do come across as rude to many people from outside town."

"Oh, thanks for that, it's helpful! I'm glad it's not a personal thing with her."

"Look, she's known as angelbreaker, that's what people call her behind her back. Well, it shows you. Everyone finds her hard to take. How about another coffee?" Lieselotte added and got up. She swung her bag over her shoulder and went to the counter.

Lene and Anni watched Liesel walk away. She was tall and strong-looking. When she stood up she seemed even taller, like people who have long legs and a shorter upper body, who surprise you with their height when they stand up.

"My dear Anni, you didn't tell me about angelbreaker!"

"I thought I'd learn to cope, but when Liesel turned up it was worth asking her. I feel so much better. It's quite tough, this course of ours. It worries me when I wonder if I can cope."

The backstabbing of the Müller government had not yet been forgotten by much of the press.

'Betrayal Proved!'

'Social Democrats Stay to Fight!'

'The Barons Take Over!' and similar headlines referred to the upheaval that had shaken the republic in recent weeks. The unemployed had time to deliver their verdict on the politics. People were standing at newspaper stands to argue about the state of things. Lene and Anni had decided to go into town. Not to Alexanderplatz, but instead they took a stroll to the Under den Linden which was not far. They had seen pictures of the street and now found themselves confronted with an imposing array of monumental buildings, which stood solidly with their grandiose presence on a sort of island between different arms of the river Spree. The two women gazed at the opera house and opposite the Pergamon museum, the Wilhelm Humboldt university and the historical museum, as if they were from a different planet. For a moment they stood still and were sunk in contemplation of the power of knowledge and cultural history that seemed imbued in the colossal stone constructions, as if the stone itself had absorbed thousands of years of tradition, art and human creativity.

"It makes you wonder - how extraordinary it is! Side by side with the shabbiness of Alexander Platz you get this stone fantasy of grandeur of human excellence, this striving for beauty - and we haven't even seen all the marvellous exhibits inside! Do you know what I mean, Anni?"

"Yes, I do, it's the same with the hospital. On the one hand there is rough angelbreaker, but on the other hand they do cure people and take care of them so that they get well."

"Humans are strange. They build huge monuments that are meant to last for ever, and don't bother with sorting out ordinary people's lives. Shall we find a drinking hole?" Lene added.

They caught a tram and arrived at Potsdamer Platz. The cafes, bars and restaurants beckoned noisily with coloured lights, jolly crowds and snippets of music. French chansons attracted them. They came from a bar with a tall ceiling and many bright lights that hung down low from the darkness. They sat down at a table in the window. The candlelight made them feel cosy and warm. A glass of Berliner beer had not been long on their table when screaming and shouting from outside disturbed the evening. They glued their eyes to the rain sodden window to peer out. In the foggy twilight they made out a group of men in brown uniforms moving quickly with truncheons and various other implements. Their arms and legs flew through the air and down on something or someone they could not see. The ferocious intensity of their attack was spine-chilling, but it was over within a minute or so, when the group ran off and disappeared. People came from all directions and bent over the victim or victims. Police vans swarmed. Sirens yelled.

"Just what we said," Lene whispered, who had gone white in the face, "the madness of evil being so close to beauty and creativity. I also saw such things happen in Gelsenkirchen." She looked at Anni, who looked back at her with frightened eyes.

"I've never seen anything like it. Who are they? What's it all about? How scary. How are we going to make it home? I'm really worried now."

"It's probably the NSDAP, the Nazis. I suppose you don't have them in a small village by the Rhine, or not yet."

Lene explained to Anni what she had seen at home and how her father had commented on the events. They had another beer before they took the tram back to Mitte. That evening Lene felt homesick. The loss of her father was in her heart. She cried herself to sleep.

CHAPTER 12

THE REICHSBANNER

Diary notes, 14ᵗʰ July 1973

A lot of things happened during the year before my mother returned. I had actually earned quite a bit of money, because my book was published, and the publisher had offered me an advance on my next novel. I was over the moon. We moved into a larger apartment with a balcony where we could grow herbs. It was still near Regents Park. My girlfriend had finished her training to become a dancer and was working with a group called 'The Forum'. My two boys were both at school and came home full of stories. The year was so full of our own lives that it seemed a much longer time before she came back. I was almost looking forward to her arrival and her next disclosures. Admittedly I had also felt quite sorry for her, when she told me of her sadness about her father. She must have loved him a lot more than I loved my father, and that was a peculiar feeling and made me question my own somewhat distant relationship with my father. I felt for her when she envied her friends having a child or speaking about having children. I had children already. My pity made me feel warmer towards her and less suspicious of her motives.

On the day of her arrival I had even bought some roses to put in her room. I was also more interested in Berlin than in Gelsenkirchen and hoped to hear lots more about that fascinating city. I don't know what mood she was in when she came. As I became more confident and ready to listen to her, she seemed more on edge and often looked at me quizzically, as if to say maybe you don't really believe me, or you're only pretending to show interest. I stopped avoiding her questions about my life. Instead I casually told her that my partner was female and that she was a dancer. My mother had become wise. She did not query the news at all, but just took the information in. Sofia was from an Italian background, dark, petite and graceful. My mother was quickly charmed by her. We had some meals together, and we celebrated the publication of my book. My life seemed accepted, perhaps even cherished, by her, I felt, and my compassion for her grew from that time on. We took the children to school and then walked straight into the park, every day. She told me about Anni, her close friend in Berlin, and I came to like her too, while with her friends Olga and Inge I had experienced a constant stream of suspicions as to why she told me about them.

End of notes.

"See you at the beginning of term, enjoy Gelsenkirchen!" Anni waved kisses. Lene could see that she was flushed with the glow of happy expectation about being back in the peacefulness of the village by the Rhine.

"Yes, and enjoy the vineyards!" Lene shouted back as they waved to each other. At home Erna pressed her younger sister to her bosom for a long time saying again and again how much she had missed her. The nurturing smell of yeast and warm bread made Lene feel delirious with a 'being at home' feeling. She had finished her first year at the Charite, and the whole family wanted to hear her stories.

"Such icy winters! You can't imagine how cold Berlin gets! Spring keeps you waiting for ever! So many people break a leg or an arm. They slip on the treacherous ground. Muck everywhere! There was lots of work using my new physiotherapy skills on the recovering patients. Some are very lazy and refuse to do exercises. You have to coax them! It's quite hard work."

Lene only realised how much she had learnt when she talked to her family. At the time it was just relentless hard graft with little time for anything else. Learning is a strange thing! You feel so ignorant and as if you'll never remember all those details. And then suddenly it has happened. You know more and can do things you never dreamt you could do. She had to describe again and again where she lived. They found her stories of Mamsell Napoleon with the carrot-coloured hair so funny and wanted to know more about her colleagues.

"Does she really have carrot-coloured hair, and what about the others?"

"Yes, really, but sometimes it was pink. She always observes everything, like a wild animal. You had to be careful she didn't find out if you left the kitchen in a state. Of all the others Anni and Liesel are the nicest ones. We didn't see much of Frau Meier, but she always wore a red and blue scarf round her neck which she kept tugging."

Lene had a lot of fun telling her stories to such good listeners. Erna cried again when her sister had to leave for Berlin and pressed her for a long time to her bosom.

She was back in Berlin and time flew. In June 1930 the Reichsbanner organised a constitution march which was very successful. Lene was careful not to overwhelm Anni with politics. Anni had a way of closing her face by tightening her mouth and looking down at the ground. She also tended to pull her shoulders up when she felt unsure or anxious. Lene learnt that those physical actions were Anni's way of saying "don't go on any more". But Anni wanted to know about the Reichsbanner.

"They're called Soldiers of Peace...."

"You just don't hear of these things in the countryside! We just deal in grapes, apples, carrots, potatoes and cabbages."

Anni gasped with frustration about her ignorance and Lene laughed. Anni had made such a funny face, and Lene thought of her own ignorance.

Lene, Anni and Liesel went to the march together. Hundreds of thousands turned up. From seven in the morning crowds filled the pavements of Unter den Linden Strasse and the 'Lustgarten'. From a quarter to eight the Reichsbanner orchestra entertained the comrades with familiar tunes at the Place of the Republic. It took until ten o'clock before all the many groups of the Reichsbanner congregated around the Victory column. The black, red and gold of thousands of flags shone in the sun. Their hearts felt warmed seeing so many celebrate the republic together.

"We will never allow anyone to take our freedom and peace away from us!" Reichstag president Paul Loebe said. There was loud applause from the huge crowd. The word peace! They sucked it in like a drug. If only words could also be actions.

When they sat later in a cafe to have lunch some people threw open the door and told the cafe crowd that it hadn't all been honey and sunshine. The Nazis had gone on the rampage!

"Where? What happened?" they all wanted to know.

"It was at the 'Neue Markt'. About one hundred and fifty Nazis had decorated themselves with social democrat badges, can you imagine! They mixed themselves into the friendly throng and began to beat up the people around them who, of course, had no idea why their own comrades had started to turn on them. These evil liars moved on towards the Victory column and carried on to attack Reichsbanner demonstrators."

The cafe was silenced with a sense of shock. How could one defeat such despicable deceipt? Lene and Anni stared at those who had announced the awful details.

Liesel tugged Lene on her arm and leant over the table.

"This is Berlin for you! We have thousands of peaceful demonstrators and fifty odd Nazi gangsters come and cause destruction. And the boots these guys are wearing are of high class quality with steel toecaps. If you get kicked by them you'll suffer severe injuries. Money is flowing in their direction all the time to pay for those expensive boots."

"Whose money?" Anni wanted to know.

"The Junkers from the Elbe, the industrialists and their American bankers, to name just some of them."

"Why would they want such dangerous and destructive groups on our streets? I don't understand, the poor police who have to deal with them." Anni looked bewildered and confused.

"You're right. Often even the police get it in the neck. They are the meat in the sandwich. The thing with the Nazis is that they are set up as a fighting machine to brutalise the people. Their hate campaign is aimed at the Soviet Union. They use the word 'Bolshevism' and show you a Russian bear to frighten people into thinking the socialist republic is our biggest enemy. In Russia they expropriated the owners of large estates and industries without compensation. That frightens the pants off the rich. It's all in the communist Manifesto," Liesel peered with a confident and interested smile at the two women. Anni looked overwhelmed. Lene thought of her father.

"I heard of that! My father was a social democrat," she said with a touch of pride and sadness in her voice. She added quickly in order to prevent being asked about his death: "He died last year, I suppose from overwork, but he also had an infection in his leg which went septic. He always analysed the political events in the evening for us, when we sat upstairs in our lounge. My sister Hilde argued with him. He often got really annoyed about her views. I went on to do political work with friends. One of them is Alfred Zingler, a journalist with 'Der Volkswille', the social democratic paper in Gelsenkirchen."

"So you already have a good idea, Lene." Liesel looked warmly at Lene and added, "Time is moving fast and there's so much to do. If you're interested, come and join me in my branch of the social democrats. We need many more people to work on our campaigns."

In her first Berlin meeting she heard chairman Breitscheid speak:

"Comrades, we have enormous conflicts to weigh up. The government is cutting wages and benefits. Bread prices are rising. This is all against our policies, but we have a bigger evil to consider, namely how to keep the fascists from getting into power. You can see the writing on the wall when you look at Italy. The pope and Mussolini's fascists have come to an agreement that allows Italians to be Catholics and still join the fascist party."

On Thursday that week Lene spotted the headline of the Berliner Morgenpost and decided to buy it. 'Heavy industry wants dictatorship,' it read. It made her think of Gelsenkirchen. How right-minded people could want the country to become a dictatorship was beyond her. She read the article at coffee break: 'Fritz Thyssen declared that only a community of people that excluded the Marxists could work.' Liesel came into the canteen, and Lene showed her the headline.

"You see, just what we were talking about! It's Marxists they are after. They don't even mince their words. The NSDAP is a sworn enemy of Marxists. What I don't understand is that the communists don't seem to have grasped how dire the situation is. They keep voting with the NSDAP and are still declaring the social democrats to be their main enemy. That must be very confusing for workers."

"It must be strange to say the least. Imagine voting for a party that is supposed to stand against fascists and then they fight side by side with them, for instance in the case of the Berlin transport strike. The Nazis are going out of their way to be look-alike lefties. Remember they wore social democrat badges at the Reichsbanner event."

When she got back to the student accommodation Lene found letters had arrived for her. They brought tears to her eyes. One was from Erna.

> *'My dear child,*
>
> *Karl-Mayer Strasse is empty without you. I miss you so much. I have the eczema again, it is driving me up the wall. I keep scratching and of course it gets worse, but I cannot stop myself. I dreamt of our father the other night. He looked young and strong and had his white hat on that he loved so much. He smiled and said 'Erna my dear, you deserve a good man to look after you.' I woke up in tears, because such a good man has still not materialised. You don't know how much I long to find someone I can love. I hope you are enjoying your studies, do write to me if you find the time. Mother sends her best wishes to you. She's as busy as ever.*
>
> *With a loving heart,*
> *Your sister Erna*

Lene's other letter was from Margarethe.

Dear Lene,

Here is a short greeting from Gelsenkirchen to let you know our work is continuing, but I miss your good helping hands. Alfred is giving many talks to encourage the workers to believe in the social democrats, but we have many clashes now with the communists. Rather than join forces with us against our dangerous enemy the NSDAP they talk wildly of overthrowing the republic, of revolution and of the SPD as being their main enemy. Such talk is so misleading. In spite of these difficulties we are keeping a positive perspective on things, in order to give our comrades hope and confidence. It's not easy. We don't like Bruening and his politics, but all the possible alternatives are worse, so we've got to support him and defend the constitution come what may.

You'll be pleased to learn that our theatre group is producing another play. Karl has agreed to do the stage design. I wonder if you're getting time to get to know the politics in Berlin. We would both love to hear from you. Keep well and take care,

With our love,
Margarethe and Alfred

Karl had also written the week before. She looked at it from time to time to feel that warm, pulsing sense of closeness coming from his loving words. She spent the evening writing her replies. She told Margarethe about her new friend Liesel who had introduced her to the local branch of the SPD and how they participated in debates, and that she had joined the party. She wrote to Erna telling her not to worry too much and that she would come and visit her in the summer. She said that Erna would certainly find a man she could love.

One sticky and windless day the German government delegation returned from Chequers in England. Chancellor Brüning and Foreign Minister Curtius were accompanied by the American foreign office spokesman Sackett. They had travelled via Bremerhaven and taken the train to Friedrichstrasse. The English foreign office spokesman Sir Horace Rumbold had joined the welcome group. A Nazi demonstration was prevented by the police. Hectic was perhaps too mild a word to describe the political machinations in June and July. France had angrily rejected the Hoover plan to stall the reparation payments. Pressure came from the chiefs of industry. What did they know and care about the many daily worries that families endured?

The emergency legislation by the Brüning government was a bone of contention. In its present form it was designed to benefit the owners of industry. Changes to the emergency legislation were demanded by the social democrats, but the Reichstag was not called to discuss these matters. The Reichstag did not even sit to debate these key issues, because the president continued to prolong the holiday sessions using article 48, as if it was a regular democratic procedure. It was just one of many small administrative paper decisions with enormous political consequences brushed aside like the flick of ashes from a cigarette.

Social democrats had to constantly weigh up whether they could afford to challenge such measures, or if it would lead directly to a takeover by the Nazis. The impoverishment of the middle classes took on frightening proportions and led directly to the huge increase in nationalist support in towns and especially in the countryside. The universities were brimming with nationalist enthusiasts turning up and disrupting lectures. Teargas bombs were thrown into seminar rooms. Three persons were injured on one such occasion. The troubles also appeared at the Humboldt University linked to the Charite, where Lene and Anni often worked in the library. It was Liesel who had initiated the setting up of a 'defend the rights to study' group. She spoke at a student union meeting attended by about fifty students.

"Colleagues and comrades, you may have heard of the troubles at many universities where the Nazis are stirring up hatred and violence. The most recent event took place in Jena, where minister

Frick appointed a racist professor to change the way subjects are taught. Nazi gangs have harassed and insulted the professors who were teaching there by disturbing lectures and turning up in uniform during teaching sessions."

Lene also spoke:

"Comrades and fellow students, we have witnessed violence and fights leading to appalling injuries at universities. These are now daily events. You will have heard of Herr Goebbels, a member of the Nazi party. This man leads a team of fascist brutes who go round Berlin with clubs, sticks and knives attacking whoever gets in their way. Their methods includes going out at night with headlamps tied to their heads which shine into people's faces so that their victim is blinded by light and can't see who's attacking them. After an attack they quickly run off into the night, leaving their victim bleeding in the street."

A vote was taken to set up 'the right to study' group. They formed small groups who took on a rota of checking on visitors. They developed good skills at spotting visitors' intentions by looking into their eyes. Anni and Lene went for a coffee afterwards. They went into the canteen and sat by the window. The clouds were drifting by as if in a hurry. It looked stormy, the plane tree branches in the park below swayed and you felt you could hear the leaves rustle. Lene could see in Anni's face that she just about had enough of politics. In fact, she was herself fed up with how it kept taking over her life. She said to Anni:

"What's so strange is you can live in the same street with people and they have no idea of what's going on around them, while you twist and turn in your sleep with nightmares about it all. So, is there a point in thinking about it, you wonder when it robs you of your sleep?" Anni looked at her, bewildered, and Lene answered her own question.

"We've got to know what's going on, but we also need time off. So how about we do something nice this weekend, go out and stuff, what do you say?"

Anni was all in favour of that. They went to see an exhibition of modern art and bought tickets for the theatre at the Schiffsbauer Damm. The weather had turned round and it was a brilliant sunny day. Both women compared each other's skirt length and laughed about how daring they were with the hem shorter than they had worn it back home. Well, here in Berlin, you could see hemlines that would be considered indecent in Gelsenkirchen, not to mention Eimsheim on the Rhine. Lene had wanted to ask Liesel to come out as well, but Anni preferred to go out just the two of them. They chatted merrily about their studies and the coming of the summer holidays.

Crowds of people were queuing up with them for the exhibition. It was very popular and they soon found out why. It was stunning. They were taken aback. The quiet countryside scenes or photographic pictures of towns that they were used to from paintings at home had disappeared. Instead loud colours, brilliant reds, blues, yellows burst forth from the frames. The people and nature scenes were depicted in broken up forms, as if through a lens in water. New names burnt themselves into Lene's brain. Wasili Kandinsky's imaginative landscapes, George Grosz, Paul Klee's fishes, Marc Chagall's floating Russians and George Grosz's prostitutes, murderers and banker gangsters looking blasé and fat staring at the observer from chaotic settings. Lene spotted a John Heartfield which she knew from the AIZ magazine. They were amused by his clever photomontage of an Adolf Hitler receiving wads of money into his Hitler greeting hand. They concluded that there was no getting away from politics in Berlin.

Later they had a sausage and potato salad at one of the many food stalls before going to Friedrichstrasse on the S Bahn (overland city train). The Schiffsbauer Damm theatre was nearby on the other side of the Spree. The Threepenny Opera was showing there. Lene had told Anni about the Gelsenkirchen production. When she saw Polly Peachum turning up on stage her heart beat fast. The dress was beautiful and had all the frills and trestles, multi-coloured skirt layers and extravagant décolleté that Katarina, the actress in Gelsenkirchen had aspired to have, but did not quite get. "She looks fantastic," Lene whispered to Anni. The ballad of Mack the Knife, the pimp's ballad and the cannon song were adorably sung. The stage set was a dingy cavern in a bare harbour warehouse. The occasional sound of a ship's horn, as if the Thames were on the other side of the stage, fired their imagination. When they emerged from the theatre they both felt numbed and elated from the eloquence of the story and drifted with the crowds hither and thither, looking at bars and taking in the warm night air. An exotic scent of jasmine from a hedge around a cafe garden filled their nostrils pleasurably. They found a couple of young men walking next to them and chatting as if they knew the young women. Lene looked carefully for any Nazi insignia, but there were none. They were far too casually dressed in corduroy slacks and open neck shirts. They had themselves been to the Schiffsbauer Damm and like them, were wandering aimlessly to find further amusements. One of them introduced himself as Heinz, and called his friend August.

"We could go to Lady Windermere's. It's near Tauentzienstrasse, not far from here. They always have some performer, either a man or a woman who is romantic or funny or both. We could sit and have a cocktail."

He added that they would invite the women. Lene insisted they pay for themselves but they would join them for a bit. Anni was all right with that. She trusted Lene in these matters. They walked down a dark set of stairs to find themselves in a cavernous basement room with a low ceiling and many small tables with candles lighting up a shadowy atmosphere filled with cigarette smoke and the low noise of chatting. It was impossible to figure out how large it was, as there were supporting columns here and there behind which there appeared to be more tables and mirrors reflecting more tables. They sat down at the side of the bar. Heinz vanished and August laughed and said not to worry, Heinz would be back.

"Are you two ladies from Berlin?" August asked. Heinz returned. He was tall and broad-shouldered with blond hair sticking up from his baby face forehead, and the beginning of a moustache curling on his upper lip, which was quite full. He was from the Baltic sea,

Rostock to be precise, which he described as a provincial backwater. He chatted merrily about the Baltic sea, the long beaches, the tide and the smoked eel and herring from the stalls. August, with sleeked-back dark hair and a sombre look on his face, turned his eyes up and rubbed his stomach to indicate how keen he was on the food his friend had described. He looked so funny while he did that in an absent-minded manner. It made Lene and Anni laugh out loud just at the moment when the bar went quiet, because a performance was about to start. A young woman arrived on stage, her face painted white with dark red lips and a long cigarette holder in one hand. She had a lovely sparkly diadem in her curly blonde hair. She smooched about close to the clientele seated around the piano and sang a sad love song. She seemed to know many people in the bar, as she kissed a number of them and sat at different tables after her song, before she disappeared. From the muddle of people that had kissed the singer a tall young man with long mid-brown hair and a casual jacket was moving towards them and suddenly stood by their table smiling beguilingly. Heinz turned and laughed:

"It's you, Christopher, I didn't see you. Meet my two lovely ladies from Berlin." He introduced his friend to the two surprised looking women and then got up, adding "My friend Christopher is from England. He loves chatting with young ladies, but you'll have to excuse us now. We've got to be off. August, stay and look after the ladies, will you?"

August nodded his agreement, smiled at them, mumbled something like 'just got to chat with this friend' and they watched him walk up to talk to another friend he had discovered.

"I'm sorry Heinz is taking me away from you, it was nice meeting you. I hope you like it here and will come back so that we can have a proper chat."

That was his friend Christopher speaking in a husky voice. Lene and Anni watched them make their way into the smoky distance of the cavern.

"How strange was that! You meet people and then they walk off like that in no time. Quite nice, in a way, to know they weren't after the usual, but odd - why chat us up in the first place?"

"I think it's Berlin. People are friendly and sociable and like to get to know new people, even if they don't have further intentions, like they could be homosexuals."

"What do you mean? Oh, you're saying they have relationships with each other rather than with women. I've never met anyone like that."

"Me neither, but I was told about all this by a friend who often travels to Berlin. She also met men who dress up as women, transvestites they are called."

They enjoyed their beer, pondering the strange colourfulness of life in the city and watched the white painted lady return to the stage and sing another plaintive song. The audience was enraptured and loud applause followed her performance. They chatted briefly about the forthcoming examinations. If you didn't pass it was the end of your training. It was very strict. As Anni was telling Lene about a fellow student Lene spotted a familiar figure coming towards them. It was Liesel. She was accompanied by a man in a trench coat and a worker's cap on his head, the likes of which Lene knew well from Gelsenkirchen. He had thick eyebrows and twinkly eyes.

"Hi Lene, hi Anni! You've found your way quickly to one of the hot spots in Berlin. This is my boyfriend Wolfgang, known as Wolfi. Would you mind if we join you for a bit? We're not staying long."

"Do, by all means! We'd love you to, wouldn't we, Anni?"

Lieselotte and Wolfgang found two chairs and sat down with them. Foaming beers were brought in large glasses.

"Wolfi is a big Wandervögel fan, he can tell you all about their recent walks. Where did you march last time, Wolfi?" He gave them a detailed description of Potsdam, Sans Soucis and the environment surrounding the park. It had been a hot sunny day, and at the end they had gone for a cup of tea and cake at the palace cafe in the park. He emphasised that they had done a good long walk first. Wolfi asked Lene where she had walked and Lene recounted one of her experiences along the Rhine. She didn't mention the nude bathing. Wolfi and Liesel suddenly grew serious. Liesel talked very quietly behind her hand:

"Be careful here, this is a fun place, but it's crawling with Nazis, as well as nice people. Look around to see who's near you. They spy on people and then when you leave they wait for you and hit you over the head and you end up in hospital."

Liesel added: "One of our friends from the social democrats left on his own last Thursday after a couple of beers. When he stepped out a man with a bright light on his forehead struck him over the head and must have dragged him around the corner to punch and kick him. He was lucky, because people saw it and called the police who came and took him to hospital. Otherwise he wouldn't be alive today."

All four of them intuitively turned to look about at the other people. They saw the candles, clouds of smoke wrapped around men in suits and women in evening dress, sitting at tables or making their way to the bar. All of it was mirrored and appeared broken up in reflections. Soft voices talked and laughter rang out. Were those uniformed men in the distance? Lene peered into the dark cavern screwing up her eyes:

"You begin to see uniforms everywhere, even if there aren't any, when you think about it. It's a really uncomfortable feeling," she pondered.

"I quite agree. It happens to me too." Liesel added, "Their presence has become so dominant in our streets, and we seem to have got used to it. I think that's the big danger. You kind of expect them to turn up suddenly. I wonder if people have a weird intuitive respect for men in uniforms. As if a man in uniform was automatically someone reliable. If they do, they are badly cheated by this lot."

"It looks very bleak for our democracy. I'm not sure if you followed the events in parliament." Wolfi had a deep frown while he continued. "The day before yesterday they now call the 'black day of German democracy', the 16th July 1930. Instead of the parties agreeing a new formulation for taxes to improve the country's finances Brüning is now using our emergency article 48 to rule on these matters. That type of misuse will eventually allow those scoundrels in by default."

"I saw the 'Volks Zeitung' comment on this. They declared this action as the birthday of a German dictatorship. Severe words! You don't want to believe them, but they haunt you," Liesel added. She looked drawn and aged for a moment but then confidence returned to her face when she concluded:

"We've got to stop them. That's all we can do, and hope. Hope against the odds."

Lene and Anni looked at them silently. A great tiredness drifted through Lene. The weight of the whole German fate seemed to lie on their shoulders. Did the countless citizens of Berlin feel the same? She suddenly felt very lonely. She looked at Anni who had shrunk into her seat, a fragile little figure.

"We've got to go home," she said. "Anni, shall we go? I feel really tired and you look exhausted."

"Yes, I'm ready for bed," Anni replied. They shook hands with Liesel and Wolfi and left. The stairs were dark and narrow. Somewhere a smell of urine drifted into their nostrils and mixed with cheap perfume. A spitting of rain met them at the entrance. They looked carefully about themselves for any uniforms. The street was deserted, as they hurried to the tram.

CHAPTER 13

STUDIO Z

Sitting in the packed audience their hearts sank. They froze into their seats. Lene and Liesel knew who he was talking about. They wished they could become invisible. Professor Sauerbruch used his keynote address to point the finger at vigilante activity at the university. Without further ado he began his seminar with a warning that students should beware of being noticed as politically motivated or active. His steely-blue eyes behind the metal spectacles seemed like searchlights, aimed to find Lene and Liesel among the throng of students. His bald head shone like a Belisha beacon.

"I am proud of our high-class establishment, and that includes you, our students, who are striving to become the best the medical and caring profession has to offer. But let me remind you that you're expected to be responsible citizens who keep away from political engagements. There are a lot of noisy orchestrations for this or that political point of view, which could seduce you to give them your voice. I must tell you that any such activity will lead, if found out, to the cancellation of your study place at this institution."

There was an uncomfortable silence in the auditorium until the professor left. What about nationalists and Nazis who had harassed students? The professor was probably just minding his career. Lene and Liesel met in the canteen. They were bent nervously over the table, their heads meeting over their cups of tea. Liesel had red blotches on her cheeks. Lene looked chalky white with coals for eyes.

"He's been told about our work. We have to be careful!"

"What a turn of events! That he'd take sides like that... we have to stop our vigils for now. He'd throw us out at once!" Lene sat pale-faced, pulling her jacket tight around her as if she was cold.

"We just suspend the rota for a bit and discuss with the others what else we can do. I wonder who told him," Liesel commented with her head leaning on her arm, her auburn bun loosened. She looked tired and fed up. Her hands tightened into fists.

"Nazi spies, or anyone wanting a favour from him, it shows you how hard it is to make a stand. Neither of us can afford to be caught..."

"No, we can't. Forgive me, I've got to rush, Lene, be careful." She picked up her bag and coat, tightened her hair back and left Lene sitting and pondering, looking out at the snow laden trees.

During the long cold Berlin winter ice flowers used to grow on the inside of the small windows of the students' rooms. Lene and Anni used to push rolled up newspaper into the gaps in the window frames. But it had actually grown milder, and they began to enjoy seeing green grass again and the first snowdrops. One evening Lene found two letters pushed under her door. They had presumably been delivered to the wrong person, who then took them to Lene's room. They knew she was from Gelsenkirchen, and the postmark showed clearly where they had come from. She was in two minds about reading them now. She was worn out and wanted to do nothing more dearly than get into bed and sleep. On the other hand she was curious and so tore open the letter from Margarethe. She had sensed correctly that the letter was going to disturb her.

My dearest Lene,

I hope very much that this letter finds you in good health and strong. You will need it to cope with the news I have to report from home. Sadly a person you love very much has been murdered by Nazi thugs. They suddenly appeared out of nowhere, beat everyone within reach and disappeared. Our dear Fräulein Bäcker, your art teacher at college, was one of the victims. It took place at our social democratic party demonstration in preparation for the election of the next President. We had stewards and our comrades turned out in their thousands. Bahnhofstrasse was packed with men and women shouting 'Hindenburg, vote Hindenburg'. It must have been about five o'clock, it was twilight just before dark. A lorry came chasing from a small side street, aiming straight into the crowd who fled in all directions. Men on top of the lorry started wielding truncheons and hitting out at those running away. Several of our comrades got seriously injured. Amongst them was your friend and teacher Fräulein Bäcker. She died in hospital from internal bleeding.

My poor girl, these are hard times we are living in, and I am afraid worse is to come. The Nazis are beyond reason and rationality. All they have is brutality and lies, aimed to put the fear of God into courageous people. It can stop people from resisting out of sheer fear.

I send you warm greetings,
From your sad friend and comrade Margarethe

Lene sat motionless. The new political reality was seeping into her life like drops of poison. Fräulein Bäcker! That dear teacher of hers with the lovely dark brown eyes, the warm smiles, the energy and passion she had for the arts! Tears rolled down Lene's cheeks. Her visit to Worpswede came to her mind and how Fräulein Bäcker had then not been quite her usual self. How happy they'd all been when she first told them the story of Heinrich Vogeler! She saw herself and Inge sitting in class and listening enthralled. She woke from her reverie and looked at the time. Good Lord! It was so late and she had to go to lectures early in the morning. She rolled herself into her blanket and tried to evoke the beautiful memory of Fräulein

Bäcker again. The next day she had to hurry, she had no excuse not to turn up for lectures. She packed her bag, put on her shoes and coat, grabbed a hat and stumbled out of the door.

The whole day was devoted to the bones of the vertebral column. Cervical, thoracic and lumbar vertebrae, the sacrum and the coccyx, the cervical curvatures and the various other curvatures. How the spine could be deformed in various ways, called Lordosis Kyphosis and Scoliosis. In her emotional state she felt curiously attracted to the cool and abstract body descriptions written down on the blackboard and repeated by the lecturer. Gratefully she wrote them down in her exercise book. The vertebrae kept her mind from wandering to the sadness inside her. She focused very hard all day and raced home as soon as lectures were finished. There was another letter to read. The second letter was from Inge, who also told her of the dreadful event with the Nazi gang driving into the demonstrators. In fact Inge had been very near where the incident happened. Her letter showed signs of tears, where the ink had run and the words had become illegible. Poor Inge! Her letter contained more bad news. Uwe, her boyfriend who she was going to marry, was seen by her brother with another woman. Walking hand in hand. Imagine that! And he said he wanted to marry me. Inge sounded almost more angry than sad. A knock on the door shook Lene out of her stupor. It was Anni. Seeing Lene's tearstained face she wrapped her arms around her mumbling:

"You should have come to see me, Lene dear, rather than suffer on your own. Have you had bad news from home? I see you've had a letter."

Lene enjoyed the hug and was glad to be able to tell Anni the story of her teacher and what a wonderful person Fräulein Bäcker had been.

"She had such warmth and passion for the arts. How she taught us about the Worpswede artists I shall never forget. Can you understand that, Anni?"

"I had a teacher like that, she also meant so much to me. She was very young, I remember her name was Frau Solinksy. Must have been newly wedded. She liked to show the ring on her finger. How she taught us music was so inspiring. It could have made me want to be a singer."

"Why didn't you go for that?"

"During her lessons, when she sang for us, I kept thinking I shall learn to sing like her. We were also in the choir. But then coming home, you know what it's like. They urge you to be practical..."

"It makes me want to scream! I wish we were all much more determined, us women. And there is my poor friend Inge. Her boyfriend Werner was two-timing her."

"So she dropped him, I suppose?"

"Yes, she did, and I think she was more angry than sad in the end, which is good."

Liesel met up with Lene in a cafe at Alexanderplatz where they had a glass of wine. It was a mild evening with a huge blue sky and small cumulus clouds spread along the middle. People ambled past, taking in the gentle air after work. They watched women in extravagant clothes, as if spring had arrived. Passers-by were pushing and shoving each other casually and excitedly in an expectation of warm weather. Flimsy dresses showing calves, high-heeled shoes, jackets over their arms the women walked arm in arm, watching the hungry glances of men out of the corners of their eyes. Liesel was uncharacteristically silent, and Lene had to chat encouragingly to get her involved.

"I've had really awful news from home, it's to do with the usual thing, the Nazis."

"What happened?" Liesel asked, tugging restlessly on her bun and throwing a long look at Lene.

"My favourite art teacher, a Fräulein Bäcker, was knocked down and killed by Nazis driving their abominable lorry into people. They were having a demonstration. Other people were also injured. My friend from the social democratic party wrote to me and described it all. I felt sick to my stomach when I read it. She was such a lovely woman."

Liesel's eyes were big and sad.

175

"I'm so sorry to hear that, Lene," she said and stroked Lene's arm on the table, bringing her hand to rest on Lene's. Lene felt the warmth and softness of Liesel's hand and burst out suddenly:

"It's men and their aggression, isn't it, Liesel? How can anyone just go and kill people they don't even know?"

Liesel's facial expression shifted from sadness to concern with a frown tightening up her forehead. She pulled back her hand and sat upright.

"Men indeed! Sometimes I wonder how we can be one species with them so different from us. But it's not all of them! My brother isn't like this lot! Your brothers aren't like that either, are they? It's to do with class. The rich and powerful! It's a class issue, that I'm sure of. If our society was run fairly and everyone had a job it wouldn't happen. You must meet my brother. He's a great person, you'd love him."

"Shall we wander for a bit, Liesel? I need to get outside, I think I'm getting a headache."

The friends paid and left arm in arm in a sombre mood. They wandered down the street to relax and ease their thoughts. They found themselves in front of a small shop. It was called 'Studio Z'. The door was open and they walked in. The whitewashed walls had a display of drawings of buildings, but also everyday items, such as tables, cups, flowers and advertising leaflets. A young man of about thirty was sitting behind a desk working on an architectural model.

"Good evening, young ladies! Do come and have a look around! We have the artist Naum Gabo exhibiting some of his work. You might find it interesting."

They became absorbed in the pencil drawing of a young man, which was clearly a self-portrait.

"Some of the work is mine. It's from my days when I studied at the Bauhaus."

"The Bauhaus?" Lene asked, surprised. Her excitement brought a smile to his face. He had large grey eyes and his sleek brown hair was brushed back. He had stood up and was a head taller than Lene.

"Have you heard of the Bauhaus?"

"Well, yes, actually..."

"Where are you from?"

"Gelsenkirchen, the Ruhr, my art teacher..."

Lene couldn't get the words out, She felt confused by a mixture of emotions that included thinking of Karl who had talked to her about the Bauhaus amidst kisses. Fräulein Bäcker was also on her mind.

"My name is Franz Ehrlich. I used to be at the Bauhaus in Dessau, but left there to set up a studio here with my friends. I suppose it's not the best time to set up a studio in Berlin right now, but we have to see..."

"I'm Lene Deppermann and this is my friend Liesel Bader. We're both studying at the Charite. I'm very interested in the Bauhaus. I've heard a lot about it."

"Lene, do you mind if I go back to the hostel now. Are you staying? I am a little tired and my foot hurts. It's these shoes."

"What's the time?"

"Five o'clock."

"Ok, I'll stay a while, Liesel, if you don't mind. I'd like to talk about the Bauhaus, you know..."

"The triangle, the square and the cylinder, they are our three basic forms. Everything stems from them. We believe in taking form down to its simplest basic characteristics..."

As Franz chatted and drew lines on paper and pointed at shapes and colours, Lene vividly remembered her conversations with Karl. An urgent desire filled her to embrace this creative man and to start working immediately on a drawing herself. The urge was so strong that she had to stand up and take her jacket off. Heat poured out of all her pores. Franz remained undeterred as he drew and explained the Bauhaus to her. Lene could have listened to him for a long time but she had to get back.

"Do come again, you know where you can find me, Lene. Great talking with you."

Berlin! The beautiful so close to the ugly, creativity next to wretchedness. Hugenberg's newspaper tirades filled people's ears with vitriol. A fever of confusion and bewilderment. 'Against the enslavement of the people'. The referendum was lost. The citizens still stood by their democratic sentiments. Hindenburg refused to support the Müller government. He got rid of him. He was replaced within three days. Newspaper boys called out the news.

"Our elected government stabbed in the back!"

"Hindenburg ousts Mueller!"

Lene and Liesel were having a coffee in the canteen.

"These people have no loyalty! They'd sell their own grandmother..."

"You bet they would! The problem is what power have we got to oppose them? We have the mass of the German people on our side, the vote showed that, but when you have the money of bankers like Schacht from the Reichsbank and that Hugenberg against them...,"

Liesel was taking a gulp of coffee from her cup and eating a doughnut at the same time. Lene looked at her. How could they lead their lives when politics shoved its ugly face into their own? She looked around the canteen at the other students. Did they all feel like that, or were the two of them just too preoccupied with the daily news? The humdrum clatter of knives and forks on plates. Gustave walked into the canteen and queued up at the counter. They immediately spotted her because of her large behind. Watching her wobble to a table with her drink cheered them up.

"She knows her stuff, though. It's a miracle she isn't having a huge cake with her coffee."

"True, she's good at the physio, but how did she get that weight..."

"If we had the right leadership, if we had a united front with the communists, I think we could do something. It's a tragedy that we haven't." Liesel sighed deeply. "Have a bit of doughnut, it's tasty, it might give you a bottom like Gustave's," she added, winking at Lene. Lene took a bite of doughnut and the jam was sweet in her mouth. She looked at the dark clouds rushing across the sky.

"They get us to go to the polls, but then do exactly as they please..."

"Yes, like install machine-gun Brüning, a captain, as a chancellor. In peace time..."

"And then they agreed the welfare payments the Müller government had demanded. They're making a mockery of democracy."

They both had to go back to their wards. The study regime was tough, and they had to practice their newly learnt skills daily. Sometimes Lene didn't see Anni or Liesel for days. So the weeks drifted by and autumn came. In the September 1930 election clerks and shop assistants deserted the wavering centre parties for the NSDAP. Fly posters plastered the cities with huge Bolshevist bears turning people's minds to fear the 'Reds'. In the town of Bremen they fell for doom-laden irrational vagueness:

"Beat the ones who bankrupt us, destroy those who ruin our national unity, get rid of those responsible for our decay."

The unemployed filled the streets Was it now three or four million? Money rolled into Nazi coffers, feeding their confidence. Violence and confusion became a toxic medicine, visible in street fights and brawling. Their lorries turned up. Men in smart uniforms jumped down with truncheons drawn. Blood was spilled. Sirens screamed. Ambulances arrived at bars, clubs and political meetings. Violence was their emblem, a trademark. It kept them in the news. People's fear, sadness and disgust became one of their weapons, as the pain was talked about. A copycat effect pulled disheartened new voters over to the Nazis. In the biting cold days of the winter of 1930/31 over four million unemployed men and women wrapped in shawls, torn coats and hats deep in their faces waited in long queues for hot soup and state handouts for their families. Trade union power was reduced with so many unemployed. What choice did they have? With the Reichstag on prolonged holidays Machine-gun Brüning had his mind on the reparation payments rather than the emergency facing his people. Ending all further reparation payments was his goal. His illustrious and wealthy friends paid large sums of money into the coffers of the Nazi party: Emil Kirdorf paid 600,000 marks. Friedrich Flick donated 100,000. Further sums came from Cuno of North German Lloyd, Baron von Schroeder, Siemens and Robert Bosch. The little known Austrian Hitler had his first audience with President Hindenburg in October 1931. He was invited by Fritz

Thyssen to make a speech in front of the industrialists on the 27th January 1932. In his demagogic pronouncements he declared war on the republic. He spoke of democracy with disdain calling it a disaster. He railed against Bolshevism. They smiled approvingly and applauded him.

Liesel was sitting in the cafeteria when Lene arrived from the library. It was a snowy February afternoon. The black tree silhouettes in the park glistened white with snow in the last beams of the sun. Lene had her coat over her arm and a large bag over her shoulder. Study materials and books weighed heavily. She felt like a packhorse. She peered past the benches and tables. Liesel was sitting by a window with a young man who she hadn't seen before.

"Hi, Lene, this is my brother Klaus. Klaus, this is my friend and comrade Lene. Klaus is in the Reichsbanner, he knows all the latest manipulations. He can tell you all about it! Sit yourself down, I'll fetch you a tea."

Lene shook Klaus's hand which he'd stretched out over the table to greet her. It was warm and firm. Klaus had a full mouth and bright blue eyes that seemed to have a humorous twinkle, as if he was thinking of something funny.

"Nice to meet you, Klaus! Have you come far? I'm sorry! I'm laden down with all these books. Let me arrange them first," and she disappeared under the table to put the bag out of harm's way.

"You seem to be very busy. Liesel told me you're studying so hard she thinks you'll get a first. You asked if I've come far. No, not that far. I'm in the Reichsbanner and trade union organisation in Potsdam. It's only a short train journey away. Have you been to Potsdam yet?"

"No, I haven't actually, is it interesting?"

"Sans Soucis palace is a must. If you ever come, I'll show you around." He smiled right into Lene's face. She had a strange feeling that he was smiling both at her and about her, as if there was something funny. It was uncanny. Before she could reply Liesel had returned with tea.

"Did you tell Lene what you heard about the secret betrayals that are handing Germany over to the Nazis? The captains of industry and the banks are determined to get the Nazis into power. God only knows what they think they'll get out of it, apart from selling weapons for a war which they're bound to start."

"It's true. They act as if they weren't responsible for a whole nation of workers, men, women and children, but only for their own estates, financial institutions and businesses. You'd have thought General Schleicher would know how to concentrate military power in the hands of the state, rather than let all manner of groups, like the Nazis, roam around with weapons. He should know that the monopoly of violence needs to be established, if you want to run a state. But what does he do? He permits the Nazis to throw their weight around, to intimidate the left. Socialism, the reds, I suppose they'd do anything to stop us having socialism here."

"Yes, the bulwark against the USSR, that's what my father used to say. American banks and industrialists have paid for the Nazis for years now. It's as if it was an international plot to sink our country into an abyss."

Liesel and Klaus looked at Lene nodding their heads, while they slurped their tea noisily. Liesel and her brother were sharing a doughnut and had placed another one in front of Lene.

"You've said it in one, Lene," Liesel remarked with fervour, her eyes glowing with anger.

"We're being taken to the cleaners, as they say. The butcher's knives are out. Makes you wonder what's going to happen to all of us. They'll lock up half the country. Have a doughnut anyway!" She looked at Klaus lovingly and added, "Klaus, you've got to be more careful, keep your head down. We're on the cusp of something we've never seen before. I worry about you."

Lene looked at Klaus. She felt anxious suddenly and wondered how her own life and those of all the people she loved were going to shape up in all this mess. Studies had occupied all her thoughts up to now, but here was something that was coming at them like a tornado.

"What do you think we should do, Liesel?" She suddenly felt like a rabbit in the glare of a headlight.

"The first thing is to try not to be noticed, if you're doing political work. Don't put your name on any register, maybe even give a false name to people. Make sure you only speak your mind when you can trust someone."

"What can I do? All the Reichsbanner ones know me. I'm a trade union official. I can only hope and be lucky." Klaus looked pensively at his sister and then turned to Lene.

"I've got to go now. There's a meeting at Invalidenstrasse headquarters. I'll see you later, Liesel, and nice to meet you, Lene. I hope we'll meet again. My sister can give you my number, if you want to come and see Sans Soucis. I hope you will!"

Klaus bent down and kissed Liesel. Lene noticed his blonde hair curling at his boyish neck. He shook Lene's hand again with a firm and warm grip. Both women sat for a moment feeling very low. Liesel was the first to find her speech again.

"You must come round for a meal while Klaus is staying at my flat, he's here for a week."

"I'd love to!"

"What about next Saturday?"

"That's fine with me."

"That's a deal then! We've got to go and enjoy ourselves while we can." Liesel had regained her positive spirit and was smiling now, giving Lene a hug, as they both left the cafeteria.

Hindenburg's seven-year period of government came to an end at the worst possible moment with mass unemployment and a government in crisis. This is when a certain Josef Goebbels demanded in a speech 'if you want everything to stay the same vote Hindenburg, if you want things to change vote Adolf Hitler'. A campaign punctuated by brutality, street fights, beatings and large scale intimidation was waged to increase the vote for the Nazis. Yet the old man Hindenburg was re-elected in spite of this orchestration of fear and chaos. The vote had a maximum turnout and the majority of the voters solidly followed the social democrats' demand to vote for Hindenburg. He won with 53% against 36.8% for Hitler on the 10th April 1932. The 'Vorwärts' newspaper warned:

"Whoever votes for Hitler votes for the last time; in the Third Reich there will be no voting." The German people celebrated the result achieved by the social democrats and the Catholic Zentrum voting together for Hindenburg. Lene had a letter from Erna who had bought the 'Volkswille' of Monday the 11th April:

Gelsenkirchen, 14th April 1932

My darling Lene,
I am thinking of you all the time and wondering how you are in that big city. I thought you might like to see what the 'Volkswille' said the other day, when the social democrats won another decisive victory in the election. I've included the piece here!

"The German workers, subjected as they are to starvation and dire need, world economic crisis and mass unemployment, is yet the only class which stands in a disciplined manner by its republic at a time of terrible stress. The attack by fascism on the Reich has been repelled."

We were relieved, as I'm sure you were.
Thinking of you,
Your sister Erna
PS I've added the 'Frankfurter' too.

Lene smiled. Dear Erna! She had such a good heart. She knew how much Lene used to enjoy her father's political debates and his readings from 'Der Volkswille'. The 'Frankfurter' commented:

"It's remarkable that in spite of Hitler's enormous effort, in spite of the wasteful energy and the use of messianic will he still did not manage to achieve success in Germany. 63% of Germans were not willing to give him their support."

'The Times' in New York greeted the success of Hindenburg with great satisfaction saying that all friends of peace would welcome this result. The 'Morning Post' in London reported that one had to congratulate Germany on its election results, and the 'Financial Times' said that one could breathe a sigh of relief about the results. The disappointing news was that the communists had stood their own candidate, Ernst Thälmann, against Hindenburg, thus resisting a united front approach.

Rushing between the wards and studies in the library Lene and Anni caught glimpses of each other, before their eyes were back in their books. Reading scientific elaborations on clavicles, scapulae, carpal bones and the ulna eased their troubled minds. Lene managed to get the Nazis out of her head, but another voice kept whispering the name of Klaus, which annoyed her. I don't even know him, what's going on? Well, Liesel said you must meet him and she asked me round, but the Saturday was cancelled in the last minute. Klaus had to leave early. Or did he not want to meet her? She tried to put all such thoughts out of her mind. Metacarpals and then the knee. So complicated.

On this occasion the forces of darkness had a setback. There was no time to waste for their supporters. To ease the path to power for Hitler the ruling generals decided to arrange German citizenship for him. The Civil Service obliged. They handed him a 'Beamten' status. He had no profession. All he had was his war experience and a prison sentence. Time was up for Machine-gun Brüning when he lost the support of the Junkers from the Elbe. The plot to remove the last legitimate government of the republic thickened in May. On the 29th of the month Chancellor Brüning turned up for work at the Reichstag for a talk with the president and was told he wasn't needed any more. When asked what this meant Hindenburg replied:

"Yes, this government must go, it is not popular any more."

Within minutes the last remnants of parliamentary legitimacy had been destroyed. Von Papen was declared Chancellor. The Barons ruled. The Reichstag was dissolved. A provocative march of Nazis from Schleswig Holstein through a working class district of Hamburg resulted in the 'Altonaer Bloody Sunday'. Communist workers and Nazis fought battles in a suburb of Hamburg. Eighteen citizens died. Many more were injured. Contemptuous and corrupt in their dealings with the lives of people 'the Cabinet of the Barons' used the incident to dismember the local parliament of Prussia in an attempt to reduce the power of the social democrats. The last bastion of reason and democracy under the control of social democrats and the Zentrum was wiped out. Bloody Sunday became the pretext to commit another act of sabotage. Not only were all the Prussian members of parliament removed from office, but the local chief of police and his second in command as well. When the matter was taken to the state court of law in Leipzig Clara Zetkin declared:

"It's like complaining about the devil to his grandmother".

The 'General-Anzeiger' paper from Dortmund spelt out what was going to happen with great clarity:

"There will be death and concentration camps for all opponents of the Nazi programme, if they carry on daring to have an opinion."

The Saturdays went by, and Lene had not seen Klaus again, but he was on her mind, more than she liked. A little voice kept reminding her of his warm and firm handshake and his boyish neck.

Lene and Anni were taking a break from their studies in town. They stood in the crowded tram looking at the people around them. Lene was bursting to speak about Klaus.

"You know Franz, the artist who I met the other day. I saw him again in his studio. He thinks the social democrats have got it all wrong. We had an argument about it. He's a communist."

"How are they different from the social democrats?"

"The strange thing is they aren't so different. They want to change the whole system to socialism now, rather than work slowly for gradual change."

Lene looked at Anni as they both held on to the leather straps in the carriage. She could see Anni wasn't sure what she was talking about, but she had to tell her about Franz, because someone else was on her mind.

"You are a one for meeting people, Lene! I don't know how you do it, when you have as much studying to do as I have." They both lurched about as the tram shuddered around a sharp corner.

"Study until the pips squeak," Gustave commented, her bottom wobbling as she spoke.

When she returned Lene met Liesel in the canteen.

"Let me get you a coffee, just find us some seats," she said. Lene could see that Liesel was dishevelled and fed up about something. Her blouse was not tucked into her skirt and her auburn bun had unravelled. They sat with a coffee in front of them, their heads almost touching the hot cups.

"Are you all right, Liesel? You look troubled."

"I do feel worried. Our exams are coming up, all that studying while we are also organising against the Nazis. But I'm most worried about Klaus. He's in such a dangerous situation, working for the trade unions. We've got to make our Saturday meal come about, Lene. The other day he had to leave early, but he'll be back again soon. Do you fancy coming?"

Lene laughed. She felt joy at the thought of seeing Klaus again and getting to know him. His cheeky smile had got to her.

"I'm just stuck inside my books until the exams. A nice evening out would be very welcome."

"OK, next Saturday for sure. I know he'll have to be in town. He's been saying he'd like to see you again."

Lene felt a warm joy inside her, but managed to hide it from Liesel.

"Great, I'll come over then. But I was also thinking of how we should respond to the goings on. The Hamburg Altona thuggery, it's so provocative to drive in people from outside and get them to demonstrate with local people."

"Don't tell me! I can't bear thinking about it. Those poor people!" Liesel shook her head, while Lene shuddered as if she was cold.

"First we get an octogenarian as a president, then we get murder in the streets of Hamburg – and no united front in sight! Things couldn't be worse."

"I wasn't in favour of supporting the old man's candidacy, but once they had decided on it, we had to vote for him. That's called solidarity in action. Ernst Thälmann received about 13%. A United Front would have added that to the social democrat vote."

"That's the big question. Why aren't the two left parties working together? It really upsets me sometimes, because I think we're heading for a catastrophe, Lene." Liesel had shadows under her eyes. The skin in her face had red blotches with tight muscles and a huge frown cutting a deep line between her brows. She was tugging on her hair, as if to pull it off. Lene stroked Liesel's arm and tried to calm her.

"We're in a desperate situation, but we're doing our best. We'll finish our studies and then become politically active again. It does give you hope to be engaged in action, doesn't it.. Hopefully it won't be too late then."

Both women fell silent. Neither of them wanted to admit what they really felt. Time was not on their side.

The next Saturday arrived. Lene woke up feeling excited and happy. She had had a dream in which she was flying. Whether it was the dream or going for dinner and seeing Klaus again, or both, she wasn't sure, but she felt exuberant. She took her time to chose a dress and a jacket for warmth. It was autumn, after all. She saw the red shoes in the cupboard and knew she wanted to wear them. They weren't autumn shoes, but what did it matter. Klaus had said that he wanted to see her again. She took good care of her hair which was full and curly brown to the nape of her neck. She put on a necklace with small coloured beads and painted her lips in a soft red hue.

When she arrived at Liesel's flat she noticed immediately how much effort Liesel had made. The flat was tidy. The table was beautifully laid with glasses, serviettes and hors d'oeuvres nibbles. Liesel kissed Lene, and Klaus shook her hand with a warm and firm grip. Again there was that twinkling in his eyes that stirred her, not knowing if he was amused by her or with her.

"How about a glass of wine, Lene?" He held out a glass filled with red wine and passed one to Liesel too. They all clinked glasses and wished each other good health.

"The journey was a bit of a bother," Lene said, "the tram stopped, some electricity problem, I think, we had to walk the rest of the way near the Schloss."

"You poor thing, have a salty biscuit." Klaus held the bowl of nibbles and smiled cheekily.

"OK, no politics tonight," Liesel ordered. Soon the food, wine and warmth relaxed them. Politics or no politics they chatted and raved about studies, Professor Sauerbruch, Klaus's work and Nazi atrocities.It was uncanny. How these butcher boys managed to attract attention through sheer brutality.

"You heard about the fight between the Nazis and the communists in Hamburg? They allowed a gang of Nazis from Schleswig-Holstein to march through a working class district. Pure provocation! Eighteen people died, many more were injured."

"They have special lorries to transport them, you wonder who pays for them."

"And how did the Barons react? The opposite of rational. They take away the last bastion of democracy in Germany with the closing down of the Prussian local government."

They could not avoid talking about politics. It was in their blood. After supper Klaus and Lene ended up on Liesel's comfortable sofa. More wine increased their passion for politics and socialism.

"A workers' republic. Like our comrades in Russia. We should be brothers in socialism."

"And sisters," Lene called out. Klaus's body was so close to her. She saw his bright eyes twinkle and his lips smile.

"You are a fellow revolutionary," he announced and slung his arms around her giving her a hug. Liesel smiled and lifted her glass.

"To the revolution!"

Lenes heart pounded. She wrestled from his arms and lifted her glass.

"To the revolution," they all exclaimed.

CHAPTER 14

THE RED SHOES

"Let me accompany you home, Lene."

Klaus looked deep into Lene's eyes. The hint of laughter in them hypnotised her. She felt warm and giddy.

"You don't need to, Klaus, it's a bit of a way on the tram, maybe walk with me to the tram stop." It was fear more than anything else that made her say that. What would happen if he came to her student accommodation? She might be tempted to let him in in spite of Mamsell Napoleon's orders.

"OK, at least I can be with you for a bit longer."

When he uttered these words Lene felt a floodgate of passion open up inside her. She swayed a little, and he took the opportunity to reach for her hand without saying anything. They walked as if in a dream. The tram stop turned up. So did the tram.

"Tuesday, can you come out on Tuesday, Lene? We'll go to the cinema. I'll meet you at Zoo station at seven pm."

"OK, let's."

He let go of her hand, and she slipped into the tram.

Musculus Piriformis, Nervus ischiadicus... Lene bent over her studies forcing the Latin words into her brain, but all she could think of was Klaus. And Tuesday.

At Zoo station a careless crowd surged in and out of the different entrances. The desire for entertainment was as strong as ever, perhaps more so because of the imminence of catastrophe. The theatres had long queues, and film studios offered world successes that had to be seen. The celebrated events were Charlie Chaplin and Metropolis. Klaus was already there. He saw Lene and a big smile shone on his face. He walked up to her and lightly kissed her on the cheek.

"Do you fancy Charlie Chaplin? That will be funnier than Metropolis. We deserve some light amusements, don't we?"

They quickly walked away from the mixture of smells made up of perfume, sausages and nicotine that hung around the station. They ambled along Hardenbergstrasse. Radio music was blaring out of a tenement flat. Beggars and net-stockinged prostitutes flashed their wares. Klaus found Lene's hand and held it tight and warm. In the cinema time was forgotten. In the privacy of darkness Klaus whispered in Lene's ear. She did not even understand his words, but she knew their meaning. They kissed.

On the sixth of November the Nazis had another setback in their election results with the communists gaining ground. In the July election the Nazis had reached 37.4%, but by November their results were down to 33.1%. In spite of the weakness of the trade unions strikes took place in many towns. In Berlin twenty-two thousand workers of the Berlin transport society went on strike for better pay. The citizens could be forgiven for thinking that the danger of a Nazi take-over had passed. The Frankfurter Zeitung wrote on New Year's day: 'The brutal national socialist attack on the state has been smashed.' The decline of the Nazi party was backed by a local election in the state of Thuringia on the fourth of December with huge losses and an enormous election campaign deficit. Large numbers of members were leaving the Nazi party. However, behind the scenes the ugly machinations were escalating. The Cabinet of the Barons, as they were called, panicked lest the Nazi movement should be lost as a tool for them. They were terrified by the surge of votes for the communists.

"Shall we ban the communists?" they wondered.

"No, that won't do. They'll all run over to the social democrats. We must keep the communists, so that the working class is divided."

It was the moment when the industrialist Schacht, the banker Schroeder, Thyssen, Voegler, general director of United Steel Industry, Reusch and Springorum from Hoesch mining felt it was time for action. They were adamant not to let the opportunity of Nazi rule pass. They wrote to the president. They asked for Hitler to be handed power. On the 4th January 1933 Hitler met with von Papen in the house of the Cologne bank manager von Schroeder. He declared:

"We shall organise the removal of all communists, social democrats and Jews from leading positions in public offices." Back-stabbing was rife among the rivals competing for power. Chancellor Schleicher learnt to his surprise that von Papen and Hitler had met secretly in Cologne. It was in the newspaper 'Taegliche Rundschau'. The meeting was arranged by the banker Kurt von Schroeder. Von Papen argued that Schleicher wanted to keep the Nazis out of government. He, von Papen, though, was actually working to help them in. Representatives from heavy industry were invited to the von Papen intrigue. A secret deal was struck. The industrialists from Hoesch AG, United Steelworks and others arranged a one million Reichsmark deposit to be paid into the Nazi bank account. The Nazi election campaign debts were solved. Hitler was declared Chancellor on the 30th January. Von Papen declared smugly: "You'll be surprised, we hired him." General Schleicher boasted: "We'll squeeze Hitler into the corner, that will make him squeal."

Lene was tired. She had not slept well for weeks. She was in a delirious state, a mixture of anguish, bliss, tiredness and exam stress. She was unable to think of anything other than Klaus. The soft blonde hair at the nape of his neck, his Adam's apple and soft lips stood cast in granite in her mind. In order to remove him from her thoughts she recited some of the bones from the legs and hips: Os coxae, Femur, Patella, Tibia, Fibula...Such reassuring Latin names, transporting her to another age far removed. Where she and her burning emotions did not exist. After the studies were done she allowed herself to indulge in looking in the mirror, when she undressed. She showered and dried her skin. She slowly ran her hands over its softness and the gentle curves of her neck, shoulders and breasts. She looked at the dark triangle of her pubis and felt a surge of desire. Who was this person? How did these powerful emotions come into her body? She felt as if she was standing outside herself looking into someone else's mind. Was she the same person, Lene, the daughter of Mathilde Deppermann? Coal-coloured eyes looked back at her out of the mirror. They glowed.

She pretended she hadn't seen Klaus rushing towards her, although she'd spotted his walk among the many passers-by out of the corner of her eye. She was trembling with excitement at seeing his smiling face. They hadn't seen each other for a month, but she felt she already knew the supple skin of his cheeks and the rolling Adam's apple on his neck. Klaus took her in his arms. They kissed passionately. It burnt deep inside her. The feeling of reciprocation was palpable for both. They needed to create distance with their talk.

"Did you see that stuff in the papers about the economy? Lies, lies, all of it!"

"I try to avoid looking at the headlines as much as I can," Lene mumbled, as she felt Klaus's arm close to hers.

"Money, money, it's the most perverse thing in life."

"How do you mean, Klaus?" They were ambling down Tauentzien Strasse acting as window shoppers, although their attention was on guarding their intense feelings. Klaus had put his arm around Lene's waist and was holding her to himself. The feeling of warmth from his body ran through her like an electric shock.

"It turns one thing into its opposite, as Karl Marx says. You can be one-legged, but with money you can have two legs. You can be ugly, but with money you can buy yourself a beautiful wife. Those with money can buy the opinion of the people and persuade them of their views."

"Yes, just like the Nazis are doing. Money has given them big trucks to drive around in and expensive ugly uniforms to wear. Don't you hate that brown! Sort of toilet colour." Lene shuddered with disgust.

"Let's talk about something more pleasant. What do you fancy doing today, cinema, theatre or strolling in the cold?" Klaus was holding Lene's hand and looked at her with a twinkle in his eyes. His hair had grown longer and hung over his ears like that of a shaggy dog.

"You need a haircut, you do! Or what style are you aiming for, a cocker spaniel's?"

She laughed out loud. He was funny and cheeky and made her laugh just by the way he was asking something. There was something broad and dependable about him, as if you could lean against him and he wouldn't fall over, but instead keep you safe. Once or twice she had nearly done it, but had shrunk back thinking it would be too forward for her to do so. He smelt nice too. The other time he'd taken one of her hands and said 'How cold your hand is. Let me warm it up for you,' and had plunged it into his deep coat pocket. It had brought her very close to him so that she could feel his strong young body next to hers. They were walking in the Tiergarten in the direction of the Victory column. You could see it glisten golden in the distance. Small tufts of clouds were drifting along the sky. It looked so innocent in its azure blue.

"I love the arts, all of them! The theatre, the cinema, art and literature. I had a very lovely art teacher at college in Dortmund. She taught us about some wonderful painters. You know, the ones in Worpswede. But she's dead now. The Nazis ran her over in one of their lorries."

"I'm sorry to hear that, Lene! Let me give you a hug." He turned round and held her in his arms. Lene pressed her head on his chest. She had imagined doing this many times. His warm body against hers, she felt a deep sound like a cello string being pulled inside her that was too powerful to bear. It took her breath away and made her feel like sobbing. For a short while they stood and the world around them was forgotten. My God, she thought! This could be so easy! I do love him so. Her convulsive breath against his chest startled them both. She turned to look at the tumult of traffic to gather her wits.

"Are you all right?" he murmured into her ear. A kind of trance enveloped them. She wriggled out of his embrace.

"I was just thinking of all the studies I still have to do..." Am I lying to him already, but how can I say what I feel. I have no words. Karl! That was different. The studio and Karl had become beautiful paintings from the past. Klaus! I love you!

"How about the cinema again? We can relax a bit with a film and then have a glass of wine, what do you think?" Klaus gently brushed a lock of hair out of Lene's face and looked at her with such longing that she knew he felt the same.

In the cinema they sat in the back row. It was crowded and warm. Some adventure film was happening on the screen, but neither of them took any notice of the action. They spent the two hours in a blissful state of hypnosis. Klaus's kisses on her neck left burn marks and his warm and firm hand held hers. An eternity went by. When they had a glass of wine afterwards they spoke little, but she heard him whisper 'I love you, Lene,' and she, even more quietly, repeated the magic words. He took Lene back to her student accommodation. They kissed, and she felt as if she was going to faint.

On the fateful day, the 30th January 1933, when the industrial bosses had delivered the German people into Hitler's hands Johannes Becher, the poet, wrote:

"Comrades, you must know: All the workers of the world are looking at you and asking:

What will you do? The worker in the Ural puts the question, and on the Yangtse the fisher in his barge. Comrades, whoever stands still today will be guilty, when it will be said 'the dead, the dead, the dead".

That night a wave of demonstrations spread like wildfire through the land. In the big cities protests, proclamations, strikes and torchlight processions lit up the streets from Berlin to Wuppertal. They were the last public expressions of protest and revulsion against the Nazis. Overnight time to plan or organise against the oncoming catastrophe vanished. Thousands of leading communists and social democrats were rounded up that same evening. On the second of February all demonstrations by communists and social democrats were forbidden. Two days later the whole country was placed under emergency legislation. Civil liberties, freedom of movement and free expression were wiped out at a stroke. The 'Vossische Zeitung' still spoke out and declared on the 31st of January:

"You cannot get rid of poverty, but you can get rid of freedom. Desperation and need cannot be forbidden, but the press can be forbidden...."

"Have you heard about all the arrests, Anni? It just shows you exactly what these monsters are like. They go straight for the whole left. They pick people out of their beds and drag them away in vans. Lock them up or murder them on the spot."

"It's so scary! I'm frightened of being out in the street, cars going past me. Thinking it's them. And I'm not even political."

"It's frightening for sure! Our social democratic meetings have been moved from one place to another to keep them secret. If they catch us we're done for. They're like animals. They seem to be everywhere, in lorries, in gangs, on loudhailers, on the radio. Just think of our comrades who have been active in the movement, like Liesel and her brother Klaus. I'm thinking of people at home, like Margarethe, my family! I feel I want to go home and protect them, but how can I?"

Both of them were sitting over a cup of tea in Lene's room, door closed, window closed, heads bent over their cups holding on to them as if the hot cups could give them security. They were still in pyjamas, on a cold Sunday morning. After a moment of quiet Anni asked:

"What's going on with you and that Klaus, Lene? I get the feeling you might have fallen in love. All that 'I'm in a rush, can't see you now,' and the way you look, positively glowing."

Lene blushed right down to her throat and looked at Anni. Anni saw in her friend's face a look that seemed torn between intense pain and supreme pleasure. Lene couldn't bear Anni's searching eyes. She got up and walked over to the window to look out at the bare trees.

"Anni, don't ask! I don't know if I can answer the question. I feel in such a state, it's making me feel breathless and dizzy to think of the…"

"Man," Anni completed the sentence for Lene. "I've been told that what you feel is definitely a symptom of having fallen in love. I was like that when I met Heiner, so I know from my own experience, but it seems to have caught you badly."

Instead of replying Lene turned and flung her arms around Anni, pressing her face to her shoulder.

"I can't work it out. It's all happened so suddenly. I had no idea I could feel like this. After all, I have a good friend back in Gelsenkirchen, my painter friend Karl who I'm very fond of, but this is knocking me over. Klaus is so sweet and cheeky. I have to laugh all the time when I'm with him, even if we talk about those gruesome Nazis, he can turn out a phrase that makes them look ridiculous and we both giggle."

Anni shook her head: "I wish you luck, Lene, because you need it! You'll have to decide whether you'll return home or stay with him?"

"Don't mention going home, Anni. I can't bear to think that far ahead. I shall just have to take it as it comes."

A few days later Lene was near to Franz's studio Z and dropped in to see how he was coping. He was, after all, a member of the communist party. Would they arrest him? She had to find out.

"Franz, how are you, I was worrying what with all these arrests of communists and left-wing people…"

"Lene, good to see you! I'm holding on, as you can see. They don't know me well enough, so I'm not on their lists. Hopefully it will stay that way. I'm very careful, but come and have a look. I want to show you something."

He took Lene into a back room behind the studio after locking the entrance door.

"We're going to bring out a newspaper or magazine for young people to educate them against the Nazis. Here are some ideas of what'll go in it. But the bad news is I'm leaving Berlin. I can't keep the studio going, it's not making enough money. I shall go to Leipzig."

"Maybe you'll be safer there anyway. I shall have to go back to see my family at some point. A magazine for young people sounds like a good idea..."

"Somehow we have to fight back, but I fear the worst. They are going to make mincemeat of the left and Jewish people, regardless of how many there are."

"You bet! It's a dreadful situation. Write to me, Franz. Let me know how things are when you're in Leipzig. I've got to go and study now." A sense of foreboding and fear veiled her eyes as she waved goodbye to him.

The war against the left was on. Communist, social democratic party and trade union offices were raided, files confiscated and the people were dragged out, beaten and locked up. The SS and SA were ordered to use weapons to shoot anyone who did not obey their orders. Then, not even a month into their rule, on the 27th February the Reichstag burnt down. Orange, red and violet flames soared into the night sky. The fire lit up the night over Berlin, and smoke filled the air. People woke from the crackling and hissing of the blaze and trembled in their beds. From its start inside the canteen it spread quickly to other rooms until the plenary hall was on fire. Fires started in many places torched through the building with alarms ringing helplessly in the winter air. The citizens came to stare in disbelief. The fire brigade fought with hoses but was overwhelmed.

"Arsonists, the enemies of the Reichstag are even stealing our building."

"Guess who they're blaming?"

"It's them! The Nazis! Sure enough, they're burning down our democracy!"

"You may think so, but guess who they'll blame. The communists, of course, they're desperate to have a good reason to get at them."

"It's warm at least, I could do with some of that wood for my stove."

"Those people don't need a reason! Haven't they burnt and butchered their way through the land for years now?"

"I'd like some of that fancy furniture, but I imagine it's too hot to get at."

"Furniture, furniture! What sort of trash are you to think of furniture at this moment, when our whole democracy is at stake?"

"Who are you calling trash! Don't throw stones in a glass house. Anyway what democracy was that we had?"

"I can tell you what's to come will be a thousand times worse."

Lene and Klaus stood huddled together and silently listened to the voices around them. She was leaning against him, as she had imagined she wanted to do, and it felt good. His strong body stood like a column of peace and certainty, a sort of beyond bodily feeling. She felt warm and happy and anguished at the same time. How could it be that one's own life was so utterly at odds with what was going on around them?

A man was arrested later that night. For the time being the fire was a useful pretext for Nazi actions. On the same night they locked up over ten thousand communists, among them many writers and artists. On the third of March the leader of the German communist party, Ernst Thaelmann was arrested. An election on the fifth of March brought little for the Nazis to cheer about in spite of all the bullying and intimidation they had mustered. They did not gain a majority (43.3%) in an event that was designed to suggest democratic credentials, although state officials were commanded to vote and all left-wing newspapers had been banned. Astonishingly the left still obtained a combined vote of one third of the population, although their leaders were already locked up or dead. All communists and social democrats were thrown out of the Reichstag. On the seventh of April all teachers, professors and judges at universities and in law courts lost their jobs, if they had been involved in democratic movements.

The Ermächtigungsgesetz (the empowerment law) gave the Nazis unlimited power. On the twenty-second of June the social democratic party was banned. 'Gleichschaltung' ('making the same') led to the disbandment of all bodies or organisations local or national.

They were in Liesel's kitchen. Klaus had his arm around Lene, as they stood together by the window looking out into Hardenberg Strasse with its tall planes, now dark silhouettes. Liesel was cooking spaghetti. She was talking into the pot of boiling water.

"Have you heard the news? They arrested Carl von Ossietzky who writes for 'Die Weltbühne' and the poets Egon Erwin Kisch and Erich Muehsam. You'd think they wouldn't dare to! These are well-known writers!"

Liesel continued eyeing her pasta and as no one said anything she carried on.

"Now they'll need more staff in the hospital, the way they are beating up people. That is, if they let them get to a hospital! It's terrifying how they were slipped into power and have changed the whole country within days. All the rights we developed over the last ten years wiped out! Shows you how citizens' rights are a very delicate thing.

"It leaves you feeling a sort of helplessness, anger and guilt. They overwhelmed everyone, but we have to rebuild our organisations."

The pasta was done. Lene and Klaus had kissed while she was talking.

"Listen to this! Our chief trade unionist, Leipart, has agreed to work with them. With a leadership like that what can be expected of the ordinary trade union member? I wish you were more careful, Klaus, you and your trade union work! Why should I lose my dear brother to these animals?" Liesel's voice was reproachful, but her eyes shone with fear. Lene wrapped her arms around her and Klaus hugged both women. Liesel turned to them.

"And you two, I can't believe it! You both look so blissfully happy, as if you were living in another world. It's a crying shame! Life could be so good. My best friend Lene with my dear brother!"

They sat down and had pasta chatting about what actions could be taken to fight back.

"We've got to produce a newsletter and contact everyone who is still free."

"An underground press, leaflets baked into bread, we've got to be creative..."

"The lists of names and addresses! They need to be guarded like gold..."

The strain of the examinations had almost taken them to breaking point. And then it was suddenly all over. Anni booked her train journey back to the Rhine for late March. She wasn't sure if she was going to have a job, but there was always work on the farm. Lene refused to think of the future. Anni embraced her warmly and invited her to come and visit her in the village back home. But she could only see an intense flame of love burning in Lene's dark eyes. Lene lived for each day. She woke up and thought of Klaus. She went to bed and dreamed of Klaus. They met most days.

"You're safer in my student room, stay here," she coaxed. Mamsell Napoleon had relaxed the rules since term ended. They bought provisions and didn't go out. Was it days or weeks? Neither of them knew. They had lost all sense of time and place. Wasn't the trade union office closed anyway? They had play fights chasing each other off the bed and then lay still, exploring their bodies. Lene trembled with pleasure when Klaus ran his warm hand along her shoulder, breast and belly. She turned round and did the same to him feeling the tiny hairs on his chest, his Adam's apple and running her hand down towards his pubis. He moaned and turned to lie on top of her and kiss her. The weight of his strong young body pressing down on her was intoxicating. She breathed in his kisses. They had breakfast in bed. Crumbs everywhere. The food was running out, the bread was dry. It was only when their hunger overwhelmed them that they started thinking about the outside world.

"I'm starving! Let's get some food."

"Kiss me first, otherwise I won't let you out of bed." He tugged at her arm and pulled her back, held her breasts in his hands and kissed each nipple in turn. Lene writhed with pleasure.

"Let me go, I'm really hungry."

She wrestled free and ran into the bathroom, locking it. She looked in the mirror. She saw her face glowing with happiness. She felt her nipples and lips kissed raw and she put lotion on them. She was without thought, because thoughts meant this blissful time would have to end. Outside the bathroom Klaus took her back in his arms, and they held each other for a long time until Lene's stomach rumbled.

"Let's go, I'm starving."

They found a stand-up food bar and ate sausages with bread and mustard. It tasted fantastic. They walked without looking where they were. Later they sat in a cafe at Potsdamer Platz. They had a bottle of red wine. She saw that he had something on his mind, and it made her stomach churn. They had to talk about things, but it was so hard. Her heart began pumping blood too fast. It made her feel nervous.

"How's things at work, Klaus? You must have heard something of what's going on."

"It doesn't look too good, but so far work is continuing, just under a different name. There have been a couple of them in the office. They literally stormed in and demanded we do this and that, used disgusting, vile language. Vermin!" He spat out the word and shook himself, as if to shake off the memory.

"You've got to watch out, Klaus! They will stop at nothing. Remember what your sister said. Just keep quiet. You want to survive this lot. We all do!"

"What about you! You're not saying what's on your mind either..."

"At some point I have to go home, like to Gelsenkirchen..."

"I was afraid you'd come and tell me this. Lene, what about us? We could build a life together. I love you very much, Lene!"

"I love you too, Klaus. I can't tell you how fond I am of you, but my family is calling me. I've got to go home soon..."

"How soon is soon?"

"In three weeks." There. It was out. She'd said it. Now it was becoming part of their life, the reality of what they needed to do. She had to leave Berlin, and he had to work in an office that was right under the noses of the Nazi party. If they hadn't spoken about it would it perhaps not have happened? Could they have stayed in her room for ever? She laid her hands on Klaus's on the table. He got hold of them and held them tight.

"I won't let you go, I won't."

"And I won't let you go! Let's not think about it now. Let's just enjoy ourselves. Maybe it'll all work out all right."

They left the cafe and walked out into the cold air.

"How about we take a trip! We'll go to the Baltic sea and have a holiday."

"Brilliant idea. I really fancy that."

The streets of Berlin were deserted after dark and a sharp wind blew cold air under their collars. Dogs were howling in some block of flats. A few streets away they heard those infamous lorries revving their engines. They looked around themselves, but their street remained silent. Sheer panic fills you - will they turn in your direction? - but the noise ebbed away. Then the haunting thought that they're coming for someone else. A communist! A Jew! Smug people hissed 'they had it coming to them'. But if they could do it shamelessly to the communists and the Jews what would stop them doing it to anyone? No one liked to face that truth. Fear stayed and ate deep into the soul.

The week before a social democrat who'd argued with a gang of Nazis in his street, when they came to take a neighbour away, was shot on the spot. They ran up into his house and shot his two sons as well. They came for several more known social democrats in the street. It was a world in reverse. Behind their curtains people stood pale and breathless and watched the wretched being dragged away. Nazi power grew like a cancer and spread through all walks of life.

Klaus organised more leave from his work to be with Lene. They wanted to make the most of the little time that remained. They decided to travel to the sea. They took the train to the Baltic Sea resort of Warnemünde.

"We won't talk about politics or the future, will we?" he asked her.

They strolled on white sandy beaches with the spring wind tugging on their clothes and hair. They ate delicious rolls with smoked eel, smacking their lips and licking each other's fingers afterwards. They sat in a pink and white striped beach basket at dusk and kissed, digging their toes into the sand. Klaus's warm soft hands held Lene tight, feeling her shoulders, the curve of her neck and her breasts. He slipped his hand under her silk blouse and pressed her nipple lightly, until she moved his hand away. She couldn't bear it. It was an excruciatingly sensuous feeling. They watched the moon rise after sunset like an orange lampion. She'd brought her red shoes. He took her feet and kissed each toe and put them on for her. They danced in a beach bar holding on to each other for dear life. The beach promenade was deserted when they stepped out to get some fresh air. The flagpole ropes clattered, and the illumination on the promenade threw light and shadow patterns on the pavement. The sea lay calm and endless. They stood and watched the shimmering distance that seemed to mirror their momentary ecstasy without bounds, endless and timeless like the ocean.

"It is so: The Allies contributed much to the Nazis gaining power. If they had shown a supportive attitude to the Brüning government at a critical time in 1931/32 the Nazis would have lost a lot of their impact."

Werner Otto Müller-Hill, 1944

CHAPTER 15

HEARTBREAK

"Why can't you just write to your family and say you've found work in Berlin?"

The grass was dry. They both sat down after Klaus had spread out his jacket. The sun was blinking through the trees lighting up the vibrant green spring leaves. He took her hand and kissed each of her fingertips. She smiled a sad smile. Klaus wrapped his arms around Lene and held her close. He pressed an urgent kiss on her mouth. She responded with such longing that stirred them both deeply.

"Lene, speak to me..." He looked at her, with both despair and bliss in his eyes. She gently pulled him down and they lay looking at the sky.

"Klaus, you know that I love you so much..." A sob stopped her words and they held each other.

"Klaus, my family... I just can't let them down. I must go and see them, spend some time with them. My mother wrote to me and asked when I am returning. My sister says there is work for me at the hospital... imagine, I could earn my own living, and here I would just be a burden to you..."

She had finally said it all, squeezed the thoughts she'd had into words. It was hard saying what she said, but she felt lighter once the words were out. Klaus was silent now, and she ran her hand through his soft doggy hair and kissed his Adam's apple. They lay together and the knowledge that they would have to part cut into their bodies like a knife.

The next days fled by in preparations and goodbyes to friends. Liesel kept saying 'I know you'll be back. You two are made for each other.' Her words were balm to their anxious souls.

"You must promise to write to me, Lene," he kept saying.

"You too, we'll write to each other every week," she promised.

Despite all their efforts to make time stop it passed, and the moment of departure for Gelsenkirchen came. Lene stood on the platform of Hamburger Bahnhof, and Klaus held her hand, warming it in his pocket as he'd done right at the beginning. He kissed her ear lobe and a lock of her bushy brown hair. He looked into her eyes and searched them for the deep glow of her love, but Lene's eyes were dark and sad. He whispered: "I love you, Lene."

She didn't respond with words but squeezed his hand in his coat pocket and leaned against his sturdy body. He hadn't cut his hair. She flung up her other hand and slipped it through the tangle. It was soft and fluffy. He caught her hand and kissed her fingertips.

"I'm glad you haven't cut it," she whispered.

But then the train pulled into the platform and masses of white steam enveloped them with a whistling noise. The engine's cacophony drowned out any words between them. Fate, the future, uncertainty and the threat of distance had all arrived with a bang. Trunks were shifted with heavy footsteps. Lene found her compartment, and Klaus followed with her suitcases. He stood looking pale for a moment. His usual easy-going humorous expression was gone from his face. It was a mask of tight anxious muscles. They hugged and kissed and looked searchingly into each other's eyes for the closeness in their hearts. People bumped into them with their cases. Late travellers nearly ran them over in their haste to get to their seats. He pressed another kiss on her mouth and turned to squeeze through the throng in the gangway to step outside. He rushed to stand outside her window. She opened it and they held hands again. The train started to move. He held her hands and then the tips of her fingers, until he had to let go. With a sinking heart Lene watched him pull a red handkerchief out of his pocket and wave it in the air. It was clearly visible amongst all the white ones that were fluttering in the windy station. Red for socialism. Red for the revolution. Klaus, my love, I shall miss you so much! A dark fear of never seeing him again enveloped her. She felt aches all over and ran to the toilet. The evening closed in on the train as it sped into the night.

They sat in Ahlsdorf cafe. The sooty Gelsenkirchen rain left smutty stripes on the window panes and dark clouds raced across the sky pushed by the storm. A clattering tin can outside cut words out of their conversation. Lene sat eyes wide, mouth agape and taking in with all her senses what Margarethe was telling her while she gazed at her good friend. Did she not look years older than when she last saw her? Her eyes were still bright and intelligent, but her skin had formed many tiny wrinkles and grey streaks made her hair look lighter and her face darker. Lene felt warm and cheerful upon seeing her friend in the familiar surroundings, yet a forlorn estrangement was besetting her thoughts as if with a fungus. The world in her home town was no longer as she had known it.

"You can't imagine how it feels living in this town now. We weren't naive, Alfred and I. You know that. We knew what the Nazis were going to do. Alfred kept telling people. Then last year he was beaten up. He had already been threatened verbally several times."

"How dreadful, how did it happen?"

"He was coming home from a trade union meeting. It was quite late on the fifth of July, when this group of Nazis ran out from the dark and started attacking him. They shouted at him things like 'you communist pig,' 'we'll get you,' and smashed their fists into his face and kicked him down. They left him in a pool of blood and disappeared without trace. One of his fellow journalists found him and called an ambulance. Without his help I am not sure if he would have survived."

"Poor Alfred, how awful that must have been for both of you! Have you reported the attack?"

"There have been so many attacks on socialists and communists. The police and the courts can't cope with it all. It's all out of control. It's criminals now in charge!"

Margarethe looked drained, but still confident.

"All the work we've built up here in town; our clubs for women, the playgroup for children, trade union support. All of it is now deemed illegal. You can't organise anything without them shutting it down immediately. Gelsenkirchen doesn't feel the same any more. The Nazi beasts have been let loose to roam the streets with no regard for human life or limb. We used to feel this was a workers' town with such a sense of unity and loyalty among us, even if there were differences. I must tell you, Lene, we're considering leaving Germany, probably for the Netherlands."

"I suppose you ought to, the way the Nazis have already attacked Alfred. You're both in greater danger, because you've done so much political work. Is the 'Volkswille' still being published?"

"Oh no! They shut it down in February this year, really as soon as Hitler was handed power. The social democrats aren't allowed to meet any more. Many of Alfred's colleagues have been beaten up, locked up and tortured. It's getting too dangerous for us. I suppose we're thinking how we can be more useful, and have decided it will be better to work from abroad to let people in other countries know what's happening here. We shall write pamphlets and keep busy. You know what we're like."

"So many have gone into exile, especially since the Reichstag fire. An obvious plot on their part! Then they used it as an excuse to lock up our best people, Carl von Ossietzky, Erich Mühsam…

Many people didn't believe they could gain power. You know what Tucholsky said about the Nazis: 'It's impossible to look so low'."

"These writers are idealists and fervently believe in the good of people and pacifism. My Alfred's an idealist too. We both are, but when you're organised in a political party you have to cope with all sorts of people and you learn to moderate your idealism a bit."

"It makes you wonder about idealism, whether we ought to stop thinking in such terms, when comrades seem so unable to..."

"No, no, Lene, don't even go there! Of course we need idealism. A vision of a better future! We need to believe that humans on earth can become free and equal! That we can get rid of exploitation! Without that we couldn't even begin to theorise and plan for what needs to be done..."

Lene felt proud and happy when she heard Margarethe make a passionate plea for the goodness in mankind. It confirmed her own deep urge for a resolute, positive vision of what humans could achieve. She felt an inkling of being at home again in this grey and dirty town. Margarethe also looked brighter with her own speech. They started laughing and even ordered a piece of Schwarzwälder Kirsch cake to share with another cup of coffee.

"What are your plans then, Lene?" They talked about Lene being offered a job at the local hospital and how Margarethe was trying to keep as much of her work going as possible by word of mouth amongst the women. Alfred continued to meet secretly with his social democrat comrades and trade unionists. Every day damning news of the situation reached their ears. As they talked their heads were bent closer over the table, almost speaking cheek to cheek, as if afraid the men in brown uniforms would suddenly turn up.

At Karl Mayer Strasse Lene found her family unchanged. It was nice, but also strange, because she now saw the world with different eyes, and wondered why they hadn't moved on at all. In her room she looked at the old chest of drawers with its forlorn items from the past: a photo of her and Erna by the sea, a small mother of pearl box and a little wooden rocking horse from a dolls house. She looked at herself in the mirror. She touched her skin, her eyebrows and hair.

She realised that she was the one who had changed. Berlin had made her a different person. She had fallen in love. She had studied. She looked at her hands, as if she was looking for her love and work to show in them.

Life was stagnant at home. Her mother, Mathilde, sat in her small office, the desk covered in orders and letters as if Lene had left her like that only the day before. Sandalwood smells wafting! The shop assistants wrapped bread in paper bags. Shoppers demanded the freshest loaf, as if the new tyranny was in another country. In the bakery young Hermann held the reins and led the apprentices with a quiet, firm but kind demeanour, just like she used to know him. He stood with his face dusted in flour and his hands covered in dough, when she ran up to him and gave him a big hug.

"Lene, it's you! Don't come too near, I'm covered in flour and dough."

"Never mind, Hermann, I know how to deal with flour and dough. It smells nice, just as it always did. Are you baking a new type of bread?"

"I'm trying all types of new things, like onion bread, but also new cakes using fruit and nuts."

His younger brother Hans had got engaged and was now working in another bakery which he was likely to marry into. Hilde had more children to look after. Her husband's cheeks and nose were redder than ever.

"My child," her mother said and let Lene give her a brief embrace, "I'm glad you've left that crazy place Berlin behind. At least here we're a small community close together. We know everyone and get on well with them. Have you been in touch with the hospital? They are very keen to have you start immediately."

Of course her mother had her mind on work, as soon as Lene appeared. She was so conscientious. Lene wondered if work had filled all areas in her mother's heart. Work could be healing and make you forget. The person she was most pleased to see again was her sister Erna. She hugged her for a long time and let the older sister squeeze Lene to her trembling bosom, like she used to do. It felt good.

They looked at each other. Erna had grown a little rounder and was wearing loose clothes to cover her extra weight.

"Sit down, my child! How have you been? You must tell me all about the big city and your studies. I hear you did well."

Lene saw Erna's searching glance, but she kept Klaus a secret. She could not bear talking about him. When Lene didn't respond Erna added,

"When they heard in the hospital that you had studied at the Charite they asked to employ you straightaway."

"Just as well, Erna, because I couldn't bear being back in the shop, to be honest."

"I don't blame you, it does get tedious. You know that I've passed my driving test and now work several days a week as a helper in the hospice, but look at my hands. They are a mess again." Erna held her hands palms down in front of Lene, who could see the red bumpiness of the eczema. Poor Erna. Maybe things hadn't really changed.

"On our course we learned that many things have to do with how you breathe and that our bodies can become poisoned by not having enough fresh air in our system. The eczema might have to do with that."

"I think you're right, Lene, that's why I keep trying to travel to St Peter Ording to breathe some fresh sea air, but I don't have the money to do that as often as I'd like. If I had a close friend with some money, I'm sure he'd take me."

All the old subjects, Lene thought. How tiring! Poor Erna is still waiting for the ideal man. If only she knew how much heartache you can have when you do find someone very nice, she might not be so eager. To avoid saying anything about Berlin was easy, because Erna was so full of her own grievances and petty local problems - getting on with her sister Hilde who came round to boss her about, Fritz her husband patting her on the bottom, which she didn't like, and her mother treating her as an extra servant. She burst into tears.

"Why does God make my life so hard, Lene? What he's got in store for me I don't know or understand. I'm trying to be patient and calm, but I find it so hard. That's why I have the eczema, I think."

At the weekend Lene took a stroll along her old route past the mine and over the railway bridge to see her friend Olga. But no one opened the door. Lene looked through the letterbox. Letters that the postman must have posted were lying all over the floor. No one had picked them up for days. What had happened to Olga and Matti and her parents? An ache seared through her stomach, as if something had cut her. Had they moved out or had they been forced out? What fate had befallen them? She felt too empty to try and talk to any neighbours. She strolled back over the bridge and looked at the bleak mine towers and the coal-smeared roads with no joy. The trolleys screeched through the air under heavy grey clouds, as they had always done. The early May green on the trees seemed limp and defeated before summer had even arrived. An ambulance was bleating in the distance. Another person had probably been attacked and left for dead by the brown uniforms.

Later, in the lounge, they sipped tea. The lights from the mine circled around the walls. Fairground lights, Lene thought, and remembered her past happy feelings. The cups clinked. The peppermint tea was strong and good. Mathilde's knitting needles clicked quietly. Erna was bent over her craftwork sewing a straw body on to the wooden head of a little boy with brown hair and eyes. Young Hermann arrived very late looking drawn and full of fatigue. A radio was now stationed on the sideboard, but no one in the house dared to turn it on, as all stations had been taken over by the Nazis shouting commands and orders through the airwaves. Lene felt a strong urge to take her father's position and raise the political issues of the day. The evening discussions about the wider world out there had been deeply embedded in her soul like a physical need for water or bread.

"Margarethe told me they're going to emigrate to the Netherlands. He was attacked and beaten up, so it's not safe for them to stay here. You remember father always read 'der Volkswille' to us. Well, they've shut down the offices and forbidden all trade union and social democrat organisations."

While she spoke her voice became louder and sharper, making them all look up from their work. She was clamping her hands on the armrests of the chair.

"Well, it does get you into a state! How can all our hopes have been wiped out by this gang of hooligans overnight?"

"Lene, mind your words! It's dangerous to speak out about them, they have ears everywhere."

"What are you saying? Are there people in the house who have sympathies with these criminals?"

Mathilde put her finger to her mouth to indicate silence, but maybe she just wanted to calm Lene down. "No, I don't think there's anyone in our house who has a liking for these fellows. But you mustn't get yourself so agitated. You might speak loosely like that in other places. I just don't want you to be in any danger."

"If everyone keeps quiet they can walk over us. That's exactly the problem. All those political parties went and dissolved themselves. No backbone! What would Father have made of that? Just as well he doesn't have to witness these developments. He wouldn't have kept quiet."

There was a proud and accusatory tone in her voice, which Erna picked up, when she responded as if on behalf of their mother.

"You should leave our good father out of this! May he rest in peace! These are very difficult times, and our mother has already a huge task to keep the household going. I know you mean well, Lene," she added, "you've got Father's spirit in you! But you should listen to our mother and be very careful about speaking out so frankly."

"This is our home! We should speak about these dreadful developments in our own home at least!"

Lene glowered at her sister, but Erna had returned to her work. So had her mother. Silence engulfed the room. It made Lene feel as if she was being frozen alive. It terrified her more than anything else so far. Finally, her mother spoke:

"Lene, forgive us, we're all very tired. Maybe another night we can talk. Maybe we just can't face the awful reality out there."

Lene slumped back in her chair, overcome by remorse. Who was she to start accusing her own family? Did they not all work hard and provide the local community with bread? They had done their best to support the republic, which had now been sacrificed on the butcher's table, cut up in pieces and thrown to the dogs. Tears ran silently down over her cheeks as she felt all her muscles become torpid and her crunched body sat like a marble figurine.

The hospital work was in many ways a welcome relief. It overwhelmed her with tasks and duties and kept her running all day on her feet. She was exhausted by nightfall. After some days she managed to get into a rhythm that allowed her energy to come back enough to go and visit her old friend Inge, who was still living at home. Her mother had died, and she had taken over the household and looked after her younger brothers. They embraced for a long time and looked each other up and down. Inge looked well, but there were sad lines around her eyes.

"Where do I start, Lene, it's been awful! It's difficult to speak to anyone now and organise. And organise we must! We must get rid of these monsters. See all those dreadful swastikas! You can't get away from them. They hang on every building in town. They're renaming our streets, community houses and halls with their own names, so you begin to feel disorientated. The communist party community house, you know, the 'Volkshaus', has been renamed 'National-Eck'. Can you imagine such a vile thing? They arrested all the communists immediately after the fire in Berlin. They killed our friend Erich Lange. I don't know if you ever met him. He was a communist. He was beaten up, shot and trampled on so much that his comrades hardly recognised him when they managed to see him in the mortuary."

They sat in silence in the old kitchen cupping their mugs with their hands.

"I can hardly bear hearing these stories, Inge. It's bad enough seeing it going on in Berlin, but my own home town... that feels very painful."

"They took revenge on him. That's what it was. Erich, you know, had joined the SS but then left when he realised what they were up to and joined the anti-fascist movement instead. He had all that insider information, and they hated him for that and for leaving them. It was in March, the Nazis held one of their obnoxious flag wavings, when they expect everyone to do a Hitler salute. If you didn't do it you were beaten up or threatened and shouted at. When they spotted him they went for him, he was beaten and kicked to death. In spite of threats two hundred comrades accompanied his coffin to the graveyard. We all cried our eyes out. But there was such a strong feeling of loyalty and belonging together; it still made me feel we can resist and somehow overcome these animals. They can't last! Our people are incredibly brave and courageous. Leaflets and fliers are stuck in letterboxes sneakily in spite of threats. It must be annoying for them, you know, that people won't just obey them. Of course if we're found out it'll cost us our freedom and maybe even our lives."

"Are you involved in these actions, Inge?"

Inge looked with big eyes at Lene, putting her hands on her friend's: "We all are, Lene! There's no stopping any of us fighting and organising against them."

"I'll join you, Inge. I want to play my part. I also helped to organise our students against the Nazis at the university. My friend Liesel joined me up in the local social democrats group. You must keep me posted about this."

"I will do," Inge replied, looking with warmth and pride at her friend. Feeling togetherness gave them both a lot of strength. Inge waved a smiling goodbye and Lene was out in the windy evening air. The soot and smoke went up into her nose and made her sneeze. As she made her way home past the forlorn crowd she thought of Klaus. The warmth of his strong body for her to lean against came back to her like a flame and burnt a hole into her heart. Happy moments with him mingled with other images, her father in his white baker's hat, walks with the Wandervögel, the theatre with Margarethe. It all seemed so distant now.

On the 5th May Alfred Zingler fled from Gelsenkirchen by night. He was picked up by a friend in a motorcar. Lene had joined Margarethe and several other comrades for some drinks at their house. They wished him good luck. He needed it, as they had learnt that an arrest was imminent.

"Rats from the gutter! They'll sink with the ship. I give them no more than a couple of years. That tyranny of theirs can't last." He seemed to be in a better mood than anyone else there, although he was the one who had to leave home.

"How are you going to travel?" someone asked.

"I'm heading via a circuitous route towards Gronau where I'm staying the night with a comrade. From there I shall make my way over the border on foot. I won't use a passport, as you know they are probably looking for me. I shall get a bus from the border to Hengelo. A social democrat from the Dutch party is going to house me to begin with. Then we shall see. I'll keep you informed."

They all left early enough to get home before it got late. That night Lene had a dream from which she woke in a heavy sweat. She was with friends who were all dressed in dark, heavy, long clothes, as if at a funeral. Agitated talking was making her feel anxious and nervous. She tried to speak soothingly to calm her friends down, when someone opened a door and masses of water started to flood into the room where they were sitting. They tried to run out, but the water kept coming in a gigantic tidal wave that grew higher every moment. Just before it caught up with Lene she woke up with a start and sighed with relief. She was in her bed at home, the clock ticking quietly on her bedside table and her clothes hanging over the chair motionless in the flickers of light from the mines.

The hospital work was exhausting. They were short of staff. One physiotherapist had to look after all the patients in the male and female wards for broken bones, fractures and accidents. Every day traumatised people arrived who had suffered the fate of meeting up with a Nazi. Their faces smashed in, arms or legs broken, they were delivered to hospital, had to be operated on by the surgeon and needed an exercise programme while they were recovering to get back to normality. Showing the patients how to begin practising to use their muscles was routine for Lene now, but seeing the emotional distress in these poor people was quite another thing. She had to be cheerful and encouraging for her own good. After such a day Lene walked out of her workplace in the evening like a zombie, worn out and emotionally drained. She walked down Husemannstrasse without seeing anyone and turned towards home by the main post office. The hated swastika banners hung sly and threatening from flagpoles. She became aware of a shop window with hats, where a young woman was decorating the manikins with a new selection. She saw herself reflected in a mirror looking tired with big dark eyes and a mop of brown hair, a beige jacket over her arm and clutching a handbag, when next to her she spotted Karl.

"Lene, you're back! Why didn't you tell me?"

"Karl! Oh God! I was daydreaming. I'm so worn out. I only came back a couple of weeks ago and had to start working at the local hospital immediately. They're short of staff. The work is really tiring, but it's great to see you," she added quickly smiling. Karl's diminutive crippled figure stood suddenly next to her. His bright face with the tall forehead beamed at her.

"Come! Let's have a coffee or even a glass of wine! I'll invite you. We'll go to a little bar I know. We can be quite private there." She wondered what he had in mind. Did he mean no Nazi listeners or neighbours snooping into their private life?

"A glass of wine would be great after all the work. You know that my friend Margarethe has followed her husband Alfred into exile in the Netherlands." How different I feel about him, she thought.

The sat down in Violetta's bar round the back of the Theatre. It had comfortable armchairs, dimmed lights and a long bar with few people at this time of the day. Karl ordered two glasses of wine, while Lene went to the ladies to check out her hair and put on some lipstick in a habitual sort of way. She looked in the mirror and saw the woman who had soaked up Klaus's kisses. Poor Karl. I like him as a friend, but no more. I hope he feels the same. She felt slightly on edge in case Karl had other intentions.

"Tell me about how your work is going, Karl. What about the arrival of the Nazis here in town. Has it affected you?"

"It's these dreadful flags that get to me! Our beautiful Gelsenkirchen is so ugly now. But I just keep on working. You know what I'm like! I carry on getting myself involved. It's a must to fight against these people. Somehow! When you left that year I had the chance to work in Sanary sur Mer in France for some time. I met a lot of artists and writers there. I joined the communist party then."

He had pulled out a packet of cigarettes and offered them to Lene, who took one. He lit their cigarettes and they toasted each other.

"I also joined a political organisation, the social democrats, in Berlin. How they carried on stopping a united front! I could never understand the logic of that," she said quizzically looking at Karl.

"I felt the social democrats kept selling out, but maybe we overestimated our strength, it's hard to know the truth," Karl said soothingly and smiled. He added,

"The Reichstag Fire! That was the start. We were still getting newsletters from artist organisations and writer friends, it was dreadful to read them. So many arrested, thrown into concentration camps and prisons. You wouldn't believe it if someone told you this is Germany today. The outside world has no idea! Literally the day after the fire. Carl von Ossietzky, Erich Mühsam, Egon Erwin Kisch, Hermann Duncker, Hans Litten, Harry Wilder. They arrested Willy Bredel in Hamburg and Wolfgang Langhof in Düseldorf. 'Die Weltbühne' published an article by Kurt Hiller on the seventh of March. The Nazis devastated his apartment the following day. He was arrested. All of it was well pre-planned and organised. There's no doubt about that. They had all the addresses ready for use. They attacked and destroyed printing presses in publishing houses."

"Horrific! Just a month after they were handed power. Culturally speaking Germany lies in ruins."

"Let's talk about more pleasant things. Tell me about your studies in Berlin, and what they qualify you to do?"

"It was hard work, Karl. We nearly gave up at times. The professor was very strict. You heard of Sauerbruch? Unfortunately, he's a conservative and is surrounded by double-dealers. He forbade all political action at the university. I made a good friend there, a woman called Anni. We supported each other. She lives on a vineyard by the Rhine." She blanked out Liesel, but as she spoke intense thoughts about Klaus made her blush. Luckily the light was so low that Karl couldn't see it or didn't notice it. All the same she felt uncomfortable now in his presence and wanted to leave before anything was said about going to his apartment.

"I'm so tired and the wine is having a very nice effect on me, but it's making me feel sleepy. Do you mind if I leave now, Karl? I'll be in touch, but I need to get some sleep now." She rose to her feet. He got up too and put an arm around her to draw her to himself. He looked at her with his grey green eyes that had the softness of the sea in them.

"I'm still very fond of you, Lene. You can come over to my place any time. It must be hard, I suppose. You still live in the bakery with all that work as well?"

Lene gently manoeuvred herself away by putting on her jacket and getting hold of her bag.

"I do, but it's not that bad, you know. I'm used to it, and Erna, well, she needs me really..."

Karl paid and they parted outside the bar. Lene felt sad. I suppose he's lonely, but what about me? I'm even more lonely. I miss Klaus badly. My friend Anni is far away on the vineyard. Olga has vanished and Margarethe has left the country.

She did not take the tram, instead she walked all the way to Karl Mayer Strasse in the dusk past the baths, shops and finally towards the Dahlbusch mine. At home a letter for her was lying on the chest of drawers in the kitchen. She looked at the postmark: it was from Berlin. She ran upstairs into her room and sat down at her desk to open it. It was from Liesel.

My dearest Lene,

It's not long since you left, but so much has happened, and sadly, there's no good news that I can tell you. Berlin is in uproar, whole streets have been emptied of our best citizens; social democrats, communists, Jewish people are being rounded up; writers, artists...the theatres are open, but there is fear everywhere; fear if a performance will be stopped, fear of actors being arrested. It seems now everything is forbidden, unless a sign says it is allowed. I don't know how you are and hope you have found your family all well and healthy, but here my worst fear has come true, and perhaps yours as well. Klaus has been arrested. As soon as he went back to Potsdam after the break he had with you, they came for him. They were literally waiting in his trade union office for him, put him in handcuffs and took him to Oranienburg prison. Don't worry too much at the moment. It may just be a temporary measure. I am trying to stay positive and feel confident that they will release him soon. I will keep you posted.

Much love,
From Liesel

Lene collapsed on her chair silently. The blood drained out of her head. Her heart pumped wildly, and she felt faint. She got up and threw herself on her bed, head in the pillows. Klaus, my darling, Klaus, can you hear me? Why do I have to be so far away from you, my dearest! What am I doing here, when I should be near you? Oh God, please hear me, help Klaus, stand by him! A prayer came into her mind without thinking. She couldn't even cry. She had to be hopeful. That is what Liesel said. She had to trust his sister. I must hope.

Diary notes, 17th July 1974

My mother interrupted her story and sat silently next to me. In any case we had to pick up the kids from school shortly. It started to rain. She sat as still as a statue and then turned towards me with tears in her eyes. I couldn't help it. A moment later we were both crying our eyes out. And held on to each other. How very sad it all was. She sobbed and sobbed. For a while we sat in the rain and gave in to our feelings of devastation.

"I shall never understand why I left him. Why didn't I just stay there with him?"

I tried to find reasons for her, but I didn't know whether she wanted to hear them.

"You wanted to be with your family. They would have never forgiven you if you'd stayed in Berlin."

"Perhaps."

"It was a terrifying time and he definitely belonged to the group of people who were at risk. You would have just been frightened all the time and worried that they would take him away, and you had no work."

"I would have hated myself if I'd left him because he was in danger. I can't permit myself such a thought."

"But you both believed that you were going to return, didn't you?"

"True, we did."

End of diary notes

CHAPTER 16

AUTO DA FE

"Brother, dressed in newspapers in exile you avoid the sun. Your suitcase in front of the door is guarded by ravens..."

Rose Ausländer, Brother in exile

On the 5th May a rabble of Nazi students in brown uniforms collected the books of several writers of Jewish and socialist persuasions in Rostock and destroyed them at a Schandpfahl (a shaming post). The book burners had arrived. Detailed plans had gone out to them on how they were to conduct the burning as a ritual with torch processions and incantations. A gruesome medieval desecration was enacted. Obliging professors spoke of a fictive purification of literature. Schalom Asch, Henry Barbusse, Bertolt Brecht, Max Brod, Alfred Döblin, Ilya Ehrenburg, Albert Ehrenstein, Ivan Goll, Walter Hasenclever, Karl Marx, Karl Kautzky, Klaus Mann, Erwin Kisch, Erich Maria Remarque, Ernst Toller, Arnold and Stefan Zweig and so many more were targeted. On the 10th May the night sky of Berlin was engulfed in flames with books, pamphlets and poets' busts thrown into the flames. They burnt symbolically that night; their books going up in flames watched by a cowering crowd of onlookers amongst the brown menace. Paper ash covered in ink symbols, ordered in beautiful and profound deliberations, in ideals of humanity's striving for justice and peace, in humour and satire, were vapourized that night. Erich Kästner watched his own books being thrown on the fire in the gloomy rain-soaked night. He commented: 'That rainy drenched night I was only one of the twenty-four poets who were going to be symbolically wiped out. I stood in front of the university by the opera, hemmed in between students in brown SA uniforms. The tirades of Goebbels, the small, infamous liar rang out amongst the buildings.'

Another poet, Oskar Maria Graf, wrote on the following day in the 'Wiener Arbeiterzeitung', after he'd found out to his horror that his name had been placed on a 'white list' of acceptable books:

"I have been put on a 'white list' and ask myself in vain: Why did I deserve this ignominy? German literature has been declared null and void; while everything that gave our art and poetry world fame is being eradicated, only to leave the narrowest of nationalism. This barbarism has nothing to do with being German. I have not earned this 'honour' of being on the 'white list'. After all I have worked for I deserve the right to have my books handed over to the pyre and not in the bloody hands and foul brains of this gang of murderers. Burn the works of the German spirit. I demand that this call is published in all the newspapers."

His books were duly burnt.

Friedrich, her father's friend, was passing by when Lene opened the bakery shop and put the sign outside. She hadn't seen him since she'd left for Berlin.

"Lene, my dear, how nice to see you. Since when are you back from your studies?" Friedrich looked bent over. His jacket was worn, his hair covered by the same cap that he used to wear, but his eyes were still bright and blue. She was very pleased to see him.

"Friedrich, good to see you! It's ages since we had a chat. You must come round one day like in the olden days. I'm only back for a few weeks. I am working full-time at the hospital."

"Congratulations to you for getting a job! What were your studies again?"

"Physiotherapy! It was quite hard work, but Berlin was also hard work – so much to see and to do!"

"I guess so! What a city with a wealth of art and culture, it must have been quite absorbing. I suppose 'have been' are the right words..." Friedrich's face darkened and he inadvertently wiped his hand over his eyes, as if to wipe a thought away. Lene noticed again his handsome large hands and long fingers. She remembered his fiancée and wondered if she was still with him.

"Very true, 'have been' are the words! Oh Friedrich! Do come round one evening, why don't you bring Wanda, and how is she anyway? I'll make you both mint tea and we'll talk."

"Wanda is very well. We got married and are now living together. I'm sure she'd love to come as well. I'll be seeing you soon. Lene. Goodbye for now."

Friedrich and Wanda came to the Deppermann's house the following week. Mathilde smiled her kind and dignified smile, expressing how pleased she was to have their company and how hard times were. They shook hands with Erna and young Hermann.

"My dear Hermann, God bless him, sometimes I am relieved that he is not with us any more. Just think how he would have suffered with this about turn in our political life in the republic that we all helped to build!"

"How right you are, Frau Deppermann! He'd never have believed it, unless he'd seen it with his own eyes. None of us thought it would be possible for this crank to get such a hold on everything so quickly. Including the news and information. You begin to look about yourself to check who is listening."

"You're all right here, Friedrich, speak from your heart! We all need it, don't we, Lene?"

Lene was just arriving with mint tea and cups on the tray.

"It's hard to keep up with it all. There's so much nasty nonsense thrown at us, one wonders how to deal with it," commented Mathilde.

Lene poured the tea and handed the cups to everyone, while agreeing with her mother:

"You can't keep up with it. People are locked up, beaten up and disappear. It's frightful."

"Did you hear that they're changing the names of many of the streets and plazas in our cities? It would be laughable if it wasn't so despicable. Calling them names like Hitler Strasse and Goering Allee. And then the book burning." Friedrich spoke with ire and exasperation, wiping the bushy hair from his brow.

"How can you burn books? What sort of barbaric act is that! Books are about learning, knowledge, human history, education, poetry and creativity." Lene's voice almost squeaked with indignation.

"Heine said it: 'Where they burn books they will also burn people'." Wanda sat up tall and straight as she spoke, and her emotion made her bosom swell and tremble. She sighed, taking a deep breath, and continued:

"He was so right; countless innocent people have already died because of them, and many more will, if they stay in power. We've got to stop them."

"We had a pretty reactionary professor at the Charite, but our student group was quite progressive and we managed to stop fascist groups being active there, until Sauerbruch forbade our actions. That brown menace was bought in with money..."

"Sure, they were! Banks and industry pushed these chaps into front line politics; financed their uniforms, their lorries, their political campaigns and so on. It's pretty obvious that they've already made their peace with big industry. No complaints from that part of the world, thank you very much."

"Still, we're giving them a run for their money. We've got a whole network of socialist families who are working with underground materials, much of it from the Netherlands, you know where the Zinglers are, but also run off in people's cellars. There's a lot of good people about, risking their lives to distribute fliers and newspapers to get the information to people."

Wanda spoke emphatically, leaning back into her armchair holding her cup on her lap. She smiled, and her rosy cheeks matched the glow of her red hair. She continued.

"You may have heard of Ernst Eck, a member of the communist party and the Red Front. I met him and his wife at one of our meetings about the distribution network. They turned up in the night and dragged people out of their flats and nearly beat them to death. Ernst was arrested in April this year. They interrogated him and then threw him into a cell with another man. That man said to him, "You must forgive me, because when I was tortured I mentioned your name." Ernst replied, "You don't need to get yourself beaten to death for me." The man replied, "If they'd beaten me to death your name would not have been said. Then he took off his clothes and showed Ernst his mistreated body. From his neck down to his heels he was covered in blood and wounds. He said 'I have participated in being hung on the cross, because they did this to me on Good Friday."

Wanda's face looked crumpled and pale with red blotches on her cheeks. She sipped the remnants of her now cold tea and wiped her red hair out of her face.

"Yes, Ernst, he's a good comrade all right," Friedrich added thoughtfully.

They contemplated this latest story silently. The whirring of the coal shuttles could be heard, as well as the screeching of a tram. The flickering lights from the mine danced around the walls like will-o'-the-wisps, making Lene feel dizzy and sick.

"Have another cup of tea, Friedrich!" Mathilde coaxed with tenderness in her voice, "we've got to stay calm and strong with this lot. We're all in danger now they've decided to take on all the working people of our country."

She looked warmly at Friedrich and Wanda, who were keeping the political work going that her late husband had been so close to. The two of them had to leave, but they all felt better for sharing their concerns, helping them feel soothed and less lonely. Lene, though, was restless. When she reached her room she felt in an agitated mood. Under her Charite papers was Liesel's letter. Something inside her made her reach for it again. It was tucked in a red leather briefcase given to her by her father. She gently folded it open and read it again word for word. She read 'much love from *Liesel*'. She discovered that it had a small postscript at the bottom, that she had not noticed before. It looked hurriedly drawn with a pencil:

> *Lene, dear, no word from Klaus for three days! The stories people tell about what they do to people in what they now call 'Schutzhaft' (protective imprisonment) are alarming. I fear for his life. Pray with me, Lene. Let's be hopeful.'*

Coldness filled her heart. She felt herself turn to ice, the walls around her growing unfamiliar, as if she had entered into a remote universe on another planet. The shape of her bed, her wooden chest of drawers, her chair and crowded desk under the shelf full of books from her studies were nothing to do with her any more. They were someone else's. She looked in the mirror. She saw the dark rings under her coal-black eyes that seemed as if two holes had been burnt into her pale face. A person she did not recognise. It was as if the life she had envisaged herself living had vacated her body, leaving it as an empty shell. The mollusc that had lived in it had moved away. Who was going to inhabit it now? She did not wonder about it, nor did she care. Klaus! My one love! She loved him more than she had known.

That same May the Nazis began their rearmament programme in earnest. Schacht, now president of the Reichsbank, created a gigantic finance project called 'Metallurgische Forschungsunion', or 'Mefo' for short, supported by the giants of industry, such as Krupp, Siemens and Rheinmetall. The build-up to a war against the Soviet Union was beginning to take shape. The trees and bushes in the parks and in the graveyard dug their roots deeper underground, and the birds sought comfort from each other. Lene went to work. She worked hard. She looked after her patients well. She taught her sister Erna some of the physiotherapy techniques she'd learnt, helping the latter to feel that she was learning something useful that might lead to work. Lene saw herself growing more and more like Erna. Perhaps the two of them would become old spinsters, never to marry or have children. She gave all the rest of her energy to the political work. In the evening she met with Inge who was well connected with the resistance groups and the emigrant press.

"Come in, quickly!" Inge whispered. "We've had a big delivery. It came with the bread van."

She pulled her friend through the door and shut it. They had tea in the kitchen. The table was covered in newspapers and pamphlets that had been baked into bread. They folded and sorted them. Later they went out and delivered them to their contacts, determined to keep the flame of resistance burning.

Margarethe's letters kept them up to date with events in the Netherlands. When Liesel wrote again Lene could barely make herself open the letter. She had written to Liesel to tell her to let her know as soon as she heard that Klaus was out of prison. Liesel's letter told no such thing. Klaus remained imprisoned. No word was heard of his whereabouts.

The heat of the July days brought no relief. The sun smelted the air as if Gelsenkirchen was a furnace. The hospital room windows were kept wide open to allow the air to circulate and water jugs were placed to encourage staff and patients to drink and prevent dehydration. Lene had a particularly hard day in the orthopaedic ward. One patient had exasperated her. He was a middle-aged man who'd had a broken leg. Not from having been in a resistance battle with the brownshirts, but from a skiing holiday! What sort of world did he come from, Lene mused and spoke to Inge about it later on that day. While everyone was trying to make ends meet and fighting against the Nazi plague here was a man who had time to casually go on a skiing holiday.

"He's quite old. He looks quite nice, but he's so irritating. He broke his leg at the lower shin end of his right leg, and it's healed, but he's quite weak on his legs now, the muscles have disappeared, so his left leg especially is as thin as a stick. It looks really funny. He's vain. When I tell him to pull up his trouser leg so I can see how he's moving his muscles and if he is doing the exercise correctly, he objects noisily and complains that he shouldn't have to do it. He knew how to do the exercise anyway. I demanded he did as he was told, and he started getting cheeky with me, asking for the chief physiotherapist. I said they were too busy to come because of a minor complaint. He went, it's not a minor complaint, that's my body, and I want it to be right again. I said OK. Calm down! It'll be all right, if you do the exercises I give you. He hadn't done them. He said he was too busy. I said we're all busy. Who do you think you are, not in those words, but meaning that. He looked surprised then. I suppose he'd never had a woman speak to him like that. OK, girl, he said. The cheek of it. Give me the exercises, I'll do them, I promise. He gave in." They laughed. Lene continued:

"He said he had been skiing in April and had been referred to our hospital because of the good name of our physio department. I thought, flattery won't get you anywhere with me."

The next time Lene visited Inge they had fliers sent by Margarethe from the Netherlands.

They worked folding them quietly for a while, when Inge looked up at Lene with a querying look.

"Lene, what's up? You're so quiet, are there no stories to tell or are you keeping something from me?"

Lene looked at Inge with guilty eyes, then cast her eyes down. She remained silent. Inge had to urge her on, saying:

"Whatever it is, just talk to me. You know you can be honest. We're friends, Lene."

Finally Lene started hesitatingly.

"You know the man I told you about with the skiing accident. He's asked me out. I can't believe it. I was cheeky and stern with him. I ordered him about and told him what for, you remember. I told you the other time. He was vexing me so much."

She stopped, then went on.

"The next time he came into hospital for his exercises and check up he was really obedient and well-behaved, quite unlike the last time. I thought, what's up with him. He kept looking at me strangely. I didn't care. It did not concern me. Then, as I said to him OK, you're improving now, you don't need to come back, and shook his hand, he held on to my hand. Can you imagine my shock! I nearly jumped out of my skin. He said to me: Fräulein Deppermann, could I ask you to come out for a glass of wine with me. You have helped me a lot."

Lene looked directly into Inge's face, full of anxious expectation that her friend was going to admonish her, but she didn't. Her face stayed friendly, urging her on to tell more.

"I was baffled. In my surprise I heard myself say, I suppose I could, but it would have to be at the end of my long shift days on a Friday."

"What happened? Did you see him?"

"I did. We went to Violetta's and had a glass of wine. He was very charming and not demanding like he'd been in the hospital. He's not our age, though. He's got a fancy job and I think earns quite a bit of money. Oh, Inge, the pull of money! It makes you feel dizzy and excited, but it also makes me feel guilty. I don't think he's one of ours. He's an engineer and runs a company in Essen like..."

"Dearest Lene, don't worry! You need to lead your life. In these hard times a good man who will take care of you is a rarity. Most of them can't afford it. If he can, well that's great." Inge had got up and put her arm round Lene holding her close for a short while, then going back to her chair.

"Do you mean that, Inge? It just feels wrong. The thought of, say, marrying and having children when all this is happening in Germany. I know my thoughts are running away with me, but he looks seriously interested in me, and made me feel very special."

"Just going out with a man doesn't have to lead to marriage. But if it does, why, you might just as well. The Nazis won't stay in power for ever and then you'll need to get back to your own life and find that you've got old before you can find a man. For myself, I've given up.

The right man never turned up and now I have my responsibilities. I wouldn't want a man to get in the way of them. But you're in a different situation. Your family's bakery is in your brother's good hands. Your mother has already a problem with your older sister not marrying, so she worries about her. She wouldn't want you to stay a spinster as well. Think of her. She'll be pleased."

"I feel so torn, Inge! I can't tell you. It's very hard. I didn't tell you, but there was a man in Berlin I fell in love with, but now the Nazis have put him in prison. It's broken my heart. I'm afraid I might never recover, and that I'll feel sad all my life. I can't bear the thought of it!"

"Just see how you feel, Lene, and whatever you do, don't feel guilty, run with your inner heart. Shall we go and distribute these now, or do you want to leave it?"

"No, let's definitely do it now. I want to finish the delivery." Lene gave Inge a hug and they quietly packed the leaflets and newspapers and left the house. Inge's brothers were expected back very late after the nightshift, so the house lay silent as they turned into the street. The lamps threw spots of white, the surroundings were drenched in darkness. They walked on quiet shoes, posting the materials into the usual addresses which they knew by heart. They were careful to check no one was lying in wait for them. There was no moon, just a dog howling in the next street, and a cat came, curling her tail around Lene's leg, only to wander back into the night.

One of the following nights Lene sat in Inge's kitchen when her brothers had an early shift, and they all had a meal together talking about politics. Inge had cooked a cabbage soup, followed by sausages with potato salad. The young men gulped the food voraciously. Their skin shone from the harsh soap and scrubbing to get the coal dust out of the pores of their faces. One man had had an accident underground, when he fell into a trolley and broke an arm. His screams were still sharp in their ears, as they were telling their sister and Lene. They looked tired, staring down at the table while they ate with their arms resting on the table top. Uwe, the younger, was the first to speak.

"This bastard caught us unawares, I can't believe how naive our people have been, the most gigantic miscalculation we have ever seen..."

"What are you talking about?" Inge inquired.

"Well, you know who, Hitler and his brown virus gangs."

"Joined together the socialists and the communists could have had a majority. But games were played to keep them separate, and they did themselves no favours. This country is going to hell, I'm telling you. With that amount of violence in all the cities people will shut up very quickly. Why risk your head to be shot on the spot!"

"At work now, don't think you can hold trade union meetings. They've shut all of that down. There are no trade unions any more, just Nazi organised meetings, even in the mine. Mind you, it hasn't stopped us. We still meet, us communists, but secretly, late, at someone's house or somewhere they don't know." Emil looked proud.

"We do the same. Our social democrat group has become small, but they're good people, you can rely on them," put in Uwe. The younger brother had followed his sister into the social democrats.

"The Zinglers wrote recently. She says that life is quite hard in the Netherlands, because their government is sympathetic towards the Nazis. If local people and socialist friends weren't so helpful they wouldn't be able to cope. There are already nearly five hundred social democrats there and many more Reichsbanner members and trade unionists, many of them with no valid papers."

Lene hesitated and then continued, while the others sat and listened full of fatigue. It was the political work that gave her a feeling of sanity and soothed her sadness. It also made her feel close to Klaus and Liesel in far away Berlin. She was proud of her many socialist friends and her association with them.

"If they get active at all, you know, politically, they can be thrown out and returned to the Nazis. You know what they'd do with them? Anyway, the Nazis also operate in the Netherlands. Even so, they produce newspapers and fliers with information to let the rest of the world know. People need to be told what's happening in our country."

"You wonder what the rest of the world makes of the Nazis. OK, they wanted him to destroy the Soviet Union and Stalin, but what if Hitler starts a war against them as well? That's all on the cards; they're producing new weapons as we speak."

By now the four of them had their heads propped up on their elbows and were staring into the distance, as if they were expecting a message from some spirit from outer space who would enlighten them as to the tasks before them. But none did. Lene had to get home and left Inge and her brothers behind in the conspiratorial kitchen.

On the way back she noticed how tightly the curtains were drawn in the windows. Her heart felt torn in two. She wished so much to speak to Liesel. Klaus, my love! But Berlin remained far away. She was without hope. She would never be able to marry him and have children with him. The Nazis had locked him up. Then she saw her patient's laughing eyes that had looked at her with such urgency. She had agreed to see him again. But was it right? She was twenty-seven years old now. And he was in his forties! She was quite old really for an unmarried woman. She thought of lovely Fräulein Bäcker, her art teacher, killed by the Nazis, like so many. Art, literature, walking with the Wandervoegel! All those good and promising times. And now? She could carry on working in the hospital, but forever? Ought there not to be something else, love, marriage, children, if she couldn't be an artist? Olga came to mind. Her married life was brief, but she had little Matti, now probably growing into a big girl and a joy for her mother. Her thoughts tailed off. It was probably not to be.

The August heatwave was relentless and hung like a soot-soaked plume over the town. The screeching of the trams and sirens from the smelting plants and mines, the shouting of the newspaper boys and car horns made Lene's skull burst, so that she sometimes felt like screaming. The chokingly hot temperatures brought people to the hospital with breathing problems. Extra hours of work were demanded to relieve those with severe problems. At the end of one such week she finally managed to go home in time to have a break before going out again. She met Heinrich one sultry and stifling evening. They met in the cafe of Hotel Vier Jahreszeiten, or four seasons, an elegant venue near the Buer district. Lene felt strangely nervous and on her guard. She wasn't going to be overwhelmed by whatever this man wanted. She wanted to check him out carefully and had decided to keep her feelings close to her heart. When she turned into the cafe area she spotted him sitting with a big smile on his face. A bunch of flowers was lying in front of him. He quickly stood up and, with his leg muscles now recovered, he strode towards her with such energy that she almost felt as if she ought to make an escape. He was right by her side within a moment, took her hand and kissed it warmly, then looked into her eyes.

"I'm so glad to see you, Fräulein Deppermann, you just don't know how much this means to me." He turned to the hotel staff and demanded:

"Waiter, could you take this lady's coat and bring the menu?"

Lene had a peculiar feeling of alienation when he addressed the man, as if another world had opened up before her, pushing her against an invisible wall. But she held back her judgement, thinking she must give him a chance. They sat down, and he showed her the bunch of red roses, saying:

"These are for you, but we'll have the waiter take care of them until later. What would you like to drink and eat? And can I propose we call each other by our first names? Mine is Heinrich."

"Yes, why not. I'm Lene."

Coffee and cake were delivered at great speed, the waiter more or less staying in attendance in case the gentleman should make another demand. The atmosphere remained stiff and uncomfortable, until Heinrich asked Lene questions about her life. She started to thaw and feel more alive, when she could talk about her beloved father and mother and then chat about her sisters. They both laughed at her amusing depiction of Hilde with her watery pale-blue eyes and stiff walk and doe-eyed Erna with her eczema and dolls. He listened, showing a lot of attentiveness and keen interest, laughing out loud at some of her jokey narratives. Time sped by, when they realised that it was supper time, and Heinrich begged Lene to stay and have supper with him. She relented. The wine was classy and the gourmet dish served thrilled her palate. Inside her a little voice whispered 'I am being seduced with luxury and bonhomie, it feels great, but so dangerous. I can feel myself falling for him against my will and better judgement.'

As the evening wore on the voice became more and more feeble, until it disappeared entirely. They were laughing and rocking with amusement. Heinrich told stories of his student years and when he spoke about having been on horseback in the First World War Lene's eyes widened. That war! The start of it all! Heinrich spoke of the trenches in Verdun, the bravery of the men and the death of one of his close comrades, Horst.

"His horse had fallen, badly injured, but he insisted on fighting on foot. Drenched in mud, his sodden rain-soaked coat dragging on him he fought on next to me, when a machine gun bullet hit him right in the head. He screamed. I can still remember his piercing voice. I turned to look at him. Half his face was torn off, blood pouring down over his coat, arms, legs. He fell to the ground. I jumped off my horse and held him. He whispered: 'Give my wife these, Heinrich, you've been a good mate,' and died with those words. I thought of that song 'Ich hat einen Kameraden...' and wept right there amidst the bullets."

Lene felt sorry for the poor man and looked at him with warmth, when he continued:

"War is war, though, and you have to overcome your soft feelings and stand by your country. Horst had been proud to fight for Germany, and so was I."

"Did you never think how useless all that fighting was? It didn't bring Germany any good fortune! In any case, to fight on two fronts, surely, was a major mistake?"

"You know, Lene, I don't like war either, but I'm a patriot, and if my country needs me to defend her then I'll do my best. You always have to do your best, don't you think?"

"Well, fair enough, doing your best is a good thing, but you need to decide what 'the best' is before you get going. Wars don't really sort out society for people, they kill people, that's all. They destroy people, homes, towns and architecture. Wars are decided upon by those in power and fought by those without it. Your poor friend Horst lost his life, but the generals did not."

"That's a fair point, but sometimes you need a war to show other countries that they can't just push your country about. We lost that war for many reasons, but not because our soldiers weren't brave. We have the bravest soldiers in the world."

"What's the good of bravery when you don't know what you're fighting for or what it's about? Most of those young chaps who ended up fighting had no idea what they were up to."

"That might be true, Lene. Let's not talk about the war, we could talk about it for ever, let's talk about us." Lene looked at Heinrich in surprise. His face was slightly reddened on his cheeks. His blue eyes shone with a flash, and his mouth had a big smile showing his teeth.

"What is there to talk about? I'd better get myself home, it must be late," she added, making a slight movement away towards her bag, when he quickly got hold of her hand and kissed it. Looking deeply into her eyes he said:

"Lene, my dear, I'm so fond of you... I'm lost for words... Lene, can I tell you I love you and I would like us to get engaged!" He leaned over the table and pressed a kiss on the astonished Lene's mouth. She stared at him, alternately blushing and going pale. She tried hard to control her emotions and said:

"Heinrich, you've caught me by surprise. I certainly can't answer your request tonight. I feel flattered and moved by your feelings for me, but I need time. We hardly know each other. Let me go home and think it over."

He looked at her with a sudden sadness that reminded her of his dead friend Horst, and moved her, but she sat silently waiting for him to calm himself. He finally spoke:

"You're right, I am a bit too fast, but by God, I am truthfully very much in love with you, and have been from the moment when we met in the hospital, dear Lene. Any waiting for you I will do, but it will be hardship. Let me take you home, but I hope we meet again soon."

"You don't need to take me home. It's my home town, I know it well, I can walk or take the tram."

"Let me take you home, I have a motorcar outside. Waiter, our coats, please. Here's your tip."

He helped Lene into her coat. The waiter brought the roses. Heinrich held the door open for her and they were out in the street. The cobblestones shone with rain, and the sharp sickle of the moon hung like a boat caught in a tree. The sky was dark with drifting clouds. There's so much I still don't know, she thought, as Heinrich gently took her arm and guided her towards a large limousine on the other side of the road. Her brain felt mushy from the wine and the coaxing and spoiling she was receiving.

"Not all the way to my house, please, that would make me feel worried, say if someone saw me, yes just drop me off here, here is fine, it's not far now."

"No, don't get out, let's say goodbye in the car." He gently squeezed her shoulders as he pulled her towards him and kissed her slowly and softly on the lips.

"Goodbye, Lene, I'll see you soon, do say I will."

"Yes, soon, I'd better get home now."

She stumbled out of the car into the street with a huge effort to get away, to have distance between her and this man. She almost ran, but tried to look dignified. Her brain was thick with confusing feelings, alcohol, pain, desire and pleasure all mixed up with a sense of forboding.

CHAPTER 17

SNOW WEDDING

"A stranger always has her home in her arm like an
orphan who she may only seek out a grave for..."

Nelly Sachs

Before Lene slipped out of the bakery to go to work her mother
caught her on the stairs.

"Lene, could you come for a minute. I have a letter to show you."

Lene followed her mother into her office, and was shown a
telegram that must have arrived early that morning. It read:

'Dear Frau Deppermann, I am overjoyed to announce
that your daughter Lene and I have decided to get
engaged. I look forward to making your acquaintance,
yours faithfully, Heinrich Hermann Berger.'

Mathilde kept holding the piece of paper in front of Lene as if it
was the length of an essay. She didn't say a word. Lene looked at her
mother, who looked furious. She had never seen her in such a quietly
intense temper. The skin of her face was white and harsh as if in a

frost. She had a deep frown between her eyes which shone with a purple rage. Her mouth was closed and pursed. Lene felt she had to say something, and she felt sheepish. Maybe this was all a mistake. Was she too young to make such a decision without her mother or did her mother have some other reasons to be so offended?

"Well, mother, it's true that Heinrich and I met up yesterday and agreed to get engaged. I didn't know he was going to send you a telegram so quickly. He could have maybe waited a bit and let me explain things to you first. I apologise to you for that. I should have told him not to, I..."

"No, you shouldn't have done anything. He should have known how to behave himself. It is not for him to ask you to marry him. He ought to have asked me first. The man has no manners." Mathilde's voice rang out loud and sharp as she vented her annoyance at having been overlooked. She was a woman with self-respect who didn't expect to be ignored by anyone. Here was someone who wasn't even from Gelsenkirchen or from local trades she knew who had bypassed her.

"Your father would have been furious about such behaviour," she shot at Lene, who stood looking like a poodle after a bucket of water has been thrown over it. "I shall write to him. You don't need to do anything."

"What are you going to write, mother?"

Mathilde's anger was evaporating, when confronted with this question. What indeed was she to write? The man was wrong, that she knew, but her daughter had agreed to the engagement. She was after all twenty-seven. She should have a husband. Maybe it wasn't such a bad thing, after all. She adopted a more conciliatory tone.

"Don't worry, I'm not going to be rude or put him off. In any case I can't undo the decision, as it is both of yours. But he must understand that I don't appreciate being the last to be told of his interest in my daughter." She turned to Lene, who was still looking miserable and stroked her face with her hand, as softer feelings emerged inside her.

"You're a good girl, Lene! I want the best for you. Only the best man out there is good enough for you. I only hope that he is such a man. You see, I don't know him, so you have to understand how I feel."

Lene put her arms round her mother and gave her a hug. "Of course you're right! He is a little impatient, but very nice and polite. You'll find that, I'm sure, when you meet him in person. He's also older than I am and maybe feels the pressure of time on him. He wants to have children and build a family."

"Go to work now, girl, it's getting late for you. It's all right. I feel calmer now. I'll let you have a copy of the letter I'm writing to him."

It was only when Lene was back at work that the storm of emotions subsided that she had experienced since her mother lost her temper. She had felt very confused all the way to work and begun to question her decision. Now that she was working with her patients, had had her lunch and chatted with her colleagues she started to feel more positive again. She was seeing Inge after work and talking about politics gave her a focus beyond her own petty life.

"They've arrested Karl Schwesig!" Inge greeted her with these words shouted in the quietest way possible. They were like a hissing in her ears that was painful.

"Karl, the artist? Are you sure?"

"Yes, I'm sure. You know my brother is with the communists. He told me. They came with a truck, bashed in the door to his studio and dragged him away after they kicked him for a while."

"Stop! I can't bear it. Poor Karl! He's such a lovely man. These monsters are without humanity." Lene's face went red with anger and devastation. She tore on a lock of her hair as if to pull it out. They held each other for a long time. They were unable to fold leaflets that evening. Instead they had tea and sat heads propped up on elbows trying to make sense of what was happening around them.

"The only way is to campaign even harder underground against them. Make sure comrades are informed about what they are up to so we can organise supportive actions when required."

241

That was a calming thought and Lene left Inge feeling less upset. The routine of work was balm. The banter with her colleagues and lunch-time gossip all soothed her raw and feverish emotional state. Repetitive thoughts of 'shall I marry or shall I not?' calmed in the presence of asthma, broken thigh bones and wrists and lungs filled with coal dust. A couple of days later she walked into the evening gusts with an urgent step to reach Inge's house. She rang the bell, but no one answered. Inge wasn't in. It can't be! She's expecting me. We have our work to do. The leaflets, the newspapers, the distribution net. She waited feeling confused and muddled. The door remained shut, as if the house didn't recognise her. Fearful thoughts rose inside her. What if Inge had been found out and arrested by the so-called 'Schutzpolizei', Protection Police. Schutzpolizei! What a lie! What an evil trick played on the population. Schutz means protection, safety. These Nazis had turned this word into its opposite by using it for foul, malicious and unprovoked attacks on citizens. Schutzhaft was the word used when you were being tortured and kept in jail without the knowledge of the outside world, often for days, even weeks, often leading to death. Klaus was in Schutzhaft. Oh Inge, where are you? Lene waited uncertainly, feeling desperate to see her friend and then left. She wandered along Bahnhofstrasse, passed a new sign saying Hitlerstrasse, when someone took her by her sleeve and whispered "Lene!" close to her ear. Lene looked around. In the half light she saw a poorly dressed youngish well built woman who seemed stooped as if carrying a heavy burden. A hat was pulled deep over her hair and made it hard to recognise her.

"It's me, your school friend Olga, don't you remember me?" said a melodious voice.

"Olga, my friend, I didn't recognise you! I looked for you and came to your house, but you weren't there any more. Well, that is a lovely surprise!"

"Much to tell, Lene! I'm not very well, as you can see. A bad back is crippling me." She pointed to her bent posture. "I've moved house..."

"Come, let's have a coffee. I know a nice little place near here. We can cheer ourselves up and have a good chat. But first let's have a good hug! Olga! It's so long since we saw each other. So much has happened, Oh Lord, what a world we live in..."

They flung their arms around each other and then looked for somewhere to go. Everything seemed to be closed early for some reason. They walked on until they saw that Walter's fish restaurant was open. They entered. The familiar decor with porcelain tiles along the walls and friendly service welcomed them. The warm atmosphere felt good and instead of coffee they had a glass of wine placed in front of them, as they leaned towards each other with the stories pouring out of them. It was not just Olga's back.

"Girl, what I've been through in the last months, I can hardly bear to tell you. My own daughter! Turned against me by those people in her school. You remember Matti, my lovely baby! Of course, she's a big girl now. She's nine years old."

"Nine years! How time passes. What happened, which people?"

"You know this Gleichschaltung thing. Well, everyone has to sing from the same hymn sheet. I'm not political, Lene, as you know. I just wanted my own life and happiness, marriage and so on. Well, you know what happened with Hubert. He disappeared. I was happy for a while, when mother and father could help me look after Matti. Then you left for Berlin. All the stuff happened then, the Nazis yelling everywhere, beating people up. Even if you just wanted to ignore them, you couldn't. They were in your face, loud, violent, demanding attention. Neighbours, good people, were pulled out of their home next door, roughed up and transported away. We never saw them again. Mother and father were beginning to get ill with the tension of it all every day, every night. Would they come to our house? They decided to move into the countryside, they couldn't bear it any longer. They thought they'd be safer there. That's why I had to move too. Not having any money myself, I was dependent on them. That's why you couldn't find me when you came back. We left at very short notice one night. Friends helped us. Mother and father helped a local farmer and have a hut on his ground. That wasn't so bad. I coped with all of that. But this year the village teachers all turned strident Nazi. Just like that, they changed. Anyone who didn't lost their job. 'Gleichschaltung', they call it. Everybody must join the Nazis and speak the same rubbish from the pulpit. German blood brothers, fatherland, victory and such hollow phrases. That you should learn to think and value different views. Forget it! Not now. Matti comes home and tells us what we should think. Can you believe it? She's very strict with us and tells us, when anyone says something against that Adolf, 'You're not allowed to speak like that, mother. I shall have to tell my teacher.' My own daughter!"

"Poor Olga, my dear, how awful is that!" Lene could barely find words to express how bitter this must be for Olga, who had started to weep silently into her wine. Lene got a handkerchief, stood up and put her arm around Olga giving her the kerchief.

"They force the children to join the Nazi youth organisations. They have to turn up to all events. If they don't someone comes round the house immediately and asks why your daughter isn't there. They train them to become spies on their own families and brainwash them. It's terrifying!"

"Shall we get something to eat, Olga, some warm soup would be good, wouldn't it?"

"You're right, Lene. Wise, you were always clever and wise. I remember you always gave good advice. I wish I had been able to follow it. Remember we were going to be singers and work in the theatre. Such nice dreams!"

"You were going to be a singer with your great voice. I was going to become a painter or a writer. Well, we have to have these dreams, even if they don't come true. They guide us hopefully in the right direction."

"What is the right direction?"

"I don't know myself, but what I do know is that we need to hold fast to our principles of working for a better future for ourselves and our children. A socialist one, where each has according to their need and gives according to their ability."

"I've never heard you say this before?"

"Maybe not, but it's been in my head a long time. My father used to say it sometimes and then in Berlin I met more people who are all communists or socialists. We learned from each other."

"That's a good principle. I like it! But how can we do anything in practice right now? I'm stuck. My own daughter preaches Nazi propaganda to me and her grandparents."

The food had arrived and they ate in silence for a while mulling over what had been said.

"What brings you to Gelsenkirchen then today, Olga?" Lene finally asked.

"To be honest, I had to get out and have a day to myself. I was going mad. Mother and father work hard helping on the farm. They are tired in the evening. They have sort of given up, just try and survive. I also work on the farm a bit, but have to deal with Matti and her new behaviour, which I try to influence. Well, we all try. But she's stubborn, maybe like I used to be. In any case she won't take 'no' for an answer. She commandeers all of us. It's a world in reverse. She tells us what to do. You couldn't imagine such a thing, unless you've actually experienced it. I said I had to meet a friend for the day and get some medicine for my back and left early this morning. It was nice to walk into Ahlsdorf, that lovely shop and look at all the goods there. Some things have stayed normal. Like this restaurant. Remember when we had my birthday here! Seems years and years ago, in a different life altogether." Olga's tears rolled silently down her cheeks. Did she have grey in her hair? Lene hoped it was the light.

"Well, look, you did go into town and you have met a friend. Isn't that a wonderful coincidence? We might never have seen each other again, and now we can stay in touch."

Olga looked up and a smile rushed over her face lighting it up. Her cheeks were becoming rosy with the food and wine.

"You're right again, Lene! It's great to have met you in the street. I couldn't believe it at first, but tell me about yourself, I haven't heard what happened to you?"

"So many stories to tell! Mm. Let me think. I suppose the most important one is I finished my studies in Berlin and came back here into a job at the hospital, working as a physiotherapist. It's quite enjoyable work and it's great to earn my own living. I really enjoy that. I still live at home and help mother in the bakery, but young Hermann is doing a fine job. He's got a good and strong young woman who is overseeing the shop, so it can all be managed without much support from me."

As she finished she realised she had lied, because the obvious story to tell Olga would have been her engagement to Heinrich. Of course Olga quickly got to the subject.

"What about a man in your life, Lene? Or are you still too independent for that sort of thing?"

Lene felt heat rising through her body making her blush and squirm. She stuttered:

"Well, yeah, mm. It's a difficult one to tell... there is a man in my life, but you know it's so new and sudden. I still don't quite understand what's happening to me."

"What on earth do you mean by that? You've got a man. That's fantastic! But you sound muddled and as if you weren't sure. Do you love him?"

"I sort of do, Olga! I find making this decision very hard. I've only known him a short time. In fact, believe it or not, he was one of my first patients when I started working at the hospital. He had a broken leg from skiing, ridiculous as it sounds, but true. Not from being beaten up by the Nazis."

"So he's wealthy and educated. Lene, you pulled the winning ticket! My, you are lucky! Does he love you?"

Lene felt encouraged by her friend's enthusiasm and regained her confidence.

"He asked me to marry him, but..."

"What but, there can't be a but! If he wants to marry you, Lene, yes is the only answer. These days few of the men have any money to marry. Good for you. That's fantastic! When's your wedding?"

"There is a but, and that is he hasn't even met my mother, but he sent her a telegram announcing that we're engaged, and she's furious with him. Like for not asking her first, you know my mother. She is very strong on good tradition and behaviour."

"Oh, she'll get over it, don't worry, he'll make it up to her."

"True, he is very good at persuasion. I can tell you, he worked his charm on me. I wasn't sure at all. In fact, I was really in love with someone else."

"You are a one! Not just one man but two. Who was he?"

"That was in Berlin. He is the brother of a Berlin friend of mine, both of them socialists. I fell in love with him, and we had a marvellous few weeks and a holiday by the Baltic sea. I intended to go back ... but the awful thing is he was seized by the Nazis and the last I heard about him is that he's still being kept in prison. His sister writes to me. She's very sad and frightened for him, and so am I."

"You do go for adventures, don't you! First no man then two, or maybe even more, and then also the politics. What about your new man? What are his politics like? Is he also going to end up locked away? I presume not if he's rich."

"To be honest, I'm not sure of his politics, as I haven't dared to have a political discussion with him, but I hazard a guess that he's not opposed to the lot that's running Germany now. I'm not saying he agrees with them, but he thinks things aren't too bad and will improve now."

"At least he won't end up in jail then. What work does he do?"

"He's an engineer and works for a company in Essen as their director."

"You've hit the jackpot, Lene! That's super! Don't dare to give him up. He can't afford to disagree with the lot at the top, otherwise he'll be out of a job. Remember the teachers I told you about. Two were summarily dismissed for not toeing the party line. The others all submitted to orders. But oil is different from educating children. You don't need to believe in many principles when you deal in oil and petrol. Maybe you should have them as well. But in education that's to do with morality all the way. How else are children going to learn to become a good person, if not by being taught by parents and teachers? Is it being a good person to spy on your own family? I don't think so! I didn't bother much before with politics, as you know. But I now think they are a gang of criminals and my daughter has to obey them. I can't bear it!" Olga had talked herself back into her own tragic situation and was now tearing on her hair as she grabbed her head in her fists, elbows on the table. Lene stroked Olga's head and gently took one of her hands into her own, making Olga look up at her.

"I so agree with you. They are evil. They won't last long, though. There is a lot of opposition... Matti is only a child..."

"Oh God, look at me, the worry of it is making me ill. I have such backaches and I'm so stiff that I can hardly move my neck. It feels as if I'm carrying a huge bag of coal on my back all the time."

"I'll have a look at your back for you, Olga, and fix you up with some exercises. They can help, really..." Olga smiled at Lene.

"You're a true friend, Lene, always positive and helpful. Let's do that. I am pushed for time now... completely forgot about having to get back, let me see..."

They paid up and left quickly. Lene walked Olga to the train station and waited till she'd got on the last train, not without taking her address first. At home several letters were waiting for her. She opened the copy of her mother's letter to Heinrich first:

Dear Herr Bergert,

> *As my daughter is a generous person and she has already agreed to the partnership between you both, it seems to me that I do not have the right to disapprove, and I have therefore accepted you as the fiancé of my daughter. My house is consequently open to your visit at any time. I hope that I will be successful in gaining the kind of attitude towards you that would allow me to have a good conscience before God and yourself. I take it you were going to ask me for the hand of my daughter, but as you already have asked her there cannot now be any sense in asking for my permission. It would not do justice to my position as Lene's*

mother to give permission to the engagement in hindsight,
when, in terms of good custom and correct behaviour this
should have been requested in the first place, before any
engagement had taken place. The situation pains me and
I request that you allow several days before your visit to
permit me to come to terms with what has happened.

Yours faithfully,
Frau Mathilde Deppermann

Lene could not help giggling when she read her mother's letter. It was beautifully written, and she was proud of her mother. That would teach Heinrich never to walk over her family. They weren't engineers, but they were a proud baker's family with customs and traditions that deserved respect. Again she could see Heinrich's impetuousness, but had to admit that she had also enjoyed it, even if she was suspicious of it. She opened the next letter. It was from Margarethe in the Netherlands.

Dear Lene,

Some news from our hiding place here near the border.
Things are difficult. The Dutch government would rather
not have German refugees. They want to keep up friendly
relations with the Nazis, so we are warned to keep our
heads down. We often meet a refugee friend of ours,
Elisabeth Hennig, who is a great political activist and
has good links back to the Ruhr, so we get news about what
is going on where you are. My poor dear, things are looking
worse, which makes me wonder if we can get rid of this
lot soon. Do you know that they passed something called
the 'Konkordat' back in July, which is an agreement with
the Pope to give up the Zentrum party as representative
of Catholics in Germany? You can imagine how much

prestige the Nazis have gained from such an agreement across the world. People probably don't realise what is going on in terms of the rights of people in Germany, if the Pope can come to such an agreement with Hitler.

On more personal matters I am not sure what happened to Inge. I did not get her usual communication about the distribution from her. Have you seen her? Please get in touch soon,

Yours,
Margarethe

It was past midnight when a just audible knocking on her door made Lene look up and say "Come in", wondering who it could be in the middle of the night. She had another letter to read and was in the middle of Liesel's latest news on her brother's imprisonment, when Erna opened the door wrapped in a blanket and stepped in, big eyes full of questions.

"Sorry to disturb you in the night, Lene, I couldn't sleep. Mother looked so irritated today, and said you'd got engaged. She never explained it much, but I had to find out from you whether it's true."

"It is true, Erna. Heinrich and I became engaged, but mother was only told afterwards and it annoyed her. We had to apologise. She doesn't want to see him until next week."

Erna rushed over and wrapped her arms round Lene who had got up and let herself be enclosed and pressed to Erna's warm soft bosom. Her sister's endearing emotional interest in her fate deeply moved her. "You lucky thing! Oh how wonderful. You're going to get married. Oh Lene, my love, I'm so happy for you. I'm sure you're over the moon about it. Anyway I would be!" she added, looking at Lene's nonchalant countenance.

"I am happy," Lene said decidedly, "but it's a big decision, Erna, and I must admit, I did hesitate. You know, leaving you and mother and all that and leading a life with someone I hardly know! I know what our life is like, but a life being married? I don't know that, do I? I'll only find out when I do it, and I've decided to give it a go."

"Gosh, fancy spending all those thoughts on it! I wouldn't have! I would have gone for the first man saying to me 'Will you marry me', but none ever came. Oh Lene! I'm so excited for you, do you know when the wedding will be?"

"Heinrich wants it soon, I reckon it will be before the end of the year."

"Good luck, my sweetie. What a big day it will be! Mother will get used to it, I'm sure. She looked calmer later last night. Must go and let you get your beauty sleep now! Night night!"

"Night, Erna, thanks for coming to see me." Lene suddenly felt worn out. She put all the letters in her desk drawer, brushed her teeth and went straight to bed, falling into a deep dreamless sleep. The lights from the coal shuttles circled through her room like the stars that rise and fall throughout the night.

It is true that Heinrich managed to persuade Mathilde of his good manners and trustworthy personality, when he was eventually allowed to present himself in the family lounge one Sunday afternoon. He brought a large bouquet of scented flowers in ochre colours and handed them to Mathilde, who was duly impressed. His affable charm, broad smile and well-spoken eloquence had their desired effect. The whole family, including suspicious watery-eyed Thilde, red-nosed Fritz and uncle and auntie, were enthralled and concluded afterwards that Lene had indeed found a good man, worthy of her. It was agreed that the wedding should take place on the fourteenth of December, leaving only a limited amount of time for preparations.

The wedding was an exuberant event. For a short day, one of the shortest in the year, place and time could be forgotten. History, past and present. Just Lene and her family and some of Heinrich's family members, but not many had travelled from Braunschweig. His sister and mother were expected. The red roses arrived at seven o'clock with a card saying 'I love you'. The family, baker's apprentices, shop assistants and maids ran up and down the stairs carrying cakes, biscuits and other tasty bits of food. Curlers, combs, cravats and jewels were lost and then found again. China for the wedding meal was carried hither and thither, together with trays, dishes and wine glasses. The kitchen table was covered with bits of garments, silk stockings, wrapping paper, pencils, rubbers, decorative bands, a coat, and an iron. Coffee cups, name labels and serviettes had to be packed. Today chaos was allowed to reign. Erna wept tears of excitement every time she looked at Lene. Her beautiful sister! How she was going to miss her! Coaches waited outside in Karl Mayer^Strasse, the horses being offered special treats from the bakery. Huge cakes laid out on porcelain plates were carried in from the back yard. The reception was to be at the town hall. A hundred guests were expected in the church.

"What a good-looking couple!" everyone said, when they looked at the two. She had her hair wrapped in a delicate silk veil held by entwined myrrh decorated with tiny white flowers curling around her head and holding the veil close to her face, her lips bright red. Her white flower embroidered dress had a V-shaped neck below which she had pinned a small bunch of myrrh twigs. Heinrich was wearing a black suit and white satin shirt with a white bow tie. Confetti mingled with snowflakes creating a magical atmosphere this very cold sunny day which would be hard to forget. Friends and family members stood and watched, insensitive to the temperature. Champagne, mulled wine and caviar canapés soon warmed the guests who had been invited to the evening meal and dance in the town hall. The swastikas outside the hall were luckily hanging flat from their masts, as the wind had quietened. Lene danced her first dance with Heinrich that evening to the Viennese waltz 'The Blue Danube'. He was as she expected an excellent dancer. The memorable tune, champagne and swirling in his strong arms while everyone watched stayed in her mind like glittering stars throughout all the troubled times that were to come, although in her later years the glitter faded.

CHAPTER 18

MASS EMIGRATION

'Fear springs out of all things. It turns to disgust,
bland and unbearable, and a bare endless emptiness
grins at me from all the walls of my room.'
Oskar Maria Graf, Sudden fright.

The newly-weds moved into Bromberger Strasse in Rotthausen,
not far from the bakery. Lene's early reservations soon dissipated.
Indeed, she felt her life to be much enriched. She had insisted on
carrying on working and took it for granted that her political work
would also continue. She found Heinrich to be a very busy man
who got up early, had a cold shower and was focused entirely on his
work at breakfast time. It left her feeling free to decide on her own
busy plans. Although he had never been with the Wandervögel his
ideas were similar to Lene's in terms of healthy living. He was also
a passionate man and often expressed how much he loved her. She
was content. Yet deep inside her the wound ached about Klaus and
what had happened with him. Love, shame and guilt lay buried in
her heart. Inge was back and had even attended the wedding. She
had not been arrested, but had been visiting a sick uncle. Olga was
unable to make the journey that day. Inge expressed genuine pleasure

about Lene's marriage, but eyed Heinrich with a certain amount of suspicion. Lene was aware of a feeling of unease about Heinrich in her presence. She heeded her warning to be careful about what she told him, but it also irritated her. She wanted to feel good about him, but when Inge started talking about the exiled poets the rosy image of Heinrich vanished.

"There is absolutely no freedom left in this country, do you realise that? Every man, woman and child is now organised by the Nazis. He'll be organised. You mark my word. They have the Gleichschaltung and you are obliged to join. But we did have a small victory."

"What was that?"

"Georgi Dimitrov proved in court that the communists couldn't have been involved in the Reichstagfire. They had to let them go. That was embarrassing for them! Here, see how they describe it in the newsletter we're distributing." Inge also pointed out a poem by Bertolt Brecht that was printed on one of the pages from his exile:

'...every one of us
Who walks with torn shoes
Through the crowd,
Proves the shame that is now staining our land.
But none of us will stay here. The last word is not yet spoken.'

"He's a great poet, can you imagine what it must feel like to have to leave your home town, like Margarethe did as well? At least it was the two of them, but many just had to get up and go. Leave all their belongings behind, including money, passport etc."

"And for a poet, a writer, they're leaving their language behind! I imagine it must be very painful."

"And their whole social life, friends, contacts..."

They were absorbed with reading to each other from the newspapers and fliers before they sorted them into streets and names for delivery. At such times Lene could forget completely that she was a married woman now with duties towards a husband.

"I know you have reservations about Heinrich, but he does really seem very modern. He keeps saying how much he appreciates that I'm an intelligent woman who can earn her own living. Then he comes and gives me a hug and adds 'but I'd love you even more if you were only there for me'. And I say to him 'how can you love me more when you already love me so much?' He then says 'you're right, I don't know how I can, but I just feel I can.' Men are funny, why is he so keen on me staying at home? I'd get bored."

"He owns you if you stay at home. Earning your own money gives you power and a potential for independent action. You don't have that if you have to ask him for money. If you're at home you are just there for him and don't have other interesting things to do, but if you go out to work, you have other interests, you might meet other men, he could lose you. I think he tries very hard to be modern, but probably isn't."

"Look what it says here on this page. They copied a letter Thomas Mann wrote to Albert Einstein in May this year: 'I am much too good a German for the thought of permanent exile not to weigh heavily indeed, and the breach with my country, which is almost unavoidable, fills me with depression and dread...For me to have been forced into this role, something thoroughly wrong and evil must surely have taken place.. and it is my deepest conviction that this whole 'German Revolution' is indeed wrong and evil...And to have warned as earnestly as possible against the elements which have brought about this moral and spiritual misery will some day certainly accrue to the honour of all of us, although we may possibly be destroyed in the process.' Shocking, isn't it, what these people are going through?"

Thoughts of the thousands who had escaped by night and in fear for their lives were engraved on their minds.

"I'm so glad we're doing this work and at least contributing something. I couldn't live with myself otherwise."

"Me too, Inge. It's good that we have each other and this work."

There was no moon, when they walked quietly in the deserted streets. Once again newspapers were delivered to those who carried on fighting the Nazi scourge. They had started to recite poems to each other which they had learnt by heart.

"Paul Zech is another poet. This is what he wrote:

'From my home, away from all I own has driven me,
not fire, nor death
Into the foggy nothingness. I took my hat and
instead of madness I took a beggar's loaf.
Insanity screamed itself hoarse in town,
Where demons now dance on a wasted, rotten and
twisted wheel.
I looked once down into the valley,
the stream and forest where all at once I saw a deer
and I turned round.
There was snow in all that wind. And when I
stepped upon the pale white ship:
There lay before me the blue Adriatic sea;
I did not see it. I came as one beat in the war,
An icy night was in my feelings, in my face.'"

"I learnt this one by Bertolt Brecht's son Stefan:
'Yellow of moon, silk of pears, pit shadows of aging.
Robbery of toys. Walk of the one who never
arrives.'"

They hugged quietly and Inge locked the front door when Lene left.

By June 1934 the elimination of the SA allowed Hitler to join forces with the army to prepare for war. The bloodbath was later justified as the prevention of a conspiracy. A month later Hindenburg died and Hitler usurped both posts of chancellor and president. The bankers and industry were busy developing a masterplan for the creation of an economy entirely focused on war preparations. The Versailles Treaty had ordained that Germany should have no more than one hundred thousand men in the army. By October 1934 there were already more than double that. On the 16th March general conscription was agreed in open confrontation with the Treaty. The British government was content to disavow the Treaty by signing an agreement with the Hitler government to allow Germany a military fleet of 35% of their own. They were allowed to build as many U-boats as Britain. 15th September saw the setting up of the Nürnberger laws which removed all rights from Jewish citizens. The abominations increased. Discrimination, repression, torture and murder. You couldn't speak out. It was a death sentence if you did. Whispered conversations around kitchen tables spoke of the evils that you had to deny outside. Anti-semitism and anti-communism were turned into daily sermons to stir up fear. The swastikas on the flagpoles smelt of blood.

Inge was washing the dishes, while her brothers were sorting the papers that had arrived from the Netherlands. Alfred and Margarethe had contact with one of the exiled social democrats, Helmut Kern, who worked for the newspaper 'Freie Presse' (free press), the paper of the Dutch socialists. They published articles that exposed the Nazi abominations openly. When Lene arrived they were just discussing Helmut's work.

"You see, Helmut worked for the 'Düsseldorfer Volkszeitung' before the Nazi takeover. The social democrats decided to send him to the Netherlands to work with the refugees. But what does that mean for the local people in Düsseldorf? If everyone runs abroad who's going to do the fighting back home? I bet he asked to leave."

"You may well ask! The poor haven't got the money to buy themselves a train ticket to get out, but the bourgeoisie have! They buy a ticket and go!" Emil looked at Lene with wild eyes, and she felt guilty for those who had left. But wouldn't he leave if he could? Why stay and be shot?

"True enough! Helmut probably found it easy to go, especially as he's probably paid for by his newspaper, but many others who are bourgeois left in the dead of night with nothing! No money! No passport! They left all their belongings behind. Do you think that was easy?"

Lene looked at Emil to see the effect of her words. She had spoken with passion, and her eyes sparkled belligerently. She thought of Margarethe's words about socialism and culture. One without the other could not be. The emigrants had precisely that meaning for her, they were defenders of both. And he accused them of having left Germany. Emil's eyes calmed. He tugged on his cap and wiped a hand over his brow.

"It's too late now to make a case for or against the bourgeoisie, I agree. We lost against the Nazis some years ago because we didn't have solidarity across the classes. Now we ought to work together. Well, I'm helping with these newspapers, aren't I, Lene? And they're written by the bourgeoisie."

He added the last sentences defensively and turned to sorting more papers. Lene noticed with satisfaction that she had found the better arguments. Inge nodded in Lene's direction to say let's leave it there. They were tired. Then she made some tea. When the brothers had left the room Lene pulled a letter out of her pocket. Her face had turned chalky white. She sat down and held her tummy as if she was feeling sick.

"Liesel wrote again."

"What's she saying about her brother?"

"Still no news of him. It's as if he has turned into thin air. Dreadful, isn't it? There's more bad news. She's heard through the network about our friend Franz Ehrlich. You know, the Bauhaus artist. They've arrested him. He's been found guilty of 'preparation for high treason'. Three years in a concentration camp!"

Inge put her arm around Lene. They held each other quietly. The warmth of their relationship was soothing, but Lene's heart was full of sorrow. Again Inge found the right words.

"We've got to be strong, Lene. They want us to fall apart. C'mon! We have each other and our work."

They slurped their hot Muckefuck coffee.

The resistance fight went on with determination although the repression worsened daily. From behind their curtains the silent and oppressed citizens watched the preparations for war being tried out on their Jewish compatriots, as they were stripped of their rights to be citizens day after day. Abroad the new weapons were being tested in the Spanish Civil War. In the autumn of 1935 preparations were made for the creation of a Popular Front against fascism based abroad. Heinrich Mann spoke at the Lutetia Hotel in Paris. The writers and poets Heinrich Becher, Lion Feuchtwanger, Egon Erwin Kisch and Arnold Zweig were there. Earlier in the year at the 'Congress for the Defence of Culture' writers from all over the world attended and discussed the issues in front of over a thousand participants including Heinrich and Thomas Mann, Maxim Gorky and Bernard Shaw. They spoke of the shame that was called Germany now. Their voices reverberated between walls of silence. The world's leaders didn't want to hear the alarm.

In the spring of 1935 Lene gave birth to her first child who she called Wilhelmine. The birth had been difficult, and she took some time to recover. Heinrich was overjoyed. His dream of having children was taking shape. He bought flowers and chocolates, praised his wife and kissed the new baby. A maid was employed. He drove to work in his automobile beaming with pride. Over supper he expressed his optimism for Germany.

"They have brilliant ideas, Lene. You've got to admit it. I know you're not so keen, but that 'Kraft durch Freude' organisation is really helping people. Admittedly, they copied it from Mussolini's 'dopolavoro'. Every worker is entitled to two weeks holidays and can apply for himself and his family to go on a cruise ship. Over two million people have already been on such a holiday. There's a chap at work. He took his family and came back saying he had a fantastic time."

"That's nice for him, but it doesn't make me feel any more comfortable about these people. They're preparing for war." Lene looked at Heinrich with tired eyes.

"All they're doing is making Germany strong again. You have to be able to defend yourself as a sovereign nation. Don't worry, there won't be a war. You look tired, my dear. Let's not argue about this now. We both need a rest."

Lene agreed with Heinrich reluctantly that she would need to give up her work at the hospital, but it left a deep-seated uneasiness inside her. Was she now owned by Heinrich, as Inge had said? She reassured herself with the thought of her resistance work. That, after all, was even more important to her than earning a living. They met most days, while the baby was asleep and being taken care of by the maid. They discussed the latest news from the resistance workers. The problem of mass emigration from Germany was so distressing for the first High Commissioner of the League of Nations, James McDonald, they learned, that he resigned his post commenting: "When hundreds of thousands of human beings are threatened by a politics of demoralisation and exile, then considerations of diplomatic correctness must give way to sheer human empathy." More than fifty thousand had left in 1933 alone. Lene and Inge knew that nothing at all was being done by those in power. They sipped their tea in silence.

"You look tired, Lene. How's the baby doing?"

"The baby's all right, but what worries me is that Heinrich's so unaware of the hardship and oppression in our country. I can't fathom it. It's like he lives in another country."

"As long as he takes good care of you and the baby don't worry about his views. They aren't important."

"True, but they affect me and how I feel about him. Now that I've given up work it bothers me more. Remember what you said to me, you'll be owned by him, if you don't work!"

Inge looked helpless for a moment, but quickly regained her assuredness.

"You can't change things now, Lene. Remember you did want children. Think of all the many women who have children and no one earning a living to help look after them well. You even have a maid and can come out to do resistance work! Just bear with it! It won't last forever. Look! Here! Thomas Mann wrote on the 14th October to Alfred Neumann about the possibility of going into exile, which he was not yet certain about. He writes about where he is 'inside, in the barrack-room rottenness of the stupid military camp that still answers to the name of Germany.' He does have a way with words, doesn't he?"

Lene knew Inge was right. It felt painful to hear her words. After all she had made her bed and was now having to lie in it, marrying a man who she did not love. Being loved was just not the same as loving someone. She thought of Klaus. Inge had spoken with such warmth, it felt good. She looked at Inge and for a moment saw her father Hermann there. She had the same way of soothing over troubles with politics just like he used to do.

They both read the article and found more information about Thomas Mann:

"That's why we need our poets! Look here, our comrades call the Nazis 'Kraft durch Freude', 'Kraft durch Schadenfreude'. That's funny! Very creative!"

"Writing is not something my brothers are into, but you see how world-changing a bit of writing can be. The leaflets and news reports of what is happening to our comrades and the victims of the Nazis who are in concentration camps, well, they all help our people to feel hope. The key thing is to show that resistance is taking place. That those who are being locked up and tortured know that we feel solidarity with them. That they are not alone."

"Maybe they won't last long! That is what all of these stories suggest. There is a lot of word of mouth going between comrades. Those who get the papers tell those who haven't got them what they learned."

"See what SOPADE, the exiled social democratic organisation, has managed to do. They're the ones who bring out 'Socialist Action' and 'New Forward'. Everyone is dying to know what tactics are being devised to fight the Nazi scourge. Did you see this? A bakery was acquired by one of the comrades which allowed them to use the delivery of bread to bring the newsprint baked in loaves to all these towns: Duisburg, Oberhausen Rheinhausen, Mühlheim, Krefeld and Essen."

"People are so inventive! It shows you how vital the resistance. Not only for those who are being helped but also for those who are doing it. They probably feel like us. It's the only way to cope emotionally with the horrendousness of what's going on around us, Lene." Inge opened her eyes in an assured way when she looked at Lene and added, "I'm proud of our circle of comrades and that we manage to carry on sharing information, in spite of the pressure."

"Yes, I'm feeling proud and good about it too. Imagine how annoying it must be for the Nazis that in spite of all their efforts and persecutions they can't stop the resistance." They both chortled with a collective sense of achievement.

"But when I go home, I change into another woman, Inge. It's like I've become two people. Sometimes I feel good about being able to be happy with Heinrich and do the secret work. Sometimes, though, it scares me to bits."

"You're doing your best, Lene. You can't do any more." Lene looked at Inge gratefully. Inge knew how to make her feel all right.

Every time Lene walked back to Bromberger Strasse from Inge's she looked carefully at each window, the brickwork of the houses, the pavement and the leaves on the trees, the stirring of branches. If the clouds moved she watched them. She was transforming herself with their help from Lene the illegal socialist comrade to Lene the mother and wife.

On another evening when they read letters and newspapers and before they sorted them for delivery they found more about Thomas Mann.

"His final decision to leave Germany was made when he wrote a comment about something a Swiss journalist had written in the 'Neue Zürcher Zeitung'. His reply had to do with an article written by Leopold Schwarzschild, who had already fled from Germany and the Nazis in 1933. He was a member of the Lutetia circle in Paris. He wrote that of all German culture only literature had been rescued. It now took place outside Germany, he said. Edward Korrodi replied that Thomas Mann's books were still being published in Germany. Then Thomas Mann adopted a strong position. On the 3rd February he sent a letter to the Swiss paper emphasising that 'nothing good could come out of Germany, while the present regime was in power, not for Germany, nor the world.' The Nazis responded instantly to his comment by removing his German citizenship and passport from him. The university of Bonn followed suit by taking away his honorary university title." Lene added, "How easy a university finds it to become accomplices of the Nazis, just like snapping one's fingers."

Inge was similarly shocked.

Late in 1936 she gave birth to another daughter called Karoline. Again Heinrich was beside himself with joy. Flower bouquets and chocolates arrived. He celebrated his wife's motherhood, and she enjoyed the exuberant love and affection that he overwhelmed her with. There were many weeks when she didn't see Inge. She didn't miss her. Life was rich and entertaining. The maid took charge of many boring tasks. Heinrich insisted that his wife must have leisure and took her out to the coffee houses and the theatre.

"Only the best is good enough for my wife!" This was one of his standard phrases. They shopped for beautiful shoes, a dress, a new coat and his happiness shone into her heart where it was dark.

Life could be easy, if Lene could forget. Forget her beliefs and ideals, her friendships, the words of her father, Klaus and his kisses. But they were always there with her, following her like her shadow. She walked the streets of Gelsenkirchen praying to the trees, leaves and clouds to help her be strong to lead her double life. She met Inge again, and they distributed newspapers as before. Her secret life grew like a plant, its roots deep inside her soul.

When the two friends met again there was more bad news in the reports. Another mass arrest led to the virtual elimination of the local organised resistance. One hundred and twenty social democrats were arrested in Recklinghausen. They were brought to court where they were beaten up. Often they were husband and wife in a family leaving their children in desperate need at home. One female comrade with abdominal cancer was dragged out of her home and put to work in a wash house. The arrested were found guilty and imprisoned in concentration camps. A few survived the camp and arrived back home, their hair grey, face ashen with swollen eyes and a broken body, but their will to resist unbroken. Chamberlain's 'Peace in Our Time' smoothed over the reality of the final manoeuvres in the war preparations. Strengthened by foreign approval from Britain and France Hitler boasted of his success in front of the German people. The news from the Netherlands was more positive. Resistance groups with names like Trepper and Gurewitch were active in Paris and Brussels with contacts in Germany. The Resistance was alive and well and gave Lene and Inge strength and hope.

One day in the winter Lene had an unpleasant surprise. She found Heinrich waiting for her in the entrance hall. His face looked flushed and his body seemed stiff and agitated, although he attempted to appear calm.

"Where have you been, Lene? I've been waiting for you."

"I've been to visit my friend Inge, which I've been doing all these years. You've never had a problem with it. Sometimes the tram is late."

"You seem to have left the children all afternoon with Marianne. Isn't that a bit neglectful? Also, what's this?" He held one of the illegal newspapers up to Lene's face. Lene's heart sank. He had become suspicious. It could be the end of her resistance work. He wouldn't approve, she knew that. How had he managed to find the paper? It must be the one I took home, because I wanted to read an article in it, written by Alfred. How foolish of me! Her thoughts flurried through her mind like a flock of birds. How can I calm the situation down? She thought very quickly and remembered that Heinrich was easiest calmed down with good food. He didn't respond to coaxing and flattery. Once he was suspicious he could be like a Rottweiler. She decided to play it cool and matter of fact.

"It's nothing, people hand them out in the street. It makes an interesting read. It's not much to bother about. How about I quickly serve you the tasty dinner I've prepared for you? You must be hungry."

This normally worked if her husband was a bit tense and tired from work. Today it didn't work.

"Lene, it's all very well, you with your activities and friends! I've never asked what they are, but I'm beginning to worry that you might get drawn into illegal actions. I'm not saying that's your aim, but you know that could get us into trouble with the Schutzpolizei. That's the last thing we want. This government is working hard with our industry to make Germany prosperous. You need to remember that."

Lene knew Heinrich well enough by now that she needed to let him have the final word, even if she felt told off like a small child. Inside her fury rose and made her feel rebellious, but she couldn't let him see how she felt. They would never agree politically. She was learning how he could become quite angry and domineering when something happened that he disagreed with. He didn't allow anyone to contradict him. For the sake of the children and her own peace of mind it was best to quietly accept his ruling. She looked up at him with a smile and said:

"Of course, my dear, you're right. Just throw the paper away, it means nothing to me."

"Promise me that you're not involved in any of these illegal distribution actions or meeting people that have been declared enemies of the state?"

"I promise, Heinrich! You worry too much. It's not good for your health. Let's just be calm and enjoy our supper. I've got your favourite sausages and red cabbage for you."

Heinrich looked more relaxed and started to smile back at Lene. She had won him round, and she was relieved. After dinner she left Heinrich with his newspapers and went into the nursery to speak with Marianne. She wondered if that woman was trustworthy. No one is trustworthy, unless they are comrades, remember that! Don't trust anyone! These were Inge's words. I must keep her words in my heart, otherwise I could be in big trouble. She felt lonely. The thought of not seeing Inge and doing paper deliveries was unbearable. Like being cut off from her own life. But this is also my own life! Something screamed in her. I live with a good man. I have two lovely girls. I am going to have a third one. I must not disappoint him. She pulled and tugged on the washing in the basket and couldn't decide whether to speak to Marianne or not. Marianne's innocent wide-eyed face. Was it hiding treachery?

She thought about Olga and Matti, but her situation was different. She had a husband who was loving, came home punctually and took a great interest in the children. It was a joy to see him play with the little girls. Olga had visited them a couple of times, but her depiction of Matti snooping on her family was not appreciated by Heinrich.

"Fancy her coming home from school and telling us to make sure to turn the radio on for Hitler's speech!" Olga laughed with her singing voice and made Lene smile, but she saw Heinrich pulling his brows together thunderously.

"Well, so she should! She's being taught in school how we must all support our government."

He spoke sharply. Olga looked at him in disbelief, and turned to Lene with a questioning look. Lene tried to signal something like 'just ignore him' to her, but the atmosphere was gone. Olga got up and Lene took her to the front door.

"He's off on his Nazi thing. I'm so sorry Olga, he's rude, but what can I do? Please stay in touch."

Olga hugged Lene and looked at her reassuringly. She knew what it was like having a man you don't understand. She eyed Lene, who looked distraught. They heard Heinrich coming and quickly said goodbye.

"Just send me messages to Inge, you know where she lives. We'll keep in touch that way."

It wasn't long after this incident that Heinrich came home and announced that they were moving house. He held a bunch of flowers in his hands and embraced Lene with a beaming smile:

"My darling, here are flowers for you! I know you're not sure about moving to Essen, but it isn't far, and we're going to have so much more room. Imagine, a whole house to ourselves! I think you'll love it. I want you to be happy there, so I hope you'll look at it positively."

Lene took the flowers out of Heinrich's hands and walked into the kitchen to avoid looking at him. She had feared this was going to happen. They had talked about moving several times. Heinrich always praising the idea, their own home, a garden, room for his mother to move in and so on. She had insisted that Gelsenkirchen was her home. She didn't need much room, and her mother was nearby, as well as her siblings. She felt fury, a sense of loss and powerlessness, but controlled herself so as not to show these feelings to her husband. She couldn't. It would cause more problems than it was worth. Heinrich was used to ruling the roost, and he would talk about his plans until he had got her where he wanted her. She put on her sweetest smile and said:

"Oh good, so you've found us a good place. When are we moving in?"

She felt that she had managed to please him with her reaction, as he excitedly continued:

"In four weeks, that's all. Isn't it brilliant! It's a beautiful house. You'll love it, I'm sure. There's a lot of space, a garden and swing for the girls, a room for Marianne and when my mother needs more help she can join us. Let's celebrate with a glass of wine, shall we?" Heinrich was full of his new house. He didn't know that her whole political life was tied to living in the Bromberger Strasse. He didn't realise what a huge blow this was for Lene. She suspected he'd speeded up his plans because he'd found the illegal newspaper. She hated him for that. She looked away and busied herself with the crumbs on the table. But he was unstoppable. He took her in his arms and kissed her on the mouth, looking deep into her eyes to check that she was also happy. She didn't know what he saw, but there was only coldness in them. She had learnt to hide her emotions with her words.

"Of course, dear! Let's have some wine. Sorry if I sound a bit low, but I'm quite tired. The children weren't well today and kept quarrelling. It's the weather, maybe."

"We'll relax now and we'll also have your family round here for a nice dinner party before we go, shall we?"

That night Lene couldn't sleep. The wine and work had soon enough made Heinrich so tired that he fell asleep as soon as he lay down. Lene, though, got up and sat at her desk in the little spare room where her books and papers were and stared out of the window. A half moon was slipping down, looking like a boat that moved westwards in the sky. She imagined she was on the moon boat and sailing with her friends Inge and Olga to meet up with Margarethe and Alfred. How much she wanted to see them again! The life of Lene, the wife of Heinrich lay like a discarded snake skin next to her. She felt he forced her to lie to him and felt disgusted. There was nausea in her stomach. She looked at the moon ship again and saw herself as a writer and a socialist with her Berlin friends Liesel, Klaus and Franz. She saw Olga and Inge. She saw her father and Friedrich and Wanda. She watched the moon boat disappear from the sky.

CHAPTER 19

KRISTALLNACHT

Diary notes, 21ˢᵗ July 1975

Today we talked for a long time about Olga. Olga is still a good friend of my mother's, but they didn't see much of each other for many years after the war. All of them had to work hard to rebuild their lives. Inge also remained a good friend. Then we talked about the silence. That silence which made me leave home years later. First she just nodded when I asked her about it, maybe to silence such a past. Then she argued that she had found it a burden at first. But then, after several of her husband's outbursts, she felt she couldn't cope with them any more. "You get used to it," she added. Then: "You can get used to anything, even Heinrich." At that point she started laughing, and I had to laugh with her. She had a sense of humour. So much had been unbearable, full of fear, confusion. All that secret resistance work. The secret love affair. The many children and the homelessness after the war. Sometimes we could hardly bear any more; telling and listening weighed so heavily on us. The loss of Anni had been traumatic, she said a few words about her. She was still hurting.

I kept wanting to ask her what had happened to them all, the people they had helped with their resistance work. But it was getting too much. We would have never finished. But I did understand one thing. The insufferable silence in the fifties and sixties stemmed from the total collapse of German culture, at least in the West. Not only the dead were silent, their songs, their poems and their pictures were also silenced. So were their stories. And what happened in the East of the country was largely ignored, unless it was derided. That Anna Seghers returned to the Eastern part of Germany and that she became a member of the Academy of the Arts in the GDR was not celebrated. Or Bertolt Brecht who also went back to East Berlin.

Today it was her last day in London, the 28ᵗʰ July. She was full of beans and chatty, but it seemed ever more difficult to get answers to my questions from her. It was as if the flow of her stories had dried up. In the evening we drank a bottle of wine and celebrated her long friendships with Olga and Inge, which had survived all the vicissitudes of the time. And Klaus? She mentioned that he now lived in the GDR, in Berlin. Liesel too. They had both joined the Socialist Unity Party. They met now and again at Friedrichstrasse station. She didn't want to say any more. Her eyes had a deep dark glow. A secret I had to leave her with.

End of diary notes

Olga stood outside the farm cottage and looked at the sky, her arms folded under her breasts tugging her cardigan close to her skin. Oily tar clouds sped like hunted animals across it. The moon was a sharpened knife blinking as if the murderer had just pulled the blade out of the sheaf. A distant perpetual howling sounded like a dog being kicked. She saw the horizon over Gelsenkirchen drenched in red. They're smelting iron into weapons all night long, she thought. They want war. She had learnt to keep quiet. She could make her face as still as a mask. Maybe having wanted to become a singer made her skilled in acting and camouflaging her feelings. Maybe it was just that she had no choice. Matti was as efficient a conscript to Nazi ideas as one can be. Only when she was in school did Olga have words with her parents about the hateful government. They couldn't even afford to joke. Matti took everything deadly seriously.

"Our Führer says we mustn't speak to Jewish people. He says they're a lower race. We had a Jewish girl in class, but she never came back in the new term."

"What happened to her?" Olga asked her daughter.

"I don't know. We weren't told."

"Shouldn't you have found out about her? She might be sick or need help."

"We're not allowed to talk about her."

"But that's inhuman, you ought to check out what happened to her."

"We have orders. We are not to speak about or with these Jewish people."

Matti was like a wall. You couldn't get through to her. It hurt Olga and her parents very much, but they were helpless. They knew that even a joke could now cost them their life. They were careful about who they talked to and what they said. Even neighbours couldn't be trusted any more. They might have joined the Nazis. Matti wasn't who they thought she had been. A trivial remark from her parents, a derogatory word repeated in school could lead to an arrest. Betrayal poisoned the air like a foul smell. Swaggering bragging about the fatherland, the blood and the soil beamed relentlessly from the radio. The broadcasters boasted about the achievements of the government. The Nürnberger Laws were celebrated and the rearmaments were trumpeted as if they made Germany into a land of heroes. If Olga didn't turn on the radio Matti expressed surprise.

"We're supposed to listen to the Führer, mother. Why don't you turn the radio on? We should feel proud of Germany."

Olga showed her daughter how she could turn on the radio and went out to look at the sky. She thought of Lene and Heinrich. Was he really sympathetic to the Nazis? Lene wasn't quite sure about it. Would Hubert have become a Nazi? Well, she didn't have to worry about it now. Her own daughter was a Nazi, to be sure, but she was only a child. She had no choice. She felt a little relieved about Matti. The thought of being married to one of them made her shudder. I have to speak to Lene, help her. A sad and tender feeling filled her as she thought of Lene.

Lene's third little girl was born in March. Heinrich was thrilled. Lene was happy and felt fulfilled. She was able to provide her husband with the satisfaction of another child. Had he not been adamant that having many children should be their goal? Were children not a blessing sent by God? Weeks went by absorbed in nursing, nappies and the warm glow of motherhood. Spring was full of blossoms. Cherry and apple trees were in full bloom, willows and birches covered in tiny green leaves. The immediacy of all the demands on her with three children left little room for the past or the future. She existed in the moment. An amnesia wrapped itself around her days like a soothing drug. Klaus, Olga, Margarethe. The secret newspaper deliveries with Inge. Reading the latest proud Resistance stories, all had vanished behind the hubbub of washing, dinner preparations and keeping on top of things. Auguste, Heinrich's mother, had moved into the house. She was old and frail, yet bossy. Another maid called Emma was employed. The radio hummed with words like 'Herrenvolk' and 'Lebensraum' in between trumpeted marches. Auguste's room was next to Emma's. Luckily she never left her room after supper. She liked to go to bed early but had a habit of ringing for a hot water bottle or a chamber pot. Emma saw to her needs diligently. Her early withdrawal from the household suited Lene, because there was no doubt that she was a difficult person. The old lady was not at all like her own mother. She was an imposing and large person, tall and broad. She chipped in everywhere, ordered people about, including Lene and expressed opinions whether requested or not. The way she stared adoringly at her son irritated Lene intensely. At least she did play with the children. Slender Mathilde was a refined and elegant person next to her. Unlike her Auguste didn't mince her words at all. How to lay the dinner table was one of her pet subjects. She maintained that Lene didn't know how to use style and elegance when laying the table.

"The damask table cloth isn't ironed well enough. You can't have supper on a cloth with these creases. And the cutlery! Haven't you learnt where to place it by the plate?"

"Look at the spoons, they're black. Haven't you heard of silver polish, my dear?"

"Go and do her the favour," Heinrich urged Lene in the kitchen where she complained to him bitterly. When Auguste started on Lene's care for her children by complaining that their hair wasn't brushed often enough and that their fingernails were dirty (which they weren't) Lene lost her temper and left the lounge. She didn't come back until the old lady had gone to bed. "Fat old bag!" Lene hissed under her breath.

"I'm not going to put up with your mother! She doesn't know how to behave! Remember I'm an adult and being patronised by your mother is the last thing I will put up with. I married you, not your mother."

Heinrich looked at her with concern. He did want her to be happy. The situation would only get worse if something wasn't done. It would have a bad effect on the children. He had a word with Auguste. She started to press her lips together tightly, when an urge to comment was on her mind. Lene watched her sharply, until she saw that the urge had gone.

On Sundays her mother visited with Hilde and her children. Coffee and cake were served. Everyone talked at the same time.

"Look at them, how tall the boys have grown, Hilde."

"Isn't Almut a pretty girl?"

"Three little girls, Lene, who would have thought..."

Her mother sat quiet and dignified holding Lene's baby, while Auguste and Hilde held forth. They were a good match as far as opinions were concerned. Both gave the appearance of knowing what there was to be known in the universe.

"Then you have to stir the dough until it's fluffy and put one egg in at a time. You've got to be careful..."

"Well, I warm up the butter first..."

Hilde's watery blue eyes scanned the dining room for its spotlessness, and Auguste scrutinised her, while she laboriously patted her lips with the serviette. Heinrich boasted about his wife and her wonderful motherhood skills. He looked at her lovingly. Lene sat next to her mother, and the two of them watched the proceedings as if they were the audience in a theatre show.

Sometimes after such a Sunday, Lene felt happy to have been with her mother, feeling that childhood closeness again. Then she waited for Heinrich to go to bed. When she was sure that he was asleep she went to the small spare room and sat at her beloved desk. She took out photos and letters from life in Karl Mayer Strasse. Her father with the new radio contraption. The sofa with the fairground lights in the lounge at Karl Mayer Strasse. Erna's warm bosom, when she pressed her younger sister to herself. Klaus and Liesel. Heat rose inside her thinking of him. Where was he now? Was he still thinking of her? She tried to piece the images from the past together with her present life, but she couldn't. Amnesia had robbed her and bits were missing. The sandalwood smell. Klaus's Adam's apple. His lips. Her life didn't hang together. Many people's lives didn't hang together any more. Many languished in concentration camps, the Jews and the communists. Many had lost everything. Where were all the poets? Homeless, wandering in foreign lands or locked up. Their freedom lost. But she had her children. She went to bed feeling sad and torn.

Outside the world of nations watched quietly while Germany metamorphosed into a monster. The mass rally of tanks and other instruments of war on the 7th September in Berlin went down like a damp squid. Hitler realised that the people of Berlin had little taste for the display of the arsenal and watched the parade in sullen silence. 'I can't do a war with these people,' he is reported to have commented. More violence and brutality would need to be applied to desensitise the population. With bellowing roaring from loudspeakers and the brown uniformed troops marching through the streets the flames of racism were fanned. The brutal rhetoric culminated in an unspeakable night of terror and destruction on the 9th November 1938. Kristallnacht. After so many nights of killing! One hundred and fifty thousand communists in the first year! Killed, incarcerated or maimed! Erich Muehsam. Erich Lange. Beaten to death. Rudolf Hilferding. Murdered. The night of the long knives! And now Kristallnacht! Places of worship were torched, ransacked and shops smashed. Homes and offices were looted and burnt. Three hundred and seventy thousand Jewish people were left without possessions, without rights, without humanity. Arrested or murdered on the spot they faced the wrath of rampaging fascist gangs that had taken leave of any sense of morality, compassion and human dignity. Young men who were trained and schooled in violence. Hyena-like they roamed in packs through the streets, drunk with a will to destroy. Pack animals, their individuality submerged under the edict of the mass. Yet in their homes people washed and got dressed as on any ordinary day. They cooked food and ate dinners. They scrubbed their floors and went about their daily work, as if life was carrying on as normal. What could they do? Time did not stand still for their sorrow. They turned on their radio stations and turned them off so as not to hear the manic broadcasts of blood and soil and 'Herrenvolk' humming in their ears.

Lene was hanging out the washing early on a September work day afternoon, when Inge stood outside the garden gate. She had asked in Karl Mayer Strasse for Lene's address. They fell into each others' arms and held each other for a long time. Life had changed utterly.

"Are you still delivering..."

"I am, I am! There are more and more contacts, new ones, even when we lose old ones who have got dragged away someone else wants to have the information. People are hungry for news of the resistance. Hungry!"

Inge's emphasis was like a breath of fresh air. It burnt like too much oxygen through Lene's lungs. It left a scalding burn. She showed Inge round the house and garden. She felt self-conscious about the luxury of her home, the brightness of the rooms, the fashionable curtains, the nursery full of toys. It was a different world to the one that Inge inhabited. Inge behaved sweetly and showed interest. She hugged the children and showed admiration for the well organised household. Lene couldn't help feeling uneasy, although Inge didn't utter a word of doubt or accusation. Children! A husband. A wealthy home. Not to have to go out to work, but yet have money to spend. She looked at Inge, who was calm and her usual self. She was dressed in clothes Lene remembered. Did Inge blame her now? She felt faint.

"What's up with you, Lene? You're pale and shaking like a leaf on a tree."

"Oh, Inge, it's nothing... I just feel so guilty. So left out. I don't know how to express what I'm feeling. I hope you don't blame me for the life I lead? I've done no political work for some time. I can't make sense of it all..."

"What are you worried about? You have everything a woman could want in life. Of course I don't blame you! I did say to you then you've got to marry him, didn't I? Well, you can't do more than you're doing. Don't worry, there will be time for political work. They'll go to war soon, you know that, don't you?"

"Oh dear Lord! I knew..." Lene gasped and looked for somewhere to sit down. Inge could see her friend was in turmoil and hooked her arm under Lene's, saying:

"Let's sit down on the bench here. Lene, dear. You need to stop blaming yourself, as if you were responsible for what's going on. There are many families like yours, and they lead a happy life and enjoy hearing Nazi marches, as if there was nothing to them. They shout 'Heil Hitler' when he demands. They are ignorant. Blissfully so! You make yourself suffer because you're not ignorant. You know what's going on and how much suffering is out there. But you also have duties to your family. They come first. There's plenty of time for politics..."

They sat down behind the apple and plum trees with their glossy ripening fruit. Inge stroked Lene's hair and pressed her shoulder with her arm around her. She felt for Lene. She knew Lene was totally loyal and dependable, and she would be that both for the socialists and the illegal work, as well as her husband and children. She realised it was a mountainous emotional burden. The colour had come back into Lene's face and Inge could feel her muscles ease. They watched Marianne hang out more washing and walk back into the house without noticing the women behind the trees. The white sheets fluttered in the sunbeams.

"Thank you, Inge, I feel better now. You're right, it's this double life. It's unbearable to think about it. I'm so glad you are visiting me, but it reminds me of what I'm missing and the thought that they'll go to war..."

"You did know, though..."

"I did. But Heinrich keeps saying there won't be a war, and I've begun to believe him. That's why I was so taken aback when you mentioned it."

"I thought as much. He's got to say it, hasn't he? How else could he defend them?"

"Don't say any more, dear Inge. It tears my heart apart..."

They were both silent for a moment thinking the same thing. Heinrich wasn't a socialist, a humanist, a defender of people's rights. What was it that blinded him to the fate of people? Was he a racist? Neither of them dared ask such questions. Lene felt a surge of energy driving through her body that seemed to lift the veil of amnesia from her. She wanted to know what was going on.

"Tell me, Inge, what's happening out there? What stories have you delivered? Who are the new groups? What are they discussing?"

"Big stuff is going on out there. Thomas Mann spoke at a mass rally in New York recently. This is what he said: "Saving the peace, that is now the task of the peoples. Hitler has to fall – that and nothing but it can only save the peace." Can you imagine - twenty thousand people, they say, listened to him. But obviously not the ones who could make a difference. The nation's politicians. Hadn't they heard that trade unionists, socialists and communists were languishing in concentration camps and were being tortured and murdered? Hadn't they witnessed Kristallnacht with thousands of Jewish people being dragged away and their homes and shops destroyed?"

"What about the newspaper deliveries and news of Margarethe?"

"We all just carry on, Lene. There's the Trepper organisation, then there's the Rote Kapelle. Lotte Schleif is in contact with them. She works in a library in Berlin. A fantastic woman, a comrade told me. She makes anti-Nazi stickers. It's not easy, as you know. They're all risking their lives. And the Nazis do everything to sweeten the life of those who choose to cooperate with them. The radio tells them about 'Kraft durch Freude', the holiday programme. It persuades many families that things are all right. Those who have disappeared are silent."

"Yes, you wish the dead could scream."

"Exactly. We try to make them scream. From exile, from hidden rooms, from cellars with printing equipment. With illegal newspapers, books, letters, any form of printed material. We circulate whatever comes into our hands."

"Have you heard stories from them?"

"There are lots of stories. About being uprooted, without work, without family, without libraries or an audience. Nevertheless they continue speaking. They describe their lives amidst a foreign language and culture. How they live like wild animals in the forest. Unreal lives. Strangers all of them. Often the only escape left to them is death. Kurt Tucholsky took an overdose in Sweden in 1935."

Lene relished Inge's news. She lapped it up like a cat thirsty for milk. They sat close together watching the pears and apples in the trees. Suddenly the fluttering sheets separated and from between them Heinrich appeared like a ghost. It was him! They couldn't believe it. It was only mid-afternoon. His face barely hid his fury. It was flushed. Even his hair, normally perfectly smoothed, stood up.

"What is it that's keeping you in the garden, Lene? The children are asking where their mother is, and you're whiling away the time with this woman. What's she doing here? Doesn't she know that you have duties towards your husband and your children?"

Lene had jumped up as if struck by lightning. Inge made a move to leave by pulling her coat close, but her bag was still in the house. In an attempt to draw his attention away from Inge Lene stepped forward to stand between him and her friend. Her confidence and quick wit came back and she replied:

"My dear Heinrich! You're back very early from work. Don't worry. My friend Inge just popped by for a short while to see our new baby. She finds the little girl very cute. She thinks she looks like you. Now, would you like some tea or coffee? It's only 5 o'clock, and sunny. We could sit in the garden. Let me call Marianne."

Lene spoke firmly and was looking straight into her husband's eyes. When she finished she pushed her arm through his and turned him around, marching him back to the house. She did this with such certainty and speed that it took her husband by surprise, as she walked him towards the entrance to the lounge. She quickly picked up Inge's handbag before he spotted it and called for Marianne to make some tea and bring the children. Before he could catch his breath she fled back into the garden.

"That's my life now. You can see what's happening here, Inge dear! Please! Forgive me! You've got to leave. I'll be in touch. It was wonderful to see you, I'm so glad to hear about our comrades, but you and he will only clash. I can feel it. It's tearing me apart, believe you me."

She pressed Inge's handbag into her arms and squeezed her hand with warmth and tenderness.

"You're my very dear friend! Don't forget that, whatever happens. We must stay in touch." Inge smiled and quickly walked towards the garden gate, closing it behind her. She turned round, smiling furtively at Lene, and vanished behind the street corner. Lene felt her heart tightening and a deep ache in its core. She pressed her hands against her loud beating chest as if to stop it splitting in two. She took a deep breath and another one and waited until the tightness had seized and the ache had lessened. She pulled down her shoulders and consciously straightened herself up to being very upright and tall. The tall feeling helped. She knew that Heinrich was probably still angry. She would face him calmly and with kindness. When she entered the lounge the two girls were around her husband, one of them sitting on his lap. It was Wilhelmine, her eldest. She seemed to be the closest to her father, and he sat smiling. Good, she thought. The children have calmed him down. Marianne brought in a pot of tea. The girls ran outside.

"What is it that you see in this woman? Isn't she the one with the illegal newspapers? I'm sure she is. I don't want to see her here again." His voice was loud and harsh again.

"She's an old friend of mine. We went to college together. She's had a hard life, had to look after her younger brothers while her mother was ill. You can't blame her for that."

"She worries me. You know me, when I get a certain feeling about someone I'm a bit touchy and impatient. This is our home, and I just don't want her here again. Do you understand?"

"I do, dear! Don't worry yourself now. You've worked hard all day and deserve to relax. Don't let these habits and friends I've kept from the past get in the way of our relationship. Come on, let's forget this now and enjoy our evening!"

She went over to him, smiled in his face and stroked his cheek. She knew he couldn't resist her smile, and she let herself be pulled down for a kiss.

"All right, but promise..."

"Of course, dear! Forget about it now, you won't see her again. I'll be a while nursing the baby."

She watched him relax. Marianne brought his slippers. Lene went upstairs and said good night to the children. Marianne read them a story. Lene left for the baby's room and closed the door behind her. She picked up little Sieglinde and smiled at her. She sat down on her armchair and put the baby to her breast. Feeding the little one was soothing. Peacefulness came back slowly with the baby in her arm and being surrounded by all her treasures from the past. The chest of drawers from Karl Mayer Strasse. Her small desk by the window. It was always locked. Hidden from prying eyes. These two pieces of furniture acted like the guardians of her other life. Their contents connected her to her past and so much that was valuable to her. Two of Erna's wooden dolls were there, her diaries and notebooks with her dreams and aspirations, as well as her letters. Both were locked up, the keys hidden. When she insisted on bringing the two old pieces of furniture Heinrich objected.

"This old stuff, you don't really need it. I'll buy you a nice new desk and chest of drawers. Also what do you need a lock-up desk for? We're husband and wife. We should have no secrets from each other. I shall be perfectly frank with you, so you should be the same with me."

"I like them, Heinrich. They come from my family home. It's not about secrets. It's just my private things, nothing important." She played their role down, but he still objected.

"You are mine and I am yours. We have our life, our children together, what more do you need? I'm just curious. I won't stop you, but why can't we be enough for each other?"

"Just call it a whim, Heinrich dear. Shall we have dinner now?" Talking of food always worked.

After she had nursed her baby and put her to bed Lene quickly pulled out a leaflet Inge had pushed into her hand before she left. It contained a poem by Erich Arendt from the Spanish Resistance after he had to leave:

'Then sighed the night. A black meteor falls deadly out of the cold starry spaces. The roofs rise up in fear, and mothers wake screaming from their dreams. The children though, never woke, when the heavy load of walls smash down on them – and blood drenched, skirts tear under the weight of rock.'

As if she'd committed an evil deed she quickly folded the leaflet, unlocked the desk and pushed it in between her letters, locking it afterwards and hiding the key. She sighed. The real world was here in her little room, but as soon as she stepped out of it the busy life of a mother and wife tore her into a thousand tiny tasks, and it was nearly time for supper. She heard Auguste speak to Heinrich. She had much to say on how to educate the little ones, but she tried hard not to make reprimands in front of Lene. She stopped when Lene arrived. The world outside disappeared. War preparations? Army manoeuvres? Callous and belligerent speeches on the radio? Heinrich heard it on the radio too, but Auguste had something to say about the dinner.

"The food isn't quite hot, is it, dear? And I wish you would put the serviette rings on the right way round."

"Is there going to be a war?" Lene asked Heinrich, looking searchingly into his face.

"War? Yes, it might have to come to that. A Blitzkrieg. It'll be over very quickly. We have an excellent army."

"You always said there wasn't going to be a war."

"I can't foresee the future, dear. But it does seem to be happening now. It won't last long."

"What if it isn't over very quickly? What will happen to us, as a family?"

"Don't worry, my treasure! You can be too negative about all of this. The Führer knows what he is doing."

"What do you mean by that?" Lene shouted. She couldn't control herself, and the blood rose in her cheeks with anger and outrage.

"You can see that he's managing Germany very well. More people have work, they go on holidays with 'Kraft durch Freude'. They celebrate him. Our industry is in good shape. We're internationally respected."

Heinrich wiped his mouth with the smooth ironed linen serviette and looked smugly from his steak to his wife.

"Yes, an industry that's taking us to war, and a country that has been deserted by most of its writers, poets, musicians, film makers, and where Jewish people have lost all their rights."

Lene was taken aback by her own courage. She had never been as outspoken in front of Heinrich like this, and in front of his mother who looked with pity and embarrassment at her daughter-in-law.

"Dear Lene, I know you have sensitivities that arise from the bakery class of people you grew up with, and I've been very lenient towards you and respected all the work you've done. But we're a well-situated household earning good money under the present government. They haven't done us any harm. Others have different lives for their own reasons. And on this matter I don't want to hear you speak of Jewish people again in front of me. I'm familiar with how they've robbed Germans of money by running the banks and smuggling themselves into people's favour. Let's leave it at that and not mention them any more here, shall we?"

He looked demandingly at Lene, his eyes cold and shiny and close together because he had a large frown between them. Lene slumped in her chair, as if shot in the stomach. Then she got up and left the room. She felt sick. She ran to the toilet and locked herself in. She heard Heinrich following her and calling out. She didn't reply. He came to the toilet door and tried to open it. She heard him apologise for upsetting her.

"I'm not feeling well, Heinrich. Just finish your dinner. I might have to go to bed early. I'm very tired."

She heard him say more, but she didn't listen, because she didn't want to hear his voice. Not tonight, anyway. He had become contemptible to her. The double life she had led had broken apart. It couldn't be done, however much she tried. How could she go on after this? In front of his mother! The old witch! She was always going to take his side, the hateful old cow! She stayed seated on the toilet breathing deeply, trying to contain her fury, fear and hatred and form them into something she could live with. It was impossible tonight. Sleep! I want some sleep. I shall sleep in the baby's room. The spare bed will do. She heard Heinrich walk away. She heard Auguste go to her room and shut the door. The house went quiet. She stayed. After a long time, she softly opened the door and walked over to the bathroom to wash for bed and brush her teeth. She put on her dressing-gown. She decided it was best to inform Heinrich of her decision. She didn't want him to burst in on her when she was going to try to sleep. Heinrich was on his own reading the paper.

"I'm not feeling well, Heinrich. I'm going to sleep in the baby's room for tonight. I am very, very tired." She hoped he was going to leave it at that, but he was incorrigible.

"Lene, dear, I just want the best for you and me and the children, that's all. And that means you respect my opinion. I'm not out to upset you, you know that. I would do anything for you. I love you."

"I know, dear, but just let me sleep on my own tonight. I'll be OK tomorrow, I promise. I'm feeling very tired, it's been a long day."

She looked at him pleadingly hoping he'd take 'no' for an answer, and he did this time.

"OK, that's all right then, Lene. Take care! You don't even have to be there in the morning. Marianne can sort out the breakfast. Just take care! We have to hold together in these hard times."

She sensed a concession in his words, admitting they were hard times and felt slightly easier. She walked up to him and pressed a small kiss on his forehead.

"Good night, Heinrich, see you tomorrow."

Up in the small room by her baby she curled herself into the narrow bed after she'd opened the window and looked out into the night. An ice-coloured full moon was strung up in the birch tree. The air smelt good, and she took a deep breath. Fresh air made her feel better. Wrapped up warm she soon fell asleep, exhausted from her mental torment.

CHAPTER 20

WAR

"...someone gets caught, he does not live any more, yet the bond between the nameless does exist, the invisible army of those who help, torture threatens, the pain is bitter, the fight back goes on regardless, they are the holy and the knights of the future human society..."

Alfred Kerr, The illegal fighters in Germany

After the confrontation at supper Heinrich came back from work the following day with a large bouquet of flowers.

"It's only politics, my darling! We love each other and that's more important than anything else. And we have wonderful children."

He smiled his most charming smile at her and kissed her gently on the lips. She had to forgive him. He looked so desperate for her approval. It made her wonder if he knew what he was doing. In her heart, though, remained a small flame of fury for all those who suffered without his recognition of their suffering. How could he! The summer sunshine hid the ugliness of the next developments. Lebensraum. Herrenvolk. Blut und Boden. Schutzpolizei. These words whined and howled constantly on the radio waves. The Soviet leadership made many attempts to forge an alliance with France and Britain, but to no avail. France and Britain weren't interested. Had Churchill not urged after the revolution to 'strangle the infant communism in its cot'? The revolutionaries had dispossessed the ruling class in Russia. That was a sacrilege. The holy cow of property was threatened. Hitler's war machine was in a good position to rectify the situation. They started by attacking Poland. Headlines announced the army's advances.

"I shall have to join up, Lene dear. You know how much experience I have, being an engineer. They need my skills. They've asked me to run the repair unit for technical equipment."

"But why do you have to go? You're not the youngest at fifty-one. You've done your bit of fighting in the earlier war."

Lene was taken by surprise by Heinrich's announcement. Luckily, he told her after Auguste had gone to bed. He was more careful these days about announcing issues publicly.

"True enough, but it means that I have plenty of experience, that is valuable. They've asked me to run a repair station in the east, I don't want to let them down."

"But you're letting us down. Your family. Your children."

"Lene, I'm doing it for us and for the children. It won't last long, I promise you."

"How can going to war be good for us and the children? I don't understand you!"

"Dear, we don't understand each other in this small matter. Trust me! I know what I'm doing. I'll make sure you're well looked after. The company will provide you with money and any help you should need."

She saw in his face that he was adamant and would not change his mind, and she felt anxious and annoyed. First he marries me then he leaves me to go to war. He's too old. He doesn't need to go. That night was the second time that she refused to sleep in the same bed with him. He pleaded with her, but she was stubborn.

"I don't agree that you have to go and join this war. It's an unjust war. It's an aggressive war. What have all these other countries done to us to make us go to war against them?"

"It's not going to be a long war. I think we shall win it very quickly."

She looked at him with disbelief. "War is war. It kills people and doesn't solve anything."

He had to leave her to what he called her whim. She locked the door and buried herself under the duvet, like she used to do in her family home. She wept hot tears and cursed her fate. She first thought that she was upset, but gradually became aware that the feeling she felt most strongly was anger. Her tears were tears of fury and powerlessness. It took her a few days to recover a sense of contentment. It was always his face with his broad and open smile that made her forgive him. That open face and big smile he could do. He couldn't be all bad. Once after making love he had told her about his enjoyment of war.

"That feeling of comradeship, the bravery and courage you get when you're with the men in the trenches."

"Yes, but you're with them while they're dying, so you keep losing them. What's the good of that?" she had said.

"But the courage you see in their faces, the togetherness, the trust you feel for each other."

"But you can feel togetherness and trust in many situations in life, while in war it just ends in death all the time. Look at what happened in the First War, it was lost. So many died uselessly."

"Let's not go there," he pleaded, worrying that they would come up with very different views on war and start to quarrel.

"I can't explain it. It's a very intense feeling having the courage of the men all around you."

By the time he left early in October 1939 she'd become used to the idea of his departure. She was even beginning to feel a sense of relief. She watched him pack his things, his leather satchel, his uniform, as if from a distance. How he smoothed the cloth lovingly! How carefully he rolled up his belongings into his knapsack! How he caressed his shiny leather boots. They kissed goodbye. He embraced Auguste and the children. Autumn leaves were falling on the wet garden path. He is following his conscience, and I'm following mine, she thought as a military vehicle stopped outside the gate and he waved. She waved back. On his face was his big broad smile. As she saw him depart she heard herself giving an involuntary sigh of relief. Her muscles relaxed. She felt like jumping up and down with lightness. Why had she tried to persuade him not to go to war? She felt guilty about her own feelings, but at the same time inside her she could feel the old strength and initiative from the years in the bakery coming back and it sent a shiver of rejoicing through her body. My conscience is definitely going to guide me, I'm not sure what it is that's guiding him, did he say patriotism? She wasn't sure.

It wasn't long before Lene's friends learnt of Heinrich's absence and visited her. They started to sit late into the night in the kitchen reading and folding papers, preparing them for delivery. Sharing news of arrested, exiled or murdered comrades consumed them totally. Lene's political passions reawakened with renewed vigour, making her feel full of energy. The old lady Auguste seemed to take her son's decision to assist the war effort to heart. She made few appearances outside her room and refused to have dinner. She needed more care from Emma, who did so with much kindness. One day she didn't wake up any more. It became one more of so many deaths as far as Lene was concerned. She wrote to Heinrich, but he was unable to return for the funeral.

Inge now visited every few days and brought reports, letters, fliers and newspapers. Their illegal work was becoming very difficult. So many of their comrades were being arrested, thrown into concentration camps or murdered immediately. They read about the Harnacks. The couple had been trying since 1933 to inform the US government of the criminal character of the Nazi regime. They met many opponents of Hitler during receptions at the embassy and started organising campaigns together with them.

"You see how many women are involved in the resistance. What they tend to do is to look after the families of men who have been arrested. Like in the Red Assistance. Standing guard is done by a man and a woman pretending to be lovers. Or having engagement parties, that's what you do to hold a meeting without causing suspicion. Women's ideas! Great, isn't it, Lene?"

"Then let's celebrate an engagement and organise a meeting."

They both laughed. Inge's warm brown eyes warmed Lene's heart. Her friend had grown her hair and was now wearing it in a long plait which often dangled at the side of her face. Lene liked looking at it. How she had missed this togetherness, but she also thought of Heinrich now and again.

"I feel quite bad saying this, Inge, but I'm relieved that he has gone off to the war. I thought I'd go mad sometimes. He could be so scary when he was angry. I began to wonder about leaving him. Then again he'd do anything to make me forgive him and love him. Apart from change his point of view, of course! It kept tearing me apart."

"Well, you've got a break from him now, so that gives you time to think about what you want to do. Look at it as a godsend. I'm just very pleased to have you back working with us. Perhaps you can come over to Gelsenkirchen sometimes. You've got Marianne here to look after the children, and you just make a wee trip. And then we'll have an engagement party!"

They both laughed again. It was so funny.

"But when they catch a woman they're even more brutal than with the men. They rape her. One prisoner described these shaking and trembling women with blood on their faces, backs and breasts and torn lips. But of course few people know about it, because no one speaks about it. The radio is silent. There is just this total silence in the country."

"Engagement party, that's a good idea, how can anyone prove it is or it isn't? But birthday parties aren't such a good idea. You only need to look into a passport to know it's not someone's birthday. Imagine how families live in fear of those brown-uniformed men kicking in their front door."

"Some of our comrades don't wish to receive any more written material, precisely because they are fearful of being found out. Our friends are trying to put together lists of our murdered comrades. Here, did you see this: Erich Muehsam, tortured to death 1934. Erich Lange, a local communist from Gelsenkirchen, murdered 1933. Hans Litten. He was the lawyer who fought in court for Nazi victims and interrogated Hitler for three hours. He was mad with this man and had him arrested. Committed suicide in the concentration camp last year. Carl von Ossietsky, murdered in a concentration camp last year. He received the Nobel price and was really famous, but that didn't help him either. That's when Hitler forbade any German to receive the Nobel price. Do you know Ernst Toller, the poet? His sister and brother are in a concentration camp. He fled to New York and committed suicide there this year."

They had become very sad during Inge's last words and held each other in a vain attempt to cope with the tale of human tragedies.

"At least they won't suspect illegal literature in the home of a man who has gone to war for them. Also we're just supposed to be mothers and housewives. It helps us, because they won't suspect us. Campaigning and politically organised women don't fit into their ideology." Lene noticed that Inge nodded in agreement, but she had another story in her mind, this time about the Zinglers.

"You're quite right, hopefully it does help us with our work! Here's something else from the Netherlands. Obviously the Nazis are there now, so all the refugees, that's tens of thousands of them, have to flee," Inge continued. "Margarethe had joined the Dutch socialist women's movement. Then they both lost their German citizenship like thousands of others. They're hiding somewhere in a farmhouse in the forest. The Nazis are on their trail, they are searching for them."

"What they're going through doesn't bear thinking about. The cold, the loneliness...I hope they've got local comrades to help them out with food and stuff. What about Gelsenkirchen? What's going on there? I haven't been out there at all, what with the children, Auguste..."

"I went to see a film in the cinema the other day. It's incredible what they show you! You could be forgiven for believing the country wasn't at war and didn't have a fascist dictatorship. It was all sweet harmless stuff about girl meets boy. No Nazis there, no Nazi salute or anything. That's how they are making the German people believe everything is in order."

Lene's household had shrunk with only her three children and Marianne living with her. The generous allowance from the company provided for a cleaner and a gardener who kept things in order. Marianne was an experienced nursery nurse. Although Lene never lost her suspicions of her their relationship improved. They shared the odd joke and chatted amicably. Lene felt Marianne was reliable enough. The thought of working in her home town with Inge was taking shape inside her. She felt she could risk visiting Inge in Gelsenkirchen and stay the night to help with visiting comrades and paper deliveries. She gave it a try one day and came back on the first train early the next morning. Once she'd managed her first journey successfully without Marianne seeming suspicious she went regularly every week.

Ringing Inge's bell and entering her dark kitchen with the old utensils hanging on the wall gave her an indescribable sense of joy. Sitting down with Inge at the old scrubbed table where they had talked so often, the same warmth of comradeship enveloped her. The smell of cabbage soup was like perfume, and she looked at the exhausted eyes of her brothers with tenderness. Emil had married and moved in with his wife's family, so the younger brothers each had their own room. The pictures of coal-dusted miners' faces hanging on

Inge's bedroom walls sent her into a deep and happy sleep. Inge was now in her mother's room, so there was plenty of space. If Heinrich found out about her visits all hell would be let loose, but he was far away. The deep rift inside her soul started to heal, making her feel less torn apart. I can manage this, take care of the children and cope with the resistance work, she mused, so why do I stay with him? The thought of leaving him grew inside her. To follow my conscience is as important to me as bread and water. Still, she didn't find it easy to explain herself to Inge.

"You worry too much. I just get on with what I have to do," said Inge.

"But how do you know what you have to do? There are so many possible courses of action."

"Funny, I don't see them. I just see my duties, I've always been like that."

The peppermint tea was in their mugs, and they sat at the scrubbed old table reading the latest information.

"The French government has handed Paris over to the Nazis, here, it was on the 14th June 1940. How do you think the French soldiers feel about that? Got into their uniform for nothing. Got worked up for nothing about the Nazis. They'll probably all be arrested, unless they start a resistance and go into hiding. And the exiled will be chased through the whole of France."

"Do you remember us talking about Willy Münzenberg? He created the publishing company for socialist and communist ideas with Leon Feuchtwanger's, Alfred Döblin's and Thomas Mann's writing. He's been found dead. It says here the Nazis hunted him all the way down to the forests near Marseilles. He was found dead in the forest not long ago."

"I'm just reading about Walter Benjamin. He was a philosopher. Again the Nazis sent troops out after him. Listen to this: He was already at the Spanish border, but they did not let him into Spain. So he walked back to Port Bou. Committed suicide in the hotel there. Can you imagine the dread, loneliness and misery he went through?"

They walked through the streets silently keeping a watchful eye on their surroundings. The comrades they visited smiled and thanked them. Many just wanted to hear stories of those who were dead or arrested. They were too afraid to participate in distributions.

When Olga visited the snow lay thick and white everywhere. The two women hugged for joy. Olga looked a lot better than the last time Lene had seen her. She beamed with confidence and stood without a bent back in front of Lene who was surrounded by her three little girls.

"Look at them! They've grown! They look very well, you must be very happy to have such pretty girls."

"I am, Olga. It's satisfying, and it gives me lots of pleasure to be with the children. It makes up for some of the harder things, when you are married to a man... but let's leave that. After all, he's away in the war now. Come and have some coffee, Olga my love. You look so well. What's been happening?"

"You'll be surprised, Lene! I've become a political animal! I never thought I'd be interested, you know what I was like, I just wanted a husband and a quiet life! But this gang of men who've taken us into war have changed me. And Matti of course! You know she started snooping on us, and we had to be very careful. It's caused a sort of rebellion in me. So I go into town now and help with the resistance. Distribute leaflets, papers, visit comrades to see if they need help, that sort of thing, also hide someone, if that's necessary."

"How marvellous is that, Olga, I'm really happy about that! But you're being careful, I mean, that you don't fall into a Nazi trap?"

"We have code words and other methods to recognise each other..."

"Yes, that's good. Well, I'm so pleased about that, Olga! I'm so proud of you. Just be really careful, we do want to survive these evil creatures... You still remember Inge from years ago? I'm often over there. We do deliveries from her house."

"Sounds good, it's true security comes first, best not to start at the same address, unless we have an engagement party. You know you can meet that way without causing suspicion."

"Yes, that's right, Inge and I laughed about that the other day. I was just going to go out for a snowy stroll with the children. Do you fancy coming?"

They had endless stories to tell. About Olga's parents who knew about her secret work and agreed with her. Matti obviously did not. Olga had met a comrade since her involvement with the Resistance.

"His name is Werner. He's a journalist, but had to give it all up. A communist. We do deliveries together. I go to stay at his place from time to time."

"Lucky you, Olga. Is it love, do you think?"

"Not like in those days," Olga laughed, "now spiritual things are more important to me. I mean, I fancy him very much, but I feel close to him because we share the same ideas."

Lene felt a pang of envy and pain at that moment. Wasn't this exactly what she was missing? There were no common ideas between her and Heinrich.

"That's so wonderful for you. It makes me realise what I'm missing. I mean with Heinrich. He's out there fighting in this war! We have nothing in common in terms of ideals. The more I think about it the more I feel I need to leave him."

"Don't rush into anything. You've got time to make up your mind while he's away. Lene, my love, I'd better get back now, but see you soon, we'll do something together."

On the following Sunday afternoon Lene visited her mother with the children. Unfortunately, Erna wasn't there, she'd been asked to travel to Hamburg to work as an assistant nurse. Lene was invited to coffee and cake. Mathilde smiled and hugged her grandchildren and Lene. She looked older and more transparent. The sandalwood scent was poignant. The cake was splendid, but Lene could hardly taste anything. They chatted about the children. Mathilde told Lene about Hilde. Lene heard her speak proudly of how well her children were doing at school. She knew what that meant. No word of Nazi propaganda. Lene forced herself to join in the conversation, but her thoughts were elsewhere. *Why can't I be like Inge and just do my duties. I can't help myself, I need love, not just duties.* Her thoughts brought Klaus to her mind. There had been letters for her at her mother's home. One was from Liesel. She kept looking at Liesel's perfect handwriting on the envelope. What news would it contain? She read them once she had put the children to bed at home. She tore open the envelope. 'Klaus is alive! They've let him out, and he's staying with me for the time being. He's very poorly but asking how you are and he wants to see you.' A wave of heat and joy ran through her like an electric current. The next letter was from Franz Ehrlich. They arrested him in 1937. He was freed. In 1939 they let him go, only to make him join the army. He's now somewhere on the Eastern front. I hope he's safe. Lene was shaking with excitement, but there was still a third letter. Lene couldn't believe her eyes. It was from her sister Erna. Since 1940 she had been asked to assist with nursing the injured.

11ᵗʰ May 1940

My dear Lene,

Here I am in Hamburg for a training course. We are staying in the Kurhaus, and I have quite a good room. We are being trained to do nursing, but I have time to work on my carvings. There is daily alarm. How much they have destroyed. It is all a terrible sight, you know we might be sent to the front, but it is better to work and help where I can than sit around twiddling my thumbs. I am thinking of you and pray to God that we all meet again alive and well before long,

Yours with hope,
Erna
PS Mother says she is well and sends you her best wishes.

Lene pressed the letters to her heart and sighed deeply. It felt so good to have had this news, the first really good news for a long time. There was hope and happiness out there after all. Klaus's face, his Adam's apple, his shaggy hair were under her eyelids. An urgent longing to be with him stirred through her, but how could it be done? Her wish to leave Heinrich rose forcefully, but not for another man, a little voice inside her said, full of doubts. I shall leave him because of my conscience, another voice triumphed. Such thoughts left her muddled but happy and very tired and she fell asleep.

In October the Nazis marched into Rumania and in March 1941 into Bulgaria. In April they attacked Jugoslavia and Greece. Then on the 22nd of June they attacked the Soviet Union. A blitzkrieg seemed inevitable. The bombastic speeches of Lebensraum und Herrenvolk squealed on the radio. Every soldier was a murderer, Lene and Inge said and read every page of news about the war against the Russian people. Leningrad froze. People huddled while the wolves lay in wait around the town. We will never give up! Shostakovich's symphony rang out loud and defiant from the wireless and warmed the heart of every Leningrad citizen. Then came Stalingrad. Each ruined house defended. Each bedroom fought over. Not one inch. The solidarity of the Red Army withstood the technological wizardry. The Volga ran red with blood. The dead were everywhere. One of the Red Army soldiers held the wires of the telephone in his mouth while he was dying. On the 31st of January 1943 the Red Army achieved victory over the Nazi army. The resonance of success surged like an ocean wave through the battle fields, concentration camps and homes. Victory over the Nazi war machine was possible! Whispers circled from inmate to inmate. A tide of renewed vigour was in every breath. The will to survive rocketed sky high. The camp guards, fearing revenge, increased their repression. The murder rate rose.

Inge was on a visit to Lene's house. The sun shone, and they could sit in the garden with the first green leaves on the trees. They had coffee and cake. Marianne had taken the children for a walk.

"There's a lot of new optimism since the Nazis were beaten at Stalingrad. It's been a turning point. The comrades feel more confident again, they are organising as much as they can."

"Yes, I think we were all a bit pessimistic when they had that success at the beginning. We feared these scoundrels would dominate us for a long time."

"But they are escalating the repression. Obviously they are mad about failing to be victorious. Have you heard of Robert Uhrig? He built up a resistance group in Berlin with over a thousand comrades. And do you remember Lotte Schleif? We talked about her a short while ago. They discovered that she was in contact with the Rote Kapelle and she was arrested in 1942. Eight years in a concentration camp! I also heard of another wonderful comrade who has done amazing work. Her name is Trude Rosemeyer. She created these links between the Rote Kapelle and other resistance groups."

Inge was beaming all over her face. She shook her head so that her long plait hopped over her shoulder. Lene looked at her and felt happy. They both laughed about the hopping plait. The relief and the new optimism felt like a drug.

"Human life means nothing to them. They're murdering more people than ever or putting them in concentration camps – they're driven by fear. They're gripped by the terror that they might lose and it's making them more vicious than ever. Fancy having made so much effort and then their great victory doesn't happen.That must feel rotten!"

They laughed. The cake tasted good. Spring perfume wafted around them. Lene saw herself arm in arm with Klaus in the Tiergarten. A lightness filled her. She threw her head back as she laughed, which made Inge laugh too. Then she grew serious again. Lene looked at her. She had something on her mind, it seemed.

"Robert Uhrig has a socialist friend who is looking for a hideaway for a few days, Lene. I wonder..."

"Of course, Inge, I'll help if I can. We've got the space here. I just have to explain it to Marianne, but we're also moving soon, to the countryside, for a short while."

"I knew you'd be a pal. At the moment he's at another comrade's in Gelsenkirchen. His name's Jonas. If you could come tomorrow evening, then you could bring him back, as if he was a friend of the family. He's from the Schulze-Boysen group. He's Jewish and still manages to fight against the Nazis under their very eyes. Remarkable!"

"Some people are astonishing. How they can hide themselves, make themselves disappear with disguises and just carry on." They both rolled their eyes with admiration for the bravery and inventiveness of Jonas and people like him.

"You can see even young Jewish people belonging to the resistance groups. It's admirable. There is Herbert Baum who's working with Hildegard Jadamowitz. She organises medicines for the illegals. Baum founded the group 'Baum' and with a lot of other people another group called 'Freies Deutschland'."

"Now that they've been beaten in Stalingrad we all know that they can be beaten. And that's a fantastic feeling. It gives us all strength." Lene felt warmth and tenderness for all of them.

"Exactly, so there's more resistance, perhaps, but also more murder. Here's another one. Have a look! He's called Phillip Schaeffer. Part of the Schulze-Boysen group, but they were murdered some time ago."

"Of course they're also being organised in the concentration camps. Resistance under the very noses of the Nazi guards. You can imagine how it drives them mad that they can't get on top of the situation and eradicate every bit of opposition once and for all..."

"I know, it's fantastic, but I've just remembered bad news about the Zinglers."

"What happened?"

"They were betrayed! It seems it was the postman who informed on them. The Nazis came for them in July. They put them in prison in Arnheim and from there to Ravensbrück."

Inge stayed for supper. They wanted to carry on reading the papers and planning their work. Marianne said little, and the girls quarrelled. Lene spent some time calming them down and putting them to bed. Later they sat for a while with their cups of tea and talked about the latest developments: the prevarications over the opening of the second front made the Allies' will to defeat Hitler look feeble indeed. The Allies probably still hoped that the Red Army might lose. Instead they were about to win the war, an entirely unexpected result. The second front! How often had the Soviet leadership asked for this to happen? How often had they been fobbed off with army manoeuvres in the desert or some other faraway war scenario? They talked about Essen where the bombing raids began in earnest in March 1943. Essen meant Krupps. They would carry on bombing until nothing was left.

"I won't hang about for that to happen," Lene told Inge. "I shall leave for Eimsheim. Anni lives there, I know her from the Berlin years. She has a vineyard and has told me that I can come and join her. At the moment we spend every night in the cellar. The children scream, and I can't get any sleep."

"Of course you must leave if you can, Lene. It's lucky that you have a friend who doesn't live surrounded by burning fires. Do stay in touch with me. It really can't last much longer. The Red Army is pushing the Nazis back every day."

The following day Lene returned to Inge's house and met Jonas there. He was a slim man of medium height with a beard. He smiled gratefully at Lene, and they left soon after for Essen at dusk. Jonas was eager to talk and seemed to have a lot on his mind. Lene looked at him from the side and thought how young he was. How much he'd already had to endure. She was proud of him. He was a member of the Rote Kapelle. They all had to have their essentials packed ready to jump out of the window or leave over the roof, day and night. She looked at him and saw that he looked older than he probably was.

"They keep finding one of us, but there are always more who join, women too. They act as if they were with a man, that's how they guard hiding places. They bring them food and documents." He looked ahead of him and breathed deeply, as if to confirm what he had said.

"I shall leave Essen in a few days' time, so then you will need to leave too."

"That's no problem, Inge already explained it to me. I just needed somewhere for a few days. I'm very grateful to you," he added and looked at Lene with big eyes.

The bombing raids on Essen began in earnest in March 1943. Nothing would be left of it. Essen looked like a huge boiling pot of roasting fires, visible from miles away. Every night gigantic nightmarish birds of prey flew over the town carrying destruction in their claws. Searchlights, explosions, tearing hissing noise, smoke, fear. Humans who burned and melted in the ferocious heat, so that the flesh fell off their bones within minutes, walking human skeletons.

CHAPTER 21

RHEINSTRASSE 3

"An oar lies on the roof. A light wind will carry away the straw. Poles for the children's swing have been dug into the yard. The post comes twice a day where letters are welcome. The ferries travel along the bay. The house has four doors from which you can escape."

Bertolt Brecht, Hiding Place

At last they were ready. They said good-bye to Marianne, because she couldn't come as well. There was no more room at Anni's. The suitcases were filled in a great rush with the most urgent and necessary things. How long would they have to stay? Would it be summer and then winter, did they need winter clothes? It was impossible to know anything. The future was a blank. The only certainty was the killing fields. The children begged for their dolls and teddy bears, so they had to be squeezed in. Lene was worn out. The fire alarms and sirens all times of the day and night, The nauseating smell of burning, the screeches of explosions sank deep into her brain. They hurried to the train station. The steam enveloped them in cloud, as they stepped into the carriage. The train journey was interrupted three times. Again and again the sirens droned. They had to rush out and wait in the station waiting room. Then they went on. At the station Anni waited and waved with her handkerchief. They embraced, a deep sigh in their breast.

"What a terrible reason to come and stay with you, Anni, I can't believe how our lives have changed."

"Lene, my love! I'm glad you've come, because you'll be much safer here. The war won't go on forever. Come on, let's rush, Rudi's here with the automobile." They packed into the car, and drove the short distance from Oppenheim railway station to the village Eimsheim up on the hill. They looked in amazement. They hadn't seen such a pleasant and tranquil sight for a long time. The fields stretched out in the afternoon sun. Wheat fields and meadows with cows soon gave way to vineyards stretching out over the hills.

"How peaceful it all looks, you could forget that there's a war going on!"

"It's true, we get to hear very little of the fighting. Fighter planes do pass over at a great height, but don't stop here. I just want to warn you, Lene, don't worry yourself about my mother. She's a bit of a dragon sometimes, but she's like that with everyone. As long as you let her call the shots she's all right. She won't tolerate anyone saying 'no' to her. You'll get used to her, we all manage, even Rudi my husband."

"I keep well out of her way. She rules the house and the kitchen garden, but not out in the fields. That's where I spend most of my time," laughed Rudi. "Her mother's quite special. She has no sense of humour. She can't understand jokes."

"Yes she can, she's just earnest. She's not that bad, Rudi."

"I didn't say she was bad, only tyrannical."

"Rudi!"

None of it mattered. Lene had no choice. She was going to be strong. They reached the farm towards evening. The sky was still bright and the birds sang, trilling in the fruit trees, a sound they hadn't heard for years. They stepped out, pale, worn out and war-weary. Countryside noises, a cow mooing, a horse whinnying, a cockerel crowing. It felt good. Lene's shoulders relaxed with a deep breath from a sense of relief. She had unconsciously held them so tight that they were aching in her neck and back. The front door was thrown open and four girls about the same age as her own ran out and surrounded the automobile, pressing their faces against the windows, full of curiosity. The three girls from Essen crept out of the small space one by one nervously. They were immediately greeted with shrieks and handshakes.

"My daughters, this one's Hella, that's Marianne, here is Ursula and the little one is Brigitte."

The terrified city children were slow to warm to the situation and shyly stood with their hands in their coat pockets. They were persuaded to follow Anni's children, to run into the house where they were shown their rooms. Two dark, narrow bedrooms, each with a massive bed in them that occupied nearly the whole space. On a heavy oak sideboard a jug with water stood next to a dish. The adults walked into the narrow low-ceilinged entrance hall of the farmhouse.

"We'll go straight to my mother's, to greet her."

Frau Krebbs was in a room adjoining the kitchen looking out towards the garden, where she sat with her sewing and darning work. She stood up to welcome the newcomers. A tall and wiry woman with grey hair tied into a knot at the nape of her neck, she wasn't unpleasant to look at, but her sharp profile revealed a narrow slightly pointed nose reminiscent of a bird of prey. Her eyes looked sternly at the crowd, but her mouth had a tight smile.

"Mother, this is Lene Deppermann, my student friend from Berlin."

"Welcome, Lene, welcome, children! You must all be very good and get on with each other. But don't worry, there'll be so much work, you'll probably be too tired to quarrel. We've prepared two rooms for you near the entrance hall which you have all to yourselves. We need extra helping hands, I'm sure Anni's told you, so in the morning I'll show you all where you can help."

For a while the children showed each other special toys, and the Eimsheim girls produced objects they'd found in the streets and in the fields. Rocket splinters, bits of metal and bullets, but tiredness overwhelmed them and they soon fell asleep in the large oak bed, all wrapped under one feather blanket. Rudi also bade them goodnight, and Lene and Anni had time to sit in the kitchen and talk over a glass of wine. The red sky of fires glowed in the distance.

"Do you remember our student hall of residence? Looking back now we had a glorious time! I had no idea what was going on politically and you kept trying to explain things to me, but I never got it. I remember you were very patient, I was so foolish. I never saw anything coming. And now this!"

"Yes, it's a disaster all right! It could have been prevented...I think I'd rather not be German at the moment. I wonder what other countries think of us."

"Why didn't they stop him? Didn't they see this coming? Did they want war? I don't understand, it's no good for them either. Their cities are destroyed, and so many dead."

"It's the Russians! They want to see the Soviets done in. That Hitler is a tool in their toolbox. The children call him Adol Fiddler. Funny, isn't it?" they laughed briefly.

"Whatever happened to your boyfriend, Lene, I think he was Liesel's brother?"

"He was locked up in prison, but luckily he's out now. I haven't heard any more. My friend Franz Ehrlich, the Bauhaus communist, was also arrested and put in a concentration camp."

"What's Heinrich like?"

Lene felt a sting going through her stomach when his name was mentioned. Was he really her husband? She felt so distant to him now. He was physically and emotionally thousands of miles away. How could she describe what went on in her heart? She wiped her hair out of her face and sat back on her chair with her hands in her lap.

"He's a charming man and full of energy and he has a nice big smile, but we are at odds over politics. He keeps saying it doesn't matter, we love each other. But it does matter a lot to me! He comes out with dreadful opinions. For instance about the Jewish people. Or the war. He actually enjoys war. Can you believe it? Thinks it's just a matter of a bit of fighting and then being victorious. Well, he's getting a few surprises now that they're losing. He also thinks he's a cut above the rest. I even feel he thinks baking is a lowly occupation."

It was odd how it all poured out of her without her realising. She hadn't wanted to say all of this, but it was as if a valve had been released.

"You seem in two minds about him."

"How right you are! I can't help it. I know he loves me, and he wants me to love him. But I feel distant from him. I even feel relieved that he's not around. I'm not sure I want him back. I sometimes felt he was spying on me. He turned up one day from among the washing in the garden to surprise me and my friend Inge. I had such a shock! He sent her away!"

"He sounds highly political. I think he also sounds quite possessive. Couldn't tolerate you having friends."

"Especially political ones not to his liking! What's your Rudi like?"

"My Rudi wouldn't even know what politics is, Lene. He just talks about the farm, the grapes, the wine making and all that. You know, I don't know much about it myself, and what I do know I know from you. So politics never comes up in our conversations. Funny, isn't it? You're troubled because you are so aware of it. If you weren't, like me, it wouldn't bother you."

"But how can the many people that had to flee Germany and go into exile, the many that were murdered or locked up in concentration camps, not bother people? That's a mystery to me, because people do know about it. You too."

Lene looked through wine-sodden eyes at Anni. The question had been like a tumour inside her, weighing her down. Suddenly it stood sharp like cut glass in the kitchen. For a moment there was silence. Lene worried that she might have upset Anni. It was the last thing she wanted. Her close friend Anni who was kind and gentle! Still, the question had popped out. It had waited inside her to get out. Anni was struggling with the answer, Lene could see that. She looked down at the table and eyed her hands. Then she rubbed her arm. Her eyes were moist when she looked back at Lene.

"Lene, it does bother me, when I think about it. Of course it does, but I try not to think about it, because what can I do, here with four children, a husband and a farm to look after?"

Lene got up and hugged Anni, while tears fell out of both women's eyes. They held each other and cried.

"Of course you're right. If you can't do anything you might as well not give yourself stress with worrying about it. I do know you care, Anni, forgive me if you thought I was criticising you. Neither of us can do much about it. We can only hope that it won't last. The war now looks pretty bad for them. I'm not sure what that'll mean for us. The Nazis probably won't forgive the Germans if they lose the war. You know what that monster of a man has said already: 'If the German people are not strong enough and able to sacrifice their blood for their existence they deserve to be wiped out by other more powerful forces.'"

"Yes, I think he really meant that."

They were both dog tired and went to bed. Early in the morning the alarm rang. Frau Krebbs was already washed and dressed in her starched apron, with a stern look on her face. She went from room to room and chased everyone out of their warm beds.

"This is no place for lazy bones. Early to bed, early to rise, that's the way on the farm. More mouths to feed, more work." She didn't disappear, but waited till she'd seen everyone rise.

"Outside, quick, for your shower, the water tap is in the courtyard by the outside toilet, I suggest the older ones first, the younger ones last."

There were no ifs or buts. She made sure each child in turn had their cold wash under the tap in the yard. And that's how it was day after day. Only out on the fields and in the vineyard were you safe from her. They all wanted to go out with Rudi, but most of the time they had to follow Frau Krebbs' instructions. In the evening they were all exhausted, only Lene and Anni often sat together after the old lady had gone to bed. Lene thought of Klaus. She began to look out for the postman in the vain hope that a letter might arrive. From him or from her friends. One day a letter actually came. She quickly hid it in her blouse and did something Frau Krebbs had asked her to do. Her face almost never expressed any emotions when she spoke. It felt uncanny and eerie, but Anni was used to that. Late in the evening she read the letter.

Lene,

I hope you are keeping strong, because you must do. The Americans and British are moving forward. The German towns are being flattened by fire and explosions. Women and children burn to death. The concentration camps are death traps, but the end is in sight. I know it. And victory won't be theirs. Here is a story I know will interest you and make you a little sad as well. It's about an artist who was with Franz Ehrlich at the Bauhaus. His name is Oskar Schlemmer. He did a famous piece of work in 1932 called 'The Bauhaus stairwell'. The Nazis stopped his job in 1933, and he had to hide from them, working quietly. The loss of friendship, colleagues, work and building his life as an artist killed him. He died last year.

But I've also got good news: I'm coming up to Oppenheim in a couple of days and I have another letter for you. Guess who it is from? Your Berlin friend Liesel! I'm sure you would like to read it soon, so I'm bringing it with me,

with love, Inge.

Lene's heart jolted from pain to pleasure while reading these lines. She was saddened to learn that Oskar Schlemmer had died of grief. What had Liesel written about? Surely news of Klaus and his whereabouts. A tumult of thoughts sped through her mind. She wanted to talk to Anni straight away but had to wait till the next evening.

"Anni, let's have some wine, I need to talk to you about something. I've had a letter from my friend Inge."

Anni didn't look well. Lene looked at her, and saw a look of pain in Anni's face. She sat down next to Lene, rubbing her back.

"I've got a backache, Lene. The harvest, my mother, you know she's not well. She's not telling anyone, because she wants to carry on regardless, but it's clear she can't. It's beginning to get to me."

"Anni, dear, can I get you something, a cushion for your back? What about Rudi..."

"Oh, he's no help, you know he just stays out in the vineyard, and afterwards he says he's too tired..."

"Let me do more work, Anni. You need to rest. But I've got to talk to you about something really important. I'm going to meet my friend Inge in a couple of days in Oppenheim. She wants to give me something, in fact it's a letter from Liesel."

"You must be excited about that! But don't let my mother know any of this. She would go mad. We'll have to invent a little lie."

"Anni, you are sweet. I'll work extra hard and take on some of your work. I'm so grateful to you."

Wine soothed their tired bodies and eased Inge's mood. Lene could see that she was very low. Lene was unable to sleep. She listened to the wind whistling under the door.

She met Inge in Oppenheim railway station. They hugged and laughed with joy. The found a bakery where they could have a cup of tea, and sat down.

"Here's the letter, Lene. Why don't you see what it says, and then I'll tell you all the other news."

Lene looked at the envelope. It was Liesel's neat handwriting. She tore it open and read it out to Inge.

My dear Lene,

The good news is we are still alive here in Berlin, and keeping our heads above the water. Klaus is feeling better at last, I had to feed him back to health first. Everything is upside down in Berlin, but we have a roof over our heads and enough to eat in spite of the restrictions. Klaus is always asking about you and wants to know how and when he can reach you. He wants to see you again, but you must say if that is possible. Write to me if you can,

Much love,
Liesel

Lene looked up at Inge. The beaming happiness in her face told all. Although it was busy and warm in the bakery she took off her jacket. She felt hot. She was still smiling. There was no doubt she was in love with Klaus.

"Why don't you write a brief letter and I'll take it with me and post it in Gelsenkirchen. You don't need to say much, less is better. And then you two arrange to meet. Would Anni help you, do you think? Is she reliable?"

"She is, I think she would help..."

"Lene, there's some other news, let me just tell you before I have to head back. You know our friend Karl Schwesig. He's been released from the concentration camp. But there's bad news about Margarethe and Alfred Zingler. Now they've been brought to Moabit prison in Berlin. He's been condemned to death. For what? For fighting all his life for a socialist future for Germany! I've also got a small article about the 'White Rose'! You know, the student organisation that distributed leaflets against the Nazis. Six of them were beheaded. They were just young kids!"

"Such brave kids. They seem to want to murder as many people as they can before their downfall, don't you think?" Lene hastened to write a note for Liesel, her hand was shaking, and they both laughed. The old conspiratorial feeling enveloped them again. Inge

309

took Lene's message and they embraced and rushed onwards in opposite directions. From that day Lene watched for the postman's arrival from the doorstep even more carefully, busying herself with sweeping or hanging up the washing in spite of the cold. She didn't have to wait long. Only a week later a letter arrived from Liesel with an insert from Klaus. He would be at Mainz station on the 16th of January. Lene puffed with air. Suddenly something could happen that she had dreamed of for so long. Yet she had never thought how it would be in reality. Her life could be thrown into utter chaos, whether she met him or not. Her mind exploded with emotions and confusions, but she sensed one thing: she had to, no, she wanted to go to meet Klaus. What might come afterwards didn't bother her. She just couldn't think that far ahead. She spoke to Anni. A plan was worked out. She might stay a night. A story was invented.

Meanwhile she ran the whole Krebbs household almost single-handed. Anni's back had worsened. She complained about chronic pain. Frau Krebbs couldn't get out of bed. She had pneumonia. The doctor called round every few days. Rudi blandly expected a dinner made come what may. Luckily the girls could help, given a bit of guidance. But guidance was also work. She had all but forgotten about Heinrich, and when her eyes fell on one of his letters she cursorily glanced at it, only to turn away in irritation. He professed to love her passionately and complimented the leadership of the army and bravery of the men, and said that victory was soon to be theirs. The victory he meant would never take place. How would he cope with the reality after the war? She looked out into the night. A snowstorm was whirling snowflakes past her window. Everything turned white. She stopped trying to explain her actions to herself and justify them. She wanted to see Klaus. That was her only thought. It was clear that if Heinrich found out about Klaus, his fury and revenge would know no bounds. Once she had indicated in a letter that Rudi had made advances towards her one evening at dusk in the garden, when Anni had gone to bed. His letter spat fire and brimstone, saying he was going to shoot the rascal.

She left the farm early on the morning of the 16th wrapped in a thick scarf and coat. Her red shoes were buried in her bag. Snow had fallen all night and lay like a thick soft carpet on the ground. A neighbour of Anni's took her to Oppenheim station. The train journey was short, but the train time-table was out of date. She had to wait, but finally arrived in Mainz. *Will I recognise him?* Then she saw him, the same shaggy dog mane! She felt as if she was in a dream.

"Klaus!"

"Lene, my love!"

"My God, let me look at you, you look well."

"My sister's good dinners, she fed me back to health..."

She noticed his Adam's apple and his smile had that humorous cheekiness that she so loved. He wrapped her in his arms and they stood for what seemed years making up for all the distance that had been between them. They walked briskly out of the station.

"Where shall we go? What about a coffee here?" Lene pointed to a small cafe.

"Yes, good idea. Afterwards I suggest we walk to the hotel, where I have a room. It's not far, by the Rhine, 'Zum neuen Schwan' on Rheinstrasse 3. We can get the key."

A hotel. Of course. He would have to stay the night. Lene had not dared to imagine what they might actually do or how they might feel. At the thought of spending a night together her heart started to pound. She had thought so little of all the details. She tried to calm herself. They chatted as before, there was so much to tell, just like years ago.

"Tell me about Berlin, Liesel and all our comrades, Klaus."

"Liesel is a stalwart, you know that, She was a rock for me to get back to and recover with her support. I don't know if I'd have been able to manage without her. They try to destroy you, you know? But I don't want to talk about it. Liesel cooked for me and fed me, until I was well. I had to be careful, they had their eyes on me. But others did fantastic work. So many groups were active, you can't imagine how courageous and inventive they are. They brought out a newspaper called 'die Innere Front'. Fantastic people like Klara

Schnabel, Arvid and Mildred Harnack, Schluze-Boysen. He was a pilot, and managed to get a job after having been arrested because of his training. He was able to get at a lot of information using the Soviet information service. Adam Kuckhoff was another one."

"Did they have contact with the 'White Rose?"

"Yes, they did, they tried to meet up with Hans Scholl in 1942. You can imagine, there were arrests all the time, which interrupted the work, but they persisted, with new comrades joining them all the time."

"What was their main work?"

"Mainly helping people that were being persecuted, distributing fliers and stickers against the Nazis, collecting information and passing it on, often by word of mouth, contacting other groups, calling for disobedience and thoughts about our situation after the war. We held a lot of engagement parties, as a cover for meetings."

"It's so good hearing about all these efforts, Klaus. We did the same. My friend Inge and I met regularly and collected information to either deliver to to talk to comrades and support them. I even hid a political refugee, a young Jewish man called Jonas, for a few days before I left Essen. He was from Berlin."

The shared stories quickly brought them back together, as if they hadn't left each other years ago. Klaus took one of Lene's hands and kissed her fingertips. She blushed with pleasure.

"It's as if we had never left each other. We're still the same with the same strong feelings for the revolution." He said revolution, but they knew he meant their feelings for each other.

"Yes, we are, that desire for socialism and everything to do with it is a very deep feeling. Tell me about yourself, what have you been up to."

"Mainly working as a clerk, just to earn a living and keep my head down. Also I was in a bad state after I left the concentration camp, it took me weeks, maybe months to recover, but let's not go there, I can't even bear thinking about it. What about you?"

She looked at him and saw that he was looking pale and worn out. She certainly didn't want to ask him any more questions of him now. When he put his last question to her, a question she had feared before, she found that the answer was actually quite easy.

"I got married and now I have three daughters. I had to get out of the bakery and was determined not to be another spinster like my sister Erna, God bless her. She was always desperately unhappy. Now she works as a nurse, and my husband is in the war. I believe he is a Nazi. That's why we quarrel so much. He was dead keen to marry me and always said how much he loved me. So I went along with it. But being loved is not the same as loving. That I now know very well. I don't really know what's going to happen, but I intend to leave him."

Klaus had searchingly watched her face while she spoke, but then the skin on his face went pale when she mentioned her marriage, and he looked down at his hands that were folding the bill into an ever smaller square. The story she told was shocking to both of them, as if they were confronted with a very loud noise, but it passed like a train going by.

"Our love seems unabated," Klaus said simply, and she nodded.

They saw that marriage can be just like other things people do, such as go to work or get themselves an education; it was not necessarily a once and for all life decision. The knowledge of that poured oil on the flames of their reawakened love.

"Let's take a stroll by the river, shall we?"

Lene hooked her arm into Klaus's and he took her hand and put it in his pocket for warming. Lene's bliss was endless. When they reached the Rhine they saw ice floes jumping up and down in the small waves, as if rolled around by a large animal. The sky was huge and filled with ecstasy. The waves murmured the word 'love' and they kissed a long and ardent kiss. Dusk threw shadows, and the street lights made the coming darkness deeper. It was as if they were in another space and time. They giggled like children, remembering the happy days they'd had by the sea. Then it had been warm, and they went dancing. Now it was war. There was no dancing in Mainz.

"You will come back with me, I mean to the hotel, won't you?" Lene just nodded. She was lost for words. She was in a dream world, as if she had no power over herself and had to follow some internal demand. They had food and wine brought up to them in their room and they toasted their love. She put on her red shoes just for fun, so that he could undo them from her feet. There was no tomorrow, there was only tonight. Tipsy and elated they undressed each other and lay naked, exploring each others' bodies, as they'd done by the sea. She kissed his Adam's apple, and flung her hand through his shaggy doggy mane, and they laughed and choked with the pleasure of it. The night was short and long at the same time. There was an eternity of love in them, but they could give each other only so many kisses in one night. Early the next day after breakfast they promised to stay in touch. Soulmates. That is how they felt.

"Lene, just let me know when you want to see me again. I do understand your situation isn't easy, so don't worry about me, but when you're ready just get in touch. Write to Liesel. That's the safest thing."

They kissed and waved. There was such promise and happiness inside them, and it made parting much easier.

Lene reached Oppenheim by early afternoon and made it to Eimsheim not long after. The children had hardly missed her. Frau Krebbs was in a coma, and a doctor had been called. Anni smiled when she saw Lene, but Lene could see the pain in her face.

"My back! It's unbearable. I've asked the doctor to give me some painkillers. Anyway, you look ever so well. I take it all went well?" "It did, Anni, we met and had a lot to talk about. He looks well too."

Lene didn't want to upset Anni with stories of the passionate night that she'd lived through. She could still feel the warmth of his body and the heat of his kisses all over her skin. She was covered in an invisible layer of loving touches from his hands.

"You have a letter from Heinrich. I put it in your room."

"OK, thanks. Let me get you something, a drink or maybe a hot water bottle?"

"Yes, both. That would be great."

She wasn't bothered with Heinrich's letter and only looked at it at bedtime. That turned out to be a mistake. It contained explosive news. He was going to come on a flying visit within a couple of days.

He was full of praise for the army, how much he loved her and how he was looking forward to seeing her and the children. She felt horrified. If she hadn't been so exhausted she wouldn't have slept, but she did.

The next days went by preparing for his arrival with special cleaning efforts. She spoke to the girls about their father and planned the visit with Anni and Rudi. All the floors were washed and the linens were ironed. He would find everything in good order. Then suddenly he stood there in the yard, as if he was God's gift, his smile as shiny as his boots. I am false, the voice inside her said, but she managed very well. She was charming and in good spirits. He lifted every child up in the air and shouted with joy at seeing them again. It was moving. But the children didn't remember him very well. He ate his supper with a good appetite. Then they went out walking with the children and had a snowball fight. He was so full of himself and his deeds that she hardly had to worry. Everything he'd done for the army, and how victory would be there soon. He eyed Rudi contemptuously and suspiciously. When they were on their own he checked with Lene about what had really happened with Rudi. He wanted to be sure, and asked again and again. How wrong he was! Once reassured he embraced her passionately and her body relinquished control under his urgent kisses.

"I love you, Lene, I shall be home soon, then we shall at last have our life together."

He whispered much like that, which Lene let drift by, as if it was the wind blowing. After a couple of days he had to leave. He kissed the children and Lene. An army automobile turned up at the yard and took him away. She sighed with relief and waved a handkerchief.

It was May 1944. Summer heat burnt the flowers into bright colours in the kitchen garden. Lene hung out the washing. She pushed her hand into her back where she had an ache. She wiped her hand over her face as if to smooth away the weariness she felt. She was cooking the dinner for the whole household from shrivelled potatoes, turnips and swedes kept in the cellar. The apples had kept reasonably well and she baked a delicious crumble in the oven. The children loved it. Anni's back was better, but she still had to be careful. Old Frau Krebbs was just skin and bones now in her bed. Her dreadful cough rattled horrifically at night. Then one morning it was finished. Anni found her dead in bed. Her funeral brought together the small community of Eimsheim for a few hours. The next evening Lene felt very sick after supper and went to bed early. She was sick again in the morning, and it dawned on her that she might be pregnant. She felt a wave of joy, followed by a wild stream of feelings and thoughts pouring through her brain. Thoughts she couldn't tell anyone. Whose child was it? It couldn't be Klaus's, they had been so careful. Heinrich's, then. But her thoughts of Klaus were stronger than those of Heinrich. It didn't matter. She wanted the child. She felt madly happy. A gift of love. It was seven years since she'd last been pregnant. This would be her peace child. It would also bring the peace. She spoke to Anni.

"Anni, I'm pregnant!"

They were sitting in the back room with a glass of wine.

"You lucky thing! It's going to make you feel good to have a little one growing. It's a message of peace. Life goes on, and there is a time to live after the war."

Anni didn't mention her meeting with Klaus and that suited Lene. She didn't want to say anything about Klaus.

"Thank you Anni, that was beautifully said. I agree with you. I'm feeling much happier, much calmer. Also I've had a letter from my sister Erna. She's being moved everywhere with her nursing duties. Listen to this:

> '11ᵗʰ June 1944
> Dear Lene,
>
> I was ill for four weeks. My hands just didn't work any more. Now I'm with a very sick man. The long awaited invasion is at last here. The Americans and English have landed between Cherbourg and Le Havre. We are here now in Brest and get the wounded from the ships to look

after. I am looking after a German soldier called Walter
from Timmerode in the Harz. He's a big strong man
of twenty-three. They threw stones at us and cursed us
'sale boches'. Slept on the ground in Tegonnec. Went on
to Rennes.'

The Allies landed in Normandy on the 6th June 1944. In July 1944 the dictator was attacked by his own men. The news sent excitement through the land, but it all went wrong. A heavy oak table protected him from the explosive's blast. The fury and vengeance he wrought on all those he deemed to be involved was terrible. The resistance groups had to exercise even more extreme caution. Lene thought of Olga and Inge and hoped they were safe. For a while Lene just gave in to her happy feelings. She only thought of Klaus and saw what was growing inside her as part of him. She forgot Heinrich as soon as he left. The thought of leaving him was like a ship well anchored. When it would travel was written in the stars. She had another letter from Erna.

5th August 1944
Dear Lene,

Brest was cut off, after bombing raids, fires and many
were injured including Dr. Dietzen. The Americans
transported us on lorries to Cherbourg. Nobody knew
where we were going or what was going to happen to us.
We got on a packed boat and looked for somewhere to sit.
We had some sauerkraut, sausages, potatoes and two pieces
of bread. It was good! Some faces went white after the food
on the rocking boat. At six in the morning we were woken
up and taken to a hospital. Nobody cursed us here. They
looked at us worriedly. We were disinfected and checked

up. After some food we were taken to a train station to go somewhere near Oxford. Must go now,

I hope you are all keeping healthy and well,
Your sister Erna

Good luck, Erna, you need it. Inge came during August. They sat out in the garden and talked hopefully of the war ending. There was more bad news.

"Perhaps you already know what they did to Alfred? They accused him of high treason and murdered him. On the 28th of August."

"Dreadful, such a good man, unselfish and creative. I just kept hoping that he would survive. They're beasts. Poor Margarethe. It's awful for her and just before the war is going to end."

The sheets and shirts fluttered in the summer breeze. Lene exuded such joy. It was impossible for Inge to ignore.

"Tell me how things have been, you look radiant."

"It's difficult for me to talk about. It's all in a whirl. You know I met Klaus in Mainz. We got on as well as years ago, in Berlin. It was magic. A few days later Heinrich came to visit. It was surreal, because he felt suspicious of that Rudi, who had tried his luck unsuccessfully with me. And now I'm pregnant."

Inge shot a quick interrogatory look at Lene, who knew what she was thinking. Whose child was it? But she didn't ask, and Lene didn't care to talk about it. It didn't matter. True love had been worth struggling for, against all the odds, and she had found it. She could see that Inge knew this now as well.

"Congratulations, Lene, I'm sure you're happy with the news. You look absolutely radiant. You're so lucky sitting up here on the vineyard hill and not in town where everything's in flames with smoke and poisonous smells. I've been to Essen. Most of it is destroyed, including where you used to live."

"Well, so be it, I thought that might happen. There wasn't much that kept me there. Luckily I managed to bring my desk and chest of drawers to safety. I'd have been sad to lose them. And my red shoes are here with me. You remember them?"

"Yes, you wore them when you visited Karl that time."

Lene laughed out loud, because Inge had made a curious face. Thinking of the red shoes always made her feel light and warm. Inge's confirmation about the house having burnt down seemed so unimportant. Lene seemed to have abandoned all worry and fear. But she added:

"Never mind, it happens to others, so it's happening now to us. We'll manage somehow."

Inge was surprised to find Lene so nonchalant.

"I'm not sure what you're intending to do, Lene, but if you're stranded without him, you're always welcome to stay at our house."

"You're very sweet, Inge. How nice of you to make such a generous offer. I have no idea what the future holds, or when Heinrich's coming back. It's all a complete mystery to me at the moment. The odd thing is that I don't even care."

Lene laughed again and Inge couldn't help joining in. There was a sense of liberation in their laughter. They sipped their wine which had remained untouched and toasted each other. Lene's bliss spilled over into Inge.

Washing had to be hung up again and again, but Lene enjoyed the work. She hung the clothes out watching the wind catching the sleeves and throwing them about like broken arms. She watched the sky and instead of clouds groups of bombers hissed through the air making the air feel boiled and tasting of poison. She shook herself in disgust. It was autumn and harvest time. Rudi was out on the hill with the girls picking grapes. Anni and Lene had their hands full harvesting the vegetables in the farm garden, curing the cabbage, digging out the potatoes, picking apples and plums, gathering the eggs from the chickens. Lene's belly was large. She was full of joy with the little one growing inside her. Erna wrote again.

13th October 1944
My dear Lene,

> *I am not sure if I've already told you that we were all arrested and taken to England. As of yesterday we are here, twenty-one of us, in a barracks-like house. There is a loo, a bathroom and a kitchen. We can't complain. Today we are getting a radio and are even allowed to listen to a German station. We are in the general hospital near Whitchurch. We are wondering when we might be able to go home and worry about our loved ones. My address here in case you get the chance to write is:*

> *H. Sister Erna Deppermann*
> *A.S.N. (31G-17217)*
> *U.S. Army, PWIB*
> *Great Britain*

Lene went into labour early the next morning. Rudi and Anni had a horse-drawn carriage ready to take her to the hospital in Oppenheim. The hour's ride from Eimsheim to Oppenheim seemed to take forever. The bumpiness of the road knocked Lene's belly painfully with every stone and hole. They kept looking anxiously at the sky for bombers, but reached the hospital safely. Several times that afternoon the air raid alarms went off and they had to seek refuge in the cellar. It was exhausting and very frightening. She had not been pregnant for seven years and had forgotten how bad the pains could be. Near midnight she was brought into the theatre. Sweat poured off her whole body, her hair stuck to her forehead.

She used all the energy she could muster to breathe deeply and was close to fainting, when the midwife called out "It's a girl!" The little one gave her first cry and was handed to her mother wrapped in towelling, when a huge thunderclap shattered the window panes. An incendiary bomb had turned the house next door into a sea of red, orange and blue flames. Thick whitish-grey smoke billowed upwards. Nurses, doctors and orderlies ran and screamed frantically to vacate the smoke-filled theatre and get everyone down into the cellar. By about three in the morning the all-clear sounded the end of the attacks.

She was supposed to be a boy, but I love her. She is my peace baby! The nurse brought her a hearty breakfast. She didn't tell her about the terrible moment when they thought they had lost the woman and her baby to shock and smoke in the dead of night. Her mother Mathilde visited with Thilde. Another girl. But they didn't say anything. They marvelled that mother and daughter had survived so well. Heinrich wrote saying he was pleased, even though she was a girl.

Post script, 14th October 2013
I have checked all the diary notes again and have determined that the last note was the one from the 28th June 1975. It is the one I mentioned last, when we talked about the uneasy silence that existed after the war. I have to say here that living in Hamburg meant being near the border with the GDR, but little of what went on there was ever reported to us in the West. What was going on there was kept from us, although more German culture was celebrated there than in the Federal Republic. Here we were overwhelmed with American culture, now simply a continuity of anti-communism. Astonishing if you think about it. I wanted to look up to see if my mother had said any more about her meeting with Klaus in Mainz, but I didn't find any further comments. I remember we both laughed and felt pleasure at their reunion, when she talked about it. She wasn't going to give away more details. I saw in the dark glow of her eyes how happy she was that her great love continued to accompany her in her life.

CHAPTER 22

THE BURNT-DOWN TOWN

Killing fields stretched across the land. It was January 1945. The snow came early and stayed for a long time, putting a white shroud over the blood soaked earth. The fighter bombers kept flying overhead making it feel as if the battle was right on top of them. On one of those icy mornings with thick clouds hiding death, Anni wanted to visit a friend whose husband had been killed. They left the village in the coach with Peter, the farmhand, in front, Anni next to him and two of her girls behind. On the frozen country lane in the direction of Mainz with no trees to protect them a fighter bomber suddenly flew very low. A deadly bomb fell down treacherously. It hit the coach and it broke apart. Peter turned to see what had happened. There was no woman next to him any more, and hardly any of the coach was left where she had been. He jumped down together with the girls and found Anni lying bleeding in the ditch under broken wood and wheels. The children stared in utter horror at their dying mother. Her abdomen had been torn open, and her intestines hung out. For a moment her eyes shone wide, her mouth looked surprised. Then she died. Peter and the girls lifted the dead woman into the remnants of the coach, wrapped her in a blanket and pulled the remains of the carriage home. Lene and Rudi stood catatonic with horror. Anni was washed and laid out on her bed, where the children and grown-ups sat with her. Lene was awash with pain. They had made it so near to the end of the war. How could it be that death came to their house now? Where a new healthy baby had been born. She couldn't comprehend it. Anni, my wonderful and dear friend! I shall miss you so much, Lene whispered again and again, as she sat next to Anni that night and suckled the baby. She pressed the baby tightly to her chest. The will to live and to love burnt like a torch inside her as strongly as ever.

At last her friend Olga visited in April. They embraced warmly and looked at each other.

"You look fantastic, Lene, considering what you've been through." She knew about Anni's death and Heinrich's visit and the pregnancy.

"I do feel well, although life on the farm has been arduous and pretty awful, especially since Anni's death. I miss her badly. But tell me about you. How's Matti?"

"Well, how's the whole country! Did you hear about the terrible fire in Dresden? Apparently the glow from the flames could be seen miles away. Burnt down needlessly, no industry there. The outcome of the war is long decided. Women, children and old men melted to death. Just like what they did to Hamburg. Matti has moved out. She's still stubbornly one of theirs. She found work in a local school. The teachers took a shine to her. I don't see her much, but all that will change when we get rid of this lot at last. A thousand years they were going to last! And how long was it? A mere twelve, but enough destruction to last us a thousand years!"

"Indeed! It's laughable how bombastic that lot was, and now they're running away from the Red Army. The Americans and the English are already near. Imagine, my sister Erna has been taken prisoner by them. Now she's in England."

"Tell me about yourself. What's up with Heinrich, is he still in the war?"

"He is indeed, still busy. He hasn't even seen our new baby yet. I'm not thinking about him much. Mostly only when I plan to leave him."

"You sound brave, Lene! But take your time. See how you feel once you see him. He'll be back, demanding his rights as your husband."

"Then there is Klaus. I've seen him again, I..."

"You don't say! Klaus from Berlin? Your soulmate? How did you manage that?"

"He got in touch through his sister Liesel, sometime after having been let out of the concentration camp. Anni helped me set up the meeting, so it was secret. No one apart from Inge knows about it. She sent me the letters – and now you."

"Tell me more, I can't believe it!"

They had reached the long kitchen table and Olga dropped herself into the chair with a deep sigh. Lene went to fetch a bottle of wine and two glasses.

"Well, fancy that, the things you get up to! But that's great. You've stayed loyal to your love. Tell me how you managed to do that."

"Anni used a fib about why I was away that night. Klaus and I arranged to meet in Mainz at the station. He had a hotel room booked in the 'Zum neuen Schwan'. We felt just like before in Berlin We walked along the Rhine as if there was no war and no problems with a husband and children. I stayed the night with him. It was bliss. He said he'd wait for me. I should let him know when I can go and see him."

"Soulmates indeed. That is for life. Like me and Werner. Whether we are together or not, we feel so close. But we don't have such a difficult situation. Heinrich won't accept it at all when you tell him."

"Goodness me, no, of course not. I couldn't. He'd kill me. He's so jealous. I can't speak to him about Klaus. I have to find another reason. And I have one. It's my conscience. But you're right, it won't be easy."

"It would be nice if one could use one's conscience as a reason, but that's not how reality works. He'd never accept that. And you can't live off love and air. You'd need to fend for yourself, and who would care for the children, unless you leave them as well?"

"I have a profession, but at the moment I'm not thinking about all that and how it could happen. First of all I need to care for my little one."

"Yes, that's true. You've got time. He's not back yet. And regarding Klaus, you have no idea how he would deal with it when you arrive with four children. A lover is one thing, but a mother is something quite different. For me, Werner is a lover. I shan't marry him or have children with him."

The wine relaxed them and they began telling each other amusing stories which made them laugh. Erna and her exzema, the actress with the temper tantrums and the cigarettes, and then Erna making her a better dress. Before Olga left they hugged warmly.

In spite of everything spring arrived and with it the end of the war. Some nights before the 8th of May they had witnessed the fires of Mainz burning, and Lene thought of the Hotel 'Zum neuen Schwan'. The sky from the horizon up was glowing crimson from the flames. Would it still be standing there by the Rhine? The tanks rolled from the distance and came nearer and nearer with thunderous rumbling. The people of Eimsheim stood in the street. The white linen bedecked village was handed over to the soldiers. The children held on to Lene who stood tall and strong with a huge feeling of relief. Whatever happened now couldn't be as bad as what they'd lived through. After the Americans came the French. The village was now run by them. Fear, hope and weariness all rolled into one messy emotional state for the villagers. Heinrich turned up at last. She looked at him. Who was this worn, thin old man with the uniform hanging on him like a snake skin not quite peeled off?

Room was made for him. He slept for many days. They had to find a place to live in. Their house had burnt down. An office space in Essen was found as a temporary home. Very few words were spoken. Then the English soldiers came for him. Under the

Denazification Programme he was declared guilty of belonging to the Nazi party and imprisoned for two years. Lene barely had the energy or time to think. Five years her husband had been in the war. Now he was imprisoned for another two. The wish to leave him had to be suspended for another two years. She couldn't really desert him as he was led off to prison. He looked so forlorn that she almost felt sorry for him. Olga was right, it was more difficult than she'd thought. She searched for reasons to strengthen her resolve to leave him. The war, the exiled poets, Alfred Zingler. The concentration camps. The murdered resistance comrades. His arrogance and fury, when he sent Inge away and forbade her to see her again. She felt full of love for Klaus and his kisses. She raked the fire of her love, which burnt like an eternal flame.

Time passed like the drops of rain that fell. There was so much rain. It seemed to rain all the time through all the seasons. The household with four children absorbed all her energy. The little one needed most of her attention. She looked at her again and again. Had she not brought her love and peace, she wondered. But after the years of dread and the conspiracy of trying to help defeat the Nazis peace came with a sense of desolation after the first feelings of joy. There was little togetherness now. Everyone was busy sorting out their lives, finding a place to live and feeling anxious about what was to come. Olga managed to visit her. It was autumn. They walked through the fields with the children.

"What about Heinrich, where is he?"

"They locked him up. He's in prison for Nazi membership. It's fine, though. I feel quite peaceful. I've got too much to do to start wondering about this now. I couldn't exactly say 'I'll leave you' as they dragged him away to prison."

Olga laughed. They both laughed. The situation had a funny side to it.

"I think you've been lucky again. You're well provided for, and you don't even have to be with him. It gives you more time to decide..."

"What about Matti?"

"Guess what! Of course, after their defeat she came home and said that she felt she had been betrayed by them. Funny way to look at it, isn't it? Well, she's her own master. She's an adult and has to find work. Like the rest of us. I'm still seeing Werner, but we haven't moved in together."

Olga caught the train in the evening. Christmas came. Just a few days before Lene found out that Heinrich was allowed a few days leave. She took pity on his tired face and weak smile. They slept together. She became pregnant again. For a few days she was in turmoil, but she calmed down into that peacefulness she'd felt since she'd met Klaus. She scolded herself. She argued with herself. Just when she'd wanted to free herself. Yet she loved the warmth of a new being growing inside her. That peaceful feeling which she'd since she'd seen Klaus again returned. Cleaning, washing, ironing, sewing, cooking, feeding. The new baby was born in September 1946. This time it was a boy.

The rain fell in long strings hanging from the sky, as if to hide the broken town behind a curtain. Heinrich finished his prison sentence in 1947 and was allowed to return to his family. The sky was still and full of moisture like eyes full of tears. Now and then the air raid sirens went off, as if to remind them of what they'd been through, an afterglow of the nightmares they had suffered. His employers had him back, but he had to move. They left for the burnt-down city of Hamburg. Ruins, empty spaces where buildings and factories had once stood. Burnt-out shells of people's homes, old burn smells, streets full of bomb craters, from which the tar had burnt off and that now just consisted of sand. Howling dogs, their owners dead or moved away. A Nissenhut was erected on a building site. They had two rooms. She wrote to Olga and Inge and missed them. Now she was a long way away from them. She wrote to Liesel telling her about her situation. Liesel wrote back enclosing a hidden page from Klaus. His love was enduring, he said. I'm going to wait for you. She repeated to herself that she would leave Heinrich. How, she didn't know. The two little ones warmed her heart, the older ones returned to school. She found one friendly neighbour who she saw often. She lived nearby in one of the few houses that were left standing. Lene admired the elegant old furniture all intact, which decorated the old lady's lounge as if the war had passed it by. It was enjoyable stepping into a warm and cosy lounge with beautiful carpets and pictures on the walls. Next door was a small corner shop. All basic necessities could be bought there, shoelaces, boot polish, sewing needles, margarine, milk and potatoes, occasionally a sausage. It was at lunch-time, when the older ones were at school and the little ones asleep, that she sometimes had a good natter with Frau Wertheim. Her son was missing, and she waited every day for news of him. Her daughter visited occasionally, but they lived in the south of the country, near Munich.

"Where the Nazis had come from!" Frau Wertheim used to point out, when she talked about her life. Lene was a good cook and sometimes took the old lady some homemade soup and boiled her a cup of tea every few days. She was a good listener and Lene confided in her. It was pleasant to have someone to communicate with. She didn't mention Klaus.

"I intend to leave him. The only reason why I haven't done so is that I seem to be unable to talk to him about anything. It's incredible, although I see him every night."

"Just think - how would you support yourself, Lene?"

"I'm a fully trained physiotherapist, I'd get a job."

"Even if you get work, who's going to look after the children? I don't think you've really thought through how it could be done practically. Also, is it right to leave the man after everything he's suffered, war, prison? After all, he didn't do it for himself personally, or what do you think?"

"No, of course not, he always said he was doing it for us, that was what was terrible. As if I'd ever wanted that war. He always used to say there would be no war. Then there was a war. We're so different. I've lost trust in him."

She went home frustrated with herself, feeling alone and angry. Was she unable to act to break out of the circus of daily chores? She cooked, washed, deloused the children, asked the older ones to lay the table and put the little ones to bed. Every supper time she became anxious. Sometimes it was even panic. What would happen if one of the older children, now in their teens and able to speak their own mind, mentioned the war? If they asked Heinrich where he'd been in the war? She spent every supper chatting eagerly, making conversation and keeping them all busy until it was time to carry the dishes into the tiny kitchen. It happened when she wasn't thinking about it. The oldest one asked innocently:

"Why were you in prison, father? What were you doing when we didn't see you in the war?"

The sound of a sharp intake of air came from somewhere. Everyone looked down at their plates that were nearly empty. Only Wilhelmine eyed her father directly and fearlessly. A stomach was rumbling and outside a lost dog barked. Before Lene could defuse the situation Heinrich screamed like a speared bull:

"I was defending you and mother and our fatherland! What do you think I was doing and who put you up to question me? I did my duty! Your mother knows how hard I worked for you. You are my children. It is not for you to question your father!"

Wilhelmine burst into tears and left the table. Lene calmed the other two. They put another one or two bites into their mouths. Normally plates had to be emptied completely but this time the other two got up and followed their older sister out of the room. Luckily the little ones were already in bed. Nobody said anything. Lene cleared the table silently. But he had more to say.

"You must have put them up to this, all these questions. What on earth are they thinking of? How dare they interrogate their father? You should have supported me."

Heinrich's face was bright purple. His blue eyes were aimed sharp and cold in her direction. Between them a huge frown wrinkled his forehead.

"I didn't put them up to this. They're growing up. They understand things. They go to school. You're taught to ask questions there. How can I back you up if I don't agree with you?"

"You're my wife. You have to support me. Whatever you think you can keep it to yourself. I was only doing my duty." Then he added in a milder voice, "Life isn't easy for us, we need to help each other."

"Why can't you just say to them what you think? You don't need me for that. Why do you get so angry with me and them? They have a right to ask questions."

She saw that he was in an inner struggle. His face had gone white, and he looked old and shrunken. He seemed to sink into the chair. It seemed his temper was almost too much for him to bear. He spoke now, quietly and hesitantly.

"You don't understand. We worked very hard to achieve something that was not to be. I still can't talk about it. It's too painful."

She looked at him with a mixture of emotions that included anger, shame, alienation and pity. How ashamed she was of him, but then again he was just a struggling worn-out human being. The words 'I'm going to leave you' almost burst out of her. It was the right moment, but it passed. The baby was crying. She left the room to pick him up. Had he also looked distraught behind his anger? He still suffered from extreme tiredness and often fell asleep soon after supper, which was a relief. It allowed her space to think. She was determined. He was never going to see how wrong he had been. She was going to start a new life, take up activities and find new tasks with her friends Olga and Inge. She fantasised about things she might do when she was away from him. But each morning she saw the rain veils around her hiding the future, the ruins around her, the barbed wire fences with their thorns. Working to feed and dress the children killed her fantasies. The mountains of small petty things, filling in forms, collecting food stamps, sticking soles on to shoes, darning socks. It all made her feel she was drowning. She spoke to Inge many times in her head, but Inge was far away. The words 'I'm going to leave you' were chiselled out of stone, but they didn't come alive. She watched him leave for work, his hair thin on his head, dressed in an old suit that she had repaired for him and that now hung on him because it was too big. He walked in the door and was a stranger who she didn't know. But he was there. The rain fell as if it would never end. The sky was colourless, an infinite grey sea of sadness. In front of her the bare sandy stretches of the footpaths had deep puddles. This was loess, earth of the ice age, in which the children played their games and where they splashed in the puddles, unaware of what had brought the ancient times back to the surface. The empty gardens surrounded by fences and barbed wire were overgrown with weeds, a green wilderness. In the distance behind their shack the army barracks still stood erect like bleak fortresses of the silenced past. A constant stream of refugees came each day and left a few days later on their onward journeys of homelessness. Lene watched them as she hung up her washing, how they staggered on, unsure of where to go. They stared with forlorn eyes that recognised nothing, that searched anew every day in the hope of finding what they were looking for. I am also searching, she thought, but we are together. At night the dogs howled as if they'd been kicked. They had fled from the fires.

Then the day came. A little sunlight blinked through the grey clouds. It was a summer lunchtime. There had been rain in the morning and the puddles shone in the mild light. The older ones had gone to school. The two little were having their lunch-time nap. Lene had made a pie and took some of it over to Frau Wertheim. The door wasn't locked and she walked in.

"Frau Wertheim, I've brought you some pie!"

"My dear Lene! That is good of you. You're a kind soul. I'd be lonely without you. How are your husband and the children? Has he gone to work?"

"Yes, he has, Frau Wertheim, and the older ones have gone to school. He lost his temper yesterday. It was awful."

"What happened?"

"My oldest, Wilhelmine, asked him why he'd been in prison and why he'd been in the war. He exploded and told her not to question him."

"Poor man. He's obviously not coping with the failures he's experienced."

"What failures? He volunteered. He decided to support the war effort. That was his choice." Lene was outraged when Frau Wertheim seemed to take his side.

"Yes, but he did it for his own reasons. It wasn't an evil deed, was it? He's not an evil man. He did what was asked of him."

"No, that's true, he's not an evil man, but what is evil and corrupted? If you think that war is wrong, you shouldn't join it. He should have known that the Nazis were evil. His actions were evil. It was against everything I believe in."

"But, Lene, it's in the past now. You've got to think of the future, not the past."

Lene stared at Frau Wertheim feeling a dissonance of emotions, Of course, she had to think of the future, but she couldn't just forget about the past, could she? Then she heard a noise outside. She listened. It was the crying of a child.

"It might be my little ones, if they've woken up. I've got to go. I'll speak to you later, Frau Wertheim."

She peeped out of Frau Wertheim's front door. The rain hung down from the sky like a net curtain. There in the rain in front of the nissenhut stood her little girl barefoot in her underpants. She was crying and calling for her mother. She was holding on to the hand of her little brother tightly. He was crying as well. Lene was spellbound and couldn't move for a few seconds. The loneliness of those two tiny humans in the rain amongst the ruins and barbed-wire fences shook her to her bones. They looked so vulnerable, so helpless.

The children, she thought. So many had died in the war. But these children were alive. They had survived. For the first time she began tareo experience her wish to leave Heinrich from their perspective. How could she leave them when they were so vulnerable? Children are like poets. Like the exiled poets in their loneliness.

Without Geborgenheit. A wave of pity, shame, hope, remorse and tenderness washed over her. Was that what Frau Wertheim meant? The fate of the poets and emigrants who had lost their homeland and their 'Belonging' were for her suddenly identical with that of the two children. They wouldn't have fought in vain. All was not lost. She stumbled towards the little ones and picked them up, wrapping her arms around them.

Lightning Source UK Ltd.
Milton Keynes UK
UKOW02n1659301015

261764UK00001B/5/P